Praise for Paul Gitsham

A Price to Pay

PAUL GITSHAM

ONE PLACE. MANY STORIES

HQ
An imprint of HarperCollins*Publishers* Ltd
1 London Bridge Street
London SE1 9GF

First published in Great Britain by
HQ, an imprint of HarperCollins*Publishers* Ltd 2020

Copyright © Paul Gitsham 2020

Paul Gitsham asserts the moral right to be
identified as the author of this work.
A catalogue record for this book is
available from the British Library.

ISBN: 9780008331160

MIX
Paper from
responsible sources
FSC™ C007454

This book is produced from independently certified FSC™ paper
to ensure responsible forest management.

For more information visit: www.harpercollins.co.uk/green

Printed and bound in Great Britain by
CPI Group (UK) Ltd, Melksham, SN12 6TR

For Cheryl.

Prologue

The branches whipped at her face as she crashed through the trees. Her breath caught in her throat, her lungs labouring to keep up. Behind her, dogs barked and snarled, and she heard the shouts of her pursuers. The further into the woods she plunged, the darker it turned, the thickening canopy of leaves blocking ever more light.

A sudden burst of pain sent her sprawling to her knees, a fist in her mouth muffling her cries.

She couldn't go on anymore.

She couldn't.

Maybe if she turned around and went back they'd forgive her.

Maybe if she begged ...

A shot rang out.

Going back wasn't an option.

She'd just seen what they did to deserters.

She'd seen what they did to women like her.

She gritted her teeth, forcing herself back to her feet. She needed to continue her flight, putting as much distance as she could between her and the following men, before running was no longer possible.

She pushed on. The dogs were louder, and she shuddered at the memory of them. Huge, slavering things – she'd seen the way they attacked the dead rabbits thrown to them; chained up all day, they

1

would be beside themselves at the prospect of a real, live prey to chase down.

The road was only a few hundred metres away; a busy, two-lane highway, the hiss of traffic was audible even at this time of night. There's no way her pursuers would risk chasing her onto it.

She stumbled again, her foot sinking into a depression in the soft earth. She tried to get up, she really did, but she was exhausted.

What had she been thinking? Nobody ever escaped. Those who tried were dragged back and used as an example to everyone else.

Another shot cracked the night sky open.

It was closer than the last, and the dogs were even louder.

The extra surge of adrenalin was enough to spur her on.

But her pace was now little more than a brisk walk.

It was the best she could do.

The sound of the road, the sound of freedom was getting louder, but the sound of the dogs was getting louder more quickly.

Another unseen obstacle, and she ended up flat on her face.

What was the point? Everything that she loved in the world was now gone. She rolled onto her back, too exhausted to care about the blood trickling down her face from her broken nose. She felt her eyes close. Just a few seconds' rest ...

This time the shot was so close, she heard the leaves above her rustle.

No! She wouldn't give in. Too much had already been sacrificed. If she gave up, if she died here, those sacrifices would have been in vain, and the memory of his selfless love would die with her.

Clambering back to her knees, she half crawled, half walked, towards the road.

This time when the pain came, there was no ignoring it.

'No, no, no,' she whimpered. Not now. Just a few minutes more.

Behind her, she heard the baying and snapping of the dogs and the shout of their handlers.

It was over. The dogs would be on her in seconds. There was no way she could keep ahead of them now. Sinking into the soil, she

2

prayed to a god who seemed to have been deaf to her pleas for as long as she could remember.

Please make it quick.

She fell to her side, welcoming the encroaching darkness, looking forward to the release from suffering.

Suddenly, bright, dazzling beams of lights cut through the trees, turning night into day wherever their dancing cones landed. Overhead the night was shattered by a loud clattering. Now she could hear the handlers shouting, calling back their snarling charges.

But she was too far gone to care, wave after wave of pain passing through her, until eventually the darkened forest turned pitch black and she remembered nothing more.

Monday 02 November

Chapter 1

It had been a fairly quiet few weeks. Some might even say boring. DCI Warren Jones felt his head start to dip and he dug his nails into the palms of his hands. Nodding off in the middle of a budget meeting before they even got to the coloured printouts of this year's projections would be rude, especially in a room full of his peers, some of whom seemed to regard it as the most exciting event in their calendar.

There weren't even any decent biscuits.

What he wouldn't give for some real policing right now. A good, meaty case he could get his teeth into, with leads to chase down and suspects to grill.

The current speaker switched slides. A quick look at the graph with its downward trends told Warren everything he needed to know. Fewer front-line officers, less money to pay for outsourced forensics services, and another cull of support staff. It didn't seem as though the cuts extended to turning the heating down in the briefing rooms, although it was a mystery to him why this even required a meeting; an email would have sufficed.

Warren resisted the urge to look at his phone sitting face down on the desk in front of him. He hated when people did that; it was the height of bad manners.

On the opposite side of the room, the door opened, and a middle-aged man with a name badge on a Hertfordshire Police lanyard came in. Apologizing to the speaker, he scuttled around the table. Warren saw glimmers of disappointment on the faces of his colleagues as the support worker passed them by. He felt a surge of much-needed adrenalin as it soon became apparent that the man was heading for him.

'Lucky bugger,' muttered the DSI sitting next to him.

The man leant down and spoke quietly into Warren's ear.

Hiding a smile of relief, Warren apologized to the rest of the attendees and made his way to the door. Clearly, somebody upstairs had been listening to his silent pleas.

Be careful what you wish for.

The crime scene was already surrounded by a cordon when Warren arrived. An ambulance, lights off, sat silently. Two paramedics sat on the back step of the parked vehicle, keeping the chill, November air at bay with a thermos of coffee. Their patient was well beyond anything they could do.

Parking up, Warren signed the scene log and fetched his murder bag from the boot. He would wait until the last minute before putting on his paper Teletubby suit, gloves, booties, hairnet and facemask. Even at this time of the year it would get uncomfortably sweaty very quickly.

Already there were swarms of white-suited crime scene investigators going about their business. He wondered if they ever got used to the protective gear, or if they just learnt to put up with it.

The smell of tobacco smoke was accompanied by the sound of rustling. Warren turned to see Detective Sergeant Shaun Grimshaw heading his way. The man's paper suit was folded down, so that only his legs were covered. He carefully stubbed out his cigarette on the edge of his packet, before placing it inside the box.

At least he wasn't contaminating the crime scene, thought Warren, though to be fair, they were still well outside the police tape.

'I take it you've been in already?'

Grimshaw nodded. 'Yeah, it's a bloodbath.' He motioned toward the paramedics. 'Nowt for them to do, that's for sure.'

'Talk me through it before I go in and see for myself.'

Grimshaw turned and pointed down the street. 'The victim's in the rear ground-floor room of the massage parlour. According to the girls who were working, it's one of the clients. A white male, mid-twenties I'd say. He was on his back, relaxing after a full-body massage. The girl servicing him said she'd popped out of the room to let him chill out for a bit and was fetching fresh towels for the next client, when she heard a scream.'

'What do you mean, "servicing him"? Are we talking sex work?'

Grimshaw shrugged. 'Supposedly it's not that type of place, but who knows? I've seen the two girls working here, and they're above the local average, if you get my drift.'

Warren let the insinuation slide; he'd speak to the Sexual Exploitation Unit later, and see if they had any intelligence on the establishment.

'Then what?'

'The girl …' he looked at his notebook '… Biljana Dragi, raced back in and she reckons there was somebody in a black hoodie removing a knife from the middle of the victim's chest. She said the window was open, and he climbed out, ran across the yard and through their back gate. She didn't see his face.

'She called for help and tried to stop the bleeding with towels. Another girl, Malina Dragi, heard her, came in and tried to help her, but they reckon he was already dead.'

'The same surname and it sounds Eastern European. Are they related?'

'Sisters, and they are Serbian nationals. With work visas. They were very keen for me to know that.'

'Where does the back gate lead to?'

'There's an alleyway. He could have gone either direction, towards the high street or into the estate behind. Jorge's already down there with a team of uniforms looking for witnesses.'

'It's the middle of the afternoon on a Monday. There should have been someone around,' said Warren. 'Presumably the killer was covered in blood, and you say he took the knife with him?'

'Yeah, the girls reckon he pulled it out. There are bloody smears on the window where he escaped.'

'Then either he's run away covered in blood, he's stopped to take his clothes off and ditched them, or he got changed. Get a team out looking for the knife and any discarded clothes.'

'Will do.'

'Whilst you're at it, get Mags Richardson to start collecting CCTV and licence plate numbers. If he didn't escape on foot, he might have used a vehicle.'

'It's a slightly dodgy area; Jorge reckons some of the houses might have security cameras out the front, so he's got his team looking for that as well. There's CCTV in the reception area and out the back, but none in the actual massage rooms. I guess you don't want that sort of thing on camera.'

Again, Warren ignored the implication.

'How many staff and clients were on the premises at the time?'

'There were no other clients at the time of the murder – it's pretty quiet this time of the week. There were just the two masseuses.'

'What about the owner?'

'She's on her way.' He looked at his watch. 'She'll be here any minute now, I reckon, in this traffic.'

'I want to speak to the masseuses when Forensics have finished with them.'

'You might need a translator. Their English is pretty basic.'

'Get one organized. Do we know who the victim is?'

'Just a first name, "Stevie", and a mobile number. They're pretty old school; they use a paper diary to book in clients.'

'Bag the diary as evidence. Send the mobile number back to Rachel Pymm and see if she can do anything with it. Who's the crime scene manager?'

'Andy Harrison.'

Warren nodded his approval. So far, everything had been done by the book.

'Good work, Shaun. I'll go and take a look.'

The rather grandiosely titled *Middlesbury Massage and Relaxation Centre* was a converted detached house, similar to dozens of small business across the town. The small garden at the front had been tarmacked over to create enough space for two medium-sized cars, whilst the large bay windows had been covered in signage advertising the services offered within, and products customers could buy to supposedly re-create the experience at home.

Warren stepped carefully onto the metal boards laid down by the CSIs to preserve any trace evidence such as footprints in the entranceway.

Inside, the wall between the entrance hall and what would originally have been a spacious front sitting room, had been knocked through to make a large reception-cum-waiting area with a desk, computer, till point and several comfy chairs. Towards the back were two small tables, each with a comfortable-looking recliner and a more practical work chair. Judging by the bottles of nail varnish and acetone on the tables, this was where the manicures and pedicures took place. Even through his mask, Warren's nose was assaulted by a heady mix of different scented oils.

Standing in the hallway beyond, Warren recognized the portly form of CSM Andy Harrison talking to another white-suited technician. The veteran CSI broke off when he saw Warren enter.

'Come in, DCI Jones. We'll have to forgo the kiss on both cheeks and the handshake; we don't want to contaminate the scene.'

The longer Warren knew the man, the stranger his sense of humour became; he supposed it was a natural response to the things the man dealt with every day.

'The victim is in the back room. We've finished the preliminaries and we're waiting for the pathologist to come and take a look.'

'What's the layout of the rest of the property?'

Harrison pointed towards the rear.

'These old houses had galley kitchens leading through to an outside toilet and coal shed. When they converted this one from residential to commercial, they made use of the existing plumbing and kept a small sink and kitchenette for staff use. The old outbuildings now house a washing machine and a tumble dryer; it looks as though they wash their towels and uniforms on site.' He rotated on the spot. 'Upstairs, the front bedroom is also kitted out as a massage suite, the original bathroom has been split in two and turned into male and female toilets, and the small bedroom has been turned into a store cupboard. It appears that the staff also keep their personal belongings in there and use it to get changed.'

Warren followed him through; Grimshaw hadn't been exaggerating, it really was a bloodbath. Here, even the scented candles, still guttering in the wind from the open window, were unable to mask the cloying smell of fresh blood.

The victim was a young man, probably in his twenties. White, with dark hair, he lay on his back, his body nude from the waist up, revealing a bulky torso that suggested hard work rather than hours spent in the gym. A gash to the left of his chest had leaked enough blood to obscure the tattoos that crossed his pectoral muscles and shoulder.

The attack had clearly been very quick. The victim's blood-

12

covered hands indicated that he had made some attempt to cover the wound.

'The pathologist will confirm, obviously, but I'd say the knife was quite large and it penetrated at least one of the chambers of his heart. I wouldn't be surprised if it was given a twist on the way out.'

Warren tore his eyes away from the wound to focus on the victim's face. The man's eyes were open, staring sightlessly at the ceiling, his mouth open in surprise. The blood loss had left his skin waxy in appearance, making the two or three days' stubble on his cheeks and chin stand out even more.

'The witnesses said that the killer escaped through the window,' said Warren. Even from his vantage point on the opposite side of the room, he could see bloody marks on the window frame.

'That's what it looks like at the moment, although we've not lifted any prints. I'd say the killer was wearing gloves. We'll look in more detail when the body's been removed, and we can move around more easily.'

Warren pointed to a number of evidence bags sitting on a chair in the corner.

'Are those his personal belongings?'

'Looks that way. The larger bags contain clothing. Blue jeans with leather belt, a black T-shirt with some rock band I've never heard of, and a brown leather jacket. He kept his socks, shoes and underwear on. The smaller bags contain his wallet, keys and mobile phone, which were in the inside-left pocket of his jacket.'

'We need to identify him, so I'll sign for those and leave the clothes with you.'

Warren collected the bags, before taking another look around the room.

His first impressions were that the murder had happened exactly as Grimshaw had stated. The killer came in through the window, stabbed the victim as he lay helpless on the massage bed, before taking the knife with him, leaving through the window.

He looked again at the victim's wide-staring eyes and his surprised expression.

Something wasn't right about the scene, but he couldn't quite put his finger on it.

Back outside in the fresh air, Warren wasted no time taking off his paper scene suit. Early evening and it was already dark. He handed the evidence bags over to Shaun Grimshaw whilst he undressed.

'We need to identify the victim. Take a look in his wallet and see if you can find a name. The bus service around here is crap, so he may have parked up nearby. Use the key fob to check the cars nearby; we might be able to identify him that way. Bag his phone and ask IT if they can unlock it. This doesn't look like a random killing, so I want to know who he's been in contact with.'

Grimshaw opened the evidence bag containing the wallet and started leafing through it.

He let out a heartfelt groan. 'You are never going to believe who it is.'

Chapter 2

The two young masseuses who had found the body were huddled together in the rear of a police van, tears streaking their faces. Their bloodstained work uniforms had already been taken by the CSIs, but even in the less than flattering replacement coveralls that they'd been issued, Warren could see that Grimshaw had a point. The two young women were very pretty, with shapely figures. Could they have been hired for their looks?

A detailed, formal interview would have to wait, as there were currently no Serbian translators available; however, the limited English that they spoke was enough to confirm the sequence of events as relayed by Grimshaw.

The owner of the parlour, Silvija Wilson, was a well-dressed, middle-aged woman. She had arrived in a brand-new Mini Clubman shortly after Warren emerged from the crime scene and was waiting impatiently outside the cordon.

'Are my girls OK?' she asked immediately. Her accent was almost pure Essex, with just a hint of Eastern European.

'They are a bit shaken, but physically they are fine,' Warren assured her.

'Thank goodness.'

'The women tell me that they're Serbian nationals,' said Warren.

'With valid work visas,' Wilson interrupted.

'I'm sure that they are here perfectly legally,' said Warren, 'however, without a translator, they haven't been able to fully answer my questions.'

'Would you like me to translate for you, to speed things up?' interrupted Wilson.

Warren smiled politely. 'That's very kind, but we're better off waiting for the translation service.'

She looked disappointed, but Warren knew better than to take her up on her offer. Given the circumstances, Wilson could hardly be considered unbiased and the last thing he wanted was for questions to be raised over the veracity of the translation.

'Why don't I just ask you some background?' he suggested.

Wilson nodded her assent.

'You are the owner, I take it?'

'Yes. I started the business from scratch about ten years ago.'

'And you are the manager?'

'Overall, yes.'

'Is it usual for you not to be present during the day?' Warren raised a placating hand as Wilson started to bristle. 'I'm not judging, Ms Wilson, I'm just trying to get a feel for the normal ebb and flow of staff and customers.'

She relaxed somewhat. 'I come and unlock in the morning and do a bit of paperwork. Except on Saturday, which is our busiest day. I let the girls get on with running the shop. They know what they are doing.'

'That's rather trusting, if you don't mind me saying so.'

'They're family from back in Belgrade. They are my sister's daughters. I sponsored them for a work visa and they joined me a little over twelve months ago, with the aim of learning a skill and improving their English.'

'How is that going?' asked Warren.

She gave a so-so gesture with her hand. 'They are very skilful at massage and the customers really like them, but the English

'… not so good. I had intended them to spend time socializing with English people, but we do have a small Serbian community here, with some rather good-looking boys …' She shrugged. 'They're young. What can I say?'

'And do you still see clients?'

'Only a few. I have a couple of older ladies who got to know me when I worked on the other side of town. They came with me when I set up this business and they're more like friends than clients.'

'So, you weren't in the shop earlier, when the attack happened?'

'No. I opened up at the usual time – half-past eight – then emptied the safe of the weekend's takings and did a bank run, before going to see my father-in-law. He's not very well and in a home.'

'You take the money to the bank yourself?' asked Warren.

'Not much choice, really. We're a small business; we can't afford Securicor to come and do it for us. To be honest, there isn't that much cash these days. Most clients pay by card.'

'So, there wouldn't have been much money on the premises at the time of the attack?'

'No. Monday's a quiet day usually, so aside from the float in the till there wouldn't have been very much.'

'I see that it's also a nail bar. Do Malina and Biljana also do nails?'

Wilson shook her head.

'No. We have a couple of girls who come and do that. They hire the space; I don't actually employ them.'

'Where were they today?'

'They weren't in. Monday is a quiet day.'

'So, the only members of staff in the shop at the time were your two nieces?'

'Yes. As I said, I was visiting my father-in-law in Stenfield. Look, can I go and speak to them? They must be absolutely terrified after what's happened.'

'Yes, of course.'

There came a tap on the door: Shaun Grimshaw.

'Just got off the phone from HQ. No registered Serbian speakers available until eleven o'clock tonight.'

Warren sighed and looked at his watch. Be careful what you wish for indeed; if he'd stayed to the end of the budget meeting, he'd probably be heading home for the evening by now.

It looked as though Susan would be dining alone again.

Back at the station, Warren held the first briefing of the case. It was eight p.m., and a lot had happened in the almost seven hours since the emergency services received the call reporting the killing. He was keen to keep up the momentum; crimes such as murder were often solved by actions taken in those first few hours.

Warren would hold a far more detailed briefing the following morning, but it was important that he bring everyone – including his superior, Detective Superintendent John Grayson – up to date, as well as introducing his rapidly growing team to one another.

Middlesbury CID was something of an outlier in Hertfordshire Constabulary, in all senses of the word. The consolidation of nearly all of the serious crime units in Hertfordshire, Bedfordshire and later Cambridgeshire into one, centralized headquarters down in Welwyn Garden City had led to the closing of most local CID units.

Warren's predecessor, the disgraced DCI Gavin Sheehy, had fought the case for Middlesbury to remain open as a first-response unit, able to deal quickly and effectively with low-level crime within the farthest reaches of the county, and at least start the ball rolling on larger-scale investigations. To that end, DSI Grayson oversaw a small, core team of detectives, led by Warren, with additional support from Welwyn when needed.

Since taking over from Sheehy four years previously, Warren had made it one of his priorities to maintain Middlesbury's unique status, growing to love a role that saw him doing far more hands-on policing than would be normal for one of his rank.

Thus far, the small unit's disproportionately high success rate had kept them open in the face of ever-increasing government cuts.

For now.

Warren started the briefing with a full-screen headshot of the man in the massage parlour projected onto the screen.

'This is our victim. Stevie Cullen, the twenty-three-year-old son of one of North Hertfordshire's most notable families. For those of you not familiar with the Cullens, "most notable" is not a praiseworthy term.'

Nods rippled around the room.

'That's a mugshot from his last arrest, and we positively identified him from his fingerprints and the tattoos covering his chest. Needless to say, the car that his keys unlocked is *not* registered to him, rather it belongs to his brother, as Stevie received his first driving ban before he was even old enough to pass his test. His mobile phone has a screen lock that IT are figuring out how to circumvent as we speak.'

Warren let the mutterings die down before he continued.

'We need to turn his life upside down, folks. This was clearly a targeted killing. Given the circles that the Cullens are alleged to move in, then that must be a primary line of investigation. The Serious Organized Crime Unit from Welwyn will be briefing us on what we know or suspect about the Cullens' business interests tomorrow. In the meantime, we need to track his movements over the past few days, as well as finding out who was in the area at the time.

'Jorge, can you fill us in on any witnesses located in the local area and the preliminary search?'

DS Jorge Martinez addressed the room.

'It won't take long, I'm afraid. Despite being a Monday lunchtime, we haven't found a single member of the public who witnessed the killer escaping the scene or recalls anyone suspicious hanging around. There are a number of small businesses in the area with inadequate parking, and public transport is poor, so residents are used to seeing strange cars parked in their streets. The lack of parking wardens enforcing resident-only parking is a long-running bone of contention amongst the locals.

'We've identified a dozen or so properties, both business and residential, that may have usable CCTV footage of the area and we're securing it for DS Richardson's team to look at.'

'Any discarded clothes or the murder weapon?' asked DS David Hutchinson.

'Nothing so far. We've emptied all the public waste bins in the vicinity, and we've secured the wheelie bins from all the local residents and businesses. First thing tomorrow, when the sun comes up, we'll have teams doing a fingertip search of all the local streets.'

'Any rumblings on social media yet?' asked Warren.

DS Rachel Pymm, the team's officer in the case – the person charged with keeping the HOLMES2 case management database up to date – shook her head.

'Nothing much so far. A few photographs have surfaced on Twitter of the cordon, with plenty of speculation about what has happened, but nobody has mentioned Stevie Cullen yet.'

'Good,' said Warren, 'his loved ones don't deserve to find out he's dead from some bigmouth on Facebook.'

Chapter 3

It's known as the 'death knock' by both journalists and the police. It was an aspect of policing that Warren rarely had to do these days, his rank largely shielding him from the duty. However, given the history of the Cullen family, he decided to accompany the family liaison team himself. He wanted to hear what the family had to say first-hand; to pick up those tiny nuances and signals that might not get passed on in the reports.

The Cullen family lived in a ramshackle farmhouse on the very outskirts of Middlesbury. Surrounded by fields, the car headlights had revealed a yard full of clusters of stacked Portakabins and shipping containers, locked behind large, steel gates. Warren's nose alerted him to the presence of pigs.

Lots of pigs.

Mrs Cullen opened the door. Spotting the uniformed officer standing behind him, she scowled.

'What?'

'Mrs Cullen?'

'Yeah.'

'We'd like to speak to you about your son Stevie …'

'He ain't here.'

She started to close the door. Warren slipped a foot between the door and the frame.

'Hey, you can't do that. You need a warrant ...' she yelped.

'We need to speak to you about your son. May we come in?' Warren paused. 'Is your husband in? Is there anyone who can be with you?'

The blood drained from her face and for a moment he thought she would faint. He readied himself to catch her.

'Seamus! It's the police.' Her voice was surprisingly strong.

A muffled voice replied from the depths of the house. 'Tell them to piss off.'

'It's about Stevie. Oh God ...'

Seamus Cullen emerged from the rear of the house, wiping his hands on a greasy rag.

He stopped dead in his tracks. Whether it was the grim expression on Warren's face, the family liaison officer holding his cap respectfully in his hands, or his wife's look of distress that told them why they were there was unclear. Either way, it was Seamus Cullen whose knees buckled and left him grabbing the staircase for support.

Coffee and a sit-down returned most of the colour to Seamus Cullen's face. Seated opposite the couple, Warren gently told them what they knew so far.

Facing them, it was hard to reconcile the family's reputation with the couple in front of him. Like most police officers in this part of the county, Warren was well aware of the family's reputation; however, he had never personally dealt with them. Most of their transgressions came under volume crime, particularly the fencing of stolen property, and antisocial behaviour, with health and safety violations and a carefree attitude to tax returns thrown in as well.

The family's nearest neighbours were almost a mile away, but Stevie Cullen in particular was still the subject of numerous

22

complaints about noise, riding quad bikes dangerously, and using threatening and intimidating behaviour. It was behaviour he'd learnt from his parents.

None of that was evident at this moment; gone were the hard edges and defiant attitude towards authority. The couple in front of him had lost a child, in the most horrific of circumstances, and their grief was all-consuming.

'It looks as though the attack was deliberate. Can you think about anyone who might have wanted to hurt or kill Stevie?'

Rosie Cullen shook her head firmly. 'No. He wasn't involved with anything like that.'

It was interesting that she'd immediately assumed he was killed due to something he had done.

'Can you think of anyone who he might have had a falling out with?'

This time it was Seamus who answered. 'Boys will be boys, and he sometimes liked a row after a few pints down the White Stag, but I can't imagine anyone wanting to kill him. Especially, you know so …' He stopped, unable to continue.

Warren made a note to question the locals down the White Stag.

'What about friends or acquaintances? Is there anyone that Stevie was particularly close to?'

The couple glanced at each other. It was clear they were reluctant to point the police in the direction of any of their associates. That was hardly surprising, given the circles they moved in, but if Warren was going to solve their son's brutal murder and bring his killers to justice, then he needed all of the help he could get.

He said as much.

After a long pause, Rosie started to dictate the names of as many of Stevie's friends as she could recall.

'What about anyone special?'

Rosie paused. 'No chance. That boy was far too young to settle down. He played the field.'

23

Seamus said nothing, biting his lip.

'Mr Cullen?' prompted Warren.

'Well there was this one girl he was quite keen on. He saw her more than most …' His voice petered out at his wife's surprised stare.

'Who?' she asked.

'Vicki Barclay.'

'What? That stuck-up blonde one from the Stag? She's far too posh for the likes of our boy. I haven't seen her around for what, six months? Besides, I thought she was engaged to that Rimington lad.'

'I'm just going by what he said to me.'

Warren made a note of all the names flying around. He recognized a few of them from the briefing reports that crossed his desk; they weren't exactly fine and upstanding citizens. However, the couple weren't telling him everything; that much was certain. Warren knew that he'd need to tread carefully.

'What can you tell me about what Stevie did for a living?'

'He helped out on the farm.' His mother's tone was firm. The couple moved closer together on the sofa.

'Did he do any other work, or have business dealings with anyone else?'

'He was a farmhand. That's all.' Her tone was icy. Beside her, her husband's face took on a mask.

They were circling the wagons. Their son was dead, and nothing would bring him back. Now it was all about self-preservation.

Warren knew that what he said next was not going to go down well.

'Would it be all right if we looked at Stevie's room?'

Again, it was his mother who replied. 'No. He's dead. I'm not having you trampling all over his room, disturbing his things.'

'I promise you that we'll be very respectful, and we'll leave everything the way we found it.'

'No. And I think it's time you left. Leave us alone to mourn our boy.'

Seamus got to his feet. 'I'll show you out.'

Warren tried to reason with them one more time. 'Please, Mr and Mrs Cullen. Your son's death was not an accident. We need your help to find his killer and bring them to justice. There may be clues in his room that will help us track down who did this to your son.'

Clues that might disappear when his parents went through his belongings to remove anything that might incriminate them.

'Not without a warrant,' said Rosie, her tone final.

Warren cursed himself all the way back to the station. He should have known the Cullens wouldn't let him search the house without a warrant. Given the family's reputation, it was entirely predictable that they wouldn't let anyone poke around their affairs; goodness knows what they would find. They'd even shunned the presence of the family liaison officer.

As Warren had driven down the driveway, he'd seen the upstairs lights in the farmhouse come on. He'd bet good money that both parents were busy tearing through their late son's room removing anything incriminating.

DSI Grayson was waiting for Warren in the station car park, the necessary paperwork clutched in his hand. He said nothing as he handed it through the open car window, but Warren could feel the disapproval radiating off him. Warren was heading back towards the Cullens' farmhouse in less than thirty seconds.

In the twenty minutes it had taken Warren to race back to Middlesbury and get the warrant, the driveway outside the Cullens' house had gained several new cars. Despite the frustration of the past few minutes, Warren was relieved. Leaving aside the parents' obstructive attitude, they had just received a terrible shock – they needed their family and friends with them now. Nevertheless, Warren intended to make a note of every licence plate he saw; he'd like to know who he was dealing with.

Warren pulled into the same spot he'd occupied moments before. Beside him, the family liaison officer, who'd maintained a diplomatic silence for the past few minutes, straightened his shirt as he stepped out of the car. It was just as well that the driveway was so large – there were several more cars and vans on their way, including a scenes of crime unit.

'Back again.'

It wasn't a question. Rosie Cullen didn't even glance at the document in his hand. The twenty minutes' delay had clearly been enough. Again, Warren cursed himself; who knew what vital clues were now locked away in the boots of the various cars sitting outside, safely beyond the scope of the hastily arranged warrant.

Chapter 4

The Serbian translator arrived shortly before eleven p.m. Warren had just returned to the station again. When he'd left the Cullens' farm, a team had been searching Stevie's room for clues. The family liaison officer had finally been allowed to do his job and was now arranging support for the Cullens over the coming days and weeks.

The newcomers had been identified as members of the sprawling Cullen family. All of them professed shock at their brother's death and described a universally beloved man entirely at odds with the intelligence reports Warren had skimmed through earlier that day. Warren had arranged more detailed one-on-one interviews with all of them over the coming days to see if that assessment changed out of earshot of the rest of the family.

The translator was a middle-aged woman by the name of Neda Stojanovi , dressed in a flowing tie-dyed dress. She shook Warren's hand as she apologized for being unable to arrive sooner.

'The only other available translator actually lives in Middlesbury. Given the close-knit local community, the agency thought it best that they send someone from farther afield.'

Warren thanked her. Police translators were registered and vetted by Language Line; nevertheless, he didn't want any potential conflicts of interest this early in the investigation. If and when the case came to trial, the last thing he wanted was the veracity of the witnesses' translation being called into question by a defence solicitor.

He decided to start with the younger of the two masseuses, Biljana, who had witnessed the stabbing. Known to everyone as Billy, the dark-haired nineteen-year-old looked tired, the adrenalin from the attack having worn off hours ago.

After explaining that she wasn't under arrest, but that the interview was being video-recorded to ensure that others could check that the translation was accurate, Warren started with a few easy questions to get them all used to the three-way conversation.

'What time did you start work this morning, Billy?'

'About eight-thirty. Aunty Silvija picked Malina and me up from our house on the way to work.'

'Malina is your sister, correct?'

'Yes.'

'What happened after you were picked up?'

'We got the shop ready and put on our uniforms. Aunty Silvija counted the money from the safe and got it ready to take to the bank. Then we put the open sign on the door.'

'What time was this?'

'About nine o'clock.'

'When did Silvija go to the bank?'

'She had a cup of coffee first. Maybe nine-thirty?' She took a sip of water.

'Did you have many clients booked in for the day?'

She shook her head. 'No, Monday is a quiet day. We had Mrs Green booked in, and that was all for the morning.'

'What about Mr Cullen?'

'He was booked in at one p.m.'

'That's not a lot of customers. I'm surprised that you open if there are so few customers.'

'Silvija says that if we start closing during the week, it sends the wrong message and that we'll lose our Saturday clients, because they think we are going to close.'

It didn't sound like a very sound business model to Warren. He wondered just how financially viable the shop was. He made a note to look into that further, in case it was relevant.

'How many staff were there when Silvija left for the bank?'

She thought for a moment. 'Two. Me and Malina.'

'What about the nail technicians?'

'Monday is a quiet day; they weren't in.'

'Sounds like it can be a bit boring.'

She shrugged. 'Sometimes. But we can do some study and talk to our friends and family on Facebook.'

'What time did Mr Cullen arrive for his appointment? Was he on time?'

'About ten to one. He was a little bit early.' Her eyes were starting to fill with tears.

'And where were you when he arrived?'

'I was in the room, getting it ready.'

'Ready how?'

'Lighting the scented candles, dimming the lights, and fetching the towels and oils.'

'Then what happened?'

Her lip trembled, and her eyes took on a faraway cast. 'He came in and took off his clothes.'

'Were you present then?'

'No. We give customers privacy. When I came back, he was in his underwear lying on the bed, with a towel across his waist.'

'On his front or his back?'

'On his front. I always start with a shoulder massage, then do his back.'

'You've had Mr Cullen as a client before?'

She nodded, the gathering tears now threatening to fall down her face.

29

'After you had finished with his back, what did you do next?'

'He rolled over and I loosened his leg muscles, before giving him a head and scalp massage.'

'Then what?'

'He likes to relax afterwards. Sometimes he falls asleep, so I turn the lights down and leave him in there.'

'What time was that?'

She shrugged. 'The massage takes about thirty minutes or so. I wasn't wearing my watch.

'Where did you go then?'

'To wash the oil off my hands.'

'Upstairs?'

'Yes.'

She took out a tissue and blew her nose. Warren and the translator waited patiently for her to compose herself. She wasn't even twenty years old yet, and Warren could barely imagine the trauma that she had experienced that day. Nevertheless, he needed her to tell him what happened next.

'I was just coming back downstairs when I heard a scream from the room, so I ran in …' She stopped, taking a deep breath, before starting again.

'There was a man … He had a knife and he was plunging it into Stevie's chest.'

'What sort of knife?'

'I don't know. I didn't see.'

'OK. Can you describe the man to me?'

'He was wearing a black hooded jumper and a black baseball cap.'

'What about his build? Was he tall, short? Fat, skinny?'

She shrugged. 'He was normal size.'

'Did you see his face?'

She shook her head. 'No.'

'Did he say anything?'

'No.'

'Then what happened?'

'He pulled the knife out and climbed out of the window.'

'What did you do?'

'I tried to stop the bleeding. Malina heard the screaming and came in and she helped me.' She covered her face with her hands and the interpreter leant closer to hear what she was saying. 'But he died.'

After a suitable pause, Warren continued. 'Where was Mr Cullen?'

'On the bed.'

'What position was he in?'

'On his back ... his eyes were open ... he was staring ...'

Again, she dissolved into tears. The interpreter looked towards Warren for permission before slipping her arm around the girl's shoulders.

After a few moments, she indicated that she was ready to continue.

The pause gave Warren a few moments to review his notes. He wanted to make certain that he had everything he needed before asking his final question, which he knew might cause offence.

'Billy, I need to ask if there is anything you haven't told me about Mr Cullen.'

'No. He was just a client.'

'Did you and Mr Cullen ever have any sort of relationship?'

'No, he was just a client.'

'I need to know if he ever asked you to perform any intimate acts or acts that you might have felt uncomfortable performing? I promise you that you won't be charged with any offences.'

She sat up straight. 'I am not a prostitute, Mr Jones.'

And that was the end of the interview.

By the time Warren had finished interviewing Biljana Dragi , it was almost midnight. He debated calling it a night, but he didn't want to let the two sisters spend too much time comparing stories. They'd already spent much of the day together, which couldn't really be helped, and he was reluctant to let Biljana tell her older sister, Malina, too much about his line of questioning.

The translator declined his offer of a coffee, saying it was too late for her. Warren knew that caffeine was the only thing that would get him through the night, although he'd pay for it when he finally got his head down.

Up close, the familial relationship between the two girls was even more marked; hair colour aside they could almost have passed for twins.

The story Malina told was nearly identical to her sister's. She could give no more details about the hooded attacker who she and Biljana had witnessed plunging the knife into the supine body of Stevie Cullen.

The older woman was less tearful, but still clearly in shock.

'After you and Biljana realized he was dead, what did you do?'

'I called the police.'

Warren had reviewed the recording from the emergency operator. The call had come in at 13.40. The female caller had a strong Eastern European accent and was so panicked it took the call-taker some time to get her name and the address of the massage parlour. It took a further minute to ascertain that the attacker had left the premises and get a basic description for officers in the area. Unfortunately, every minute of delay had allowed the attacker to cover his tracks more efficiently.

'Where were you before the attack?'

'I was in the front at the desk.'

'Where there any other clients with you?'

'No. Monday is a quiet day.'

'What about other members of staff?'

'No. Only Billy and I were working.'

'What about the technicians in the nail bar?'

'They do not work Monday. It is a quiet day.'

'And you ran in immediately when you heard Billy scream?'

'Yes.'

'How well did you know Mr Cullen?'

'Not well. He was a client.'

'Did you ever give Mr Cullen a massage?'

'No. Billy always gave him his treatments.'

'Why do you think that was?'

'He liked Billy. If a customer has had a good massage, then we try and make sure they have the same person next time.'

'Did Billy and Mr Cullen have any sort of relationship?'

'I don't know what you mean.'

'Did she ever see him outside work?'

'No, of course not.'

'You sound surprised that I asked. Are you not allowed to make friends with clients?'

She paused. 'We can be friends with anyone we like, but my sister was not friends with Stevie.'

Warren paused. Again, he had a feeling that his next question would bring the interview to a close.

'I'm sorry, but I need to ask. Did you or your sister ever have a more intimate relationship with Mr Cullen? You won't be in any trouble.'

'No. Just because we work in a massage parlour does not make us whores.'

She seemed as angered as her sister at the suggestion.

She settled back in her chair, her arms folded.

Whatever the truth of the relationship between Stevie Cullen and the two masseuses, he could see that he wasn't going to get any more from her at that time of night. He'd review the interview tapes in the morning with the team, but already he had identified several discrepancies in their accounts.

He was far from finished with the two women.

Tuesday 03 November

Chapter 5

Despite his late night, Warren was in well before the start of the eight a.m. briefing. Much to his surprise, the coffee that had sustained him through the late-night interviews had not stopped him from falling asleep as soon as he clambered into the bed in the guest room. Susan had been sound asleep before he arrived home and they had barely exchanged a dozen words and a kiss outside the bathroom before Warren had left again. Once again, part of Warren was starting to regret wishing for more excitement. On the other hand, this was what he lived for; nobody joined the police to sit in overheated meeting rooms discussing quarterly projections. Nevertheless, the timing could have been better. He double-checked that his calendar was still free on Thursday morning for Susan's appointment.

He was well into his second cup of coffee by the time he called the briefing to order.

The first thing the team reviewed was the previous night's search of the Cullen farmhouse, specifically Stevie Cullen's rooms. Warren's fears that the delay between obtaining the search warrant and the scenes of crime unit gaining access to the house had proven well founded. The search team had said that his parents were adamant Stevie hadn't owned a laptop, but they didn't really believe them. Who knew what else had been spirited away before the team started their search?

Forcing the self-recriminations to one side for the time being, Warren moved on to the previous night's interviews with the two young masseuses.

'The timing of events seems to be a little muddled,' he said. 'Biljana claims that she heard Cullen scream and that was why she rushed back in; however, she then says that she saw the killer plunge the knife into his chest as she re-entered the room. If her account is correct, that suggests that he screamed before he was stabbed.'

'Maybe the killer startled him? A hooded man standing over you with a knife would do that, especially if he was half-asleep,' suggested Martinez.

Warren acknowledged the theory, before moving to his next point.

'Her sister, Malina, says that she was in the reception, when she heard her sister scream; she then rushed in also and claims to have seen the killer stabbing Cullen. There was only a single stab wound. Biljana claims to have screamed when she saw him being stabbed, so I don't see how her sister could have been in the room when he was stabbed if she only ran in when her sister screamed.'

The room was silent for a moment, before Martinez spoke up again.

'I still think it could work.' He leant forward. 'In her interview, Malina doesn't mention hearing Cullen scream, yet Biljana heard him from upstairs. Maybe Malina actually heard Cullen scream, not Biljana and so entered the room only just after her sister? That way they could both have seen him being stabbed. You know how unreliable witnesses are in stressful situations, especially when it comes to how long things take.'

The room was silent again, before Grimshaw spoke up.

'I hate to admit it, but Jorge might be right. We should also get someone else to review the translation. Maybe Serbian is one of those funny languages where past and present tenses are all muddled up?'

'A good suggestion – I'll see about sending the videos for a second opinion,' said Warren. It would cost money, but it was essential that the women's accounts were as accurate as possible. The last thing Warren wanted was for a canny defence team to pounce on a misinterpreted verb ending.

Grimshaw was on a roll now. 'If you ask me, those girls have something to hide. They were far too defensive when the boss asked if either of them had slept with Stevie Cullen.'

Opposite him, Warren could see DS Rachel Pymm rolling her eyes.

'Well wouldn't you be, Shaun? It had to be asked, but it was tantamount to accusing them of being sex workers.'

'I'm with Rachel,' said Martinez. 'Workers in legitimate massage parlours must put up with those insinuations all the time. The Sexual Exploitation Unit said that as far as they are aware, the parlour is a legit, professional business.'

'I'm just saying it as I see it,' said Grimshaw defensively. 'Even if the shop is a perfectly lawful business, the girls are on their own all day. They could easily be offering clients a "happy ending" for a few quid bonus, with the owner none the wiser. Maybe that's why Cullen always requested Biljana?'

Warren raised a hand to stop the argument getting out of hand.

'Shaun has a fair point.' He ignored the man's smirk towards Martinez. 'It's something we should look into. Given the discrepancies, I think we have enough to request the phone records of Biljana and Malina. I'd like to know if either of them has contacted Cullen on their personal phones. Let's not forget that so far, we only have their word that Cullen was killed by an intruder.'

'We should also request the records for their aunt and the business line,' said Pymm.

'Good idea. Rachel, can you do a RIPA request?' asked Warren. 'Get DSI Grayson to sign off on it. Moray, work with her. I don't think you've done one of them yourself.'

Moray Ruskin nodded; the young detective constable eager as always to get stuck in.

Warren moved on. 'Next up, where are we with the searches and the CCTV? Jorge?'

'The fingerprint searches restarted at first light. No sign of the weapon or discarded clothing yet,' replied Martinez.

'Mags, what about CCTV?'

'There is CCTV footage of the front half of the reception area, although the angle of the camera doesn't look too helpful.'

'What about out the back?' asked Martinez.

'Nothing, the camera is broken.'

'That's convenient,' said Ruskin. 'When was it broken?'

'They reckon ages ago,' said Richardson. 'If it was deliberate, it shows some serious premeditation. The digital video recorder has been seized as evidence; IT are retrieving the data as we speak.'

'Good. See if they can get some footage of when the camera was broken, so we can see if it's linked to the killing,' instructed Warren. 'What about ANPR?'

'It's going to take some time, and it'll cover a huge area. The junctions in the immediate area around the massage parlour aren't covered by cameras, so we'll have to cast the net pretty wide. The main roads that are covered are very busy, especially that time of day. I've got a team down in Welwyn tracking all the cars in the vicinity. They've identified the car that Stevie Cullen was driving, and they're reconstructing his route that day as best they can.'

'Good. Extend that over the past few days. Clearly, he's upset somebody enough for them to kill him. I'd like to know where he's been recently – perhaps we can find a motive?'

'We've had our eye on the Cullens for some years,' said DCI Ian

Bergen, an investigator in the force's Serious Organized Crime Unit. A balding man, with an impressive moustache, Bergen had travelled up to Middlesbury from headquarters in Welwyn that morning to brief the team on the Cullen family.

'I'm sure that many of you have come across them in one way or another over the years, although as a rule of thumb if it's anything more serious than public disorder, petty vandalism or driving offences, the case is handed over to us as part of our ongoing investigation. Unfortunately, in terms of the serious crime pecking order, they are quite far down the food chain, and so we've struggled to justify putting the resources in. They also tend to steer clear of drugs, so we're cut off from that funding source.

'In a way it was very helpful of Stevie Cullen to get himself killed yesterday; it means we can get you folks to do some of the legwork for us. I've been itching to get a warrant to have a wander around their farm for years.'

The room remained silent. Realizing his humour wasn't appreciated by the team who would be dealing with the bloody aftermath of the previous day's killing, as well as liaising with a grieving family, Bergen moved on quickly. 'It's good to see a few familiar faces here that I recognize from days gone by in SOC. Your familiarity with the family will doubtless be invaluable.'

Shaun Grimshaw touched two fingers to his temple in a mock salute and Jorge Martinez nodded in acknowledgement.

Bergen gestured towards a family tree projected on the board behind him. 'As you can see, the immediate family is quite large; Mr and Mrs Cullen have five kids. Stevie was the youngest at twenty-three. Expand the family out to include cousins, in-laws and partners and it gets large and complicated very quickly. Not all the people listed here fully partake in the family's extra-legal activities, but generally speaking most are involved to some extent. Given that one of the sons, Patrick, was convicted of shoplifting nappies a few months ago for his sister, you could even argue that the youngest member of the family – eighteen-month-old Tyler – is probably involved in the handling of stolen property.'

Warren recognized the man that Bergen was pointing to from his visit the previous night.

'The head of the family is the father, Seamus Cullen. He's sixty-two years old and has done a handful of short stretches in prison for handling stolen property, and his supposedly peripheral involvement in an armed robbery on a Post Office some twenty years ago. He was convicted of helping the actual robbers store the stolen money, but his defence solicitor successfully convinced the jury that he was only involved after the fact and that he had no idea what he agreed to look after, so he only got a couple of months. Total bollocks, but the evidence was lacking. He tries to cultivate an image as a hardworking simple farmer struggling to eke out a living, but make no mistake, he's a clever and slippery bugger, with a nasty temper to boot. He always seems to be one step ahead of us.'

He moved over to the next slide. Mrs Cullen.

'Which brings us to the next person of interest, Rosie Cullen. She is also sixty-two, and mother of Seamus's five children. Unlike her husband, she's never seen the inside of a prison, although she's found herself occupying a custody suite a few times over the years, mostly for affray, antisocial behaviour and some petty shoplifting.

'The two of them have been married for forty-odd years, although it's questionable whether we could describe it as a "happy marriage". On a couple of occasions, when officers visited the property, Rosie answered the door with fresh bruising to her face. She refuses to admit to being hit and reacts angrily to any suggestion that she may need help. As you know, there is very little we can do in those circumstances.'

Warren had seen no evidence of any abuse when he'd visited the night before, but he knew that they would need to be vigilant in future. A shock such as this could have devastating effects on a family's dynamics; he made a note to ensure that the family liaison team were fully informed.

'As to the kids, on paper Stevie was a farmhand, but he spent an awful lot of time driving around Middlesbury and the surrounding villages, visiting other local farms. He's clearly got other money-making ventures on the side. We have our suspicions about what he's up to, but we can't be sure exactly what he's doing.

'The other four kids range from their eldest Lavender, who is forty, to their next youngest, also a daughter, Saffron, who is thirty-two. I'll let you draw your own conclusions about what four kids in eight years, then a nine-year gap before Stevie came along suggests about his place in the pecking order. Between them are two more sons, including Patrick, usually known as Paddy, aged thirty-four and Frankie, his twin brother.'

Warren reviewed his notes from the previous night. Lavender had not been present; however, he had briefly met Saffron and her husband, and both of the twins.

Bergen was still speaking. 'Paddy lives and works at the farm when he's not inside for stealing; the bugger will nick anything. He also has two convictions for violent offences, both drink-related. He was convicted of affray six years ago and got away with a suspended sentence. A month after the suspension expired, he was involved in yet another pub fight. Witnesses claimed he had a knife, but he didn't have one on him when he was arrested, and the CCTV angle was wrong. Unfortunately, Stevie Cullen, who was also present, managed to leave the scene without being searched; we suspect he took the knife with him.

'Given that he didn't use the knife and that nobody was seri-ously injured in the fisticuffs, the CPS dropped the more serious charges and again, he got a suspended sentence.'

Warren made a note of the man's details. Stevie Cullen had been killed by a stab wound. Could his brother be the killer?

'What about Frankie?' he asked. He remembered the man from

43

his visit to the farm the previous night – it was hard to believe they were even brothers, let alone twins.

'Frankie isn't known to us officially. The family don't like to speak about it, but my understanding is that he has some learning difficulties. He works on the farm, and apart from the odd trip with his brothers to the pub, isn't really on our radar.'

That certainly matched Warren's impression of the man. Unlike the rest of the family, Frankie was huge. The man had remained seated and stared into space during the time that Warren was with the family, but it was clear to see from the length of his legs, the width of his shoulders and the size of his hands, that he dwarfed even Moray Ruskin.

Warren made a note to find out more about this second brother. Learning difficulties could mean anything, and he'd need to know more before ruling him out as a suspect, although surely the masseuses would have mentioned the attacker's exceptional size if Frankie was the killer?

'What about the sisters?' asked Hutchinson.

It was a good question. Although the attacker was described as male, neither of the two masseuses had given a detailed description. A baggy hoodie could easily conceal a person's figure. They could also be the driving force behind the attack, even if they weren't the person wielding the knife.

'Lavender, the eldest, lives a few miles away in Bishop's Stortford. She's married with two young children. She has a fairly close relationship with the rest of the family, but as far as we know runs a perfectly legitimate small business. Her husband also isn't known to police, other than through his association with the Cullens.'

It was still an avenue worth exploring, decided Warren.

'The youngest daughter, Saffron, lives in a cottage on site with her husband and three toddlers. They are both farmhands, and Saffron also takes the family's produce to market. She has no convictions, although the Food Standards Agency have taken an

44

interest lately, after a wedding party she supplied came down with the shits.'

Warren remembered meeting her: a slim woman, in loose clothing, she could probably be mistaken for a man, especially in such a stressful situation. For that matter, her husband was of average build also.

'We know that the family employ a number of itinerant workers on their farm, particularly during the harvest season. We did a joint visit to the farm a couple of years ago with HMRC who are interested in the family's tax affairs, but only found a couple of workers, all with valid National Insurance numbers. It's bloody obvious that there are other, unregistered workers, probably working cash in hand, but there was no evidence and HMRC have bigger fish to fry.

'All joking aside, we'll be grateful for anything your team find out and we'll support your investigation in any way that we can. We've been after the Cullens for years.'

After a few more questions, Warren thanked Bergen for his time. In his experience, SOC tended to play their cards close to their chest, allowing CID to do all the hard work, before claiming all the credit. He'd said as much to Grayson before the briefing. Time would tell if Bergen's words were more than just platitudes.

'The killing of Stevie Cullen wasn't some random act,' said Warren. 'It could well have been business-related, or the result of a family feud. I want to know where all of the family members were at the time of the killing and who he's been doing business with. Jorge, I want you and Moray to start turning his life upside down. Work with DCI Bergen and his team in Welwyn.

'Shaun, liaise with the Social Media Intelligence Unit. See if you can find us some more suspects to interview. I'd also like you and Rachel to keep on top of the mobile phone companies; they've been served with warrants and I want the call logs and GPS from everybody's mobiles.'

'I've arranged for the family to come to the station to give formal interviews starting at midday. If any of them were involved, I don't want to give them too long to get their stories straight, so we'll be interviewing them separately and simultaneously. But let's be sensitive, people; regardless of our suspicions they've just suffered a bereavement and they are probably still in shock. Rachel, Mags and Hutch, I'll split the interviewees between us, with a view to feeding back at evening briefing. Reconvene here at eleven to go over interview strategies.

'DSI Grayson has arranged for uniform and non-uniform bodies from Welwyn to support us, so put them to work.' He glanced at his watch. 'The killing happened less than twenty-four hours ago. Let's start rattling cages before the killer has time to cover his tracks. Feed everything back to Rachel so she can keep HOLMES up to date.'

Dismissing the team, Warren headed back to his office. A moment later, there came a knock on the door: Shaun Grimshaw.

'Can I have a quick word, Boss?'

'Of course, Shaun.' Warren settled down in his chair.

'I know all the social media stuff is important, but I wondered if I could join Jorge's team investigating the Cullens? Jorge and me worked for months with Ian Bergen and his team when we were down in Welwyn. I'm familiar with a lot of the players and I can help bring the rest of the team up to speed.'

Warren contemplated his request. Grimshaw and Martinez had transferred to Middlesbury earlier in the year. Both detective sergeants, the two men had worked together extensively before joining Warren's team. By all accounts, their partnership had been forged from their earliest days in training college, when they'd bonded over a shared love of Manchester City Football Club. The two men had worked alongside each other as constables, before transferring to CID together. They'd taken their sergeant exams at the same time and were now both in the early stages of their inspector training.

Their partnership had been effective over the years, and they were both ambitious and hardworking. Nevertheless, their close relationship had caused some disquiet. Dubbed the 'Brown-nose Brothers' by some, their ambition to get noticed was a source of some amusement, and occasional exasperation. The two had gained a reputation for hanging around in the lobby at head-quarters so that they could catch the same elevator as more senior officers, ensuring that even as constables their names were known by those who mattered, and they were always the first to volun-teer for high-profile roles in investigations.

They had been assigned to Middlesbury to gain experience and fill a vacancy. With DI Tony Sutton on long-term sick leave, Grayson had agreed to take them on and allow them to start 'acting up', taking the lead in investigations and preparing for their next move. The close-knit structure of Middlesbury CID was an excellent place for them to stretch their wings.

But Warren had concerns that the two men spent too much time working together. To be effective leaders, they needed to work with a wide range of colleagues, not just one another; that was why he had been deliberately separating them, giving them their own, independent roles.

Warren's wife Susan found the whole situation highly amusing. As a schoolteacher, she spent a lot of time breaking up friendship groups within her classes, stopping students from getting too comfortable with one another. Her pupils didn't like it, but it forced them to develop new skills and not rely too much on just one or two individuals.

However, there was no question that the men complemented each other. Grimshaw was, to be charitable, rather a blunt instru-ment. Forthright and outspoken, he didn't suffer fools gladly and gleefully played up to the stereotype of a gruff northerner. It was a ploy that often worked well in southern England. He was a lot cleverer than his demeanour sometimes suggested.

By contrast, Martinez was quiet and softly spoken, with only traces of his upbringing in his accent. Where Grimshaw typically looked as though he'd just rolled out of bed after a heavy night and dressed in the dark, Martinez wore sharply tailored suits, expensive aftershave and kept his short, neat hair immaculately trimmed. When watching the two men interviewing, Grimshaw would tend to take on the role of 'bad cop', unsettling the interviewee, with Martinez offering a more sympathetic ear. It was an effective strategy, and made Warren feel the absence of Tony Sutton all the more; he'd lost count of the number of times the two of them had played those roles.

All that being said, Grimshaw had a valid point. He and Martinez knew more about the Cullen family and their acquaintances than anyone else on his core team. It would be silly not to take advantage of his experience.

'That's a fair point, Shaun. I still want you working through the social media and phone records, but make sure that you keep up a close dialogue with Jorge and his team. Let's see if DCI Bergen is as good as his word.'

Chapter 6

From the outside, the White Stag looked like a typical country pub. Within walking distance of the Cullens' farm and several local houses, the small front car park was nevertheless full, although it was too early for the two-for-one offer on pub grub. The chilly November air meant that the weathered picnic benches were unoccupied, save for one middle-aged man puffing on a pipe whilst he read the newspaper and supped a pint of bitter.

Jorge Martinez parked his Audi TT in one of the few spaces left in the overspill car park to the rear, locked the doors, and followed Moray Ruskin into the crowded bar.

Despite the relatively early hour, there was little space. Immediately inside the doorway, a group of men stood in a loose circle, staring into their pints.

'Speak of the devil,' muttered one of them, scowling at the new arrivals. Clearly, news of Stevie Cullen's death had made it to his local.

'Ignore him,' said the woman serving behind the bar.

As always, Ruskin was surprised at how he was immediately identified as a police officer. He supposed he shouldn't be; he and Martinez were the only people in the bar not dressed in work clothes. Several of the men wore mud-stained jackets and boots.

A black and white Border collie looked over, yawned then rested its head back on its paws.

'I guess you're here about Stevie,' she continued. It wasn't a question.

'That's right, Ms ...' confirmed Martinez, introducing himself and Ruskin.

'Gweneth Rain. I'm the landlady.'

'I understand that Mr Cullen was a regular drinker here,' continued Martinez.

'When he wasn't barred,' called out the same man who'd spoken as they entered. The smattering of chuckles were muted and half-hearted.

'That happen very often?' asked Martinez.

'No, not really,' she replied, glaring at the man who'd called out. 'He could be a little argumentative after a few, and I told him not to show his face for a week a couple of times.'

'Did he have run-ins with anyone in particular?' asked Ruskin.

'He'd argue with anyone and everyone, but nobody for a while,' she said. Ruskin couldn't decide if she was being evasive or not.

'Hell of a bloody shock,' she said. 'They say he was stabbed in some massage parlour. Any idea who did it?'

'Investigations are ongoing,' said Martinez. 'We wondered if any of his friends or other customers could suggest why he was killed?'

'Probably some pissed-off husband or boyfriend,' interjected the man again.

Turning to him, Ruskin could see that it was obvious that the nearly empty pint of lager in the man's hand wasn't his first of the day.

'Why do you say that, Mr ...?'

'Benny.' The man shrugged. 'Common knowledge. Stevie was a complete fanny rat; 'scuse my French, Gwen.'

'Is there anyone in particular who may have been upset with him?' asked Martinez.

Benny looked at him blearily. 'Take your pick; any new bit of skirt came in and he'd be after her like a rat up a drainpipe. More than a couple of blokes have told him to piss off and leave their missus alone.' His voice cracked. 'Stevie reckoned it was a just a bit of fun …'

Elbowing past Martinez, he placed his pint glass on the bar with the exaggerated care of the habitual drunk.

'I'm going for a fag.' He turned and headed towards the door.

'Don't pay too much mind to Benny.' Rain lowered her voice slightly. 'He and Stevie have been best mates since primary school. He's pretty cut up about it.'

'If you could give us his full name, we'd be grateful,' said Martinez. 'I'd like to talk with him again when he's in a fitter state.'

'You'll be waiting for a long while,' she warned, as she wrote his name down in Martinez's notebook. Ruskin didn't doubt it; even if he and Stevie had been in different years at school, Benny looked a lot older than he should. Ruskin suspected that the lunchtime drinking wasn't just because his friend had died.

'Does anybody else have any ideas about why Stevie was killed?' asked Martinez.

With Benny gone, nobody else seemed willing to contribute.

Martinez fished out a stack of business cards and handed them around to the group; everyone took one, although judging by the lack of eye contact, Ruskin suspected they'd end up in the bin after they left.

'I appreciate that this has all been a big shock to you,' he said, raising his voice slightly, 'but if any of you have any information – no matter how insignificant it seems – please don't hesitate to call. We want to bring Stevie's killer to justice, and we need all of the help you can give us.'

Still none of the men made eye contact, but at least a few of the cards made it into trouser pockets.

Thanking the landlady for her time and securing a promise that she'd also call if she heard anything, the two police officers headed outside. Neither Benny nor the pipe smoker were anywhere to be seen, and there was no trace of tobacco smoke in the still air. Ruskin hoped Benny hadn't driven himself home.

'That was a waste of time,' said Ruskin, as they headed back to the car park at the rear of the pub.

'Maybe not,' said Martinez. 'It confirms what his dad told the boss last night. It could just be a jealous spouse.'

'Seems a bit extreme, and yesterday was hardly a crime of passion,' countered Ruskin.

Martinez shrugged. 'I've seen worse done for less,' he said opening the car door.

He paused. 'Hold on.'

A black wooden door marked 'staff only' had opened. A flash of blue hair was visible above the pale white face of the teenaged girl who'd been collecting glasses as they'd spoken to Gweneth Rain.

The girl looked nervously around, before glancing one more time over her shoulder and coming out. Ruskin strolled back across the car park.

She swallowed, before clearing her throat, and introducing herself as 'Selina'.

'I saw Stevie arguing with someone a few weeks ago.' Her voice was timid, and she stared at her feet.

'Can you be any more specific?' asked Ruskin quietly.

She looked around again. 'It was a weekday lunchtime. I don't know the name of the man, but he comes in here quite often for a bite to eat. He runs one of the local farms.'

Even without a name, that narrowed the pool of suspects.

'Do you know what they were arguing about?'

She shrugged. 'I only heard some of it, but the farmer was unhappy with a bill that Stevie had charged him. He said something about not paying for work that had only been half-done.

52

Stevie said that was bollocks and that everything had been finished.'

'Any idea what the work was that Stevie was charging him for?' Martinez had now joined the two of them.

'I don't know exactly, but he said something about the job taking twice as long as necessary and then he said, "Where was that bloody brother of yours?" and something like "I don't have time to keep on chasing and nagging." That's all I can remember.'

Her piece now said, Martinez gave her one of his business cards, telling her to use his direct number or email address if she had anything else to share.

Back in the car, Ruskin mulled over what the girl had told them. 'It could be a business disagreement,' he suggested. 'Do the Cullens organize labour for other farms?'

'I don't think so,' said Martinez, 'but I'll look into it.'

'It's also a bit premeditated, don't you think?' said Ruskin. 'I can see them getting into a disagreement that gets out of hand, but tracking him down to a massage parlour weeks later … that doesn't seem right.'

'I'll see if I can locate this farmer and have a word,' said Martinez, 'but I doubt he's linked.'

Chapter 7

The interviews with Stevie Cullen's immediate family took up most of the afternoon, so Warren called a late briefing to share the findings.

Rachel Pymm went first, having interviewed Saffron, the sister closest in age to Stevie.

'She was absolutely broken,' said Pymm. 'She could be acting, but if she is, she deserves an Oscar.' She took a sip of her drink – an evil-smelling brew that reminded Warren of the mess he'd cleared out of a leaking gutter the previous weekend – and flipped open her notepad.

'She said that she was nine when Stevie was born and that she fell in love with him immediately. She used to pretend he was her own baby and would dress him up and carry him around with her wherever she went. She claims to have been in town delivering vegetables to a local grocery at the time of the murder and says that her husband was at the doctor's with their youngest, at that time. We'll check it out, of course, but I can't see it being her.'

'Could she shed any light on a possible motive?' asked Warren.

'No. To hear her speak of him, he was universally loved by everyone he met. A bit of a rogue, but nothing too serious. I'll be honest, I can't work out if she really did see him that way, or if she's hiding something.'

'OK, we'll interview her again in the future and see if she's changed her tune,' said Warren. 'Hutch, how did your interview go?'

'Not much better. Paddy was less effusive in his love for his brother, but he just shrugged when I asked him about a motive. He was shifty, but with his past record that could just be because he was in a police station. Given the lack of detail from the two masseuses about the appearance of the attacker, we can't rule him out, but it'll never stand up in court.'

'What about an alibi?'

'None. He claims to have been working with his dad all day, cleaning the pigs pens out and doing chores around the farm. He just laughed when I asked about any CCTV footage or other witnesses.'

'Not too surprising,' said Warren. 'Unfortunately, given what we know about the family dynamics, I can't see his old man admitting it, even if he did disappear during the day. He's never going to rat him out.'

'There was one interesting thing, which may or may not be important.'

'Go on.'

'When I asked him if anyone had threatened his brother, he shrugged then said, "Just the odd jealous husband." He made like it was a joke, and wouldn't elaborate, but I think there may have been something in what he said.'

'That agrees with what Moray and Jorge heard from the staff and customers at the White Stag. It's certainly something we should check out,' said Warren. 'If Stevie was in the habit of hitting on other men's partners, that might be a motive. People have certainly killed for less, although it seems a bit of an elaborate method.'

'It also fits in with what the eldest sister, Lavender, told me,' said Richardson. 'Lavender said that Stevie was a real charmer.

She said that he'd been doing it since he could talk. She claims that as the youngest, he was rather spoilt and that "as far as Mum and Saffy were concerned, he couldn't do any wrong". I tell you, there's a lot of pent-up resentment there. Once she started talking, I didn't think she was going to stop. I felt more like a counsellor than a police officer. She was obviously very jealous of the attention Stevie got.'

'How old was she when he came along? Sixteen, seventeen?' asked Rachel.

'About that,' said Richardson.

'My cousin was about that old when her little brother was born,' said Pymm. 'She was a full-on teenager at the time. She used to claim that the baby crying all night was why she did so badly in her exams. It had nothing to do with the fact that she spent every evening hanging around the local park drinking cheap cider when she should have been revising.'

'That's a long time to hold a grudge,' said Hutchinson.

'Not for a teenage girl,' said Richardson, 'but to be fair, she still seemed really cut up about his death. My gut tells me she wasn't responsible.'

'What did she say when you asked her about motive?' asked Warren.

'Not a lot, she sort of clammed up. Again, I can't tell if she really has no idea why someone would kill him, or if that's just how she is around the police.'

'She doesn't have a record,' pointed out Hutchinson.

'No, but given the track history of the rest of her family, it's hardly surprising that she is uncomfortable cooperating with us.'

'What about an alibi?'

'She claims to have been working at home and looking after her two kids. She runs a small business and says that she was on her work phone all day, a landline. I'm going to put in a request for the phone records. She lives miles away, so we can probably rule her out if she was at her desk making a call around that time.'

'What about her husband?' asked Hutchinson.

'Doing a shift in their local Sainsbury's – he's a manager. I'll send someone over to check that out; he'd need to have been absent for a lengthy period of time to get to the massage parlour, commit the murder and then come back.'

'What about Paddy's twin, Frankie?' asked Hutchinson.

'I didn't get anything out of him,' admitted Warren, 'unless he too is a skilled actor, he's got serious learning difficulties. He came with his mum, Rosie, but he was absolutely terrified. Every time I asked a question, he looked at his mum and started to cry. I wonder if he even really understands what's happened. Besides, he's absolutely huge; if he wasn't Paddy's twin brother you wouldn't think they were even related. There's no way he could fit the description of the hooded attacker that the sisters gave us. Come to think of it, I doubt he could have even climbed through that window.'

'That matches what Lavender told me,' said Richardson. 'I think another reason she resented Stevie when they were younger was because she was already playing second fiddle to Frankie. She said her dad spent all of his time looking after Frankie. He still works with him all day now. I think that may have been why she left the farm to set up her own business.'

'Speaking of business,' interjected Warren, 'DCI Bergen and Moray and Jorge suggested that Stevie might have interests outside of his parents' farm. Could anyone shed any light on that?'

'I asked,' said Pymm, 'but Saffron said that he was just a farm-hand, working with his dad and his twin brothers.'

'Same here,' said Hutchinson.

'Lavender said the same thing,' said Richardson.

'Which sounds suspiciously like they are all toeing the party line on this,' said Warren. 'I want to know more about why he spends so much time travelling to other farms. Hutch, can you organize some bodies to interview the local farmers in the area, and see if they can shed any light on what he was up to? See if any of them are known to Organized Crime. DCI Bergen promised us full cooperation; let's test that, shall we?'

'Will do.'

'What a family,' said Warren. 'The youngest brother has just been brutally murdered. Either they know who did it, and they're covering for him, or they don't want to help the police as a point of principle.'

He looked at his notes. 'Right, well we'll see if they become more cooperative as time goes on. We also still don't have a definite motive. I want to know more about his business dealings and I also think it's interesting that his brother Paddy suggested that he might be a bit of a ladies' man, which chimes with what was said down the pub. His father mentioned last night that he might have been seeing someone. His mother seemed surprised, since she thought that woman was already engaged. I think a visit to this lady friend might be in order.'

According to Seamus Cullen, his son had been seeing Vicki Barclay, a relationship that his mother was apparently unaware of, and which she probably would not have approved of. That alone made Warren want to speak to her. Add to that the fact that she was supposedly engaged to somebody else, and there was already a potential motive that needed exploring.

Barclay had clearly been expecting a visit, answering the door to Warren and the family liaison officer within seconds of the first ring of the doorbell. Unfortunately, the make-up that she had clearly spent significant amounts of time applying was unable to entirely conceal the swelling on the side of her face, in the same way that the baggy cardigan she wore was unable to conceal the swelling of her belly.

Vicki Barclay came from Kent; her accent alone enough to mark her out as 'posh' in the eyes of Rosie Cullen. Up close, she looked even younger than her nineteen years.

Warren pointed to her face. 'What happened?'

'I slipped in the shower.'

The tone was defiant, but again her eyes filled with tears. She pulled a shredded tissue from her cardigan sleeve.

'Do you know why we are here?' asked Warren gently as the family liaison officer offered her a fresh one.

She nodded. 'It's about Stevie. Somebody killed him.' She sniffed loudly. 'I expect you're visiting all of his friends.'

'We are,' confirmed Warren, 'but you were more than just a friend, weren't you?'

She opened her mouth, as if she was about to deny it, before closing it again. 'How did you know?'

'Things that people have mentioned.'

'Oh, God …'

Warren chose his next words carefully. 'I also hear that you are engaged to be married.'

She looked down at the large shiny ring on her left ring finger, as if surprised that it was still there. 'Yeah.'

'Vicki, who did this to you?' He pointed to the bruising on the side of her face.

'I told you, I hit my head on a cupboard.'

'No. You said you slipped and fell in the shower.'

She paused. 'I hit my head on the bathroom cupboard when I slipped in the shower.'

Warren said nothing, waiting as the tears started to gather again. He felt bad about pushing her, particularly given how heavily pregnant she was, but he knew that there was information she was holding back. Information that might be crucial to the investigation.

'We both know that isn't true, Vicki. Tell me what really happened.'

The pause this time was longer. 'Anton and I had a row. It was my fault really, I shouldn't have said what I said.' She looked away. 'He's not a violent man. Not really. He's never hit me before …'

'What was the row about?' Warren asked softly.

She shook her head. 'It was silly really. I can't even remember.'

'When did the argument take place?'

'Sunday night.'

Warren took a deep breath. 'Vicki, is the baby Stevie's?'

She let out a small gasp. 'No!'

Warren waited.

'No. It can't be, we were careful.' She looked down at her hands, her voice becoming a mumble. 'The midwife must have got the dates wrong, that's all.'

'Vicki, look at me,' instructed Warren, his voice kind but firm. 'Please tell me what happened. Somebody killed Stevie and it was really brutal. He deserves justice. To get him that justice, I need to know everything about him. Even if you don't think it's relevant or important.'

She gave a tiny nod but said nothing.

'Let's start with Sunday night. What started the fight?'

She sniffed. 'We were looking at the scans.' She smiled. 'We were trying to choose a name that fit the picture.'

'Who's we?'

'Me and Anton of course.'

'Sorry, carry on.'

Her face fell again. 'The picture from the scan had the dates on. They calculate it from when you had your last period, but everyone knows it's not accurate.' She paused. 'On the date it said I conceived, Anton was visiting his mum in hospital. He was away all week. But we had sex the night he came back, so you see it could be his …'

'But Anton didn't believe that.'

She shook her head sadly.

'Did Stevie know about the baby?'

She nodded.

'And what was his response?'

She bit her lip.

'Vicki?' Warren prompted.

'He said I should pretend that it was Anton's, and that we should still get married.'

'But why?'

She looked away, suddenly becoming fascinated with her fingernails. 'He said that once we'd been married for a few months, we could get a divorce. Then Anton would have to pay me child support.'

Warren could barely believe his ears. 'But surely a DNA test would show if the child isn't his?'

'We didn't think he'd ask for one. Besides, Stevie and Anton look alike They have the same-coloured hair and the same-coloured eyes … The baby would look just like him.'

Her tone was defensive, but he could see that she knew in her heart, that the plan had been crazy.

'And Anton figured out he mightn't be the father Sunday night?'

She nodded.

'Does he know that Stevie might be the father?'

She shrugged.

'What happened after he hit you?'

'He went out.'

'Where?'

'I don't know. He isn't answering his phone.'

'Do you know where he is now?'

'No. I haven't seen him since Sunday.'

Vicki Barclay had already provided Warren with a potential motive, but he knew that she had more to share. Warren helped the FLO make them all a cup of coffee whilst Vicki composed herself.

'When did you last see Stevie?'

She placed the mug down on a coaster that urged her to 'Keep Calm and Carry On', with a picture of Sid James' face laughing. Warren's matching coaster had Barbara Windsor in a scene from *Carry on Camping*.

'Not since last week. Anton had the weekend off, so we went shopping for the baby.' Her face crumpled, and Warren handed her another tissue.

'Was that the last time you spoke to Stevie?'

'No. I tried to speak to him on Sunday night, after … you know. To warn him that Anton might know about the baby.'

'What did he say?'

'He didn't answer. He left me a voicemail Monday morning saying he had to go and see a few people, but he'd ring me later so we could meet up. But we never did …'

The tears were coming back, so Warren jumped in quickly. 'Do you know who he was going to see?'

'No. He never really spoke about business.'

After a few more minutes, it became clear that he wasn't going to get much more out of her. He gave her his card, gaining an assurance that she would call him if she heard any more.

As she stood to let him out, she winced slightly, grabbing her ribs.

The tissue that she'd used to wipe away her tears had smudged her make-up slightly, revealing the bruised skin underneath.

'Vicki, do you have anywhere you could perhaps stay for a few days? Just until things calm down a bit?'

Whether her fiancé was involved in Stevie Cullen's death or not, Warren didn't feel comfortable leaving her alone.

She bit her lip.

'What about your parents? Perhaps you could go and stay with them?'

She shook her head violently.

'What about a relative, or a friend?'

Her lip trembled, her eyes filling with tears again, and Warren's heart went out to her. He had no idea what her circumstances were, but as he looked around the tiny one-bedroom flat, he could feel the loneliness. Young, pregnant and apparently cut off from her family, the probable father of her unborn baby was dead, the man she was due to marry already violent.

He motioned towards the FLO. 'Constable Dennell and her colleagues are trained to help women in your circumstances,' he said gently. 'They can even help you find somewhere safe to stay.'

She continued chewing at her lip, before finally shaking her head. 'I have a cousin in Cambridge. Maybe I could stay with her …'

'Does Anton know where she lives?' asked Dennell.

She shook her head again. 'No, he's never met her, and I don't think I've ever mentioned her.'

'Then why not give her a call? Do you have a car?' asked Dennell.

'No, I don't drive.'

'Then I'll arrange for someone to take you there. Why don't you put some things together in a bag?'

An officer trained in domestic abuse could meet the FLO and take Barclay where she needed to go, perhaps even convincing her to accept more help to extract herself from her situation. As she went into the bedroom to start packing, Warren made the necessary calls. Barclay was a potential witness; she needed to be kept safe. Warren couldn't imagine raising his fist against Susan under any circumstances, especially when pregnant. But according to the statistics he'd seen from the Domestic Violence Unit, one of the most dangerous times for an abuse victim was when she was pregnant or when trying to leave her partner.

As he hung up, he knew that if he was honest, there was another reason he wanted to keep her on his radar. She could well have been more involved in the death of Stevie Cullen than she admitted.

Chapter 8

The air in the mortuary was chilled and filtered, the astringent smell of disinfectant a welcome alternative to the odours that would otherwise fill the space.

As a rule, Warren preferred to delegate witnessing the autopsy to somebody else, such as Tony Sutton. Unfortunately, that wasn't an option and all of his sergeants were busy elsewhere. Moray Ruskin was always keen, but Warren didn't feel the young DC was quite ready to undertake the task unsupervised yet.

At least there was a familiar face behind the mask.

'Good to see you, Warren,' Professor Ryan Jordan, the American-born pathologist greeted him. 'How's Susan?'

'She's doing well, thanks, Ryan. I hear you've become a granddad again?'

'Yep. Number three was born three days ago. Still no name.' He chuckled. 'For the past nine months they've been convinced it would be a girl. It never even crossed their minds to have a boy's name ready just in case! We'll be flying over to Germany for kisses and cuddles in a few weeks.'

Warren followed him into the white-tiled room. He wore gloves and a red splash suit, although he had no intention of prodding anything too squidgy.

Stevie Cullen looked much as he had when Warren had last seen him at the massage parlour.

'There's no mystery about the cause of death,' stated Jordan, pointing toward the gaping wound on the man's chest. The Y incision had been angled to avoid disturbing the entry wound.

'Massive blood loss caused by the penetration of the left ventricle by a bladed implement. It entered between the fourth and fifth ribs, before being twisted and removed. The blade nicked the fifth rib on the way out. He would have been dead within seconds.'

'Pretty brutal. Does the fact that it entered so neatly indicate that the killer had a working knowledge of anatomy or some sort of training?' asked Warren.

'Not necessarily. I'd say that most reasonably educated people are aware that stabbing downwards on a person's chest like they're impaling a vampire would be difficult to accomplish because of the breastbone; a right-handed person standing above the victim would naturally come in from that side. The blade appears to have been very sharp, so it wouldn't have required huge strength.'

'What else can you tell me about the murder weapon?'

'Unfortunately, the twisting of the knife makes it hard to be specific, but it was clearly very sharp and non-serrated. Judging by the depth of penetration, it has to be a minimum of fifteen centimetres. I've taken images of where it hit the rib, which should allow me to match any potential knives that you uncover. Beyond that, I'm guessing.'

'What else have you found?'

'Overall, the subject was in reasonable physical health, falling within normal height and weight for a white, Caucasian male. His musculature suggests a manual worker, and a full body X-ray reveals a healed fracture to his right collarbone, probably dating back to childhood. No signs of liver damage, although there was some scarring on the septum of his nose that suggests he may have been a cocaine user. I've sent off for drug and alcohol screening.

'I've also observed what appear to be small, fresh bruises on his left arm. I can't be any more precise on the timing, but they would be consistent with him heavily falling on the floor within a few minutes of his death.'

Warren pondered that for a moment. Had Cullen bumped himself before his massage? Or had he fallen during the attack? How did that sequence of events match what the two sisters had claimed had taken place that day?

Jordan's findings had given him much to think about. The pathologist had used his experience, and the application of science, to persuade Stevie Cullen to tell at least some of his story from beyond the grave. In a way, Jordan had allowed the victim to help them find his own killer. Now it was up to Warren to finish the job.

Chapter 9

The 'Golden twenty-four hours', crucial to any investigation, elapsed Tuesday afternoon. From now on, as time ticked by and the scene grew colder, the likelihood of a quick resolution started to decrease rapidly.

Warren arrived back at CID early evening. In his absence, the wheeled whiteboards in the briefing rooms had started to be filled in. The first board was the suspect board. At the centre was a headshot of Stevie Cullen, with lines drawn in marker pen leading off it. The first photo that Warren had found was the one taken the last time he was arrested. He'd decided not to use that picture, because not only was it a couple of years out of date, but also because of the negative connotations of such a photo. Instead, he'd replaced it with one a few weeks old culled from Cullen's Facebook page. This picture showed a smiling, carefree twenty-something. It was a reminder that no matter what crimes he had committed when alive, he was still a victim. Warren had seen the look of terror on the dead man's face – nobody deserved to die like that, and no parent should have to bury their child.

To Cullen's right were the two masseuses, Biljana and Malina Dragi , and their aunt and owner of the massage parlour, Silvija Wilson. All three women still had questions to answer in Warren's mind and he was looking forward to checking their phone logs and social media usage. The latter would likely be complicated by the need to translate much of the material from Serbian, and DSI Grayson had grudgingly authorized the cost of fast-track translators.

On the left of the board were Vicki Barclay and her erstwhile fiancé Anton Rimington. The latter was still not answering his mobile phone and Grayson had authorized an alert to be issued for his whereabouts.

Barclay was now safely en route to her cousin's house up in Cambridgeshire. The story that she had told Warren was certainly compelling and had given him a new direction to look in, but he was not going to take it at face value.

A second whiteboard had photographs of Cullen's known associates, including his parents, siblings and extended family, and drinking buddies from the White Stag. A written column headed 'Business interests' had a growing list of names of local farmers that Stevie Cullen might have been working with. Many of the headshots were taken directly from the Police National Computer – those were the circles that he moved in. Any individuals who proved to be of more than passing interest would be moved to the suspect board.

'Mags, how are Traffic doing?' started Warren. Before her move into CID, Richardson had worked in the Roads Policing Unit. She had been there during the sudden explosion in the volume of evidence from Traffic cameras and video footage and had maintained an expertise in that area since. Richardson was now Middlesbury's primary link with headquarters' Video Analysis Unit down in Welwyn.

'It's early days. They've done a data dump of all the static number recognition cameras in the area, as well as mobile ANPR units, but coverage is pretty poor in that area,' Richardson cautioned. 'They're still doing pattern analysis, working out what cars were in the area at the time and cross-referencing with usual patterns of movement, to see if anything stands out, but they were able to give me a preliminary report on Stevie Cullen's movements on the day of his death.'

'Well give us what you've got,' said Warren.

'First off, we're assuming that Stevie Cullen was driving the clapped-out Ford Fiesta registered to his older brother, Paddy. It was parked down the street from the massage parlour, and he had a key to it in his pocket.'

'That makes sense,' said Pymm. 'Stevie Cullen was banned from driving.'

'In that case, could he have been a passenger?' asked Ruskin. 'The driver could have dropped him off.'

'Then why abandon the car?' asked Richardson. 'The car was still there hours after the attack. And Cullen had the keys in his pocket.'

'His most recent conviction was for driving without a licence and insurance six months ago,' pointed out Pymm. 'He clearly has no respect for the law in that regard.'

'What if the driver killed him?' asked Ruskin. 'They drop him off, wait until they know he's vulnerable, then go in, kill him and run away, leaving the car behind. Stevie uses the car sometimes, so he has a spare key on his key ring.'

The idea had enough merit for Warren not to dismiss it entirely. 'Hutch, tell your door-knockers to ask if anyone saw the car, and if Stevie was alone,' he ordered. 'In the meantime, what else have we got from Traffic? Anything on Anton Rimington?'

'Nothing,' said Richardson. 'We've run the licence plate from his car through the databases, but the last time his car was pinged was Sunday evening, driving away from Vicki Barclay's place.'

'I don't suppose it gives us a clue as to where he's holed up?' asked Warren.

'No, not really. He could be anywhere that side of town. They'll trawl the data for any other cars that he may have access to, but as far as we can tell, he didn't use his own car to cross town to the massage parlour the day of the murder.'

'Thanks, Mags. Anything else on the video front?' asked Warren.

'IT are still examining the parlour's digital video recorder, but they've sent me the footage from the hours before and during the attack.' Mags Richardson started the video on the main screen.

'You can see the two girls and their aunt arrive at the shop just after eight-thirty.'

The camera position was less than ideal. Placed up in the left-hand corner of the reception, its angle meant that much of the right side of its field of view showed nothing but wall; the remainder showed only the front of the reception area, going as far back as the desk. It didn't record sound.

Richardson increased the speed of the footage to sixteen times.

Little happened for the next few minutes. The two masseuses flitted in and out of shot, still in their street clothes, straightening the customer waiting chairs and opening the window blinds. Biljana, easily identifiable by her dark brown hair, rearranged some bottles of massage oil on the cabinet in the front window, fixing what appeared to be a poster to the glass. Warren remembered seeing a printed sheet advertising buy one, get one free on selected oils.

During this time her aunt, Silvija Wilson, took up position at the computer on the front desk. Opening the customer ledger, she appeared to be transferring information from the A4 diary into the computer.

'Do we have a copy of the spreadsheet, or whatever she was using on the computer?'

'IT bagged the desktop computer as evidence, along with the video recorder,' said Rachel Pymm. 'I'll ask them to scan the hard drive for anything of interest and send it over.'

At a quarter to nine, the two women disappeared, reappearing about ten minutes later wearing the black uniforms that were currently undergoing investigation in the central forensic unit down in Welwyn Garden City. Whilst they were getting changed,

Wilson disappeared briefly, before reappearing with what appeared to be a wad of cash, which she slipped in an envelope. After writing on the envelope, she placed it in the zip-up compartment at the front of her bag.

'Looks like she's getting ready to do the bank run,' observed Grimshaw. 'We should check that she actually made it.'

'I'll do that,' volunteered Martinez. 'I'll keep it discreet; we don't want to spook her by asking her questions about her finances.'

'Good thinking,' said Warren.

At nine o'clock on the dot, Biljana turned the sign over on the front door.

A few seconds later, her dark head popped briefly back into view as she passed over a cup of coffee to her aunt. Just before nine twenty-five, Wilson picked up her bag, and called over her shoulder before leaving through the front door.

Moray Ruskin looked up from his notepad. 'So far that sequence of events seems to match what the two girls told us.'

The video continued, Richardson increasing the speed to maximum.

'Monday really is a quiet day,' observed Martinez, as the counter on the clock raced ahead with nothing happening on the screen.

Shortly before eleven a.m., a middle-aged woman in jeans and a dark T-shirt arrived. Malina greeted her at the desk, before the customer walked past her. Richardson slowed the video to normal speed.

'I really wish that camera was installed properly,' muttered Richardson to no one in particular, as she sped the camera up again. Even at high speed, Malina sat stock still, staring at her phone, the only movement visible her blurred fingers across phone's touchscreen.

At twenty-five past eleven, a second woman entered the shop and Richardson slowed the video again. Dressed in a flowery dress, she looked to be elderly, with a wooden walking stick.

Sitting down on one of the reception chairs, she greeted Malina at the front desk. They spoke briefly, before Malina turned and called something over her shoulder. A minute or so later, a flash of brown hair signalled the arrival of her sister with a glass of clear liquid.

After finishing her drink the woman rose to her feet, and using the walking stick for support headed off screen. Malina followed her.

For the next few minutes, the picture remained unchanged, the reception desk empty. No customers entered the shop. At 11.40 the woman in the jeans and T-shirt reappeared, walking out of the front door without a second glance.

Again, the picture returned to a static image, and Richardson sped past the next fifty minutes, until Malina returned to the front desk. Two minutes later, the second, older woman joined her. Leaning her walking stick against the table, she rooted around in her bag before producing her purse. Malina entered something on the till, then handed over a credit card reader. After returning her purse to her bag, the woman waved goodbye before heading out of the door.

'I want to know who those two women are,' said Warren. 'Rachel, check the customer records and see if we can identify them.'

The display now showed 12.32. Biljana joined her sister at the front desk, placing two white china mugs on the wooden surface, before pulling over one of the waiting chairs so that she sat opposite. Opening her bag, she handed her sister a foil-wrapped parcel, and a packet of crisps, which the older sibling opened and placed on the desk between them.

As the two women tucked into sandwiches and shared the crisps they chatted. Melina turned her phone around and showed something to Biljana, who laughed and passed her own phone over. Unfortunately, there was no way to see the phones' screens.

The lunch break lasted until ten minutes to one, when the

door opened. Both women quickly stood up. Stevie Cullen had just entered the shop. Dressed in a brown leather jacket, blue jeans and a dark T-shirt, he stood in front of the desk.

After speaking to him for a moment, Biljana headed off-camera in the direction of the back rooms. Cullen said something, and Malina followed her sister. She mustn't have gone too far as Cullen kept on speaking.

Shortly before one, Cullen stopped speaking and headed off screen. Moments later, Malina resumed her place at the front desk.

'Going back for his massage,' said Ruskin.

'And whatever else he's paid for,' said Grimshaw.

This time they kept the video footage running at no more than four times its normal speed. Again, Malina sat almost unmoving, staring at her phone screen. Warren wondered if she was watching a video; perhaps a favourite TV programme from back home?

At ten minutes past one she suddenly sat upright, half turning in her chair. She sat still for a few seconds, her head cocked, before quickly getting up and disappearing off-screen. Warren would have given anything for the camera angle to change, or for there to be sound.

An agonizing twenty-six minutes of nothing but an empty reception desk passed, before a visibly flustered Malina reappeared, leaning over the computer. She placed her phone on the desk in front of her.

Warren squinted at the screen. 'Can we pause it and zoom in?'

'It's pretty low quality,' warned Richardson as she complied with his instruction.

'What the hell is she doing to that computer?' asked Hutchinson as the video resumed. On screen the young masseuse was tapping away at the keyboard and manipulating the mouse.

After a minute or so, Malina stood up and headed back off screen.

Moments later, she reappeared, her arm around the shoulder of her sister. Even on the poor-quality video it was clear that Biljana was sobbing.

Still holding her distraught sibling, Malina manipulated her phone, placing it to her ear. Warren noted the time stamp: 13.40. 'That's the 999 call.'

Malina remained on the line, leaving her sister briefly to lock the front door, as instructed by the call handler, before resuming hugging her sister tightly. Four minutes passed until Malina returned to the door and opened it again. Two of the constables that Warren recognized from the crime scene entered, batons drawn.

Warren signalled for Richardson to pause the video; the specialist team at Welwyn would be reviewing the video in far greater detail than his team were capable of, but it had given them plenty to get started with.

'The most important questions I have are, what the hell were the two girls doing in the almost thirty minutes between Malina disappearing off screen and the emergency call being made. And what was so damned important on that computer?'

Wednesday 04 November

Chapter 10

The morning briefing of the second day of the investigation still had that new investigation buzz about it, although for Warren, it was already partly fuelled by caffeine. He'd slept poorly, the stress of the case adding to the anxiety he was already feeling about tomorrow's upcoming hospital appointment. Weeks of waiting would soon be over, and the timing of what he feared was going to be a long and arduous investigation couldn't have been worse. At a time like this, he should be spending as much time as possible with his wife. Nevertheless, he had a job to do, and he forced his attention back to the matter in hand.

The seconded officers from Welwyn had been formed into small groups led by the experienced sergeants on Warren's own core team, and so the first part of the briefing necessitated bringing everyone up to speed. Warren worked his way down the list of tasks from the previous day, starting with Rachel Pymm.

'Through a combination of wit and charm, I persuaded IT to give me a raw dump of the massage parlour's hard drive. They're still going through it properly, but I have access to documents such as the appointment lists and the emails et cetera.'

'Good. We seized the handwritten customer ledger from the reception desk as evidence. Cross-reference the appointments with her records. I want to know how often Stevie Cullen used to visit the massage parlour, and if there was a predictable pattern to his visits. I also want to know who those two other customers were – maybe they saw or heard something. Have you got the records back from the two sisters' phones yet?'

Pymm made a face. 'No. The phones are registered to some cheap overseas carrier based in Eastern Europe. We'll get them, but it'll take time.'

'Bugger. Well keep at it; prioritize them when they arrive,' Warren said. He turned to Hutchinson next.

'The alibis from Stevie Cullen's two sisters and their husbands check out,' said the veteran sergeant. 'Lavender's phone records confirm that she was making and taking calls from her landline all day, and we found plenty of staff at the supermarket where her husband works to confirm that he was on shift when Stevie Cullen was killed.'

Hutchinson flipped over the next page in his notepad. 'We've also got positive sightings of Saffron at the grocer's that she visited that day to sell the farm produce. One of them was even obliging enough to show CCTV footage of her at about the time that the murder occurred. The GP surgery confirmed that her husband had an appointment that day with their youngest, and they were running behind. The surgery uses one of those electronic booking terminals, so we have corroboration that he booked in shortly before Stevie was murdered and confirmation from the GP, the receptionist and the practice nurse that he stayed in the waiting room during that time. There's no way that any of those four could have been the killer, or even directly involved.'

Warren drew a line through the names on the whiteboard. It was a symbolic gesture, but he knew from experience that the deluge of information coming into an investigation, particularly in its early stages, could feel overwhelming. Visibly chipping away at that growing pile helped the team feel as though they were making progress.

'We should speak to Benny Masterson, Stevie's best friend,' suggested Ruskin. 'I thought I'd try and track him down later today when he's slept off yesterday.'

'Well don't leave it too late,' cautioned Warren, 'or from what you told us yesterday, he might have started drinking all over again. How are we doing tracking down that farmer Stevie was seen arguing with?'

Moray Ruskin flipped open his notebook. 'Jorge's narrowing it down. The White Stag pub is near a busy junction. I reckon there are about six farms or smallholdings that are close enough to consider the White Stag a local. I'm going back there to get a better description of the bloke Stevie was seen arguing with. The landlady, Gweneth Rain, seemed to be willing to cooperate; I reckon if I catch her before any of Stevie's mates turn up for their mid-morning pint and pork scratchings, she'll help me out.'

'Well don't dismiss the other farms out of hand,' said Warren. 'If any of them did have dealings with Stevie Cullen – business or otherwise – they might have useful information.' He turned to Rachel Pymm. 'Any progress on tracking down Anton Rimington, the fiancé of Vicki Barclay? If he was as angry as she said he was when he figured out that somebody else might have got her pregnant, who knows what he could do?'

'His mobile phone has been turned off since Sunday night, when Barclay claims he stormed out,' said Pymm. 'We have a list of his known associates from around the time of his arrest. He doesn't have any close family that we are aware of in the area, so if he is staying with someone, rather than holed up in a Travelodge, it'll be a friend. I'll get a team ringing around and, if necessary, door-knocking, but even if he is with one of these charmers, I don't know how cooperative they'll be.'

'Well we won't know if we don't try. Prioritize finding him; he's one of our strongest suspects at the moment. And if nothing else, I want to know what sort of risk he poses to Vicki Barclay. He has form for violent offending in the past.'

'Speaking of which, how certain are we that Vicki Barclay is innocent in all of this?' asked Martinez.

'Well she's very obviously pregnant,' said Warren. 'It would have to be a pretty baggy hoodie to fool the two sisters into thinking that the killer was a man.'

'Maybe she was working with Rimington?' suggested Martinez. 'Imagine this scenario: Stevie Cullen gets Vicki pregnant. Realizing that she is never going to hide this from Rimington, she decides to tell him that Cullen raped her. She says she doesn't want to go to the police, knowing that Rimington has such a temper on him, he may well go and solve the problem for her.'

'Blimey, Jorge, you need to stop watching so many soap operas,' said Grimshaw.

Warren placed a hand up to stay the sniping between the two friends. 'Don't dismiss it out of hand; let's work through it,' he said, although it seemed a bit far-fetched.

'OK,' started Grimshaw, 'why would she go to all of that trouble, when she could just get an abortion? Surely that would solve the problem?'

'That *problem* is an unborn baby,' said Pymm, pointedly. 'That's a big step for many women to contemplate.'

'Bigger than killing the baby's father?' countered Grimshaw.

'Killing Stevie Cullen might solve one problem,' said Hutchinson, 'but surely it opens up a whole load more. If her plan was to create a plausible reason for falling pregnant, so that she could then live happily ever after with Anton Rimington, that only works if Rimington gets away with the murder. Otherwise, Rimington goes to prison and she has nobody to support her.'

'You're assuming that she wants support from Rimington,' said Richardson. 'She might feel that she would rather bring up the baby on her own. Getting Rimington to kill Cullen would take them both out of the picture.'

'Or maybe there is a kernel of truth in what happened. Maybe Stevie Cullen actually did force himself on her?' said Martinez.

'So why didn't she go to the police?' asked Grimshaw.

'Lots of rape victims don't, you know that,' said Martinez. 'By all accounts, they had a more than friendly relationship. She might have felt shame, because she felt she had led him on, or maybe she just thought that no one would believe her. Perhaps she couldn't face the thought of a "he said – she said" court case.'

'Not to mention the whole evidence-collecting process,' said Richardson.

'She could also have been too frightened,' said Hutchinson. 'The Cullen family have a hell of a reputation around here. Accusing one of them of rape would take some guts.'

'OK, it's a theory worth pursuing. Anton Rimington is our number-one suspect at the moment. Let's see if we can find him. In the meantime, keep looking into the two sisters; something isn't right about them. I want to know if there is any link between them and Rimington. But remember, we still only have their word that there was even an intruder.'

No matter how many times he did them, press conferences still didn't get any easier. The press briefing room down at police HQ in Welwyn Garden City was surprisingly full; testimony perhaps to the unusual circumstances of Stevie Cullen's death, and the man's own reputation. The briefing was short and factual, and primarily a plea for witnesses. They had decided not to mention Anton Rimington yet, because if he was involved – and that was far from certain at the moment – they didn't want to spook him. If they didn't find him in the next day or so, they would need to revisit that decision. In the meantime, Cullen's name had been circulating on social media for at least twenty-four hours, giving the assembled journalists plenty of time to dig into his, and his family's, somewhat colourful history.

Warren had come straight from the Cullen farm where, as Senior Investigating Officer, he had taken it upon himself to visit the grieving relatives and update them on the investigation's progress personally.

The family had finally given in to the entreaties of the family liaison team, although they remained suspicious of the police. Warren respected their wishes, but felt he had a duty to at least keep them informed.

The cramped kitchen of the farmhouse had been thick with cigarette smoke, and Warren regretted wearing his best suit. It would need to be dry-cleaned before its next outing. Rosie and Seamus had been joined by their eldest daughter, Lavender. Beside her on the table was her laptop. She was obviously working from her parents' that day. Warren's phone had already shown that the house had Wi-Fi, suggesting that Stevie may well have owned a laptop and it had indeed been spirited away the night of the murder. There was no sign of either of the twins, Paddy and Frankie, or the remaining sister, Saffron.

Warren's welcome was less than warm, his repeated condolences ignored; he was the only person in the room without a cup of coffee in front of him. Helping himself to a chocolate Hobnob from the packet on the table was completely out of the question.

Regardless, the Cullens listened to what he had to say, and when he left after half an hour, Seamus Cullen had at least shaken his hand and wished him luck in finding his son's killer. His wife had remained stone-faced throughout, grief and anger rolling off her in waves. Lavender had avoided his gaze, her eyes shining with the threat of tears.

The Cullens had declined the opportunity to attend the press conference but had agreed to a written statement to be read out on their behalf. Warren was acutely aware that Stevie Cullen was likely to be dissected mercilessly in the press over the coming weeks, and he was keen to build sympathy with the public, knowing that their cooperation could prove vital. Two days into the investigation, and they had yet to find any witnesses.

Nevertheless, he winced inwardly at the eulogizing statement that the family had composed along with the family liaison officer. Grayson, dressed in his crisply tailored uniform, had generously handed over the reading of the short testimony to Warren.

'Stevie was a much-loved son, brother and friend who will be sorely missed by all who knew him. A hardworking and honest man, we cannot understand who would want to hurt our beautiful boy. Somebody out there must know who killed Stevie, and we beg that you come forward and help the police with their investigation, to ensure that he gets the justice he deserves.'

Warren finished reading the statement and looked up, studiously avoiding the smirks on the faces of some of the local journalists, many of whom had made a good living out of reporting the various misdeeds of the Cullen family over the years.

The statement might have been somewhat over-flattering, but Stevie Cullen was a victim and deserved justice. Warren was determined to get it for him.

Chapter 11

At the same time that her old team were receiving their first briefing of the day, but on the other side of town, DC Karen Hardwick stared at the envelope. The crest in the corner told her who the sender was without any need to open it. She sat down, her legs suddenly weak. She'd filled in the forms weeks ago, then forgot all about them until the invitation to come and visit. Even then it hadn't seemed real; more of a cosy chat than anything serious. But she'd enjoyed it and realized how much she'd missed that life.

For the past few years, almost her whole existence had been the police. First a constable on the beat, then a sideways move into CID as a detective constable. She'd enjoyed the intellectual challenge of working cases and DCI Jones and DI Sutton had been tremendous mentors.

And then there had been Gary. Awkward from the moment they'd met, it had been obvious the more experienced constable had fancied her from the outset, but she had been too engrossed in her new role to think about things like that. Besides, workplace romances were never a good idea, were they?

Of course, it had been nothing more than idle curiosity that had led her to looking up Hertfordshire Constabulary's policy on relationships between colleagues. To her surprise it turned out that as long as there were no line management conflicts of interest and supervisors were apprised of the relationship, there was no problem at all.

In the end, there had been no need to inform DCI Jones of their burgeoning romance; he and the room full of detectives they worked with had seen the direction their friendship was going in before even she and Gary had realized what was happening.

The next two years had been the happiest of her life, as the two lovers had moved in together and started planning for a future that would forever include the two of them.

Tears pricked at her eyes, and she gently touched the diamond band on her left ring finger.

Fifteen months.

Fifteen months since a week that had seen the two of them reach new levels of happiness.

Fifteen months since her surprise discovery had turned their world upside down and made everything else seem trivial and unimportant.

Fifteen months since a glimpse at a future of love and excitement had been cruelly snatched away.

Fifteen months since a senseless act of violence had destroyed all of their futures.

As if sensing his mother's distress, a fussing came from the baby carriage next to the armchair. Karen held her breath; she'd only finished feeding him twenty minutes before – at eight months old, Oliver was no longer so demanding, but he was still hard work. He continued to grizzle for a few moments before settling back to sleep.

She turned her attention back to the letter, picking it up and weighing it in her hand. Judging from the thickness of the envelope, it contained a single sheet of A4 paper folded three times.

What did a single sheet mean? Yes or No? For the first time

since she had started the process, she realized that she was truly at a crossroads. The answer contained within the envelope was just one of several options, and whilst in theory she had until February to decide what she wanted to do, she needed to make her mind up sooner rather than later.

She placed it back on the table and walked over to the kitchen counter to fill the kettle, suddenly needing to do something – anything – rather than open the envelope. The threatened tears now started to roll down her cheeks again.

Fifteen months and sometimes the grief was as strong as the day that he'd been killed. Outwardly she appeared to be coping amazingly well; she'd lost count of the number of times she'd been told that, as if burying one's true feelings and carrying on as if nothing happened was something to be proud of.

But inside ...

Inside it was a different matter.

When Oliver finally went down for the night, and the bedroom door closed, she crumpled, climbing into her bed – their bed – and crammed the duvet into her mouth to muffle the sobs as she pressed her hands against her ears, trying to blot out the memory of the sound of Gary's death; the deafening crash that cut him off in the middle of the last conversation she'd ever have with him.

Fifteen months and she still imagined she could smell Gary on his pillow.

Fifteen months and she could convince herself that any moment now she'd hear his key in the lock; the metallic chink as he dropped his key, coin wallet and ID badge into the bowl on the kitchen table. Then the quiet creak of the bedroom door as he slipped in, tired after a long shift but still wanting to steal a quick kiss before clambering into bed beside her.

What she wouldn't give to have him here now. Gary would help her decide. Gary would listen and help her make up her own mind without pushing her either way, and even if he disagreed with her decision, he would support her one hundred per cent. But that was no longer possible.

Who else could she ask for advice? Who else would be an impartial sounding board? Everyone who loved her wanted the best for her, but they all had their own views about what she should do.

She knew what her parents would want. They'd be delighted if she moved back to where she was brought up. Since her grandmother's passing, the small, self-contained granny flat that she'd spent her last few years in had been empty. It would be the perfect size for her and Oliver. Her father had never been anything but one hundred per cent supportive of her career choices, but she knew he had been disappointed when she'd joined the police, rather than continuing the career in science that she'd seemed destined to follow since childhood.

Then there were Gary's parents. They'd be equally delighted if she moved closer to them. Oliver was the only living evidence that their son had once walked the earth. They meant well, but sometimes she just wanted to scream 'leave us alone'. If she accepted the offer in the letter, living in Middlesbury was no longer an option. Gary's Mum and Dad had already promised to help her with the deposit on a flat if she moved nearer; it would also mean free childcare as both his parents were retired. Their offer was generous, and God knows it would be one less worry, but she wasn't sure she wanted to be that close. She loved the couple who would have been her in-laws to bits, but sometimes she felt smothered as they sought to lessen their grief by focusing on Gary's legacy.

And what about DCI Jones? Over the years, she'd come to value his opinion and guidance on so much, but she knew he couldn't be impartial. He was desperate for her to return to Middlesbury CID. But could she face it? Could she go to work every day in the same office where she'd met and fallen in love with Gary, working for the man who'd held her fiancé's hand as his life ebbed away? She'd heard everything that happened over the open telephone line and she'd remember Jones's panicked response until the day she died.

But then again, did she want to work in a different unit or even a different force? Middlesbury was unique, and she wasn't sure she'd ever find a team she'd feel as comfortable in.

In a way, the direction that she chose was less to do with her future career and more to do with a more straightforward yet more difficult choice: should she try to pick up the pieces and continue as before, or make a clean break of it?

She picked up the envelope again. Over the baby monitor, she could hear the quiet rasp of Oliver's breathing. The contents of the envelope were as important to his future as hers. She took a sip of her coffee. Lukewarm already.

Time to stop procrastinating.

Before she could find another excuse to delay, she slipped her finger under the flap and pulled the two edges apart. She removed the sheet of paper, unfolding it as she did so.

The top third confirmed the identity of the sender on the right and her mailing address on the left. A single line before the fold.

Dear Ms Hardwick,

Hands trembling, she turned it over.

After a successful interview, we are delighted to offer you a place studying for the degree of Doctor of Philosophy in the School of Biosciences at the University of Nottingham for the academic year commencing September 1st 2016.

We would be grateful if you could communicate your intentions to us no later than Friday December 4th 2015.

Chapter 12

Vicki Barclay's fiancé, Anton Rimington, had been located as soon as he powered up his mobile phone mid-morning. Sitting on his best friend Leroy McGiven's sofa, where he'd been sleeping since Sunday, he was valiantly fighting a hangover with black coffee, a fizzing glass of Alka-Seltzer, and if that didn't work, what appeared to be a line of cocaine.

Despite his fragile condition, and the fact he was only wearing a pair of boxer shorts, he declined to attend the station voluntarily, and was forcibly arrested after throwing a punch at one of the arresting officers and trying to escape through the kitchen window.

Possession of suspected class A drugs and assault of a police officer was enough to ensure that he could be detained for the next twenty-four hours without charge, giving Warren and his team plenty of time to plan their next move.

By midday, Rimington had found himself a solicitor and been pronounced fit and healthy enough to be interviewed. Already, his friend's flat and both men's cars were being searched by a CSI team.

After Grimshaw had finished setting up the recording, Warren got straight down to business. 'Anton, can you tell me your whereabouts Monday afternoon?'

Rimington blinked in surprise. 'Why? What's it to you?'

His solicitor looked similarly puzzled, as well he might. 'According to the charge sheet, I was under the impression that Mr Rimington was here in relation to alleged drug possession and an alleged assault on a police officer. These incidents supposedly occurred early this morning, and my client strenuously denies them both.'

'We will get onto that in due course, but in the meantime, I would like to deal with another matter.'

Warren awaited the solicitor's response but didn't take his eyes off Rimington.

The lawyer looked over at his client, who shrugged. His expression and his body language both suggested that he was confused. Did he really have no idea why the police had arrived that morning and what had happened Monday afternoon, or was he just a good actor?

'This is most irregular, DCI Jones. My client has a right to know what he is being accused of.'

Doubtless the solicitor would put a complaint in, but Warren knew that his strategy was on the right side of the law.

'Mr Rimington? Could you tell me your whereabouts Monday afternoon?'

'I can't remember.'

'It was only forty-eight hours ago,' prompted Warren.

'Yeah, well, I've been on a bit of a bender since Sunday night.'

'Would that be the night you punched your fiancée?' asked Grimshaw.

'What's the bitch been telling you?' snapped Rimington.

'Why don't you tell us what happened Sunday night?' suggested Warren.

Rimington took a breath. When he spoke again, his tone was conciliatory.

'Look. Vicki and me had a bit of a tiff, Sunday night. Nothing too serious. I decided I wanted a bit of time to think, so I came round to Leroy's. He said I could stay for a bit. You know, just until things calmed down.'

'What was the row about?' asked Warren.

'Just the usual. Nothing important.' His tone was a study in nonchalance. 'It's hardly worth talking about.'

'It was important enough to leave Vicki with a black eye,' said Grimshaw.

'Is that what this is about? Seriously, she's pregnant. You know what they're like when they're up the spout. Hormones and all that shit. She's just pissed at me. She's so clumsy, she probably bumped her head on a cupboard.' Again, his tone seemed forced. 'Anyhow, I haven't been back around there since Sunday. I definitely wasn't round there Monday afternoon.'

'I thought you said you were on a bender? How do you know if you weren't around there Monday?' asked Grimshaw.

'Look, I've been on the piss and the days are a bit blurred, but I'd remember if I went back around there.' He settled back in his chair and folded his arms.

'Tell me, do you know a Stevie Cullen?' asked Warren.

There was a sharp intake of breath from the solicitor, who'd clearly just started to put the pieces together.

Rimington gave a shrug of the shoulders. 'Yeah, he drinks in the White Stag sometimes. Can't say I really know him.'

Again, his attitude was forced, but Warren had caught the flash of anger as it crossed his face. Once again, Warren was glad of the decision to upgrade the interview suites to include video evidence. Micro-expressions could be persuasive to a jury.

The question was, what did the anger signify?

Warren now needed to be careful with what he said. It wasn't clear from his interview with Vicki Barclay whether Rimington definitely knew that the likely father of her unborn child was Cullen, or even that she had confirmed that her fiancé wasn't the father. On the one hand, if Rimington appeared genuinely surprised that Cullen was the father, that potentially removed his motive. On the other hand, confirming his suspicions potentially placed Barclay in even more danger, should Rimington be released on bail or without charge. He probably already thought that she had reported him for assault. The man's record suggested that he wouldn't take kindly to that.

At the moment though, something else bothered him about the man's reaction.

His solicitor clearly recognized Cullen's name. The murder at the massage parlour had been on both regional and national news bulletins, front page of the local newspaper and all over the internet. Although Cullen's identity had only just been released formally, it had been freely circulating on social media for the past twenty-four hours.

Yet Rimington gave the impression that he was unaware of the man's demise. If he really had been on a forty-eight-hour drinking session, and his phone had been turned off during that time, then unless he had been told by a friend or he was directly involved in the killing, he probably wouldn't know about the murder. In which case he was probably not involved.

So, was he truly innocent, or just a very good actor?

Warren called an impromptu team meeting to discuss the interview with Anton Rimington. He'd already proven that he had a violent streak – Vicki Barclay's swollen cheek was clear evidence of that – but was he capable of murder? If he was, the murder was cold-blooded and pre-planned. It marked a change in his offending pattern. Anton Rimington had two previous convictions for violence, both against previous partners. The first had resulted in a suspended jail sentence, the second in a three-month spell inside.

'What is it about these bastards?' Moray Ruskin voiced his disgust. 'He's got two convictions for domestic violence already; why do women think that he'll behave differently with them?'

'Maybe she didn't know his reputation?' said Rachel Pymm.

'She wasn't brought up locally; she moved here from Kent, a couple of years ago.'

'And she was definitely vulnerable,' said Warren. 'From what I can tell, she left her family after some sort of row, answering a job advert she saw online. That lasted six months, by which time she had met Rimington. He's six years older, not bad-looking, and earns a decent wage as a slaughterman.'

'He just gets better,' snorted Grimshaw.

'Either way, he pops the question and when she's threatened with eviction for not paying her rent, he swoops in and lets her move in with him. She probably didn't even know about his previous convictions,' said Warren.

'And that's why these bastards need a tattoo on their forehead,' said Grimshaw. 'The word "wife beater" in big black letters should make a few women think twice.'

'It's not often I agree with Shaun, but I think I'll make an exception today,' said Pymm.

'Regardless, I think he has to be our number-one suspect at the moment,' said Warren, bringing the meeting back to the main topic at hand.

'He's clearly a violent and dangerous man and I'd imagine he's pretty handy with a knife, and not too bothered by the sight of blood,' said Grimshaw.

'Animal blood, not human blood,' Warren reminded him.

Grimshaw shrugged.

'Does it fit his offending pattern, though?' asked Pymm. 'Domestic abusers are usually pretty cowardly. Can you see him attacking Stevie Cullen? Cullen was a fit, well-built farmhand. That's a lot different to hitting a tiny, pregnant woman.'

'Cullen was also helpless on his back, probably half-asleep,' pointed out Ruskin.

'His previous assaults have also been heat-of-the-moment,' said Pymm. 'Killing Stevie Cullen would take significant planning. He had to know that he was going to be in the massage parlour at that time; he also needed to know that he could get in through that back window.'

'Has Rimington been to the massage parlour before?' asked Ruskin. 'If he has, he might know that the back window is accessible.'

'That also means he'd know the two sisters,' said Hutchinson.

'I'll check the ledger,' said Pymm.

'That still doesn't explain how he knew that Cullen would be there,' said Warren. 'Even if Cullen had a regular appointment, I'd still want to know how he knew that.'

'Maybe he just got lucky?' said Grimshaw. 'He could have been following Cullen all morning, waiting for him to wander down a dark alley so he could stab him. Most murders aren't committed by some great criminal mastermind; hell, he might not even have intended to kill him. He might just have been planning on confronting him.'

Martinez was already shaking his head. 'The girls claim that he climbed in the window and killed Cullen before he could react. No, the bastard was definitely out to murder him.'

'Then let's see if we can pin him down to the area,' said Warren. 'Mags, can you add any vehicles that Rimington had access to, to the CCTV and ANPR search? Hutch, give Rimington's picture to the door-knockers; see if anyone spotted him in the area.' He thought for a moment. 'Give them a photo of Vicki Barclay as well. If she was involved, then a pregnant woman might jog a few more memories.'

Chapter 13

It had been forty-eight hours since the death of Stevie Cullen, and the crime scene investigators had finished their first search of the massage parlour. Warren decided to drive over and do a walk-through with the crime scene manager, Andy Harrison.

'We've been focusing particularly on the blood spatter, trying to establish the position of the victim when he was stabbed, and any movements afterwards,' started Harrison. The two men were dressed in white scene suits at the threshold of the back room where Stevie Cullen had his final massage and met his demise.

The building was a converted residential property, and the space they stood in had probably been a dining room once upon a time. Decorated in soothing pastel shades, with thick, blackout curtains, the room had a cosy, almost womb-like feeling. The main ceiling light had been supplemented by dim, wall-mounted uplighters controlled by a separate switch, and wooden shelves with tea-lights. A CD player with speakers sat on a corner table, covered in a cloth. Two days after the killing and the faintest traces of scented oils and perfumes still lingered in the air, valiantly competing with the smell of dried blood.

The scene was exactly as Warren remembered, but now the

room was covered in numbered yellow markers. Powerful portable lamps lit up even the dimmest corners.

'The witnesses stated that the victim was lying on his back on the massage table when he was stabbed,' said Harrison. He pointed to a pool of blood smeared on the covered table. 'He certainly bled out on there, but he didn't stay on there throughout.'

Harrison crouched down, pointing to another large bloodstain a little over a metre from the table and a series of markers between the stain and the edge of the table.

'Aside from the obvious pool of blood, there are blood spots on the floor here, consistent with dripping from a height of less than half a metre.'

Harrison turned on the spot.

'There are more drips here, this time hitting the ground at an angle, indicating that the victim was moving back towards the table.'

Warren frowned. 'Are you saying that the victim wasn't stabbed on the massage table?'

Harrison shook his head.

'Not necessarily. The knife was stuck into the victim's chest. It's not uncommon for there to be little blood released at the moment of entry. The major blood loss occurs when the knife is removed, especially if it's twisted.'

'Which we know the killer did, as the knife wasn't present when we arrived. The witnesses claimed that the killer took the knife with him when he left,' said Warren.

'Exactly, so it's possible that our victim was stabbed on the table, tried to get up and then collapsed on the floor here. Then the killer retrieved the knife, which caused a more significant loss of blood.'

'So how did the victim get back on the table?' asked Warren.

'Two possibilities. Either the victim clambered back to his feet, then crawled back onto the table. Or he was lifted back on by someone else.'

Warren thought back to the interviews given by the two sisters. They had both stated that they tried to stem the bleeding from Cullen – bloody towels had been bagged as evidence. Neither had said they helped move him back onto the table. Nor had they said that he got up off the table after being stabbed and collapsed onto the floor. He made a note to put the question to them when they were interviewed again.

'What about the killer's escape?' asked Warren.

Harrison moved over to the window.

'You can see the blood smears on the window frame, consistent with the killer lifting it and climbing out. Unfortunately, there were no fingerprints. Interestingly, there are no blood spots leading to the window, or on the ground outside. Assuming that the killer took the knife with him, it must have been wrapped in something or held so it didn't drip.'

'Assuming?'

Harrison shrugged. 'Just keeping an open mind. We haven't found the weapon on site, but we only have the witnesses' testimony that tells us the killer took it.'

'What else have you got?'

'There are plenty of bloody footprints in here, and in the corridor and the kitchen. We've eliminated the first responders, now we're going through the rest, but I wouldn't hold your breath, most of them are partials. So far, we've only found impressions consistent with the flat shoes that the two workers were wearing. Assuming the killer was a man, it looks as though he managed not to step in any of the victim's blood on the way out of the window.'

Warren thanked him. The lack of trace evidence was worrying. Was the killer just lucky, careful, or was there more to what had happened than they had been told?

Chapter 14

'I spoke to the landlady down the White Stag again.' Ruskin sounded excited. 'She's convinced that the farmer her glass collector Selina overheard arguing with Stevie, is some guy by the name of Ray Dorridge. He runs a farm about a mile and a half from the pub.'

'Any idea what they may have been arguing over?' asked Warren.

'That she didn't know. I also spoke to Selina again, but she can't remember anything else.'

'I think we need to have a word with Mr Dorridge.'

Ray Dorridge was a short, compact man in his late thirties. Warren eyed him across the table as Moray Ruskin fussed with the PACE digital recorder. The description of the killer from the massage parlour was maddeningly vague – Warren tried to imagine Dorridge in a shapeless hoodie; he couldn't rule him out.

'Thank you for coming here, Mr Dorridge,' Warren started.

The man in front of him grunted. 'I didn't have a lot of choice, did I?'

'I have explained that you are not obliged to be here, and you are not under arrest.'

The man grunted again. From the moment Warren had appeared on the farmer's doorstep, the man had been surly.

Warren slid a photograph of Stevie Cullen across the table. 'Do you know this man?'

Dorridge gave a loud sigh. 'That's Stevie Cullen.'

'And how do you know Mr Cullen?'

'He sometimes drinks in the White Stag.'

Warren nodded; Dorridge had said as much before agreeing to accompany Warren to the station.

'How would you describe your relationship with Mr Cullen?'

Dorridge gave a big shrug. 'Didn't really have one. He'd be in the Stag sometimes when I popped in for a pint after work. We'd occasionally exchange a few words.'

'What sort of words?' asked Ruskin.

Dorridge shrugged again. 'You know. Talk about the footie if it was on the telly.'

'Do you own Dorridge Farm?' asked Warren.

'Yes. Or at least the bank does.'

'And how long have you run it?'

'About ten years. My old man died suddenly, and I took over.'

'And you live there alone?'

'What does that matter?' Dorridge scowled.

'Forgive me, we coppers are a nosy bunch.'

Dorridge's scowl lessened slightly. 'Yes. Mum passed away a couple of years ago. It's just me and the dog now.'

'And you don't have a partner?'

Dorridge glared at him. 'I work fourteen hours a day, 365 days a year, and I still haven't got a pot to piss in. Funnily enough, that's not a big turn-on for women.'

For the first time, his expression changed from one of irritation, to one of bitterness.

'What about brothers and sisters? Or farmhands?'

'I'm an only child and I hire in workers as and when I need them. Like I said, it's just me and the dog.'

99

'You say that you knew Mr Cullen, from the White Stag pub.'

'Yes.'

'Any idea why someone would attack him?'

Dorridge paused. 'He wasn't a nice bloke.'

'In what way?'

'He was a bit mouthy and he'd start arguments with people.'

'Over what?'

'Anything really. He liked to take the piss – sometimes he'd go a bit far. Like if someone's football team lost – he'd wind them up big-time until they finally snapped and told him to fuck off.'

'What about women?'

Dorridge's lip curled. 'Yeah, there was that as well. He'd screw anything in a skirt. Sometimes he'd just wind people up for the fun of it. He'd buy people's girlfriends a drink when they went to the toilet and flirt with them really loudly.'

'Sounds like he was ripe for a punch on the nose. I'm surprised he wasn't banned,' said Ruskin.

'Yeah, you'd think so, but they weren't the sort of family you mess with. Especially that brother of his, who went everywhere with him.'

'Which one?'

'Frankie – dumb as a bag of spanners but built like a brick shithouse. Bigger than you.' He nodded toward Ruskin.

'Why wouldn't you mess with the Cullen family?' asked Warren.

'You know why – you don't need me to tell you about their reputation.' Dorridge leant back in his chair and folded his arms. 'Are we nearly done here? It gets dark early this time of year and I've still got to feed the pigs.'

'We won't keep you any longer than necessary, Mr Dorridge.'

Warren made a show of flicking the page over in his notebook. 'You say you didn't really know Mr Cullen?'

'That's right.'

'So, what was it you were talking about when you met for lunch in the White Stag?'

'We didn't meet for lunch. We were both in there at the same time, and he sat down at the same table.'

'That sounds rather friendly, given that you barely knew each other.'

Dorridge shrugged. 'The place was nearly empty, I guess he wanted some company.'

'So what did you talk about?'

'This and that. The weather. Farming stuff.'

'According to witnesses, the two of you were arguing.'

Dorridge shook his head. 'They must have been mistaken.'

Ruskin flipped over the page in his own notebook. 'Apparently there was a disagreement over a bill?'

'Nope. They must have been getting me confused with someone else.' He folded his arms.

'OK. Thank you for clearing that up,' said Warren.

Dorridge shifted in his seat before making a show of looking at his watch.

'I appreciate you giving up your time, when I'm sure you're busy,' said Warren. 'Just one more thing before you go.'

Dorridge sighed again.

'Where were you Monday afternoon?'

'Out on the back field.'

'Did anyone see you?'

'Does the dog count?'

'OK, Mr Dorridge, thank you for your time.'

After Dorridge had been signed out of reception, Ruskin turned to Warren. 'I think we've just been told a pack of lies, Boss.'

'I agree. I think that Mr Dorridge knew Stevie Cullen a lot better than he's willing to admit.'

'I can't say I'm surprised that he doesn't have an alibi. Do you reckon he could have done it?'

Warren tugged his lip, thoughtfully. 'It's hard to say. But he's definitely on the suspect list. Let's see if any of his vehicles were near the scene. Check his phone records for links to Stevie and see if we can track his movements by GPS. Also, speak to his neighbours, such as they are. SOC said that they observed Stevie travelling a lot between local farms; maybe they can shed some light on his relationship with Dorridge. And ask Rachel to check the massage parlour's ledger – see if he ever visited.'

'Will do.'

Benny Masterson, Stevie Cullen's best friend, arrived unprompted at the police station mid-afternoon.

'I heard you were looking for me,' he said to a surprised Warren.

The farmhand had been on the list to interview but had been missing from his bedsit when Moray Ruskin had gone looking for him.

He claimed to have got drunk the night before and ended up crashing at his sometime girlfriend's house. The lack of a phone charger accounted for his phone going straight to voicemail.

The faint miasma of alcohol fumes surrounding him, and his bloodshot eyes, lent some credence to his story. His companion, who had dropped him off at the station, corroborated the rest of his story.

Despite his apparent hangover, he proclaimed himself fit to talk.

'I've known Stevie since we were kids.' He slurped at his coffee, wincing slightly at the heat.

'My parents ... they weren't great you know? They liked a drink, and Dad had a bit of a temper. But Stevie's Mum and Dad would have me over for tea most evenings.' He glared defiantly. 'I know their reputation and all that, but I don't know what I'd have done without them ...'

He rubbed his nose with the back of his hand. 'Stevie was a good mate you know? He had a bit of a temper, and he was a bugger with the women, but when you needed someone ...'

Warren gave the man a moment to compose himself.

'Somebody obviously didn't feel the same as you. Can you give us any idea who might have been angry enough with him to kill him?'

Masterson sighed. 'I've been thinking about it since the moment I heard, but nothing makes sense.'

'You said in the pub that he had a bit of a reputation for going after other men's partners. Could that be a reason?'

'I was drunk. I didn't really mean it.'

Warren could see that the man was talking himself out of something.

'Please, Benny, help me out here. Was there anyone in particular who you think might have taken offence to Stevie hitting on their girlfriend?'

Masterson was silent for a few moments. 'You didn't hear this from me, right?'

'We'll do our best to be discreet,' said Warren.

'Most of the time it was a bit of fun you know? A few blokes threatened to punch him, but everyone knew his family's reputation. Most people wouldn't want to mess with him, and he knew that.'

'Most, but not all?'

Masterson bit his lip. 'There was this one bloke. He's a bit of a psycho. Did some time in prison for assault. He's engaged to this girl. She's pretty and all that, but not worth the aggro. Stevie … well he liked the challenge.'

'What happened?'

'Stevie would wind him up a bit. He'd buy her drinks, text her stuff. The guy told him to leave it out, but that just made Stevie chase her more.'

He sighed. 'I didn't think there was anything in it. Usually, Stevie was all mouth – he knew where the line was. A few months ago, she stopped coming to the pub. I figured her fella had put his foot down and didn't think anything more about it.'

'But?'

'A few weeks ago, I heard a rumour that Stevie had been seeing her behind his back. I asked him, but he denied it.' Masterson looked at the table. 'I think it's the only time he's ever lied to me.'

'Does this man have a name?'

'Anton Rimington.'

Thursday 05 November

Chapter 15

The day was finally here. Neither Susan nor Warren had slept for more than a few minutes at a time the night before. Late-night fireworks from their neighbours' bonfire celebrations had hardly helped matters. By unspoken agreement, neither had mentioned what the morning might bring, as if sharing their hopes and fears might curse them.

They could have had a lie-in; both of them had booked the morning off, but by mutual assent, they got up at the same time as usual. Nevertheless, it took all of Warren's willpower not to access his work email on his phone; today was about him and Susan. Everything else could take a back seat.

The later start meant they had time for a leisurely shower and a decent cooked breakfast. Neither of them had enough appetite to finish it.

Warren looked at his watch. 'Let's go – we don't want to get stuck in traffic and end up being late.'

It would have taken a traffic jam the likes of which Hertfordshire had never experienced before, for them to be late for their ten o'clock appointment. Susan stood up immediately and picked up her bag.

'Let's leave the dishes until we get back.'

Arriving early had its advantages. No sooner had they sat down, than they were being ushered through the double doors to the ward.

'We had a cancellation this morning, so we may as well see you now. Never hurts to get ahead of ourselves!'

The nurse was breezy and cheerful; Warren imagined that regardless of the overwhelming pressures on the NHS from years of cutbacks and under-funding, generally speaking she probably enjoyed her job. Warren tightened his grip on Susan's hand; neither of them managed more than a perfunctory smile. That another couple had cancelled a scan reminded them that despite her upbeat demeanour, the nurse didn't just deliver happy news.

Two hours later it was all over. Sitting in the clinic's car park, the shaking in Warren's hands had subsided enough for him to start the car engine.

'I can lend you some mascara to fix your eyes,' Susan teased.

'Bugger off,' said Warren, unable to stop smiling.

Twelve weeks in and finally, after years of trying, everything was going to plan.

And if a man wasn't allowed to shed a tear or two during his wife's ultrasound scan, when could he?

'Silvija Wilson is a bit of a naughty girl,' said Rachel Pymm triumphantly.

Warren moved around to stand behind her chair. He'd arrived back at the station just minutes before and had only just taken his coat off; his heart wanted nothing more than to stay at home with his wife, but Susan had only booked cover for the first part of the day, so there was no point in Warren staying home alone. Hopefully he'd get back at a decent hour, so they could celebrate properly. Moments later, Grimshaw, Martinez and Ruskin also joined him and Pymm.

Pymm's workstation had three large screens arranged in a horseshoe. Each screen had a different spreadsheet on it.

'What a waste – this would be the perfect set-up to play video games on,' remarked Martinez.

'Alex is into 3D gaming,' remarked Ruskin. 'He's just bought a headset.'

'I can't wait to see what the porn industry does with that technology,' said Grimshaw.

'And there you go, lowering the tone again,' said Pymm, her voice cold.

'Shaun, save your fantasies for outside work,' warned Warren. Grimshaw smirked.

'What have you found, Rachel?' asked Martinez.

She pointed at the three screens in turn. 'This is a copy of the handwritten appointments book for the past three months. I've listed the names of the customer, the treatments, the appointment times, contact numbers, the amount paid and the payment method. I have identified the older of the two customers that we saw on the CCTV prior to the killing, but her phone keeps going to voicemail. No luck with the other woman yet.'

'Well keep at it,' said Warren.

'You'll be interested to know that both Vicki Barclay and Anton Rimington have had treatments recently,' continued Pymm.

'So, they would know if the window to the massage parlour was routinely kept open, and presumably would know the two sisters,' stated Warren.

'Exactly.' She moved to the next screen. 'This is the accounts spreadsheet, detailing the numbers of treatments each day and the cost, including the payment method. In addition, it includes sales of consumables such as scented oils, gift bags, bath salts et cetera.' She moved to the third screen. 'This is the online banking spreadsheet. The cash deposited, and the electronic payments, match the accounts spreadsheet. It also includes the business costs.' She paused. 'After paying her overheads and her staff, most months she doesn't make much of a profit from what I can see.'

'So, the business was struggling?'

'According to these spreadsheets, I'd say so.'

'What are you holding back, Rachel?' Warren knew the sergeant had a flair for the dramatic.

'The handwritten appointments book doesn't match the accounting spreadsheet. There are a significant number of appointments in the book that don't appear in her accounts.'

'Could they have been missed appointments?' asked Ruskin.

'Possibly, there's no way to tell,' conceded Pymm.

'Could they have been from the nail bar?' asked Warren. 'They just rent the space. Maybe they record appointments in the book, but they pay the nail technicians directly?'

'Not from the treatment descriptions. They use their own shorthand, but they don't sound like manicures or pedicures. The abbreviations also seem to match treatments that are paid for by card and recorded on the spreadsheet.'

'So, she's under-reporting some of her cash sales. Sounds like a clumsy attempt to avoid tax,' said Warren. It was certainly interesting, but he doubted it had anything to do with their investigation.

'I expect you're wondering why I think this is interesting,' said Pymm.

'Practising your clairvoyance skills again, Rachel?' said Warren.

'Some customers seem to always be treated off the books. Want to have a guess who?'

'Stevie Cullen,' said Ruskin.

'Stevie Cullen had a complicated personal life, but I think it important at this stage that we keep an open mind as to suspects and motives,' said Warren.

'I'd like to know more about his connection to the massage parlour,' said Hutchinson. 'There's a reason he was either getting

110

complimentary massages or he was paying cash and they were keeping it off the books.'

'I still reckon he was enjoying services that weren't advertised in the shop window,' stated Grimshaw.

'That explains why he was there,' said Pymm, 'but where's the motive? Does it mean the workers in the parlour were involved in the killing?'

The team pondered the question.

'Maybe they were accessories?' said Ruskin.

'In what way?' prompted Warren.

'Maybe they tipped off his killer that he was there? They might not even have thought he would be killed?'

'That would explain why they were so shocked,' said Pymm. 'I've only seen the video recordings of their interviews, but they seemed genuinely horrified.'

Warren found himself agreeing. Over the course of his career, he'd met many killers. And he'd be the first to admit that he'd been fooled more than once, but his gut was telling him that the shock expressed by the two young masseuses was real. Nevertheless, he was reluctant to dismiss their involvement yet.

He said as much.

'That still leaves us looking for a motive,' said Pymm.

'Let's go back to the basics, then. Why do people kill?' asked Warren.

'Sex,' said Grimshaw immediately.

'Money,' said Pymm.

'Revenge,' said Hutchinson.

'Jealousy,' suggested Richardson.

'Blackmail or extortion,' said Grimshaw.

'All of the above,' said Ruskin.

Warren tapped his pen against his teeth in frustration. Aside from random or chance killings, or mistaken identity, one of those core motives was usually at the heart of any murder. And where there was a motive, there was usually a suspect.

He dismissed the notion of a random killing almost immediately – the attack had to have been premeditated in some way. Even if the killer didn't know who he was targeting, they had to know that there was a customer in that room at the time, and that the room was accessible from the rear of the building.

'If we assume sex, and/or jealousy were the motives, that could lead back to the girls,' said Grimshaw.

'In what way?' said Warren, ignoring Pymm's sigh.

'If they were servicing Cullen, maybe one of them had a jealous boyfriend?'

'Shaun could be right,' said Hutchinson. 'I reckon we should look into the girls' personal lives a bit more. Did either of them have a boyfriend or significant other who might be jealous? It might also explain why their descriptions of the attacker were so vague; they could be protecting him.'

Despite Pymm's misgivings, Grimshaw's theory had some merit.

'Keep on looking at their social media accounts, Shaun. See if you can identify anyone of interest. Rachel, give him a hand. I'll get DSI Grayson to authorize some more translation assistance. Any news on their mobile phone records?'

'Still waiting,' responded Pymm. 'Bloody overseas providers are a nightmare to deal with.'

'Well it can't be helped,' said Warren, knowing that Pymm had a tendency to take such things personally. 'Hutch, we're going to need some boots on the ground. The girls were part of our local Serbian community, so put some feelers out. Speak to their friends and acquaintances but keep it discreet.'

'Should we bring them in for questioning again?' asked Ruskin.

'Not just yet, let's see what we uncover first. I don't want to go on a fishing expedition and scare them off. I don't want them disappearing or tipping off the killer that we're looking in their direction.'

'If sex or jealousy weren't the motives, what about money?' said Pymm.

'Organized Crime have been looking into the family's business dealings for some time,' Hutchinson said. 'Given their history, they could have pissed someone off.'

'He could even have been blackmailing or extorting someone,' suggested Ruskin.

'I can look into that,' volunteered Martinez. 'I'm familiar with the team working that angle.'

'Do it,' ordered Warren. 'In the meantime, I think another chat with Benny Masterson is in order. He was Stevie Cullen's best friend, and I think he has a lot more to share with us. If he and Stevie were as close as he claims, he may know why he visited the massage parlour. He might even be persuaded to tell us about any business dealings.'

This time Benny Masterson was asleep in bed in his bedsit when officers turned up to request his presence at the station. Following a heads-up, Warren was waiting for him with a strong cup of coffee and a packet of paracetamol.

The man's eyes were bloodshot, and the smell of stale booze was even stronger than before. Fresh scratches and mud on the side of his face suggested that his journey home after being kicked out of the White Stag the night before hadn't been entirely without incident. However, he appeared sober and willing to help.

'Thanks again for your time, Benny.'

The farmhand grunted in response.

'We took the information you presented us with seriously, but we are still pursuing other lines of inquiry. We are particularly interested in why Stevie was present at the massage parlour where he was attacked. Can you shed any light on that?'

'Why does anyone go to one of those places?' asked Masterson.

'Why don't you tell us? It's not the only place in town offering those services. Do you know why Stevie chose that particular place?'

Masterson shrugged, but his eyes remained fixed on the table.

'Did you ever go there with him?'

He shook his head. 'Not my kind of thing. Seems a bit pricey for smelly candles and baby oil.'

'Did Stevie ever talk about it?'

'No. Why would he?'

Masterson looked up, but his eyes were clouded.

He's hiding something, Warren decided.

'Did Stevie visit there very often?'

Masterson shrugged again. 'Dunno, I never asked him.'

Warren let the silence stretch a little longer.

'Do you know if Stevie had any … special relationship … with any of the workers at the parlour?'

'I just said, we never spoke about it.'

Noting the edge to Masterson's voice, Warren decided to change the subject slightly. Aware that the man was there voluntarily, he didn't want him leaving before he finished asking questions.

'OK, let's leave that to one side. How did Stevie earn his living?'

'He worked on his mum and dad's farm.'

'Doing what?'

'A bit of everything you know. Working the fields, feeding the pigs, looking after the farmhands, that sort of thing. It doesn't exactly come with a job description.'

'And that's all he did?'

Masterson picked at a dirty thumbnail. 'Like I said, he did a bit of everything.'

Warren let the silence stretch again; he could see that Masterson was conflicted.

'Benny, help us out here. Your best friend was killed brutally. I need to know why. What was the motive? Was it a jealous boyfriend, or was it something else? I understand that he may have been doing things he shouldn't have. He might even have been doing things you didn't agree with. But unless you help us, we might never find out who did this to him.'

He paused. 'You said before that his parents were kind to you when you were a kid. Have you visited them since he died?'

Masterson nodded, his eyes wet.

'They're hurting, Benny,' Warren said softly. 'You're hurting. Stevie didn't deserve this; I want to bring his killer to justice. For him. And for you. But I need your help.'

Masterson was silent. Warren said nothing. He could see that his words had got through, but he needed to give him time.

'There was something going on with the massage parlour.'

'Like what?'

'I don't know. He wouldn't tell me.'

'Was it sexual?'

'I really don't know. Maybe.' A flash of pain crossed Masterson's face. 'Stevie didn't always talk to me about those sorts of things. He said …' Masterson cleared his throat '… he said I couldn't be trusted. He said that I couldn't keep my mouth shut when I'd … you know, been drinking.'

Warren could see how much the admission had cost the man.

'Thank you, Benny,' he said quietly.

Masterson stared into space. To Warren's surprise, he started talking again. 'Stevie had ambitions, you know?'

'What sort of ambitions?'

'He wanted something better. Better than working for his mum and dad. He used to say, "farming's dying". He's right. There's no future for small farmers these days, not with the supermarkets pushing their prices down. The profit margins are too narrow. His parents work twelve hours a day, seven days a week, and it still isn't enough. They got out of milking when they ended up selling the milk for less than it cost to produce. It's why they do all the other stuff, you know?'

Warren didn't know, but he could hazard a guess based on

what Ian Bergen from Organized Crime had told them during his briefing.

'What was he doing?'

'He wouldn't tell me. But I know he was visiting all the other farms in the area regularly. He used to carry two mobile phones, one just for business. I never knew the number.'

Masterson took a sip of his cooling coffee and made a face. 'One day I saw him over at Dorridge Farm, talking to Ray, where I was doing some work. I asked him what it was about, and he changed the subject. I asked him if he needed some help – it's tough to get work around here with all the Eastern Europeans sometimes; they push the wages down – but he said he had nothing going.'

Masterson pushed the polystyrene cup away. 'I'm not an idiot,' he said, his voice dripping with self-loathing. 'Everyone sees me down the Stag and they think I'm some sort of drunk ... maybe I am. But I work hard, and I'm never late for work no matter what I did the night before.'

He wiped his nose on his sleeve. 'I just want a chance you know? And I thought maybe he could give me one.'

Warren hated seeing the man in front of him crumbling, but he knew he couldn't afford to let that stop him.

'Witnesses saw Ray Dorridge arguing with Stevie a few weeks ago. Do you have any idea what that might have been about?'

Masterson wiped his nose again. 'I heard some rumours. About dumping.'

'Dumping?'

'Yeah, fly-tipping. It's big business now. The council charge a fortune to dispose of rubbish for you, and they're really fussy about what they'll take. If you can't load a van and take it down the dump what can you do?'

'He was involved in illegal fly-tipping?'

'Yeah. I don't know how it works exactly, but if you look online you can find mobile phone numbers you can call. You ring them, give them some cash and they'll take it away for you, no questions asked.'

Warren was aware of the growing problem. It seemed that every time he and Susan drove out to their favourite country pub, new rubbish had been dumped on the side of the road. Mattresses, old fridges, even bags of builders' rubble filled the lay-bys. But he couldn't see the connection with Dorridge.

'Apparently, if a farmer or landowner reports fly-tipping on their land, the council takes it away for free. Sometimes farmers get a cut of the money paid to the fly-tipper, sometimes they don't.'

'What about Mr Dorridge?'

'Dunno. It was just a rumour I heard.'

It seemed far-fetched, but perhaps Dorridge had objected to Cullen using his land for illegal dumping. Yet that didn't seem to match the comments that Selina, the glass collector at the White Stag, had overheard about him not paying a bill for a job half-done. If Cullen was using Dorridge's land for his illegal dumping, wouldn't he be paying Dorridge? Unless Dorridge was paying Cullen to get rid of his waste?

And what did Dorridge mean by 'the job taking twice as long as necessary' and not having the time 'to keep on chasing and nagging'? Either way, killing Cullen seemed extreme.

'We can rule out Vicki Barclay, Boss,' Grimshaw greeted Warren as he came back into the office, shrugging off his jacket. As usual, a fug of stale cigarette smoke hung around him.

'She claimed that she was at an NCT class at the time of the murder. NCT, in case you're wondering, stands for the National Childbirth Trust and it helps prepare women for having a baby.'

Warren fought down a smile. He knew very well what NCT stood for, and after that morning's good news he was looking forward to attending classes with Susan in the not-too-distant future.

'The class meets up at the community centre at midday and runs for about an hour. I went and spoke to the woman running it.' Grimshaw smirked. 'After class, Barclay went out for lunch with a few of the yummy mummies-to-be. I spoke to a couple, and they reckon it was a pretty leisurely affair. There's no way that she could have been over at the massage parlour within at least an hour either side of the killing, longer if you factor in the fact that she doesn't drive.'

The news wasn't a big surprise; even allowing for the two sisters' muddled accounts of the events that day, it was unlikely that they could have failed to notice that the killer was heavily pregnant.

Nevertheless, it didn't rule her out of the killing entirely. Her fiancé, Anton Rimington, was still a suspect; it wasn't beyond the realms of possibility that she had conspired with Rimington to kill his rival. Her name would stay on the board for the time being at least.

Thanking Grimshaw, Warren headed back to his office. Unfortunately, he didn't walk quickly enough to miss Grimshaw's aside to Martinez.

'I tell you what, Jorge, I might start going to those NCT classes myself. There's something about a pregnant woman that does it for me.'

Warren paused; he was losing count of the number of times he had spoken to Grimshaw about inappropriate 'banter' in the office. He looked over his shoulder. Nobody else seemed to have heard Grimshaw's comment and Martinez was studiously ignoring his colleague's boorishness. Warren sighed; he'd bring it up at their next meeting. He didn't have the time right now.

Chapter 16

Malina and Biljana Dragi arrived at the station promptly for their follow-up interviews. They met Neda Stojanovi , the translator who had sat in on their original interviews on the night of the murder.

The two sisters looked tired and nervous but were soon put at ease by Mags Richardson's breezy efficiency, and Moray Ruskin's friendliness. Warren had decided to downplay the importance of the interview, in the hope that a more relaxed atmosphere would make the interviewees more open.

Both interviews started with the women being shown a headshot of Ray Dorridge, the farmer that the White Stag's glass collector, claimed to have seen arguing with Cullen.

Both women denied knowing, or recognizing, Dorridge. Warren wasn't entirely surprised. There was no record of his name, or his contact details in the massage parlour's ledger. Neither his phone records, nor the massage parlour's, gave any indication that he had ever visited, or had dealings with the business. Inquiries were ongoing to see if there were any other links, but so far it seemed that he largely shunned social media, so was unlikely to have had contact with either of the two women, or for that matter Stevie Cullen, that way.

The only app that he used with any regularity was an online dating site. They had requested the records from the site to see if he could have socialized with either woman that way, or their aunt, who would seem to be more in his age range. The app also catered for same-sex relationships, so they decided to check if Stevie Cullen was also a member. It would be embarrassing to say the least if they missed a connection because they were too old-fashioned to think of it.

In the meantime, Warren chafed at the continued delay at retrieving the mobile phone records for the two sisters; he wouldn't be entirely satisfied until they arrived.

When specifically asked if Dorridge could be the black-clad killer, the two women had shrugged and admitted that he might be. Neither had sounded confident.

Turning to the events at the time of the killing, the two women largely repeated what they had said before about hearing Cullen scream.

'I still don't think the timings add up,' said Richardson, in the post-interview debrief, agreeing to disagree with Martinez, who again theorized that Malina had heard Cullen scream, not her sister.

'I'm more interested about what happened after Cullen was stabbed,' said Grimshaw. 'They've changed their story on that.'

'I wouldn't say changed,' countered Martinez, 'they've just remembered more details.'

'Still, don't you think it weird that they both suddenly remember all those extra details about what happened?' said Grimshaw.

'Not really, they've had a couple of days to process it,' said Martinez. 'You know how unreliable witnesses are. It's not uncommon for them to remember things weeks or even months after the event. And they've probably talked about little else since it happened.'

Grimshaw scowled but conceded the point reluctantly.

'Whatever the reason, their accounts match the evidence that we saw better,' said Warren. 'Stevie jumped off the table after being stabbed, then collapsed with the blade still in him – which would account for the bruises on his left side. The killer then removed the knife and fled the scene.' He looked at his notes. 'Cullen then got back to his feet, and the sisters helped him back onto the massage table, where they tried to stem the blood flow. He then bled out on the table.'

'It certainly matches the evidence at the scene,' said Martinez.

Warren was forced to agree, but something in his gut didn't sit quite right.

They really needed those phone records.

Friday 06 November

Chapter 17

'I'm still not happy about Ray Dorridge,' said Warren.

The team were seated around the main briefing table. Warren took another swig of his lukewarm coffee – his third cup that morning. The previous evening's bonfire night celebrations had carried on late into the night, with random bangers that sounded more like a car bomb than a firework, being set off well into the early hours. Not that he and Susan had been in much of a mood to sleep. The enormity of the upcoming changes to their lives had finally hit home, and they had spent much of the night talking and planning for the future.

It was still a bit early for them to start choosing baby names, but both of them had lists of names that they didn't want; Susan's were largely based around former pupils whose passage through the school had made a lasting – and negative – impression. A number of them overlapped with Warren's own list – for largely the same reasons.

Forcing himself to focus on the task at hand, Warren continued, 'So far, we can find no link between Dorridge and the massage parlour, but when Moray and I interviewed him, he was clearly holding something back.'

'After what Benny Masterson told us yesterday, I called the

council,' said Ruskin. 'Apparently he's complained about fly-tipping on his property three times in the past twelve months. Each time, the council shifted a lorry-load of rubbish; everything from fridges to mattresses to building rubble from kitchen or bathroom refits. They routinely go through it to see if there's anything they can use to track down the original source, but it's been picked clean. It's definitely a professional job.'

'So, the question is whether Dorridge is a victim of illegal dumping, or if he partnered up with Cullen to make some money on the side,' said Grimshaw.

'It's not much of a reason to kill someone,' said Martinez, 'especially if the council takes it away for free.'

'Fair point,' conceded Grimshaw.

'What else do we know about him?' asked Warren.

'He received a police caution back in February,' said Pymm. 'It resulted from an argument leading to minor damage in the Café Rouge on the high street. The person he was arguing with left before the police attended, and Dorridge refused to name them. There isn't much else on the PNC.'

'Get onto the arresting officers and see if they can add some more information,' ordered Warren. 'I'm particularly interested in who he was arguing with. How's his alibi looking?'

'We just got his phone records through,' said Pymm. 'No calls to Cullen's smartphone that we retrieved from the murder scene, but plenty of calls to unregistered numbers. Including one number that he speaks to regularly; including twenty-four hours before each of his three complaints about fly-tipping.'

'Now that's interesting,' said Warren. 'If he was working a fly-tipping scam with Cullen, that could be Cullen's business phone.'

'Which was nowhere to be found when we searched his room,' said Hutchinson.

'Run it by Compliance and see if we have enough to justify a request for the phone's records,' said Warren. 'If it is his phone, we might be able to use it to identify anyone else he has dealings with. We might even be able to track his movements.'

'What does the GPS on Dorridge's phone show for the day of the killing?' asked Hutchinson.

'It shows the handset as largely present on the back field from first thing in the morning until about an hour after the murder,' said Pymm.

'Which confirms his alibi,' said Martinez.

'Not necessarily – he could just have left the phone in his tractor out in the field,' said Hutchinson. 'The killing was clearly well organized and premeditated. Leaving his phone behind would be the least of his preparations. I'm no farmer, but presumably if he was trundling up and down his field all afternoon in a tractor, the GPS would show movement. Did the handset move during that time?'

'The data's ambiguous,' admitted Pymm. 'The GPS signal is only accurate to a few tens of metres, and the phone signal out there is too patchy to narrow it down any further. I can send it off to IT to see if they can be any more precise.'

Warren thought about her suggestion. He knew from experience that such analysis was far from guaranteed and could be costly and time-consuming. However, Hutchinson's question was a good one. They could very well catch Dorridge in another lie.

'Do it,' he ordered. 'In the meantime, Mr Dorridge stays on the suspect board. Somebody arrange for him to be picked up. I want another chat with him.'

Warren took a sip of his coffee. 'Next up, what about Anton Rimington?'

'He hasn't done himself any favours,' said Ruskin. 'He turned his mobile off Sunday night after his argument with Vicki Barclay and after he'd rung his mate to say he was coming around. That's when they started drinking. He switched it back on a couple of times on Monday, including ringing in to work to claim he had the flu, but he was obviously sulking and switched if back off again after ignoring Barclay three times. He didn't switch it back on again until Wednesday morning, which was when we ploughed in and arrested him.'

'So, we can't use his mobile phone to track his movements the day of the attack?'

'Nope, he could have been anywhere.'

'Which begs the question, did he turn it off to avoid the missus or was it to help build an alibi?' asked Martinez. 'There can't be many people who don't know that we can track their phone's location these days.'

'What does his mate say?'

'Again, no help. He reckons they drank the house dry Sunday night. He somehow managed to make it to work for eight and didn't get back until gone seven p.m. He rang Rimington at about lunchtime, to see how he was, but it went straight to voicemail. When he got back, he says Rimington was already pissed again. He reckons he'd been drinking all day.'

'How would he know that if he hadn't been with him?' asked Pymm.

'Good point,' admitted Ruskin.

'He wouldn't be the first person to commit a murder and then drink themselves into oblivion to forget what they've just done,' said Martinez.

'What about people in the neighbouring flats? Did any of them see Rimington at the time of the killing?'

'Nobody we've spoken to was around during the day, and there's no CCTV. The flat has its own door, so Rimington could easily have left without being seen by the neighbours.'

'OK, let's carry on testing his alibi,' said Warren. 'In the meantime, he would have needed to get to the massage parlour. His mate's flat is on the other side of town.'

'It'd be a walk of several miles,' said Richardson, pointing out the pins on the wall map. She placed her tablet on the table. 'His car's licence plate wasn't recorded on any ANPR cameras that day. The locations of the fixed cameras on that side of town make it impossible to travel more than halfway to the massage parlour without being tracked. If he did use his car, he'd have had to have parked it so far away from the murder scene, you'd have to ask what the point of driving was.'

'Did he have access to any other cars?'

'His mate took his own car to work that day – probably unwisely given how much he claimed to have drunk the night before. His place of work is in the opposite direction to the massage parlour and we have him on a fixed camera arriving and leaving work at the time he said. His car stayed in the car park all day.'

'What about friends and relatives?'

Richardson pursed her lips. 'His fiancée, Vicki Barclay, doesn't own a car, nor does his mother, who is his only close family. As for somebody else … we're looking at CCTV and ANPR in the area around his flat for a link to anyone who could have given him a lift, but we don't really know what we're looking for.'

'Could he have changed the licence plates on his car to avoid cameras?' asked Ruskin.

'That would have required some serious premeditation,' cautioned Grimshaw.

'It's worth pursuing,' said Warren. 'Check the PNC for reports of stolen licence plates – or even stolen cars for that matter.'

'Unless he stole them off a car the same make and colour as his own, then wouldn't that show up as a mismatch between the vehicle on the DVLA's database and the car caught on camera? I'd like to see him explain that away,' suggested Ruskin.

'If you want to visually match all the cars in the area to their records in the DVLA database, be my guest,' said Grimshaw.

'It's a good idea, Moray,' said Warren quickly, not wanting the probationer to lose heart, 'but a big job. Let's see what Forensics say first; they may be able to tell us if the car's plates were tampered with.'

'What about other methods of transport?' asked Martinez.

'I've already contacted the local bus companies for their CCTV to see if Rimington was a passenger that day.'

'How about cab firms?' asked Grimshaw.

'There are no journeys recorded on the app on his phone. There are also no calls to cab firms on his mobile or his mate's landline,' said Pymm. 'I've arranged for his mugshot to be circulated amongst local firms to see if anyone did a pick-up off the street, although as you know, only black cabs are licensed to do that. We've had mixed success getting drivers to admit to illegal pick-ups in the past.'

'Well Benny Masterson also fingered Stevie Cullen as potentially the father of Vicki Barclay's baby,' said Martinez. 'If even the village drunk had worked that one out, how likely is it that Rimington didn't know until Sunday night? I reckon he still has the biggest motive out of all of them.'

'Let's not narrow the suspect field prematurely,' cautioned Warren. 'There are still plenty of other people who probably aren't mourning the loss of Stevie Cullen, not least Ray Dorridge. I'd also like to see the sisters' reaction to a mugshot of Rimington. We'll see what they have to say next time we get them in for questioning.'

Chapter 18

Ray Dorridge put up a good show of merely being irritated at his time being wasted, but the way he fiddled with the polystyrene cup of water belied his nervousness.

'He's lawyered up, this time,' Grimshaw observed before they entered the interview room. 'Feels like a man with a guilty conscience.'

Warren chose to ignore the Americanism – Grimshaw was a big fan of US cop dramas. 'Or he's a sensible person who is concerned about being questioned for a second time, and a search warrant being executed on his property.'

This time, Dorridge was interviewed under caution, although he still hadn't been arrested. He'd come willingly, and Warren didn't want to start the custody clock ticking until he needed to.

'In our last interview, you said that you only had a passing acquaintance with Stevie Cullen?'

'Yeah, that's right.'

'Just drinking buddies?' asked Grimshaw.

'We both liked a pint down the Stag,' agreed Dorridge.

'But you were aware of his reputation with women?' Grimshaw pressed.

Dorridge shrugged. 'It's hardly a secret.'

Warren leant back slightly in his chair. 'I'll be honest, you aren't the first person who's mentioned his, shall we say, "philandering nature". Can you tell me a bit more about it? Who else might he have annoyed?'

Dorridge also leant back in his chair, visibly relaxing. 'Form an orderly queue. As I said before, he'd target anything in a skirt.'

'So he had numerous affairs?' pressed Warren.

Dorridge made a slight rocking motion with his head. 'Not necessarily affairs. I think it was more about taking the piss. Some of the women he hit on clearly weren't his type; he was just winding up their husbands or boyfriends.'

'How did they take it?'

'It varied. Some blokes were all right with it. I reckon they knew he was just being a prick and it wouldn't come to anything. Others … well I guess they probably felt a bit threatened. He was a good-looking bloke, and he usually had a wad of cash in his back pocket. I imagine a few were worried that it might go somewhere if they weren't careful.'

'Was there anyone in particular who got upset?'

Dorridge thought for a moment. 'Harry Raynor was pretty annoyed with him one night. He and his missus, Teri, had had a row earlier that evening on the way to the Stag. He went into the back room to play pool and left Teri in the bar area. When he came back Teri and Stevie were drinking, and were sitting pretty close, if you get my drift. Harry called Stevie a wanker, grabbed Teri's hand and took her home. Didn't even finish his pint. I reckon it might have got a bit more messy if Stevie's brother Frankie hadn't been in there. Stevie shouted something like "Facebook me if you need something bigger" and waggled his little finger. I heard that they broke up a few days later, although everyone knew they'd been having problems for a while.'

'Do you know if anything came of it?' asked Grimshaw, writing down the names.

Dorridge shrugged. 'I've no idea.'

'Do you know of anyone that he definitely did have an affair with?'

Dorridge looked uncomfortable.

'It would really help us, Ray,' said Warren. 'We just want to know what sort of man Stevie was. He's beginning to sound like a real bully.'

Dorridge sighed. 'Look there were rumours that he might have been seeing someone more seriously. I don't know, because she stopped coming to the Stag. Her fiancé had a bit of a reputation for hitting women. I heard he may have even spent some time in jail for assaulting an ex.'

'Can you give me some names?'

Dorridge paused before answering. 'Anton. Rimington, I think. His missus was called Vicki. She was a bit young for him if you ask me. Stevie was probably more her age, if that makes any difference.'

'And you think the relationship was more serious than just a bit of flirting down the pub?'

'Yeah, that was the rumour. A couple of people reckon they saw him near their flat when Anton was away, visiting his family.' He paused. 'Somebody also reckoned she looked pregnant. Draw your own conclusions.'

Warren glanced at Grimshaw. Yet another person aware of Cullen's affair. It was getting harder and harder to believe that Rimington was unaware of his fiancée's infidelity. Perhaps that was why he put the pieces together so quickly when looking at the baby scans. Rimington's lack of alibi was looking more and more problematic.

In the meantime, Ray Dorridge's relationship to Cullen hadn't been fully explored yet. With the farmer apparently at ease, Warren decided to wrong-foot him.

'You've been really helpful, Ray, although from what you've told us, the list of people that Stevie Cullen angered is getting longer. We're going to need another suspect board!'

Dorridge joined in with the chuckles from Warren and Grimshaw.

'There are going to be a few relieved husbands and boyfriends now that he's no longer making a nuisance of himself,' said Grimshaw.

'Yeah, there were probably a couple of blokes who have thought about killing him over the years,' said Dorridge.

'Were you one of those people, Ray?' asked Warren.

'Sorry?'

'You told me last time we spoke how hard it was to find a woman, what with all the hours you work. I'll bet you were really annoyed when Stevie turned up in Café Rouge last February and scuppered your date. Tell me, did you ever see that woman again, or did she decide that your little temper tantrum was a turn-off?' asked Warren.

'How did you …'

'Bit of a kicker two days before Valentine's day,' said Grimshaw. 'I'd have been pretty annoyed.' He looked towards Warren. 'According to the witnesses in the police report, she left shortly after Cullen.' He turned his gaze back to Dorridge. 'Say, you don't suppose she caught up with Cullen, do you?'

Dorridge's solicitor had clearly been unaware of his client's caution; nevertheless he attempted to step in.

'This seems to be rather flimsy, DCI Jones. Do you have any more substantial allegations?'

Warren and Grimshaw both ignored him.

'What happened that night, Ray?' asked Warren.

Dorridge scowled and folded his arms. 'Not a lot, I'm sure it's all in the report.'

'I'd like to hear your side of the story, Ray, because it sounds to me as though you might also be on the list of men with a reason to want Stevie Cullen out of the picture,' said Warren.

'Oh, come on! That happened months ago. We settled it there and then. End of story.'

'Settled it with a police caution for you and nothing for him,' replied Warren. 'Why didn't you tell the arresting officers who you were fighting? Seems a bit unfair that you get the criminal record, whilst he gets off scot free.'

'This is old ground,' interjected the solicitor. This time all three men ignored him.

'Fine. You want to know what happened? I'll tell you.' Dorridge glared across the table. 'You're right, it is bloody hard to find a good woman, so yes, I was really pissed off when that prick Cullen decided to mess things up.' He took a sip of his water.

'I met Carrie online about a month before the … incident. It wasn't our first date; we'd gone for coffee the Saturday before. We'd got on really well and she agreed to come out for dinner on Friday night after work. Nothing too serious, just a bite to eat in Café Rouge and maybe a drink afterwards.' He turned his glare towards Grimshaw. 'And yes, I was thinking about asking her out again on Valentine's day, although it was on a Sunday, so I thought I might offer to cook, rather than try and book a table somewhere.'

'Go on.'

'Well the restaurant was busy two days before Valentine's, and we were on a little table squeezed into the front window. Everything was going great, then suddenly, Stevie's standing next to me. He'd clearly been drinking, and he starts asking me to introduce him to my "lovely friend". He obviously wasn't going anywhere, and I didn't want to be rude in front of Carrie, so I introduced him. Then he starts asking if we were "on a date".'

Dorridge's lip curled. 'He was like a teenager. Carrie laughed, although I couldn't tell if she was being polite or not. Anyway, I persuaded him to clear off and leave us alone. At which point he took her hand, kissed it and said "*enchanté*" in a really embarrassing French accent.'

Warren watched Dorridge closely; it was clear that even nine months later, the memories of that evening still angered the man.

'Then what happened?'

'I got up to use the toilet, and when I came back the bastard was sitting in my seat, pouring Carrie a glass of wine. He must have just moved around the corner to the bar and waited for me to leave. I don't know what he was saying to her, but she was laughing.'

Dorridge stopped, looking down at his hands. His ears were flushed a dark red.

'Then what?'

'You know what happened.'

'Tell us in your own words.'

'I was so annoyed with him. I'd been paying a subscription to that damned matchmaking website for years, and I'd had three proper dates out of it. All of them lost interest when they realized what being a farmer really meant. Carrie was different. Her family used to be in farming. She wasn't put off.' Dorridge paused. 'Then along comes fucking Stevie Cullen, and he thinks it'll be funny to mess it up for me. I don't think he was even that interested. To him it's all just a game.'

'What did you do?'

Dorridge cleared his throat, the redness of his ears spreading to his cheeks, the base of his throat turning a blotchy pink.

'I told him to piss off. He got up and said that was no sort of language to use in front of a lady, then turned to Carrie and said, "I'll see you again. Maybe we can finish that drink."

'So, I threw a punch at him.'

Dorridge closed his eyes, briefly. 'I can't believe I did it. It was like I was back at school again, and the bullies were stealing my pencil case and throwing my bag out of the window to get me into trouble. I don't know what I thought would happen, but that big ape of a brother wasn't with him, so I guess I thought I stood a chance.' He snorted. 'I haven't thrown a punch since I was a kid. I missed him completely and ended up sending the table of the couple next to us flying. He didn't even try to hit me; he just gave me a shove and sat me down on my arse. By the time I got back to my feet, the bar staff were running over and Stevie was legging out of the door laughing and blowing kisses. Carrie left about a minute later.'

Dorridge's voice hardened. 'In all my life, I've never been so humiliated. It cost me two hundred quid by the time I'd paid for everything, and I have a fucking police record. In answer to your next question, no I didn't see Carrie again. I called her to say sorry, but she said that her ex had had "anger management issues" and she didn't think it would be a good idea to continue the relationship.

'So yeah, I fucking hated Stevie Cullen. But that was nine months ago, and I'm not going to suddenly kill him over a ruined date.'

Ray Dorridge's solicitor suggested a short break; Warren and Grimshaw moved into the corridor to discuss what they'd learnt.

'It might have been nine months ago, but he's clearly still furious,' said Grimshaw.

'But is he furious enough to kill Cullen?' asked Warren.

'Maybe he hooked up with Anton Rimington?' said Grimshaw. 'He's lied to us about how well he knew Cullen, I'll bet he knows more about Rimington than he's letting on.'

'I can't see it,' said Martinez, who'd been watching the interview remotely. 'I still can't imagine him killing Cullen over a date.'

'Well that might not be the only motive,' said Warren. 'Let's go back in and see what else he has to say.'

'When we last spoke, you denied having any sort of business relationship with Mr Cullen,' said Warren.

'Yeah, that's right,' Dorridge had regained his composure during the short break.

'However, witnesses claimed that you and Mr Cullen were seen arguing in the White Stag pub over the payment for services.'

'And I said they must be mistaken.' Dorridge's tone was defiant.

Warren opened the folder in front of him and removed a sheet of paper. 'According to Middlesbury council, you reported illegal fly-tipping on your land on three separate occasions last year.'

Dorridge shifted uncomfortably in his seat. 'Yeah, dirty bastards. They'll dump their shit anywhere.'

'We've spoken to a witness who confirms Mr Cullen ran a business that involved collecting rubbish from households and businesses for a fee, and then dumping the rubbish illegally on land, such as farmland, where the council would ultimately pick it up for free.'

'I wouldn't know anything about that.'

Warren removed a second sheet of paper. 'This is a copy of your phone logs.' He pointed to three highlighted entries. 'You received calls from this mobile number two or three days before each reported incident of fly-tipping.'

'So?' Dorridge's tone was defiant.

'The timing seems rather coincidental. Who does the number belong to, Mr Dorridge?'

Dorridge's eyes darted around for a few seconds, before he suddenly relaxed. 'It's one of my neighbours. He spotted the rubbish on my land and kindly called me to let me know about it.'

'Who is this neighbour?'

Dorridge shrugged. 'I couldn't tell you.'

'Do a lot of strangers have your mobile number?'

'You don't have to answer that, Mr Dorridge,' interjected the solicitor. 'In fact I fail to see the relevance of this line of questioning.'

Warren ignored him.

'We did a search online for this mobile phone number, and it turns out that it's the contact number for a "Middlesbury Refuse Disposal Service". One phone call and they'll take any unwanted rubbish away and dispose of it properly. They promise to beat any quote.'

'And?' It was clear Dorridge wasn't going to make it easy for them.

'We have been unable to find any licensed disposal services with that name or linked to that phone number. Tell me, Mr Dorridge, do you know the owner of this telephone number?'

Dorridge swallowed. 'No.'

'Are you sure about that?'

'Positive.'

'Well that's strange, because not only did you receive calls from this very helpful – but unknown – neighbour, you also made calls to them on a regular basis.'

Dorridge had turned a pasty white colour. He licked his lips.

'Does this number belong to Stevie Cullen?'

Dorridge looked over at his solicitor, who gave a tiny shake of the head.

'No comment.'

Warren fought to repress a smile of triumph; Dorridge had all but confirmed that the number belonged to Cullen. The question was, did the relationship – which he had been denying – extend beyond the fly-tipping scam?

'Why were you calling this number?'

'No comment.'

'I'll ask you again, Mr Dorridge. Did you have a business relationship with Mr Cullen?'

'No comment.'

Warren gave a big sigh. 'Look, Mr Dorridge, we have already established that you lied about how well you knew Mr Cullen the last time you were interviewed. You need to help me here. I'll be honest, I'm not that fussed about a bit of illegal dumping. All I want to do is work out what happened to Mr Cullen.'

'No comment.'

'Are you sure about that, Mr Dorridge?' asked Warren.

'What are you hiding, Ray?' asked Grimshaw.

'No comment.'

'I would remind you that my client is here voluntarily,' interrupted the solicitor. 'He has already made it clear that he doesn't wish to discuss his dealings with Mr Cullen. He is not under arrest, and so you shouldn't be drawing any inferences from that decision. Mr Dorridge has been very cooperative, not least in allowing you to search his property for evidence linking him to Mr Cullen's death.'

'The search has been authorized by a warrant,' Warren reminded the man.

'Which I would question, on the basis of what we have heard so far. In fact, I'd go as far as to suggest that this is a fishing expedition, and request that you cease the search.'

Dorridge looked over at his solicitor and licked his lips. 'I want to take a break.'

Chapter 19

Whilst Dorridge spoke to his solicitor, Warren and Grimshaw met other members of the team who had been watching the interview remotely.

'He's shitting himself,' was Grimshaw's considered opinion.

Warren had to agree. But over what? Getting the council to remove illegally dumped waste was definitely a crime, and he'd be liable for a large fine, but Dorridge had looked terrified.

'How's the search of Dorridge's farm going?'

'Nothing so far. They're going through his wardrobe and laundry basket to see if there's any clothing matching the description of the killer. They've taken several knives, and they're dismantling the sink traps and the washing machine to look for any blood.'

'It's a farm,' said Grimshaw, 'he could have just hosed himself down in the middle of a field, and burnt his clothes, and we'd never be any the wiser.'

'Let's hope he isn't that smart,' said Warren.

'Assuming he's even the killer,' cautioned Martinez. 'I still think he's an unlikely fit, based on what we've seen so far.'

'Well let's allow Forensics to do their job,' said Warren. 'It's too early to dismiss him just yet.'

'What if he continues no commenting? Do we have enough to arrest him?' asked Grimshaw.

Warren thought for a moment. 'Enough to arrest, yes, but not enough to charge within the next twenty-four hours, and we haven't got enough to extend his custody yet. I'd rather not arrest him until we've got more.'

The custody sergeant poked his head around the door. 'He's back.'

'Well at least it appears that he's decided to stick around for a bit,' said Warren, before finishing the last of his coffee in one big gulp. 'Put your fags away, Shaun, let's strike while the iron's hot.'

'Stevie's been dumping on my land for the last few months. I'm not the only one. At least half the farms in the area have been dealing with his crap.'

Ray Dorridge looked tired. He'd regained some of his colour, but he sounded weary. The statement matched the records from Middlesbury council, who'd recorded almost two dozen incidents of fly-tipping on farmland in the past financial year alone.

'Tell me how it works,' said Warren.

'The first time it happened, I didn't know anything about it until I stumbled across it.' Dorridge thought for a moment. 'That'd be about a year or so ago. The bolt on the gate down by the small field had been cut through. There's an unpaved, single-track road, with a turning circle down there. It's pretty out of the way if you don't know the area, and I can't see it from the house. It looks as though somebody had ripped out their kitchen, including appliances. I knew immediately that it was a professional job, because there was too much to get in the back of a car.'

'What did you do?'

'I spent all bloody morning loading up my trailer, before hauling it down to the tip. At which point they told me that they don't accept commercial waste, and I ended up paying two hundred pounds to get it disposed of properly.'

'How did you find out that it was Stevie Cullen that was responsible?' asked Warren.

'I was complaining about it down the Stag, and one of my mates told me the same thing had happened to him. I said I was going to go to the police about it, but he said that I didn't want to go upsetting the Cullens.

'Anyway, I figured I'd just have to leave it, but I couldn't afford to keep on paying out two hundred quid every time the bastards dumped it on my land. If it kept on happening, I wouldn't have any choice.'

'So, what happened?' asked Warren.

'Stevie must have heard that I was badmouthing him, and so one night he confronted me in the car park outside the Stag. Him and that bloody great brother of his. He told me to keep my gob shut, or there'd be consequences. I was still pissed off with him and told him what to do with himself and drove off.'

Dorridge shook his head. 'I knew as soon as I said it, that I shouldn't have. I spent all night awake, wondering what they were going to do to me. I mean you know their reputation as well as I do. I figured even if I didn't get a kicking, they'd probably burn my barn down.

'Anyway, the next morning, I was in the house having lunch when the doorbell went. Who's there, but Stevie Cullen and his brother? I don't mind telling you, I nearly shat myself.'

'What happened?'

Dorridge snorted. 'Oh, he was all smiles and apologizing. His brother didn't say anything of course. He asked how much it had cost me, and when I told him, he just pulled a wad of notes out of his back pocket and counted out two hundred quid. And then he left.'

'And that was it?' asked Grimshaw.

'Of course it bloody wasn't. And I knew it wasn't going to end there. A couple of months later, my phone went. I've no idea how he got my number. He said he wanted to meet up for a pint and a chat. What could I do?

'We met up, in the Rampant Lion this time. Again, his brother was with him. The first thing he asked was if I'd said anything. I said no, of course. I'm not that stupid. Then he said that he had a proposal for me. He said that the council would take away any rubbish dumped illegally on a farmer's land. He said that as long as I reported it, and pleaded ignorance, there'd be no problems. He said all I had to do was lock the gates with a bit of chain; he wouldn't even cut the padlock. He'd call me after he'd done it, and then I just needed to report it a couple of days later.'

'And you agreed?' said Warren.

'What else could I do?' Dorridge looked down at his hands. 'Besides he gave me fifty quid for my trouble, every time he did it.' He shook his head. 'I can't believe I was so stupid. Now I couldn't go to the police, because I was part of the scam.'

Warren could see the dilemma that Dorridge had faced; the problem was it moved him further up the suspect list, not down. It seemed that for the most part, Ray Dorridge was a hardworking, law-abiding farmer. Stevie Cullen had cleverly manipulated him into joining his conspiracy; even if the money hadn't been enough to persuade Dorridge to keep quiet, by accepting the bribe he had become complicit in the fraud. Add that to the debacle in the restaurant, and Ray Dorridge had plenty of motive to hate the man.

'When was the last time this happened?'

'Two weeks ago.'

Martinez had been right that an incident in a restaurant nine months previously – no matter how embarrassing – was an unlikely reason to kill Cullen, but the latest of his dealings with him had been only a fortnight ago. Could that have been what finally tipped Dorridge over the edge? There were plenty of holes in the man's story that needed filling.

'I take it the argument in the White Stag over payment was related to this?'

Dorridge nodded eagerly. 'He was late paying me for the latest tipping. I said he was taking the piss and wanted my money. It got a bit heated.'

'I see. And this – arrangement – over waste dumping is the only business arrangement that you had with Mr Cullen?'

Dorridge nodded again. 'That's it. Just some dumping.'

Warren said nothing for a few seconds, watching as Dorridge relaxed. 'I'm afraid I don't believe you, Ray.'

The smile dropped from Dorridge's face. 'What do you mean? I can give you the names of other farmers he was bribing. Maybe one of them killed him.' He scrambled in his pocket, bringing out his phone. 'Look at my call logs. You were right about that number being Stevie's mobile. You can match the dates that he called me, to the dates that I called the council to report the dumping.'

'We already did,' Warren reminded him, gesturing toward the folder in front of him.

'It also shows that you called him on several occasions throughout the year. Now why would you do that? From what you've told me, you actively avoided the man where possible, and he was the one to call you when he had a load that he needed to dump.'

Dorridge fell silent. Warren said nothing, allowing him to dig himself deeper. He wondered if Dorridge knew that his left foot bounced around when he was trying to think of a lie.

'Sometimes he was a bit late paying, I rang him to remind him.'

'None of those other calls match the dates around the dumping,' said Warren, his instincts telling him that Dorridge was starting to panic.

Dorridge was silent again. Warren could clearly see the man was trying to think of another plausible excuse for calling Cullen.

'Some months, things got a bit tight. I asked Stevie if he had any more loads that needed dumping.'

'So, you'd get your fifty quid?'

'Yeah.' It was clear that it sounded weak, even to Dorridge's ears. He looked over at his solicitor, who maintained a professional poker face. Whilst it was his duty to advocate for his client, and ensure that he was fairly represented, he couldn't advise on how to lie to the police.

'Going back to the conversation overheard in the pub, the witness was quite clear about what they heard.' Warren took out another piece of paper. 'They said that you were unhappy with a bill that Mr Cullen had charged you. I thought that Mr Cullen paid you for the fly-tipping?'

'They must have misheard.'

'Apparently, you said that the job had only been half-done and that it had taken twice as long as necessary. You then asked, "Where was that bloody brother of yours?" and said that you "didn't have the time to keep on chasing and nagging".'

'What job was only half-done, Mr Dorridge? And who were you chasing and nagging?'

Dorridge's eyes were now dancing around almost as much as his foot. When his answer came, his voice was barely a whisper.

'No comment.'

'I think it's clear to everyone in this room that you and Mr Cullen had a business relationship that went far beyond what you've already admitted to. Why don't you tell us what it was? Then we can get this all cleared up, and everyone can go home.'

The last bit was a bit of a stretch. Depending on the nature of Dorridge's business dealings with Cullen, he might well be charged with an offence. Nevertheless, he would probably be released on bail – although he'd have to find somewhere else to stay whilst the search of his farm continued.

For a moment, Dorridge looked tempted, before shaking his head again and repeating, 'No comment.'

Warren waited for a few moments longer, but Dorridge had clearly made his mind up.

After a short discussion with Grayson, Warren decided not to arrest Dorridge yet. Nevertheless, the man stayed on the suspect board.

In the meantime, the interview had thrown up a wealth of new leads.

'At least we know that Dorridge and Cullen had strong links, and Dorridge had several motives for killing him,' said Warren, 'and we've caught him out in a lie at least once.'

Martinez was already shaking his head. 'I'm sorry, Boss, I'm still not convinced. What have we actually got here? An embarrassing incident over a woman in a restaurant nine months ago, and him being strong-armed into committing an offence that'll probably result in no more than a fine.'

'That's only the motives we know about,' pointed out Pymm, 'and besides, he implied that he felt threatened by Cullen and his brother. People will do extreme things if they think they're in danger.'

'He lied about the fly-tipping until we pushed him on it,' said Ruskin. 'I'd like to know what he and Cullen were communicating about so frequently, and what they were arguing about in the White Stag. Maybe they had a bigger disagreement over money than Dorridge is letting on. He's been lying to us all along.'

'Place yourself in his shoes,' persisted Martinez. 'Stevie Cullen was brutally murdered, then we take Dorridge in for questioning. He must realize how bad it looks for him, and so he lied to protect himself. He wanted as much distance between himself and Cullen's murder as he could.'

'Blimey, Jorge, you've gone all liberal on us,' said Grimshaw. 'You need to stop reading *The Guardian*.'

Martinez ignored his friend's jibe. 'Besides, even if he had a motive, how would he know that Cullen would be at the massage parlour at that time? Even his best mate, Benny, didn't know about that.'

The room went quiet. Martinez had made a good point.

'Well, let's keep digging. I won't be satisfied until we can rule him out,' said Warren. 'I'll request a warrant for his financial details – I suspect most of his dealings with Cullen were cash in hand, but let's not assume that. Hopefully we have enough reason for one to be granted.'

'Let's not put all of our eggs in one basket, though,' said Martinez. 'I reckon Anton Rimington is still worth a look. If even the local gossips in the White Stag suspected that Cullen had got his missus pregnant, I can't believe that the first time Rimington suspected anything was amiss was when the dates on the ultrasound scans didn't match.'

'Thank you, but I wasn't planning on placing all of our eggs in one basket, *Sergeant*,' said Warren, a little more waspishly than he'd intended.

Martinez flushed pink. 'Sorry, didn't mean it to come out like that.'

'You're right though. Rachel, check if Ray Dorridge knows Anton Rimington or Vicki Barclay beyond what he has already admitted. And whilst we're at it, we should take a closer look at that couple Cullen supposedly helped split up. It's another potential motive.'

Chapter 20

'Decision time, Warren. Have you got enough to charge Anton Rimington or not?'

Warren sighed; Grayson was right.

The case against Rimington was circumstantial at best. So far, forensic analysis of his clothes had yet to find any traces of blood and a thorough search of his friend's flat and car had failed to find anything suspicious. They had no evidence placing him at the scene of the attack, or even in the area. Ruskin's suggestion that Rimington had used his own car but had changed the licence plates had all but been ruled out by Forensics who were confident that the dirt and grime coating the car had been building up for weeks or months.

The man was clearly a bully and a nasty piece of work – and Warren had genuine concerns for the wellbeing of his fiancée, even if she had gone to stay with her cousin – but he could see no justification for charging him. With the custody limit fast approaching, Warren had no choice but to release him.

'Cut him loose on bail, pending further inquiries,' said Grayson.

It was a good suggestion; it would ensure that Rimington could be called back at any time for further questioning. It might also make him think twice about harming his pregnant fiancée if he thought he was on still on the police's radar.

And if Rimington thought he was no longer a person of interest and free to go, he might relax and slip up.

Four days after the murder of Stevie Cullen, the massage parlour where he met his demise was ready to be reopened. No longer a crime scene, a specialist cleaning firm was due the following morning to remove the bloodstains and make the room usable again.

Whether that would be enough to attract clients back again remained to be seen; Warren couldn't imagine relaxing in a room that had witnessed such a horrific crime.

Something still bothered Warren about the scene though, and so before driving home for the day, he decided to drop by one more time.

The massage parlour was dark by the time he arrived. The crime scene tape still fluttered outside, but there was no longer a police presence. The cold November night made Warren tighten his coat as he used a spare key to open the front door. He disabled the alarm, using the code, and flicked the lights on.

Several days without heating had sucked the warmth out of the building, and the smell of massage oils had faded away, leaving only the tang of dried blood.

Standing in front of the reception desk, Warren mentally replayed the CCTV footage of Stevie Cullen as he entered through the front door. He took a pace forward and turned on the spot. This was where Cullen had stood, for several seconds, speaking to someone behind the reception desk, and off the edge of the poorly positioned camera's field of view.

With the desk in front of him, Warren tried to work out who Cullen had been talking to. There was clearly no one at the desk, so that left someone in the space behind. There were two nail stations to his left; the open doorway through to the rest of the house was on the right. The carpet that covered the reception area, gave way to a more hard-wearing, wooden laminate in the nail bar area. Easier to clean up spillages, Warren supposed.

Thinking back to the video, Cullen was clearly angled to the left. There were no other customers and the nail technicians weren't working that day. Perhaps one of the two masseuses was sitting on one of the nail technician's chairs as she waited for a client to arrive? Warren cursed the poorly installed camera.

Giving up on the question for the time being, Warren continued through to the back room. Switching the lights on, he could see that whilst it wasn't the worst murder scene he'd been to, the clean-up crew would probably have to completely redecorate. The raised massage bed was certainly a write-off.

Warren pulled on a pair of gloves and slipped on some plastic overshoes, the precaution more about protecting his clothing than avoiding contaminating the crime scene. Again, the feeling that something wasn't quite right struck him.

He walked around the room carefully. The massage bed was in the centre of the room, the head towards the window. The walls of the room were painted a pale, pastel yellow, with small shelves holding vases of flowers or scented candles. Thick velvet curtains covered the windows, and concealed the door, muffling sound and blocking out any light. A second light switch activated a number of shaded spotlights. Warren switched the main lights off and found he could easily imagine Stevie Cullen drifting half asleep, relaxed from his massage, enjoying the smell of the scented oils and the soft music floating from the concealed speakers.

Moving over to the window, Warren undid the security bolt and pushed up the sash; it barked loudly against the wooden frame, letting in a blast of chill night air. His coat brushed against the windowsill as he leant out.

The backyard stretched into the darkness beyond, the security gate and fence nothing more than a dim outline against the night sky. To the right, the wall of what would have been an outside toilet and coal scullery when the house was originally built extended a few metres beyond the room he was stood in now, knocked through to make a store cupboard. A couple of rickety-looking chairs sat next to a metal sand bucket studded with cigarette butts. Warren estimated the distance between the window ledge and the uneven paving slabs below to be closer to four feet than three feet.

It was then that it struck him what was wrong with the scene. And it changed everything.

Saturday 07 November

Chapter 21

Warren had been too excited to sleep properly. In the end, unwilling to disturb Susan who relished her Saturday morning lie-in, he'd moved to the spare bedroom. Eventually he'd given up entirely and gone in to work to prepare for the morning's briefing.

Word had got around that the there was a major shift in the investigation, and the room buzzed with anticipation, and so as soon as the team were assembled, Warren put them out of their misery.

'We are now pursuing the theory that it was an inside job, that the two sisters running the massage parlour that day were either responsible for, or complicit in, the murder.'

After the murmurs had died down, Warren filled everyone in on his insight the previous night.

'The murder took place on a chilly November day. According to the two women present at the time, the killer came through the window, attacking Stevie Cullen where he lay. The room has a sash window that makes an absolute racket as it's slid open. Even if the bolt securing it was undone, I can't believe it was open on such a cold day. So, how did the killer open the window without alerting our victim?'

Warren let the team digest that for a moment.

'Not only that, the window is covered in thick, blackout curtains. How did the killer know that Biljana had left the room and Stevie was alone? For that matter, how did the killer even know that he was going to be there? His appointments were infrequent. Only the two sisters and their aunt were likely to know that he had decided to come in.'

Martinez raised a hand. 'He could have been followed. His killer could have been waiting and just guessed at when he was alone. Or they could have been listening at the window.'

'That still doesn't explain how the killer surprised Cullen,' countered Rachel Pymm. 'Biljana has stated repeatedly that the killer attacked him whilst he was lying down.'

'Biljana could have killed him as he lay helpless,' said Ruskin, 'and Malina came through and helped her tidy up and concoct a story. That would account for the time between the CCTV showing Malina running back and the 999 call when they said the attack had only just happened.'

'Malina could even have been involved in the killing,' pointed out Hutchinson.

'Even if the two sisters weren't responsible for the actual killing, they could have opened the back door and let the killer in – and then helped him escape,' said Grimshaw. 'The whole business about coming through the window could have been staged.'

'And the CCTV cameras are broken out the back,' said Richardson.

'Which suggests premeditation,' said Pymm.

'Exactly my thoughts,' said Warren, pleased that his team hadn't found any major holes in his reasoning.

'The two sisters have been upgraded from witnesses to suspects, and Rachel's team have finally got hold of their phone records; that's a priority.'

Taking her cue, Pymm took over, drawing the team's attention to a wheeled whiteboard divided into columns and covered in different-coloured Post-it Notes and pen marks. Seated in front of it, she used her walking stick to highlight her findings.

'The left column is a timeline from when the parlour opened that morning until late afternoon. The next column is what we observe on the CCTV cameras in the reception area and the time that it took place. Besides that, we have the call logs from the two masseuses – pink Post-its for Biljana, yellow for Malina. Then we have the timings from the girls' statements.'

In seconds the assembled team started to spot the discrepancies.

'I definitely reckon the murder happened at 13.10,' said Pymm. 'Biljana's been out the back with Cullen for ten minutes and suddenly her sister runs back there. She makes no mention of that in her statement. In fact, she claims not to have left the front desk in all that time.'

'In which case Biljana lied about finishing the massage and heading upstairs at half-past, with the murder taking place roughly five minutes later,' said Hutchinson.

Ruskin pointed at a yellow Post-it Note. 'According to the call log, Malina phoned an unlisted number at twelve minutes past one for twelve minutes. Who the hell was she calling and what were they talking about for that long?'

'I'll bet that whatever they were talking about had something to do with whatever Malina was doing to the reception computer, since she calls that number again for two minutes whilst she's using it,' chipped in Richardson.

'The same time that Biljana supposedly heard Cullen scream and saw him being murdered,' said Ruskin.

'Could they claim that they were just a bit confused over the timings?' asked Martinez.

'They can try, but I looked at the video again; after she finished using the computer she goes back off-screen again,' said Pymm. 'Malina's defence might claim that was when she heard her sister call out and she went back to investigate.'

'I listened to the 999 call at 13.40,' said Ruskin. 'Malina clearly tells the operator that the murder only just happened. The operator tells her to stay on the line, but she hangs up.'

'Can we identify the owner of the mobile phone Malina called?' asked Warren.

'It's an unregistered pay-as-you-go,' said Pymm. 'I've asked for its logs, to see if that gives us a clue. Fortunately, the carrier is one of the major UK networks, so we should get them quicker than the sisters.'

'Why don't we just ask her about it?' said Ruskin.

'My thoughts exactly,' said Warren. 'Time to bring them both in.'

Chapter 22

Biljana Dragi and her older sister Malina were still in their pyjamas, eating pizza and watching *Love Actually* with Serbian subtitles, when a team of uniformed officers appeared on their doorstep. Within an hour, the two women were sitting in separate interview suites, awaiting their solicitors and translators. Grayson had grumbled about the cost, but had agreed to foot the bill for two different translators. The last thing the team wanted was for the same translator to work with both suspects, and inadvertently pass information between them. Similarly, the two masseuses had been appointed different duty solicitors. Warren had worked with them both before, and he trusted them to play by the rules; there would be no communication between the two interviewees without his say-so.

In the meantime, Warren and their team planned their interview strategy.

'We'll play them against each other if necessary. I want to interview them both, so the interviews need to be staggered, but we can pretend that the other sister is spilling the beans next door.'

It was a dirty trick, but legal as long as the team was careful not to bend the truth or lie outright.

'We'll tackle Malina first. I want to know who she was calling during that twelve-minute call and what the hell she was doing to that reception computer. We've confiscated her phone already, so I want to know her PIN.

'Biljana is the younger of the two, and supposedly came across the body. She has to be the number-one suspect at the moment. We'll take her back through the timings and see if we can trip her up. I also want to ask them some more about Anton Rimington; if there is a link between them, I want to know what it is.'

The interview suite was crowded with five people in it. Ruskin had set up the video and audio recorders, and everyone had introduced themselves for the record.

Warren started the interview by going through the sequence of events the afternoon of the murder. The older sister stuck rigidly to her previous statement, her answers sounding fluent and practised to Warren, even though he didn't speak a word of Serbian.

'Let's go back over the moment that you said you heard Biljana call out. You said that happened a little after one-thirty. After your sister had finished the massage and gone back upstairs to wash her hands.'

'Da.'

Even without the translator, Warren had picked up that meant 'yes'.

'You then called the emergency services a few minutes later, after you and Biljana tried to resuscitate Mr Cullen?'

'Da.'

'According to your phone log, that was about one-forty. Correct?'

Malina shifted slightly in her chair. That was the first mention that Warren had made of her call logs.

'Where were you before you ran to help your sister?'

'I told you already, I was sitting at the reception desk.'

'Doing what?'

She shrugged. 'I already said. I was watching a video on my phone. It was quiet, there were no customers.'

'And you didn't leave there between Mr Cullen arriving for his massage, just before one p.m., and hearing your sister scream?'

'Ne.'

Warren pressed start on the video screen behind him.

'I'm showing Ms Dragi exhibit 2015/12/NH6382-12, surveillance footage taken from the camera mounted in front of the reception desk.'

In front of him, the young Serbian masseuse paled, and started to chew her bottom lip.

'As you can see, at twelve minutes past one, you sit upright, before running in the direction of the massage rooms. That's about twenty minutes before you said that you heard your sister scream, and nearly thirty minutes before you called the emergency services. That's quite a discrepancy.'

Warren waited patiently whilst the translator relayed his comments. The young woman paled even more. After a few moments' consideration, she started to speak again.

'I must have been mistaken. I wasn't wearing a watch.'

'What were you doing in those thirty minutes?'

'We were trying to stop the bleeding.'

'For half an hour? Why didn't you call an ambulance immediately?'

'We panicked.' Her bottom lip trembled, and Warren could see the pinpricks of tiny tears starting at the corners of her eyes. 'We were confused and scared. We thought he might come back and kill us.'

'Who was this man? Tell me again what he looked like.'

'He was dressed in black and he wore a hooded sweater. That's all we saw.'

Warren opened the folder on the desk and produced a colour

headshot. He slid it across the table. 'Do you recognize this man?'

She glanced at the picture, then away.

'No.'

Warren waited a moment, before nodding his acceptance. 'OK, so let's go back to this man dressed in black. You say he climbed in the window?'

'Yes.'

'How do you know that, Malina? You were at the front desk.'

She paused. 'Billy told me.'

'According to your sister, she had finished Mr Cullen's massage, and had gone upstairs to wash her hands. That means the massage lasted barely ten minutes.'

Even as he waited for the translation, Warren could see that she had already understood enough of what he'd said to realize their error.

'She must have been mistaken. Maybe she went upstairs to get some more oil, or another towel?'

Everyone in the room recognized the lie, but Warren decided not to address it. He'd let her sweat about it for a while.

'OK, let's move on.'

He removed a sheet of paper from his folder. 'I am showing Ms Dragi exhibit 2015/12/NH6382-18, a mobile phone call log. Is this your mobile phone number?'

She glanced at the top of the page and nodded.

'According to the call log, you made a twelve-minute call to this number, two minutes after you heard your sister scream, and you ran back to help her. Who was the call to, and what did you discuss?'

The pause after the translation was even longer this time.

'I can't remember.'

'Really?'

'I can't remember. It was confusing and Billy was screaming.' She brightened slightly. 'Maybe I dialled the wrong number.'

'The emergency service number in the UK is 999. Mobile

phone numbers are eleven digits long. That's a very big mistake to make, Malina.'

'Maybe I pressed the wrong button and called a recent number?'

Even before the translation came through, he could see in her eyes that she knew she'd misspoken. If the number was in her recent call list, then surely she knew who it was?

'And you didn't hang up for twelve minutes?'

'I was panicking.'

'According to the log, you called that number a second time, eleven minutes later, this time for two minutes. Another wrong number?'

She nodded, the tears now starting to flow. She'd backed herself into a corner, and she knew it.

Warren turned to the screen again. 'I'm showing Ms Dragi more of the surveillance footage, starting from one-thirty-five, the approximate time that she initiated her second phone call to the unidentified number.'

The video ran forward silently, showing the empty reception area. Everyone in the room stared at the screen; the translator in unabashed fascination, the solicitor scribbling notes on his pad, Malina wide-eyed in panic. She knew what they would see.

Unable to tear her eyes away, she watched herself re-enter the frame, her phone clamped to her ear. Pressing a button on her phone, she laid it beside the reception desk computer, before manipulating the keyboard and mouse. After just over a minute, she left again. Warren stopped the playback.

'What were you doing to the computer, Malina?'

She shook her head and said nothing.

'You should know that our Forensics team are currently examining the computer as evidence. You can save us all a lot of time by telling us what you did to it, and why you did it.'

Even with her accent, 'No comment,' was clearly understandable. Warren wondered if her solicitor and translator had introduced her to the term before the interview commenced, or if she had picked the phrase up watching English TV.

'There are still another two minutes before you called the ambulance, Malina. What were you doing in that time?'

Again, she shook her head. 'No comment.'

Warren sighed. 'Look, Malina, you must tell us what happened. It's clear that you have been lying to us. In fact, I'm starting to wonder if there even was a mysterious man who climbed through the window. Lying to the police is a serious offence in this country. Come clean and tell us the truth, and it will go better for you.'

She said nothing, shaking her head as she buried her face in her hands.

'What really happened? Are you protecting your sister?'

Silence.

'Who were you calling? Maybe if we get their side of the story, they can help you.'

Again, nothing.

Warren tried again. 'We know that Stevie Cullen was a nasty man. Did he do something to Billy? Are you trying to protect her?'

She took a deep breath and looked up, staring Warren directly in the eye. 'Mr Cullen was killed by a man who climbed through the window. Billy and I had nothing to do with it.'

She folded her arms and sat back in her chair.

Warren waited for her to say something more. She didn't.

'Interview suspended.'

Malina Dragi was led back to a cell, whilst Warren and the team regrouped.

'You've just been fed a pack of lies,' said Grimshaw, who'd watched the interview on a monitor.

'I won't disagree with you,' said Warren. 'The question is what is she hiding?'

164

'I think she's protecting her sister,' said Grimshaw. 'I reckon Cullen did something to her and she killed him. Now they're both trying to cover it up.'

'Which would explain a lot,' said Ruskin, 'but it clearly wasn't just them involved. Who was she calling? Never mind the cock-and-bull story about dialling a wrong number, surely she'd have just hung up and tried again, instead of staying on the line for twelve minutes?'

'My money's on her aunt – who else is she going to call?' said Grimshaw.

Pymm shook her head. 'I don't think so. She called her aunt after they had been interviewed at the scene. I've identified that call on the log, and her Aunt Silvija is a different number entirely.'

'Then we need to find out who that number belongs to,' said Warren.

'I'm hoping to get the call log back from that number sooner rather than later, as it's another UK-based carrier,' said Pymm, 'but it's a tiny little provider and they're notoriously poor at responding quickly. As soon as I've got it, we'll see if we can figure out who it belongs to and where they fit into this.'

'And what about the computer? We really need to know what the hell she was doing to it,' said Warren.

'I've flagged it as a rush job,' said Pymm, 'but Pete Robertson says they're snowed under. They just seized a half-dozen computers full of suspected kiddy porn, some of which is recent and may show ongoing abuse. That's the priority at the moment. He might get something to us by next week.'

'By which time, we'll have had to either charge them or release them on bail,' grumbled Grimshaw.

'Can we get it looked at by an external contractor? They're usually quicker,' said Ruskin.

Pymm made a rude noise. 'No chance. I suggested it to DSI Grayson, and he nearly had a stroke. They'll never authorize the cost for the likes of Stevie Cullen.'

What she said was sad, but true. Despite the best intentions of Warren and teams like his, funding was a political issue; not all murder victims were equal. Sometimes, he wished that the accountants could meet a victim's loved ones face-to-face. Rosie and Seamus Cullen's grief was as raw as any he'd encountered.

'We still don't know if either of the two girls was involved in the killing,' said Richardson. 'We know that Anton Rimington has visited the parlour for a massage, so Malina is probably lying about not recognizing him and neither could rule out Ray Dorridge when we asked them about him before. I think both of those men are still suspects, alongside plenty of other pissed-off husbands and boyfriends.'

'Does this "man in black" even exist?' asked Hutchinson, his tone sceptical.

'If he does and he threatened them, then that could explain the time discrepancy,' said Ruskin. 'He could have demanded that they delay calling the ambulance for thirty minutes to give him some more time to escape.'

'And it might explain why Malina still won't back down from her story,' said Ruskin. 'What's the betting that the two of them got a really good look at the killer and are protecting his identity? If he's still out there, they're probably terrified that he'll come back for them.'

'Which brings us back to the question of who they were calling,' said Hutchinson. 'Presumably the killer had scarpered by then. I can't imagine him letting them use their phones until he was gone.'

'Of course, it could still be a conspiracy,' said Richardson. 'Ray Dorridge, Anton Rimington, or somebody else angry with Cullen arranged with the two girls to have him killed. You said that you thought it was an inside job, Sir.'

'That would answer the question of how come the killer knew that Cullen was having a massage at that time,' said Ruskin. 'If he was killed within fifteen minutes of arriving, as the CCTV suggests, that doesn't leave the killer long to figure out he was there.'

Warren let out a puff of breath. They were going in circles; did the man in black exist, and if so, did the two women know him? Were they involved directly or indirectly in the killing, or were they just parties to it after the fact? And if the man in black didn't exist, which of the two sisters wielded the knife, and why?

The room fell silent.

'The killer could have followed Cullen,' suggested Martinez after a while.

'On the off chance he goes somewhere suitable to kill him?' scoffed Grimshaw.

Martinez scowled at him.

'If it was a conspiracy, then that clears up something that was bothering me,' interjected Warren hastily, eager to stop the two men from bickering again. Was it just his imagination, or were the two friends becoming more argumentative? Could it be due to competition between them to become the next DI, if that vacancy became permanently available?

Warren continued, 'How was the killer able to open that squeaky window, without alerting Cullen? If Biljana said that she needed to open it for some fresh air, say, then she could have done it without raising Cullen's suspicions.'

'If it was a conspiracy, then there must be some previous link between the suspects and the massage parlour. Rachel, can you go back through the customer records again and see if any other names of interest have booked a massage there? Look for initials, maybe, or unknown mobile phone numbers.'

'I'll have another look,' said Pymm, but her tone was doubtful. 'We already know that Vicki Barclay has had massages there in the past, but she always seemed to come in with Anton Rimington; it'd take some guts for her to come in with Cullen,' said Pymm.

'Maybe Cullen liked the danger,' said Ruskin. 'He seemed the type.'

'Ray Dorridge doesn't strike me as the sort of bloke to enjoy a relaxing, scented back massage,' said Martinez.

'Don't be so judgemental,' said Grimshaw. 'Farming's a hard job.'

'OK, we all have plenty to do,' said Warren. 'Team leaders, be sure to dole out the work to our visiting colleagues from Welwyn. Moray, shall we go and see what Biljana has to say for herself?'

The interview with Biljana Dragi started in exactly the same way as that with her older sister. Like her sister, she gave precisely the same account as she had the night of the murder. By now it was clear to Warren that the two girls had rehearsed the story between them.

However, as before, she too was unable to account for the discrepancies in the timing. By the time Warren had finished picking apart her story, she was tearful and uncooperative.

'Billy, you really need to help us here.' Warren hoped that the use of her nickname might make her feel more trusting.

'We know that you and your sister have been lying to us. Stevie Cullen was a very unpleasant man. Did he do something to you? Or are you protecting someone else?'

Biljana shook her head again.

Warren decided to change tack. 'The video shows Malina doing something to the computer after Stevie was murdered. What was she doing?'

'I don't know, I wasn't in there.'

Inwardly, Warren punched the air. It was the first time that one of the two sisters didn't fully back the other up. It was also the first time that either girl had admitted – albeit rather obliquely – that Stevie Cullen had died before they originally claimed.

'It seems a strange time to do something to the computer. Who was she speaking to on the phone?'

Biljana dropped her eyes. 'I don't know.'

'It must have been important; she called the same number twice. Once, immediately after Stevie Cullen was killed, for twelve whole minutes, then again whilst she was on the computer.'

'I don't know.'

The set of her jaw suggested that her next reply was likely to be a 'no comment'.

Warren went back to cajoling. 'Billy, I really want to help you here. We all know that Stevie Cullen behaved very badly towards women. If it was self-defence, then tell me. In this country, juries are very sympathetic towards victims, but they don't like liars. Help us to help you.'

'I did not kill him. Malina did not kill him.' Her reply in English was halting, but emphatic.

'Then who did kill him?'

'I told you, I don't know.' Again, the reply was in English, and she glared at him angrily.

'OK, let's go back to the attack. You said that you were upstairs when you heard Mr Cullen scream?'

'Yes.'

'You ran downstairs, and then what did you see?'

'He was stabbing Stevie in the chest.'

'Where was Mr Cullen when he was stabbed?'

'He was lying on the massage table.'

'Was he there when you left him after the massage?'

'Yes.'

'Was he on his front or his back?'

'On his back.'

'What was he doing?'

'He was resting after the massage.'

'And what about when he was stabbed? What position was he in?'

'He was still on his back. Then he fell off the table. We helped him back onto the table and tried to stop the bleeding.'

Warren made a note of her statement. It was almost

word-for-word identical to the account given in her previous interview. Beside her, her solicitor was also writing furiously.

'How did the attacker get into the room?'

She paused. 'He came in through the window.'

'How do you know that?'

'The window was open.'

'Was it open when you went upstairs?'

She shook her head firmly. 'It was too cold.'

'So how did the attacker open the window from the outside?'

She paused. 'It was unlocked, so that I could let some fresh air in after Stevie left.'

Warren nodded. 'And how did the attacker leave?'

'He jumped out of the window again.'

'Billy, do you know the identity of the man who killed Stevie?'

She shook her head.

Warren again pushed the headshot across the table; he watched her carefully as she looked at them, before looking away. Like her sister, she claimed not to know Anton Rimington, which he was certain was a lie.

Warren softened his tone. 'I know you're scared, Billy, but we can protect you. The sooner we catch Stevie's killer and put him in prison, the safer you and your sister will be.'

She shook her head again.

Warren sighed. 'Interview suspended.'

The team had gathered for another briefing. The inclusion of real-time video links in the interview suites, streamed to officers' desktop computers, had been a real revolution, and Warren was keen to get his team's insights as soon as possible.

In front of him, he had a pad on which he'd recorded the outstanding issues.

'We've interviewed them both now, and I'll be honest, I don't think they realize just how much trouble they are in. They are still stubbornly refusing to change their accounts to fit the video

170

evidence, or admit to knowing Anton Rimington, something we can almost certainly prove is a lie.'

'That'll be their downfall,' opined Grimshaw.

'I also gave Biljana every opportunity to change her story about how she found him. Leaving aside the discrepancy between her claiming to hear him scream, and her then going downstairs to witness the stabbing, she's adamant that he was flat on his back when he was stabbed. The autopsy can't rule that out, although the blood spatter indicates that he started to leak blood when he was on the floor, which matches the account that she just gave me about how he ended up on the floor after being stabbed.'

'How compelling is the evidence?' asked Grayson. 'Juries can blow hot and cold over blood spatter.'

'It's pretty good, but it also fits the common-sense test. That window makes an absolute racket when it's opened. There's no way you could surprise someone by entering quietly. If the attacker had come in through the window, I'd have expected him to be sitting up at the very least, which would fit the evidence.'

'But she insists that Stevie was lying down,' said Grimshaw in satisfaction.

'If we go down the conspiracy route,' continued Warren, 'she's already admitted to leaving the window unlocked, although I'd question that story. There are blood smears on the window frame, but no clothing fibres. I looked at the height of that window from the outside and that an average-sized person would need to climb to get in and out. I'd expect more trace evidence. The only fingerprints on the frame belong to the two women.'

'The rest of the room was covered in dozens of different fingerprints and loads of mixed DNA profiles,' said Ruskin.

'Which is what you'd expect inside the massage parlour,' said Grayson, 'but how many customers open and close the window?'

Warren acknowledged his point.

'If the attacker didn't clamber though the window, then the easiest route would be through the back door,' said Hutchinson.

'We know from the CCTV that they didn't come through the reception area.'

'That door is locked from the inside, which again points to conspiracy,' said Richardson.

'Forensics didn't find any footprints from men's shoes leading out of the door,' said Richardson.

'Here's a suggestion,' said Ruskin. 'Could the killer have already been in the building? Perhaps waiting upstairs?'

The team fell silent, contemplating the suggestion.

'If the killer was already in there, then either the girls are lying to protect themselves, or we're back to conspiracy again,' said Grayson.

'Well we've got enough to charge, but there's no rush,' said Warren. 'With what we've got so far, we can get the full extension to ninety-six hours easily. In the meantime, I want to know who the hell Malina was calling, and what she was doing to that computer.'

Chapter 23

'How are you doing with the social media, Shaun?' asked Warren.

Grimshaw was slouched in his chair, shirtsleeves rolled up, his tie nowhere to be seen.

'Losing the will to live, Boss.'

Beside him Martinez openly sniggered at his friend's plight.

'Those two girls practically lived on their phones: Facebook, Instagram, WhatsApp, SnapChat, Twitter – and those are only the ones I'd heard of. Some of their social media apps aren't even English-language based. I've sent them off for translation. The Social Media Intelligence Unit are doing deep data mining of their contact lists and building a network of their friends. So far, neither of them seems to be friends or followers of Stevie Cullen, so now they're looking to see if they share any common friends, such as Ray Dorridge, Anton Rimington or Vicki Barclay. Muggins here is looking to see if Cullen appears in any of their photos, or if there are any other people of interest.'

'Slow going?' asked Warren, with some sympathy.

'Like you wouldn't believe. The only good news is that they were obsessed with tagging their friends, so I'm saving pictures with anyone they *haven't* tagged for later analysis.' He turned to look at Warren. 'I'll send those to Welwyn and see if they can do anything with them.'

It was clear from his tone that the sooner he washed his hands of the task the better.

'Well at least the time window is relatively short. They didn't move to the UK until last year.'

He turned to leave, but it was clear Grimshaw hadn't finished.

'Seriously, what is it with kids these days?'

'Kids?' repeated Warren. Grimshaw was thirty-five – he sounded like an old man. Beside him, Martinez let out a sigh – he'd obviously been listening to Grimshaw grumble all day.

Grimshaw continued, either missing or ignoring Warren's teasing.

'Yeah, when we were their age, when somebody told you to pose for a photo, it just meant smiling or sticking your fingers up at the camera. These two stage mini-photoshoots. You just know the photo we're seeing is only the best one from about twenty. And what's with these bloody filters? Even the ones without cartoon bunny ears and dog noses are processed to hell. Nobody has skin that smooth.'

'Oh for the good old days, eh?' interjected Martinez. 'When you had to wait two weeks for the photos to return from Boots to find out you'd cut somebody's head off or they'd blinked. I tell you Shaun, it was all downhill from the moment the photographer no longer needed to hide under a black cloth and hold the flashgun above his head.'

'Piss off, Jorge,' muttered Grimshaw, as Warren laughed.

'I tell you one thing,' Grimshaw muttered darkly, 'if my old mum is right, then should the wind ever change direction when these girls are pouting for the camera, they'll end up permanently looking like goldfish.'

Suppressing another laugh at his colleague's misfortune, Warren patted him on the shoulder.

'Well you're doing a fine job, Shaun. Keep me up to date on

anything interesting,' said Warren leaving the disgruntled sergeant to his work.

As soon as Warren was out of earshot, Grimshaw twisted his monitor around so that his colleague could see it more clearly.

'There is one compensation to this job.'

'What's that?' asked Martinez, knowing that if he didn't indulge his friend, he'd never get any peace.

Grimshaw grinned. 'They take their camera phones to the beach with them.'

'Seriously, Shaun? You're perving over suspected murderers now? Some days I worry about you, I really do.'

After the arrest of Malina and Biljana Dragi , search teams had moved into the flat that they shared. After seeing the size of his email inbox, Warren decided to stop by; he was in no mood to look at budget projections. Crime Scene Manager Andy Harrison's deputy, Meera Gupta, was in charge of the search and gave him a tour of the property, alongside David Hutchinson, who had been supervising door-to-door inquiries with the neighbours.

'According to the woman next door, their Aunt Silvija has owned the flat for years,' said Hutchinson. 'She often rents it out to young Serbians and Eastern Europeans. Before the two sisters moved in last year there were many different residents. She thinks that a lot of Silvija's extended family send their kids over to learn English and gain work experience. Silvija was something of a mother figure to them.'

That fitted with what Silvija Wilson had told them the night of the killing.

'Were they good neighbours?' asked Warren.

'Not too bad, apparently. They liked to party, but were usually considerate enough to turn the music down when it got late.'

'What about regular visitors? Boyfriends or girlfriends perhaps?' asked Warren, remembering Wilson's comment about the young women being distracted by male friends and not socializing enough with English speakers.

'Difficult to say. The layout of the flats means that she can't see who comes in and out of the communal door. I showed them headshots of Rimington and Dorridge, but she didn't recognize either of them. She also doesn't recall seeing anyone pregnant.'

Warren wasn't surprised; it had been a long shot anyway.

The flat was on the first floor, and was a small affair, with two tiny bedrooms, easily identified as belonging to the two sisters. The compact kitchen was untidy, but clean, its cupboards stocked with a mixture of supermarket own brands, and unfamiliar items, some with Cyrillic script.

'Looks like a few comfort foods from home. They probably use the little Serbian deli around the corner,' said Harrison.

'Check if the shop workers know them. I really want to know if either girl had a partner, or someone special. A jealous boyfriend could be a suspect and lend weight to the conspiracy theory.'

A cantilevered door revealed a tiny, but well-organized bathroom, with a shower, toilet and sink, with a mirrored medicine cabinet above it. A white-suited CSI was busy dismantling the sink trap to check for trace evidence, whilst another technician took photographs of the medicine cabinet.

'We'll see what we find, although from what we know of the aftermath of the killing, the girls presumably still had traces of the victim's blood on them when they returned home,' said Gupta.

The living room, familiar from the pictures that the girls had shared on social media, had a sofa bed, a small TV and DVD player, and a couple of bookcases filled with DVDs; a mixture of familiar Western films and others, again with titles in Cyrillic or a complex Roman script, presumably Serbian.

'Looks as though they were fans of *CSI*,' remarked Warren looking at a battered boxset.

'Andy calls *CSI* the "Open University for Burglars",' said Gupta. Warren agreed. The popular TV series, not to mention the countless true-crime series that now flooded the airwaves, had doubtless contributed to the rise in more forensically aware criminals that he and his team were now encountering.

'So far, we've found no obvious trace of the murder weapon; however, there are spaces in the knife block in the kitchen. The problem is that the knives that are present are a real mix and match, probably bought individually, so it's unclear if the gaps are due to missing items or if they were never filled.'

'Well keep on looking. We haven't found the murder weapon yet. You never know, they might have smuggled it back to dispose of it later.'

It was a long shot, but murderers, even those who planned their attacks, often didn't fully think through the aftermath of their actions.

Standing in the middle of the room, Warren did a slow circle, his plastic booties rustling on the carpet.

In his mind's eye, he could picture the two sisters seated on the sofa bed, watching TV together, taking a seemingly endless series of selfies as they played with the photo filters on their camera phones.

The photos that he had seen on Grimshaw's screen had painted a picture of two young women enjoying their time in England, working and partying with friends.

What had gone wrong?

Neither of them seemed like a murderer. But then, they rarely did.

Janice, Warren's unofficial PA, snagged him as soon as he returned to CID. 'Silvija Wilson is waiting in reception, Sir. And she's not a happy bunny.'

'Good, that saves us going to the trouble of tracking her down. I've got a lot of questions to ask her.'

'Not a happy bunny' was an understatement. Warren had only spoken to her briefly on the day of the murder, and he spent the time that it took to set up the interview room for recording to look at the woman fuming in front of him.

Silvija Wilson was a woman somewhere between forty and sixty years old, Warren guessed. It was hard to be sure, given the amount of make-up she was wearing and the liberal use of age-defying cosmetic surgery. Up close, her red hair was clearly not her natural shade. A couple of inches shorter, and a good bit heavier, than her nieces, the family resemblance was nevertheless obvious to see.

'What is the meaning of this? Those girls have been through hell, and you arrest them? After what they saw, they are as much a victim as that poor man.'

Wilson's English was perfect, but her native accent, buried under years of living in England, could be heard trying to break through.

'Mrs Wilson, Malina and Biljana are key witnesses in this investigation.' Warren's tone was firm. 'At present, they are helping with our inquiries. Key aspects of their story don't add up. Perhaps you can help explain what happened, and then maybe they could be released?'

Wilson sat back in her chair, her arms folded. She continued to glare but said nothing.

'You've turned up voluntarily, Mrs Wilson, but if you wish to have a solicitor present, you are welcome to do so. We can provide one, if you can't afford to pay for one.'

Wilson looked at him, before shrugging. 'I have nothing to hide. And neither do my nieces.'

'OK, well let's start by you telling me a little about your business. Are you the sole owner?'

'Yes. I owned it with my husband, until he died three years ago.' She paused. 'Owning our own business had been our dream, ever since we married. At the time we met, I was a nurse. I specialized in midwifery, but when we found that we couldn't have children … it was hard.'

Warren felt a wave of sympathy. He could imagine how difficult it must have been, surrounded by women welcoming their children into the world, all the time knowing you would never do the same. God knows, he and Susan had stared into that abyss enough times in recent years.

'Anyway, I tried retraining, but I didn't enjoy my new job, and I started to suffer from depression. One day I saw an advert in the local paper advertising courses at the local college teaching massage. I'd always loved the hands-on aspects of nursing, and so I decided to give it a go. I loved it.

'After a few years working at different parlours, I really wanted to set up my own business. Ten years ago, my husband was offered redundancy, and we took the plunge. He did the accounts and that side of it, and I did the massage. We were a really good team.'

She cleared her throat. 'And then three years ago he died suddenly. No warning.'

Warren gave her a moment to compose herself.

'You said that Biljana and Malina are your nieces?'

'Yes, I have a big family back in Serbia. I haven't lived there since I left as a young woman to join the NHS. Then I met my husband and stayed. But recently, my nieces and nephews have started coming over to England to learn to speak English or go to college. My husband and I owned a small flat, and so I can put them up. I only charge enough to cover the mortgage. It works out very well for all of us.'

'Do you have anyone else staying at the flat?'

'No, just Billy and Malina at the moment. It only has two bedrooms, so there isn't enough space for anyone else.'

By now, Wilson had relaxed somewhat. Her indignation had largely subsided, and so Warren decided to move on.

'You said that you were looking after your mother-in-law, the day of the attack. Where was that again?'

'My father-in-law and he lives in a hospice in Stenfield.'

'I apologize. Did you visit him on your own?'

'Yes. My husband didn't have any brothers or sisters, and his mother died many years ago. His father is all alone.'

'And how long were you with him for that day?'

Wilson frowned in concentration. 'I went there after the bank run, then stayed until mid-afternoon.'

'According to Malina, she called you just after half-past three. Yet you didn't arrive at the massage parlour until twenty-to-five. It's only a fifteen-minute drive, why did it take so long?'

'I had taken my father-in-law out for the day. I had to return him to the home. And then I got stuck in traffic.'

'Forgive me, Mrs Wilson, but I'm a little surprised that you didn't drive immediately to the massage parlour and bring your father-in-law with you.'

'My father-in-law has dementia; he gets confused very easily. I couldn't really bring him to the massage parlour after what had happened, could I?'

'I suppose not,' said Warren. 'What do you know about the events that took place that afternoon?'

'Only what the girls have told me.'

'Which is?'

'That Mr Cullen arrived just before one p.m. Billy gave him his massage, then went upstairs. Whilst upstairs, she heard him scream. She and Malina then raced into the massage room and saw a man dressed in black stabbing Mr Cullen.'

'What happened after that?'

'The man jumped out of the window. They tried to stop the bleeding, then called an ambulance.'

'Do you know if they called anyone else before the ambulance came?'

Wilson shook her head. 'I don't think so.'

'Do you know what time they heard Mr Cullen scream?'

'A little after half-past one.'

'So, the massage had finished, and Biljana had gone back upstairs?'

'Yes.'

'What was Mr Cullen doing at this time?'

'I believe he was resting after his massage.'

'Is that normal? I assumed he had paid for a full hour?'

Wilson paused. 'It depends on the type of treatment he paid for.'

Warren nodded understandingly. 'I believe that Mr Cullen had been for treatments before?'

'Yes.'

'And he always asked for Biljana?'

'I believe so.' Wilson's tone was wary.

'Do you know if the girls knew Mr Cullen on non-professional terms?'

Wilson scowled. 'They are not prostitutes. They told me what you asked them the night that you interviewed them. I don't run that sort of establishment, and I certainly don't pimp out my own nieces.'

Warren held up a placating hand. 'Of course, Mrs Wilson, I never meant to imply otherwise. I meant socially, outside work?'

'No, I do not believe so.'

'What about you?'

'No.'

Warren thought about what he wanted to ask next. It was tempting just to dive in and ask her about why Stevie Cullen seemed to be receiving his massages off the books, but he knew he had to be careful. There was no evidence that Wilson was involved in the events of that afternoon, but if she was, the last thing he wanted to do was tip her off. Similarly, asking her about Ray Dorridge might alert her to the direction that their investigation was taking.

Furthermore, even if she wasn't involved, she clearly cared deeply about her two nieces. The last thing the investigation needed was her trying to protect the two sisters by destroying evidence or muddying the waters with lies. He thought briefly about chancing his arm and arresting Silvija Wilson as a precaution, but he knew that they had no compelling evidence to suggest that she was in any way involved. Even if the custody sergeant agreed to her initial detention, they'd never get an extension beyond twenty-four hours.

Besides which, after his sudden realization the previous night, the massage parlour remained sealed as a crime scene and the girls' flat was still being searched. On balance, there was probably little that the concerned aunt could do to interfere with the investigation.

'Thank you for coming along today, Mrs Wilson, you've been very helpful.'

'When can I see the girls?' Her lip trembled, and Warren was reminded of the reason she had turned up that day.

'I'm afraid that won't be possible until we've completed our inquiries.'

Wilson looked as though she was about to object, until her shoulders dropped, and she nodded quietly.

Warren felt a flash of sympathy, quickly suppressed. Silvija Wilson was clearly worried and upset about her two nieces. But that was nothing compared to the agony being experienced by the family and loved ones of Stevie Cullen.

Warren had finished for the day. It was a little later than he'd intended, but as soon as he finished filling in Grayson on the day's events, Susan would be picking him up.

There was a quiet knock at the door.

Ruskin. 'Sorry to interrupt, Sirs, but I thought you'd want to see what I've found.'

'That's a bright lad; he'll go far,' opined Grayson after Ruskin had left.

Warren agreed, although he couldn't help feeling disappointed. With a cast-iron alibi, Rimington was no longer a suspect. He made a note to ensure that somebody warned Vicki Barclay that her potentially violent ex was no longer a person of interest. He hoped that she was right about Rimington not knowing where her cousin lived.

Ruskin had recalled Rimington's friend saying that the two men had drunk the house dry Sunday night. Yet Rimington had found something else to drink on Monday. A quick trip to the small shop a five-minute walk from the flat had yielded CCTV footage of Rimington buying cheap cider and cigarettes at almost exactly the time that Stevie Cullen had been bleeding to death on the other side of Middlesbury. Furthermore, Rachel Pymm had yet to uncover any overlap between Rimington and Barclay, and Ray Dorridge.

Ruskin had also eliminated Harry and Teri Raynor, the married couple that Ray Dorridge had suggested Cullen might have come between. It would seem that Benny Masterson was wrong, and despite Cullen's best efforts, the couple were still together – they were currently enjoying a two-week cruise in the Caribbean. As alibis went, that was even stronger than Rimington's.

Chapter 24

The past forty-eight hours had been a challenge for Warren and Susan. As a rule, Warren was a private man; yet it had taken all of his willpower not to announce to the world that after years of trying, he was finally going to become a dad. Despite the all-consuming nature of the investigation, Warren found his mind drifting at quiet moments. More than once, he'd had to force a smile off his face. It was all he could do not to pull out his phone and stare at the black and white image.

As for Susan, she'd already had to confide in her lab technician, Janina, the first week of the school year. That way she could avoid some of the more toxic chemicals used in school science practicals. At least it got her out of teaching radiation to a rather challenging year eleven group; demonstrating the differing properties of the school's radioactive sources was a definite no-no.

Janina had also discreetly placed metal wastepaper bins behind the fire exits on all of Susan's teaching labs, and even briefly covered her class for her a couple of times as Susan felt the physical effects of her pregnancy.

However, Susan had resisted the temptation to announce her good news to the rest of her colleagues and friends. They had long ago decided that one special person needed to know about the pregnancy before anyone else.

The car scrunched up the drive to the small visitors' car park at the rear of the home. Saturday night traffic on the M6 hadn't been as bad as it could have been, and they'd made good time once Susan had picked Warren up immediately after finishing work.

Warren hated leaving in the middle of a case, even for short periods of time, and so he'd sat in the back of the car, juggling his smartphone and printouts, whilst Susan drove.

'If we do this again, I'll have to get you a chauffeur's cap like Parker out of Thunderbirds,' Warren suggested.

'I'll dress like Parker if you dress like Lady Penelope,' had been Susan's response.

After an hour or so, Warren had given up trying to read, mild travel sickness making him feel nauseous. He wondered if that was how Susan felt first thing in the morning. He decided it probably wouldn't be wise to ask.

The Fir Tree Terrace Respite Home was intended as a stopgap. A step on the way back to the home he'd lived in since he'd married his sweetheart seventy years ago. Granddad Jack had made it clear that he intended to live out his final years at home, dying in the same bed his beloved Betty had passed away in just a few years earlier.

Eyeing up the frail ninety-one-year-old, Warren had no idea if that would be possible.

The broken leg that Jack had suffered back in March was healing remarkably well, and he'd avoided any of the potentially fatal complications, such as pneumonia, that long-term bed confinement could result in.

Nevertheless, Jack looked even smaller than the last time Warren had seen him, barely a fortnight previously. As before, he was sitting in the wing-backed chair next to his bed, fully dressed. A copy of the *Coventry Telegraph* lay open on his lap, although Jack's eyes were closed, his reading glasses hanging from a thin chain around his neck.

'Jack, Warren and Susan are here to see you,' the carer announced loudly.

Jack's eyes opened immediately, a smile spreading across his face. 'Just resting my eyes.'

Despite his appearance, his voice was strong, and clear of any confusion. According to the staff, he'd been in the common room playing cards with other residents earlier in the day. Next week, they were hoping to take him for a short walk around the gardens with his new walker. Nevertheless, progress was slow and there were concerns that Jack's heart wasn't really in it.

An active man all of his life, he'd eventually got over the death of Nana Betty by lavishing his attention on the small garden at his home. Now even that would be taken from him. Jack was no fool. Although the specialists spoke of him living independently again, they all knew what that meant. Sitting in his house, alone, waiting for his visits from the carers or whoever else was able to stop by. On a nice day, he may be able to sit in his beloved garden, but its upkeep would now be somebody else's job.

Aside from Jack, Warren's closest living relative, who he was in touch with, was his cousin Jane, yet she had her own family and had recently moved to Nottingham.

After the death of his father, Nana Betty and Granddad Jack had become Warren's *de facto* parents. In his later teenage years, he'd probably spent more time around theirs than he'd spent with his mother and his increasingly absent older brother.

Moving to Middlesbury to further his career hadn't been an easy decision, and now Warren wondered if it was time to contemplate a move back to West Midlands Police. Susan's parents still lived in Warwickshire; they'd be delighted if she moved closer to them. With Susan's impending maternity leave, maybe now was the time to consider a change?

After handing over some mail that they'd picked up from Jack's house on the way over, Warren looked at Susan. It was time to reveal the real purpose of their visit.

Jack stared at the black and white photograph for almost a minute. When he finally spoke, the tears clogged his voice.

'Is this ...'

'Yes, Granddad.'

'Oh, my. I never thought I'd see ...'

He stopped, unable to speak any further.

Warren and Susan took one of his hands each, the three of them crying freely now.

'When?' His voice was a croak.

'May,' said Warren.

Granddad Jack squeezed his hand tightly and Warren felt the surge of resolve from him. They'd just given him a reason to fight.

'It gets better,' said Warren. 'There's going to be two of them.'

Visiting hours at Fir Tree Terrace finished at nine. Normally Granddad Jack was beginning to flag by that point and it was all he could do to keep his eyes open as he bid them farewell. It was after nine-thirty when a member of the care team chased Susan and Warren out. Granddad Jack was more chatty than Warren had seen him since before the death of Nana Betty.

Neither of them knew if the next people they told would be as excited.

It was after ten p.m. when they finally arrived at arrived at Susan's parents' house. Warren squeezed Susan's hand.

'They'll be over the moon, you'll see.'

'I know. It's just Mum was so set against us having IVF ... She still thinks it's a sin.'

'Then we don't tell her,' said Warren firmly.

Susan snorted. 'And what about when she asks? Do we lie?'

Warren opened his mouth, then closed it again. Susan was right. Lying to Susan's mother, Bernice, was a non-starter. Susan had a reputation in school for being able to wring the truth out of even the most skilful liars. Warren had no idea if such a thing could be passed down genetically, but there was no doubt Susan had acquired the skill from her mother.

Despite the late hour, the living room lights shone through the thick curtains. Since Susan's father had finally taken full retirement, the couple were now busier than ever, with Dennis regularly marvelling that he couldn't figure out how he'd ever had the time to work. The couple's sole concession to their new lifestyle was a shifting of their sleep patterns; gone were the six a.m. starts, with them now regularly staying awake until midnight or later, and enjoying a more leisurely morning routine. Typically, when staying over, Susan and Warren went to bed well before her parents.

The security light over the front door gave away Susan and Warren's presence as soon as they pulled up and Dennis was by the car boot lifting the couple's overnight bags out before Susan had even managed to say hello properly.

'Come in, you'll catch your death,' admonished Bernice, silhouetted against the open doorway.

'You're later than usual. Is everything all right?' she asked. 'Jack seemed a bit tired when we saw him earlier in the week.'

'Everything is fine,' Warren reassured her, as he gave her a hug. 'Granddad was in good spirits, so we stayed a little later than usual.'

On the way over, Warren and Susan had discussed at length when to break their news. Should they wait until the morning and spend all night worrying about it, and risk offending Bernice and Dennis who would wonder why they hadn't been told about it immediately?

Or should they tell them immediately and risk a big row with Bernice right before going to bed?

In the end, Susan had decided to play it by ear.

Ushering the two of them into the living room, Bernice picked up the open bottle of red wine on the coffee table. 'Would you like a glass?'

Susan shook her head. 'Not for me thanks.'

Bernice turned to Dennis and smiled in triumph. 'See, I told you so. A mother always knows.'

Sunday 08 November

Chapter 25

In all the years that he had been married to Susan, Warren couldn't recall a time when he'd been more reluctant to leave his in-laws' house. Bernice was, to be charitable, hard work, and as much as he loved her, he was usually rather relieved to bid his farewells.

But this time, their brief overnight stop had been different. Despite the couple's exhaustion, they had stayed up late, the copies of the black and white ultrasound image sitting pride of place on the dining table as they discussed the future.

Bernice and Dennis were already grandparents several times over, yet they were as excited as the time Susan's sister, Felicity, had first announced her good news, years before. Bernice had insisted on sending a picture of the ultrasound to Felicity, and it was all that Warren and Susan could do to stop her from announcing it to the rest of the family.

'What are you hoping for, Warren? Boys or girls?' asked Dennis over breakfast the following morning.

'I'll be honest, I don't really mind,' admitted Warren. Truth be told, the ups and downs of the last few years had left him doubting if they would ever become parents, and he'd shied away from thinking about it too much. He guessed he was just superstitious. Over the past couple of days though, it had suddenly become real and now he was starting to realize how much his life was going to change.

'If they are boys, I hope you're going to bring them up as Coventry City fans,' teased his father-in-law, knowing that Warren's understanding – and interest – in football was limited at best.

'It's the twenty-first century, Dad; girls can watch football as well, you know,' admonished Susan. 'Besides they might prefer rugby.'

Warren grinned. His father-in-law was not a fan of the oval ball.

'Well, I'd like some more granddaughters,' said Bernice. 'I have to put all of my best china on the top shelf when Felicity brings the boys around.'

'Maybe we'll have one of each,' said Warren, diplomatically.

'When will you know?' asked Dennis.

'When they are born,' said Susan immediately. She and Warren had decided long ago that they wanted to be surprised.

Dennis frowned slightly. 'I can understand that, but twins take a lot of preparation. It'll help if you know what you'll be getting, so you can paint the nursery and everything.'

'And I have to start knitting two of everything,' said Bernice. 'I need to know what colour wool to buy.'

'White will be fine,' said Susan firmly.

'The most important thing is that they are healthy,' said Warren quickly, not wanting the moment spoiled.

'Of course,' said Dennis, taking his daughter's hand and giving it a squeeze. He smiled. 'Let me know when you want me to come down and help you get the small bedroom ready. I've just bought a brand-new drill; I've been itching to put it through its paces.'

'As far as we can tell, neither Biljana or Malina Dragi or their aunt, Silvija Wilson, had any online social connections to Stevie

Cullen,' said Grimshaw. Warren and Susan had made good time on the motorway, leaving her parents shortly after breakfast. It was now just after midday and Warren had scheduled a briefing. He'd been gone barely eighteen hours, yet the pace of the investigation made it feel longer. By the time he'd poured himself another coffee, he was fully in work mode, the previous evening with his in-laws a distant memory.

'Their social media contacts don't overlap with his, and neither do any of their closest friends,' continued Grimshaw. 'He doesn't obviously appear in any of their shared photographs, nor they in his. Their text and phone logs don't list any calls linked to either of the phones that we know he used. There are some texts and calls to unlisted pay-as-you-go phones, and we can't rule out that either they or he had another handset that we don't know about.'

'From what we've learnt about Stevie Cullen so far, a burner phone would be just his style,' said Ruskin.

'Cullen *did* call the massage parlour business line on a regular basis, using his personal phone,' continued Grimshaw, 'but these calls were short and broadly corresponded with times that we know he had appointments. If either of the girls, or their aunt, had a social relationship with the late Mr Cullen it was either offline or they used a different phone. Similarly, we're drawing a blank on Ray Dorridge.'

'Thanks, Shaun. Wilson was adamant that they had no relationship with Cullen outside of work; if they did, we've caught her in a lie. Have we identified the girls' friends for interview?'

Grimshaw nodded. 'If their contacts are anything to go by, they pretty much socialized exclusively with the local Serbian community. We've identified a list of about ten that they seem to meet on a regular basis.' He passed across a list to Warren.

'Anybody particularly special? Boyfriends or girlfriends?' asked Pymm.

'Nobody obvious. They're a tactile pair; especially after a few drinks, they seem to be hugging everybody. I asked the translation team to keep an eye out for terms of endearment that might give us a clue.'

'Good work. Hutch, can you arrange for these people to be interviewed? Use translators if necessary. I want to know if they were aware of any contact with Stevie Cullen and his family. I also want to know if they've seen or heard anything about the killing or have any suspicions.'

'There are also two other, unidentified people that I think we should look at,' said Grimshaw.

'Go on.'

Grimshaw held up two sheets of A4 paper, both with several coloured images. 'The girls tended to tag most of the people appearing in their photographs. Anyone who wasn't tagged in a photo, I was usually able to match to a name by looking for them in different pictures where they were tagged.' His lip twisted slightly. 'That's a large chunk of my life I'll never get back.'

'But these two couldn't be identified?'

Grimshaw shook his head. 'The first is a young woman. She only appears in a few of the more recent photos, usually in the background.'

He passed the sheet of photographs around.

The woman appeared to be slim, with dark hair, and of average height. Even the best photographs had only a three-quarter profile. Warren hoped it was enough for someone to recognize her. The chances were that she was just an occasional friend that the girls hadn't yet 'friended' on social media; regardless, Warren wanted to know who she was.

'The second is an unknown male, of average build and height, probably in his mid-twenties. He appears in several different pictures from various parties that the girls attended in the first few weeks after they arrived here. If I had to guess, I'd imagine he's one of the Serbian community. He stopped appearing in the photos about three months ago.'

'Well he fits the physical profile of the supposed attacker,' said Ruskin.

'So do half the men in Middlesbury,' said Pymm, 'and that's assuming the girls' accounts are even accurate.'

'If he did have a relationship with one of the girls, that might explain why they tried to cover for him by giving such a vague description, and it might explain his motive,' said Martinez, ignoring Pymm. 'He could have been jealous of Cullen.'

'If they wanted to cover for him, why not say the attacker was a twenty-stone black man? That way we'd be looking for someone completely different,' countered Pymm.

'If they made the description too distinctive, we'd soon question why we haven't had any eyewitness sightings or CCTV of the attacker. As it stands a nondescript, average bloke might just have slipped through the net,' said Grimshaw.

'That sounds a bit sophisticated to come up with on the fly,' said Hutchinson.

'Who says they came up with it on the fly?' asked Grimshaw. 'They could have been planning it for months.'

'And besides, we know they didn't call the police immediately,' agreed Martinez.

'OK, OK, people, let's not get carried away,' said Warren. 'We're building a very flimsy house of cards here, based on not a lot.' He took a breath. 'First of all, let's find out who he is. Show those photos to someone else who was at one of the parties he attended, see if they can identify him. Next, let's ask why he no longer appears in their most recent photos. Is he even in the area anymore?'

'Could they have deleted photos that he appeared in?' asked Hutchinson. 'They could have done the most recent ones and not quite managed the earliest ones.'

'It would certainly be a big enough job,' said Grimshaw. 'They've posted hundreds over the past year or so, on several different social media platforms.'

'Nothing's ever completely deleted,' said Ruskin. 'We could raise a warrant and ask for the data from Facebook and Instagram.'

A chorus of groans rang around the room.

'You'll be collecting your pension by the time that comes through,' said Martinez.

'Besides, why was he the only person not tagged? If they deleted him as a contact, would that have automatically untagged him?'

There was a silence, followed by a series of shrugs around the room.

'We'll need to find out if that's the case,' said Warren.

'Sounds like a job for young Moray,' said Grimshaw. 'Us old folks find these new-fangled social media platforms far too complicated.'

Chapter 26

'I've figured out who Malina was calling immediately after the murder,' said Pymm, triumphantly, the moment Warren re-entered the office.

Warren hurried over to her desk, the rest of the team also dropping what they were doing. Mags Richardson sat next to her, a satisfied look on her face.

'It was a team effort,' said Pymm, turning to Richardson. 'You tell them, Mags.'

'No, you tell them, you had the brain wave.'

'Ladies …' warned Warren; Pymm's flair for the dramatic and her inability to pass up the opportunity to tease had started to infect other members of the team, including Richardson.

'The number was saved in the address books of both Malina and Biljana's handsets, which IT finally figured out how to open. Thank God for dirty fingers and swipe access. The problem was that I don't read Cyrillic or Serbian for that matter. Translation services are really swamped at the moment, so I figured why not use an online translation tool whilst we're waiting?'

'Good idea,' said Warren.

'Anyway, I started copying the Cyrillic entries into a translator one at a time to see what came out.'

She maximized her internet browser, which was open on a page with two boxes, side by side.

'Now look at this.'

There were two words, neither of which meant anything to Warren, the Cyrillic completely meaningless to him.

Pymm pressed translate, and the translation appeared in the right-hand box.

Aunty Silvija.

'That's the number we already have for Silvija Wilson, and it's the number Malina called that afternoon after she had been interviewed. So next, I tried translating each individual word, and it seems that this one, pronounced "Tetka", means Aunty – specifically a maternal aunt – and the other word, is the Cyrillic form of Silvija.'

'OK.'

'Well this is what's recorded next to the unknown number.'

She clicked on another entry.

'I assumed of course that was another aunt. I figured that for whatever reason, she'd decided to call another relative, perhaps for advice, but when I enter the other word, which I won't even try to pronounce, this comes up.'

Copying the Cyrillic into the left-hand box, she pressed translate.

The result was clear: *Aunty – job.*

'And before you ask, she doesn't have an aunty called "Job", it means job as in work.' She smiled smugly. 'Aunty Silvija has a separate work phone, and Malina phoned it immediately after Stevie Cullen was killed.'

'I want to know what Silvija Wilson was doing on the day of the murder,' said Warren.

Grimshaw flicked through his notepad. 'She told us that she

had been with her father-in-law all day, after completing the bank run first thing.'

'Do we have an address for him?' asked Warren.

'No, but we know he's in a care home out in Stenfield,' replied Grimshaw.

'Speak to that helpful neighbour again; she seems to know the family. Now we know that the phone belongs to Silvija, I want you to track its movements that day.' He thought for a moment. 'You could also try cross-referencing its location with Silvija's personal phone that we definitely know belongs to her.'

'I'm expecting the data any time soon,' said Pymm.

Warren thought back to the aunt's arrival the evening of the murder. 'Mags, see if you can also track down her car's movements that day.'

'I'll run it through the ANPR system, Sir.'

'We've interviewed all of Biljana and Malina Dragi 's friends,' said Hutchinson.

'Give me a summary,' said Warren.

'Well the good news is that most of them spoke sufficiently good English not to need a translator.'

That was very good news; translation services weren't cheap and DSI Grayson was already dropping none-too-subtle hints about budget constraints.

'What did they know?'

'Not a lot, to be honest. They'd all heard about the murder, obviously, but most hadn't spoken directly to either of the girls or their aunt since it happened. None of the people we interviewed admitted to knowing Stevie Cullen, or even hearing of him and his family before the attack. Which is probably not too surprising – they are all college kids or bar workers in town. Most don't even own a car, so they're hardly going to be driving out to the White Stag for a pint and a plate of scampi and chips. I can't see how their social circles would ever overlap with the Cullens.'

'What about anyone who has spoken to the girls since?' asked Warren.

'Three women, identifying themselves as the girls' best friends, had been around to see them. We asked them what they knew about the incident and all three parroted exactly what the girls told us in their original statement.'

'Which we know was incorrect,' interjected Grimshaw.

'Do you think they were simply repeating what the girls told them, or do they know more than they're letting on? You say they describe themselves as the girls' best friends. Could the girls have confided in them what really happened? Did they look cagey at all?'

'Sorry, I really couldn't say,' said Hutchinson. 'They were all quite nervous and excited about the whole affair.'

'I'm surprised they didn't ask you to pose for a selfie,' muttered Grimshaw.

'OK, we'll take a look at the video interview again, and see if there are any obvious signs they're lying,' said Warren. 'Now, what about these two unidentified people in the girls' social media posts?'

'I think we can rule out the young man. Several interviewees positively identified him. Apparently, he didn't live here; he was the cousin of one of the regular gang, over for a long summer holiday to practise his English. He turned up to a few parties, but nobody really knew him. He was a bit of an idiot apparently, which is why no one friended him on Facebook. We've spoken to Border Force who are tracking him down to make sure he wasn't in the country at the time.'

'What about the unidentified young woman?'

'Less luck. Everybody claimed not to know who she is, which is strange given that she was in several different photos, taken over a period of time.'

'Gut feeling?'

'I spoke to the interviewing officers and they reckon that at least a couple of them were lying. Exactly why, they weren't sure.'

Warren pinched his lip thoughtfully. Something didn't seem quite right. 'Could it be an immigration issue?'

'That might explain the caginess. All of the people we spoke to were keen to stress that they had the correct visas or were British citizens.'

With Serbia not part of the EU, the correct visas would be necessary to live, work or study in the UK. Had the mysterious young woman overstayed her visa? Was she in the country illegally? If so, that might explain why she was keeping a low profile and her friends were reluctant to acknowledge her existence.

'Keep on digging. It could be nothing, or it could be something.'

Chapter 27

Mags Richardson grabbed Warren the moment he set foot back in CID. It was late afternoon, and the toast and marmalade he'd had at Bernice and Dennis' seemed a long time ago. As much as he loved custard creams, he'd needed something more substantial. The franchised coffee shop that had taken over from the station's canteen had sold out of anything Warren considered remotely edible hours ago and he'd been forced to seek sustenance from the local garage.

The excitement on Mags' face meant the sorry-looking ploughman's sandwich he'd finally settled upon could wait. Half of it would be going in the bin anyway, after he'd dismantled it and discarded the superfluous lettuce, tomato, cucumber and red onion.

Richardson had moved her workstation next to Pymm, so the two of them could work more efficiently. Judging by the piles of printouts, and the fact that all three of Pymm's screens were filled with data, the two sergeants had been busy.

'Forensic IT have been going over that security footage from the massage parlour on the morning of the murder, and we think we know what Malina was doing at the reception desk after the attack. But I warn you, you're not going to be happy,' said Richardson.

'Go on,' said Warren, warily.

'The keyboard, mouse and monitor for the desktop computer are also connected to the digital video recorder for the surveillance system. They use a switch to swap between the two.' She looked apologetic. 'I've watched the footage back in slow motion and it's clear that she flicks the switch before she starts typing.'

'For fu ...' Warren bit his tongue. It was hardly Richardson's fault. 'And nobody thought to tell us this before?'

'Sorry, Boss. Don't shoot the messenger.'

Warren sighed; he had a good idea where this was going.

'The video surveillance system is a pretty basic system: two cameras, the one we've already watched from the front of the parlour, and another over the back door, which has supposedly been broken for weeks.'

Warren noticed the qualification in what she said.

'You don't think it has been broken for that long?'

'Nope. According to the techs, this CCTV unit is really simple. The disk has enough space for about four weeks' footage from a single camera. Plug in two cameras and it'll store about two weeks from each input. You can add up to four cameras and it records on a rolling system – the newest footage overwrites the oldest footage. If you disconnect a camera, the system automatically allocates that unused disk space to one of the other cameras and overwrites what was there before. The system tries its best to fill as much of the disk as possible.'

'OK, so what's the discrepancy?'

'Silvija Wilson claims that the rear camera has been broken for weeks. If that was the case, the stored data from the working video camera in reception should have overwritten the unused hard disk space from the broken camera.'

'And it hadn't?'

'Nope. In fact, almost exactly half of the disk is empty.'

Warren would be the first to admit that he wasn't a technical expert, but even he could see what Richardson was getting at.

'The camera was broken that morning, and the video footage deleted. Before we got there.'

Warren was irritated by the delay to what could be crucial evidence, and he ordered Richardson to light a fire under IT and get the deleted footage recovered as a priority – he figured they owed them a favour now.

In the meantime, it was clear that the two sergeants had more to show him.

'I finally got the call logs and cell-tower positioning data back from Silvija Wilson's work phone. I really wish criminals would stick with the big four mobile phone providers; it's taken ages to get an answer from that dinky little network,' said Pymm.

'Well you've got it now,' soothed Warren. 'What've you found?'

'It's early days, but I've managed to unpack some of the data.'

Warren moved around to see Pymm's screen.

'What am I looking at?'

'This spreadsheet shows the calls to and from that phone for the last twelve months.'

'OK.'

Pymm pointed to a series of entries highlighted in yellow. 'I haven't identified every number yet, but these are the calls that she received from Malina that afternoon.'

Both the twelve-minute call immediately after the killing, and the two-minute call whilst Malina fiddled with the security system, were listed.

'OK, that confirms that we have the correct phone data.'

'Well there's a bit more. These next entries take place over the next two hours, before Malina called her aunt on her personal mobile phone to let her know what happened.

There must have been over a dozen calls, to multiple numbers. Some lasted seconds, others several minutes.

'Is this a normal level of traffic for this phone?' asked Warren. There was no point getting excited over her day-to-day business calls.

'No. This number usually only makes or receives a handful of calls a week, mostly from the same half-dozen numbers. I took a quick look at her personal mobile phone, and she receives and makes many calls each day, from lots of different numbers. That's the phone that Malina and Biljana also usually call. I haven't even started properly identifying the callers yet, but it looks to me as though the unlisted number is a private line that only a few people know about, and she actually conducts most of her business on her personal phone.'

Warren contemplated what he saw on the screen. Two phones, one of them public, one of them clearly private, and she had obviously taken some measures to keep the private phone unlinked to her. Why? Her nieces had stored the numbers on their phones under 'Aunty – job', implying that it was to do with her work, and that had been the number that Malina had immediately rung when the murder took place.

Warren's gut was telling him that this phone was the key to unravelling what had happened that afternoon.

'We've also tracked Silvija Wilson's movements on the day of the murder,' said Richardson.

'First of all, the cell-tower location data shows that Silvija Wilson's unlisted work phone and her personal phone always move in tandem,' said Pymm.

'Which proves that the unlisted phone is definitely hers,' said Richardson.

'Good, that should stop her playing silly buggers and denying the work phone belongs to her,' said Warren.

'It looks as though her day started exactly as she said it did,' continued Pymm, pointing to one of her screens. A large map of Middlesbury and the surrounding villages was covered in red dots, joined by dotted lines. Floating textboxes showed the timestamps.

'She was at home until just after 7.50 that morning. She sent a text message to Malina, then travelled – presumably by vehicle judging by the speed – to the girls' flat. It took her about eight minutes. She spent just under five minutes there, before leaving. Both of the girls' mobiles moved with her.'

'Picking them up for work,' interpreted Warren.

'Exactly. All three mobiles arrived at the massage parlour at 8.25. The traffic would have been building up with the school run at that time.'

That fitted with the sisters' account that they arrived at work at about 8.30.

'The girls' mobiles stayed at the massage parlour until they left after being interviewed following the murder. They then returned home at 17.30 with their aunt. They stayed there until they were picked up later for their formal interview.'

'OK.' He looked at the two women. 'Don't keep me hanging – what are you not telling me?'

'Look at Silvija Wilson's two phones.'

Warren squinted at the timeline.

'The car's movements are confirmed by ANPR cameras along the route,' said Richardson.

'Bloody hell.'

'And look at the call logs for her two phones,' said Pymm, pointing to a second screen.

Warren switched his gaze. 'Bloody hell,' he repeated. 'I'll get DSI Grayson to authorize search teams along that route. Mags, get a team down there to seize any CCTV.'

He turned, about to head towards Grayson's office.

'Oh, just one more thing that I thought you might be interested in.'

Warren stopped. He knew that tone of voice. 'You're worse than bloody Columbo,' he muttered.

'I'll take that as a compliment.' Pymm pointed to another high-lighted entry. 'This number called her "job" phone about once a week. She occasionally called it. Does the number look familiar?'

Warren squinted at the number, before standing up sharply.

'Find Silvija Wilson and arrest her.'

Chapter 28

Unsurprisingly, Silvija Wilson's first action the moment that she was arrested at the small house she had shared with her late husband, was to insist upon a lawyer. She angrily rebuffed the offer of a translator.

Search teams moved into her property the moment she was taken into custody.

In the hours between Richardson and Pymm's piecing together of her movements on the day of the murder, the pace of the team had increased even more, with dozens more officers racing up the A1 from Welwyn to assist in the searches along her route. Mags Richardson was coordinating the retrieval of yet more CCTV evidence and David Hutchinson was organizing more house-to-house inquiries.

The time pressure was all the more acute with the initial extension of the two masseuses' detention fast approaching its end. He would have to prepare a request for the local magistrate to detain them longer. It was almost certain that the two sisters would be charged, rather than released, but Warren knew from experience that when that happened the dynamics of the situation would change dramatically. He really couldn't predict the effect that charging Malina and Biljana would have on the three women;

would the sudden dawning reality of their true situation cause the two sisters to become more cooperative, or would they shut down and refuse to answer any more questions? What effect would it have on their aunt?

Warren started Silvija's interview by going over the sequence of events that the two masseuses had given when first questioned, and then stuck to, despite the evidence to the contrary. Silvija Wilson repeated precisely what she had said before – there was no way that she could know how her nieces' stories had started to unravel.

Again, she denied any relationship with Stevie Cullen, and claimed that the first she had known of the attack was Malina's call to her personal mobile phone at 15.35.

Warren was pleased. It was always nice to start an interview with a few easily provable deceptions that he could use later. His casual inquiry at the start of the interview whether the number of Wilson's personal phone was correct and if she owned any other mobile phones that they could contact her on if necessary was met with a denial. The perfect place to start, he decided.

'Do you recognize this mobile phone number, Mrs Wilson?'

He recited the number of her unlisted work phone.

'I don't think so.'

An interesting response. He could see the calculation in her eyes, and knew exactly what her defence would be.

'It's just that it's unlisted and we can't identify it.'

She shrugged.

'You see, I think that this is your phone.'

Wilson said nothing. He could see in her eyes that she was frantically trying to work out whether he was guessing that it was hers, or if he knew for sure.

'I'll ask again, do you have access to another phone, Mrs Wilson?'

She swallowed. 'I have another phone that I occasionally use for business.' She brightened slightly. 'I use it so rarely that I forgot about it and didn't recognize its number.'

Her relief as she was able to use her defence was short-lived.

'Did you have it with you on the day of the murder, Mrs Wilson? Did your nieces try to contact you on it that day?'

She licked her lips. 'I don't think so.'

Her response was textbook. Caught in a potential lie that could have serious repercussions, she was now trying to row back slightly from her original position and hoping not to commit herself further.

'According to the phone's call log, there were two incoming calls from Malina's phone.'

'She must have called that number by mistake. I didn't have the phone with me, so I didn't pick up.'

'You left the phone at home?'

'Yes.'

'It seems a bit strange for you not to carry your business phone on a workday.'

'I don't get many calls on it, and I only carry a small handbag. I just check it for messages when I get home in the evening.'

A jury would probably raise an eyebrow at her definition of a 'small handbag'; Warren could probably pack enough for a long weekend away in the bag that she had been carrying when she'd arrived at the crime scene.

'The calls were rather lengthy. The first lasted twelve minutes, the second over two minutes.'

She paused. 'They must have left a voicemail. I haven't checked that phone since the day of the attack.'

Warren nodded understandingly. 'But you did have your personal mobile phone with you?'

'Yes, I always carry that with me.'

Warren placed a stapled pile of paper in front of Wilson.

'The column of numbers on the left are the coordinates of your personal mobile phone from the twenty-four hours beginning at

211

one minute past midnight on the day of the murder to midnight that night.' He paused. 'The column on the right shows the coordinates of your business phone at the same time. As you can see, the coordinates at each time point are identical.'

'I don't understand.' It was the weak denial of a person backed into a corner. Warren could see that she clearly did understand. Her solicitor undoubtedly understood.

'It shows that wherever your personal phone was, your business phone was within a few metres, even when you left the house. You were carrying them both that day.'

She swallowed. When that didn't work, she took a gulp of water. Her tongue still sounded thick when she spoke again.

'I must have been mistaken. Maybe I picked it up by accident and put it in the bottom of my bag without thinking that morning? It's always so busy first thing, and the girls are never ready on time, and I had a million things to do. I had to go to the bank …' Warren let her ramble on.

'It's an easy mistake to make,' he said, 'but the phone would normally be at home?'

'Yes.'

'That's strange. I don't know if you are aware, but mobile phone companies are obliged by law to keep data such as this for twelve months, just in case we request it. My officer in the case loves stats, and she reckons that over the past year, your two phones have been close enough to one another to return the same coordinates to the cell tower for 98.4 per cent of that time. I'd say that you routinely carry your two phones.'

Even under her thick make-up, Wilson was now visibly grey.

'Yet you say that you never spoke to either of your nieces on that phone, that day. You must have known that they were calling you.'

'It was in my bag on silent. They must have left voicemails.'

'We have been unable to find any voicemail recordings from that day.'

'Maybe they weren't saved?' Wilson's tone was desperate. It was getting painful; beside him, Moray Ruskin was watching with fascination as Wilson's story collapsed around her. And they hadn't even got to the good stuff yet.

'The reason there are no voicemails, is because the phone was answered. The call log tells us that the phone was picked up both times. What were you and Malina talking about when she called you? Twice?'

It had been a long time coming, but Wilson's next response was no surprise. She looked over at her solicitor, who said nothing.

'No comment.'

'Come on, Silvija, what was so important that your niece phoned you twice that day?'

'No comment.'

Warren was keen to stop her falling into a no-commenting cycle. He decided to see if he could lay the groundwork for catching her in another lie later.

'According to your niece's account of events, Mr Cullen was killed a little after one-thirty. Is that correct?'

'Yes.'

'The first call made to your phone by Malina was at twelve minutes past one, for twelve minutes. Presumably, Mr Cullen was having his massage at that point?'

'Yes.'

'So, what were you speaking to Malina about when her sister was with Mr Cullen?'

Warren had given her a possible way out. Would she take it, or would she go back to no commenting again?

Wilson sighed. 'It's all a little awkward. Malina is unhappy in England, but she doesn't want to leave her sister.' Wilson paused. 'She'll deny it of course if you ask her and I'd rather you didn't mention it to them – especially Billy, she'd be very upset.'

Warren had to give her marks for effort. Wilson had even tried to stop him from asking the two sisters questions that they might contradict her on.

'Of course,' he said, 'and what about the second call?'

'More of the same.'

He nodded. 'That conversation must have taken place just as Mr Cullen was being murdered.'

'Um, I guess so.'

'Did you hear anything in the background that could help us?'

She thought for a moment. 'I don't think so.'

'According to the call log, the call was ended by Malina. Do you know why?'

'No.' Wilson paused. 'She just said she had to go.'

Warren said nothing, waiting to see if Wilson would fill the silence.

'Maybe she heard Billy finishing the massage and going upstairs?' she said eventually. 'She wouldn't want her sister to overhear the call.'

'Yes, that makes sense,' said Warren. 'Well you've been really helpful, Mrs Wilson. You've cleared up a lot of discrepancies.'

Wilson relaxed.

Her solicitor didn't.

'Are we done now? Are the girls free to go?'

'Not just yet, there are just a few more things I'd like your help with.'

'Of course.'

'Do you know who this mobile phone belongs to?'

Wilson squinted at the number. She swallowed. 'No, I don't recognize it.'

'It's an unlisted number from your business phone's call log. You ring it regularly, and it also calls you on a regular basis.'

'I'm sorry, I don't know who it belongs to.' She shrugged and managed a half-smile. 'Who knows people's phone numbers these days? Can you not trace it?'

'It's an unregistered pay-as-you-go phone.'

214

'Maybe if you tell me when it called, I could go home and look at my diary and perhaps work it out who it belongs to?' she said hopefully.

'That won't be necessary; we've already done that. Mrs Wilson, at the beginning of the interview you said that you had no relationship with Mr Cullen. Are you still saying that's the case?'

Wilson's shoulders slumped.

'We've traced this number to Mr Cullen's own unlisted business phone. Tell me, Mrs Wilson, how did you know the man who would later be murdered in your massage parlour, and why did you lie about knowing him?'

Silvija Wilson's solicitor requested a break. Warren agreed – it had been an intense experience on his side of the table also. It was getting late in the evening, and he decided to finish for the night. Wilson was on the back foot. A sleepless night staring at the ceiling of a prison cell often changed a person's perspective. Besides which, he wanted to see what else his team could find to bring to her next interview.

True to form, Shaun Grimshaw was the first to comment on how well the interview had gone, miming someone tying a noose around their neck.

'Cracking work, Boss. You've given her so much rope, she could hang herself twice. I hope you were taking notes, Moray. She must have ticked every box on the "signs someone is lying" form.'

Warren thanked him politely. Despite the success of the interview so far, it was far from in the bag. He also felt slightly sad. They still didn't know why Stevie Cullen had been killed, or by who. His feeling was that Silvija Wilson was desperately trying to protect her two young nieces, who she clearly loved dearly.

He took a long slurp of the coffee that Grimshaw had made him. He grimaced at the bitter taste; Grimshaw obviously thought he needed the caffeine boost and been extra generous with the coffee powder.

'I plan on resuming tomorrow morning. Is there anything else that I can hit her with?'

'I've got some financials back from Silvija Wilson's personal account,' said Pymm. 'I've only skimmed them so far, but it makes interesting reading. I have a team ploughing through her mobile phone records, putting names to numbers. I expect to have a list first thing tomorrow.'

'CCTV is coming in from the route that she took that day. It's being processed as a priority,' said Richardson. 'I think we'll be able to join the dots by tomorrow morning.'

'Search teams are out and about along the route,' said Hutchinson. 'It's dark now, so they're a bit restricted. I'll keep you posted.'

'What about her car?' asked Warren.

'It's in the pound. They're looking it over,' said Hutchinson.

'And her house?'

'A team's in there now – nothing yet.'

Warren looked at his watch. Malina and Biljana Dragi had been arrested nearly thirty-six hours ago. They would have to either apply for another extension or charge them.

'Anything from the two sisters?'

Richardson answered, 'I sent someone down there to rattle their cages an hour ago, like you asked, but nothing.' She shook her head. 'They're both tearful, but they are refusing to say anything. I think they're in denial, hoping it will just go away and we'll release them after the ninety-six hours expire. Even their solicitors are getting frustrated.'

'Well unless either they or their aunt come up with something new, they're going to be in for a rude surprise when that custody limit rolls around.'

'Boss, I think you might want to come and hear this.' Ruskin sounded excited over the phone. Warren had been putting his coat on, looking forward to going home. He was tired, after a

216

long weekend, but he knew that Ruskin wouldn't have called him if it wasn't urgent.

'Where are you?'

'I'm in the smart meeting room speaking to one of the missing customers from the massage parlour. She just turned up at the main desk. I was free, so I said I'd come and see her.'

It took Warren less than two minutes to make it downstairs to the so-called 'smart meeting room', a pleasantly decorated space where they took grieving relatives or important visitors. Its little machine served the best coffee in the building, bar John Grayson's legendary personal stash, and at Warren's nagging insistence now also stocked custard creams and Garibaldis alongside the packets of shortbread and ginger stem biscuits. It was the little victories that made life worth living, he decided.

Rebecca Green was an older woman in her late sixties, or early seventies, Warren judged, sporting a healthy glow that in November could only be the result of time spent abroad in sunnier climes. Two customers had used the massage parlour that morning; of the other there was no record, but Green's name had been noted along with her mobile phone number in the customer ledger.

'I hear that you have some information for us,' said Warren once the introductions had been made. At first quiet and a little shy, she soon started to relax, becoming chattier as she wolfed down more custard creams.

'I was just telling Constable Ruskin here that I'm sorry that I didn't return your calls sooner. We've been away you see, cruising in the Mediterranean, just a few days to take the chill off before the winter. It was a last-minute deal in the travel agent's. Somebody dropped out apparently.' She caught herself. 'Sorry, I'm sure you're very busy. You haven't got time to hear me wittering on. Anyway, when I'm abroad I only use my phone for text messages. I never make calls. Did you know that the mobile phone companies will charge you just for answering a call?' She tutted. 'My friend Gladys from the club went to Spain for a month last winter. She isn't daft, she used a phone card to call home. But her daughter phoned her each week, just to check in, and she didn't think to call her back on the pay phone. Well you wouldn't, would you?' Green lowered her voice. 'Her phone bill when she got back was almost a hundred pounds.' She laughed throatily. 'Now that's what I call daylight robbery. Those are the real crooks you should be chasing.'

'Tell me about the day you went for your massage,' Warren prompted.

The smile fell from Green's face. 'Such a dreadful thing – poor Silvija and the girls, it must have been a dreadful shock. Of course, I didn't know anything about it when we were away. We try not to keep up with the news when we're on holiday. It's all so miserable these days. John gets a copy of *The Sun* for the sport, but we don't read the rest of the paper. Besides, he says that the only thing he trusts in *The Sun* is the football scores.'

'So how did you find out about the murder?' prompted Warren. Important or not, he still hoped to get home at a decent hour.

'From Joanna, my eldest. We drove over to see her and her girls for Sunday lunch, and she told us what we'd missed when we were away. Anyway, she told us about the murder, and she said, "Isn't that where you get your massage done?" And I said yes. Of course, she couldn't remember what day it happened. Then I remembered that I kept on getting voicemails when I was away, so I listened to them and realized that you'd been trying to get in contact with me. John said we should pop in on our way back from visiting her, so here I am. I'm sorry it's so late, but she lives in Kent and the Dartford Crossing was blocked. Two hours we sat in that traffic jam.'

'We? Where is your husband, Mrs Green?'

'Oh, he's sitting in the car listening to the radio. Don't worry, he's quite happy.'

'Then I'll try not to keep you too long; it's cold outside. Perhaps we can start by you telling me about your visit to the massage parlour?'

'I've been going once a month ever since I slipped on the ice, about five – no tell a lie – six years ago. I hurt my hip and my back, and it's never been quite the same since.' She motioned towards her walking stick.

'And do you always have the same masseuse?'

'Yes. Originally, I had Silvija herself, but she doesn't do as much these days. Then last year, her nieces came to work with her. I was a bit wary at first, because Silvija did such a good job with my back, but Malina has such gentle hands. Now I can't imagine having anyone else.'

'Tell me what happened that day.'

'Well John dropped me off a little before my appointment. I don't usually go on a Monday morning; I normally go on a Wednesday lunchtime and catch the bus there after my club. It's a bit of a walk from the bus stop, but the exercise does my hip good. Anyway, I wanted to get a massage in before we went away on the Tuesday, so they booked me in for the Monday morning.'

'What time was your appointment?'

'Eleven-thirty, but John dropped me off a few minutes before, because I didn't have time to catch the bus and walk.'

That matched the video footage. Mrs Green had arrived at eleven-twenty-five.

'Then what happened?'

'They offered me a cup of coffee, which was sweet of them, but a bit silly.' She chuckled. 'What was I going to do with a cup of hot coffee when I'm having a massage? I just thanked her and asked for some water.'

'And did your appointment start on time?'

'Oh yes, I went through and got changed, then Malina did my massage.'

A thought suddenly occurred to Warren. 'How long does the massage last? Do you get the full hour?'

'Well not really. It takes a few minutes to get undressed, and then re-dress at the end.'

'And does the massage last for the rest of the hour?'

'About that. They give me a few minutes to just relax afterwards, before getting dressed again.' She frowned. 'I would say she's working on me for about forty or forty-five minutes.'

'Do you know if Biljana follows the same sort of schedule?'

'Well I can't say for sure, but both girls were trained by their aunt, and that's how long she used to take.'

Warren filed that away for future consideration. According to the statements given by the two women, and repeated later, Stevie Cullen's massage had only lasted about half an hour, before he was left to relax. Although the CCTV evidence suggested that was patently untrue, Warren wondered at the story presented by the two suspects. Would Cullen's massage ordinarily only take half an hour, rather than the longer massage favoured by Mrs Green? After all, Mrs Green had medical issues that she was trying to manage. Or were they lying about the length of his massage to explain why he was alone when they claimed the attack took place?

'What time did you leave?'

'About twelve-thirty. I tried not to dawdle, as John was picking me up and there are double yellow lines outside. I paid Malina at the till and then left.'

Again, that matched the video footage.

'Who else was there when you were there? Was anyone else having a massage?'

'I don't think anyone was having a massage.'

The video had clearly shown another, as yet unidentified, woman enter at eleven o'clock, before leaving forty minutes later.

'How do you know?'

'Well Malina was with me, and Biljana was sitting chatting to the lady having her nails done.'

Monday 09 November

Chapter 29

Warren felt exhausted. He'd barely slept a wink the night before, awakened repeatedly by disturbing dreams. Eventually he'd got up again, and moved to the spare room, unwilling to disturb Susan, but had just lain there staring at the ceiling, consumed by the worries that the nightmares had provoked.

The dreams had been a smorgasbord of images and themes, melded together by his subconscious, all of which had a common theme: fatherhood. The excitement of the pregnancy had given way to a feeling of dread and fear and guilt.

First there was the dread from the thought of suddenly being responsible for the care of two helpless beings. Warren had never been a father before. What if he wasn't up to the task? He'd certainly crossed paths with enough men in his time as a police officer who had been unable to step up to that obligation. But leaving that aside, he worked outrageous hours during investigations. Could he juggle that with his responsibilities as a parent? Warren's own father had been absent for much of his childhood, pursuing his career and leaving his mother to do most of the parenting. Warren felt that his father had missed out, that his mother had been unfairly stifled in her own ambitions, and that he and his brother had paid the price. He had vowed not to let that happen to him.

And what about Susan? She had been working as a head of science for several years now; her next career move was likely to be as an assistant or deputy head. Would she want to pursue that at her current school, should an opportunity arise, or would she rather move back to the Midlands? To his chagrin, Warren realized he'd never really asked her.

The support network of Susan's parents and family would certainly make juggling home life and work life easier, particularly with twins, but it didn't really solve the problem of Warren's own contact time with his children.

That being said, Warren knew that if he moved back to the West Midlands, his hands-on policing approach would have to end. The circumstances of his position in Middlesbury were all but unique; in other forces, nobody would countenance a Detective Chief Inspector even interviewing suspects, let alone going out into the field to track them down. He'd miss it, and it was unquestionably an approach that worked, but should he be delegating more? It would certainly make his work hours more manageable.

Modern communication technology meant that he wouldn't have to spend as many hours at the station as he did; calls could be routed to his mobile phone, and he could keep a track of his email just as easily at home, whilst watching a sleeping baby, as he could at work. God knows, DSI Grayson spent enough time out of the office. Perhaps a change in working patterns would mean that he didn't need to move back to the Midlands?

Warren didn't need the services of the counsellor he'd been seeing sporadically since the death of Gary Hastings to identify the trigger for this sudden introspection. The worries about fatherhood had been there since the moment Susan had emerged from the bathroom, her cheeks flushed with excitement, holding the pregnancy test triumphantly. The issues from the loss of his father, although largely resolved in recent years, still haunted his dreams occasionally, and his guilt over the death of Gary Hastings had lost much of its rawness.

However, anticipation of today's visitor had brought all those feelings together and triggered the previous night's dreams.

Warren cleared his throat to bring the briefing to order, then took a swig of water to combat his suddenly dry mouth.

'Before we get started, I just want to welcome back a former member of the team, Detective Constable Karen Hardwick.'

Karen Hardwick smiled self-consciously as everyone in the briefing room turned to face her. Her hands on her lap felt clammy and her stomach was tight with nerves. She'd been awake since four a.m., but for once Oliver hadn't been the reason for her lack of sleep. In recent weeks, he'd been sleeping through until almost five a.m. most days. When he'd finally awoken, she'd been almost glad of an excuse to get up.

After changing him, she'd prepared several bottles of formula, ready for her parents who would be taking care of him that day. By six-thirty, an hour before they were due to arrive, she was showered and ready, despite having spent far longer than usual choosing what to wear.

She'd felt like it was the first day of a new job, and she had tried on three different trouser suits before settling on a smart, charcoal two-piece. If anything, the suit was larger on her than it had been before she had Oliver. Grief had a way of helping shed the baby weight.

Of course, it had all been for nothing, as her beloved son had decided to be sick down it five minutes before his grandparents were due to arrive, and she'd ended up grabbing the nearest clean suit to hand.

Perhaps it was for the best. Suddenly finding herself running late had pushed her worries to one side, and she'd arrived in CID flustered, but oddly nerves-free.

Looking around the room, most of the faces were new to her; seconded officers from Welwyn. But everybody knew who she was. Everybody knew what had happened to her. Everybody knew about Gary.

She felt a sudden rush of dizziness. She couldn't be here. What was she thinking?

Officers on maternity leave were entitled to up to ten keep-in-touch days, but they weren't compulsory. She didn't need to take them. She could have just started back the day her leave finished, no questions asked.

But she had wanted to come in. She'd spoken to her Federation representative a few weeks previously and gone through the rules surrounding return from maternity leave. Her terms of employment clearly stated that if she chose not to return to work after her leave, then the extra maternity pay that she had received, above the statutory legal minimum, would be forfeited. She would have to pay the money back.

Her rep had suggested that the unique circumstances of her leave – coming as it did after her bereavement leave following the death of her partner on duty might mean the force could be persuaded to treat her sympathetically, if she chose not to return. But it was at the force's discretion, and in these times of ever-tightening budgets, it was far from a given.

The loss of the money wasn't her over-riding concern, however. She knew that her parents, and Gary's parents, would cover that in a heartbeat. Instead, she needed to know that leaving was what she really wanted to do. The offer of a place at university had left her torn by indecision.

Was a career in the police what she truly wanted now? She was Oliver's sole parent. Didn't she have a responsibility to make sure that he didn't lose both his mum and his dad? A responsibility to keep herself safe and out of harm's way?

Perhaps she could move to a different, less hazardous position? The force would doubtless be sympathetic to her request for a transfer, and casting aside false modesty, she knew that she was a well-respected, highly competent officer, with many skills.

But did she want to leave front-line policing? Would she feel fulfilled in a different role? And if she did decide to stay in CID, should she – could she? – return to Middlesbury and continue working there, now that Gary was no longer with her?

She hoped that today might help her decide.

Walking back into CID after all this time had been a surreal, emotional experience. The layout of the office had been completely changed. She understood why; nobody had wanted to sit at the desks once occupied by her and Gary, but leaving them empty, as some sort of shrine, was neither desirable nor practical. She was glad somebody had made that decision for her. Nevertheless, she found herself unable to look over at the corner where they had once sat.

Greeted with teary hugs by Mags Richardson, and David Hutchinson, and warmth by John Grayson, her meeting with DCI Jones had been stilted and awkward. He still blamed himself for Gary's death, and she knew that no matter how often she told him that she didn't hold him responsible, her presence would forever be a reminder to him of what happened that day. She noticed that he too seemed unable to look over at her former workspace, now housing a set of filing cabinets and a photocopier.

Hardwick focused on her breathing, until finally the oxygen drove away her light-headedness. Eventually she was able to turn her attention back to the briefing.

'… Wilson wasn't particularly forthcoming in her interview last night, but we hit her with evidence that we knew she had been lying and left her to sweat overnight. We know that she wasn't present at the time of the murder; our belief is that she is lying to protect her nieces. I think we need to start using that as leverage more. None of them seem to fully appreciate just how much trouble they are in.'

Warren took a sip of water.

'As mentioned at the beginning of the briefing, the information given by Mrs Green yesterday evening, alongside the recovery of the deleted CCTV footage from the rear of the property, is a potential game-changer.' There were nods of assent around the room. 'I intend to hit Wilson with those revelations to break the stalemate. I think we can be cautiously optimistic that Wilson might finally break and give us what we need.'

Hardwick felt a brief moment of panic, worried that she had missed something, before relaxing. She was just an observer today.

As the meeting broke up around her, she had a sudden feeling of dislocation. What was she supposed to do? Everyone else seemed focused; they all had specific jobs to do and left with purpose in their stride.

She remained seated where she was. DCI Jones had already left, talking as he walked to Moray Ruskin. She knew him from the previous summer; the huge, bearded Scotsman had worked alongside Gary on the Meegan case. Gary's last case. She forced down the sudden rush of grief. Behind Ruskin and Jones, she recognized the Brownnose Brothers: Grimshaw and Martinez. She'd never worked with them, but she knew them by reputation. Everyone knew them. The two had been keen to be seen during the briefing, the first to ask questions. Their ambition was a source of some amusement on the force's grapevine. Their contrasting appearances – one sharp-suited and clean-shaven, the other rumpled and stubbly – easily allowed her to distinguish between them.

Finally, the room was almost empty, with only Mags Richardson and one other person left behind. There was no need for the introduction, her crutches meant that she could be only one person.

Hardwick swallowed.

'Karen, I don't believe you've met Rachel Pymm, our full-time officer in the case, I was hoping that you might work with us today.'

Karen shook the other woman's hand, forcing herself to smile. She blinked, trying to drive away the tears that suddenly threatened to appear. She could convince herself that Ruskin was just another DC, ignoring the obvious fact that he was there, in part, to cover her and Gary.

But Pymm was different; she was Gary's direct replacement. In the last few months of his career, Gary had been fulfilling the role of officer in the case on a part-time basis, having taken over from Pete Kent. He had been hoping to make a switch to that position full-time, if he was promoted to sergeant. Unbeknown to him, he'd passed his qualification hours before his death. Karen was grateful to DSI Grayson and DCI Jones for insisting that Gary's final rank be recorded as detective sergeant on the police memorial on the corner of St James's Park.

As the three women left the room, Pymm touched Karen's arm. The older woman's face was creased with concern.

'I know this must be hard for you, but I just wanted to say that the whole team still talk about Gary. I never met him, but he's left some big shoes to fill. And I'm looking forward to getting to know you.'

Karen said nothing, her throat too tight to let her speak.

Chapter 30

It was clear that Silvija Wilson hadn't enjoyed much of a night's sleep, the bags under her eyes accentuated by the remnants of the previous day's tear-streaked mascara. Warren could sympathize. Quite apart from the many other reasons for his insomnia – and despite it being several days after November the 5th – the local idiots were still letting fireworks off late at night, which then set off the neighbour's dogs, who howled for the next two hours.

'Why don't we start by talking about what you did that day?' Warren started. Beside him, Moray Ruskin gave no indication that he'd had anything less than eight hours' uninterrupted beauty sleep, despite leaving work at the same time as Warren the previous night and going for his usual morning run before starting early. Warren's pang of jealousy at the man's remarkable stamina was tempered somewhat by the appearance of Shaun Grimshaw that morning; he was living up to his nickname 'the Grim Reaper' even more than usual.

Ruskin was a freak. Warren had decided that long ago.

Wilson described her movements the day of the murder exactly as she'd stated previously. She'd left her house at ten to eight, arriving at her nieces' flat just before eight. As usual, the two young women weren't ready, and she'd sat in her car for five minutes waiting for them. They'd then crawled through the morning rush hour, arriving at the massage parlour at eight-twenty-five. Her account matched the tracking data from both of her mobile phones and those of the two sisters.

She'd left to take the weekend's takings to the bank at nine-thirty, her phones showing that she spent fifteen minutes in the Lloyds Bank on the high street, presumably in the queue. After that, she'd travelled directly to the River View care home, where her father-in-law was a resident.

'What did you do after you arrived at the home?'

Wilson looked down at her hands, before finally answering. She must have known that her story for that day was falling apart, but it seemed that stubbornness ran in the family.

'I spent a bit of time watching TV with my father-in-law, then took him out for some fresh air and then to lunch.'

'Where?'

'I can't remember. Some pub that we drove past.'

'What did you do when Malina told you about the death at the massage parlour?'

'I drove my father-in-law back to his home, then drove to the parlour.'

'Are you sure about that?'

'Yes.'

'Well according to the care home, you didn't take your father-in-law out to lunch that day; Monday is cold beef sandwiches left over from the Sunday roast. It's his favourite.' Warren took out a printed map from the folder in front of him.

'This is a map of Middlesbury and the surrounding villages. In red is the route that your two mobile phones travelled that day. The asterisks mark automatic number plate recognition cameras that registered your car, with the time stamp next to them. At fourteen minutes past one – approximately two minutes into your call with Malina, your phones left the care home. This is confirmed by the care workers, who said that you didn't even finish your sandwich. According to our colleagues in Traffic, the journey time to the massage parlour from the care home should take about thirteen minutes. You arrived ten minutes later, at one-twenty-four. Coincidentally, that was the time that you ended the call to Malina. What did Malina say to you that made you drop everything and race to the massage parlour so quickly? You passed the speed camera in the thirty zone on Fairfax Street at sixty-three miles per hour.'

Wilson looked over at her solicitor pleadingly. He said nothing. This was all news to him.

'No comment.'

'Thirty-three minutes past one, you left the massage parlour, and headed back towards your nieces' flat. This time you drove a bit more carefully; it took you six minutes. In fact, by our calculations you were travelling well under the speed limit.'

'No comment.'

'Were you travelling so slowly because you were talking to Malina again on your business phone? We know that you can do that legally, by the way; it's paired to the car's hands-free system.'

Wilson was starting to breath heavily. 'No comment.'

'What happened in the nine minutes that you were in the massage parlour?'

'No comment.' Her voice was little more than a squeak.

'What were you and Malina talking about during those two minutes, as you drove back to your nieces' flat?'

'No comment.'

Warren nodded to Ruskin, who pressed play on the video screen.

'I'm showing Mrs Wilson exhibit 2015/12/NH6382-12, CCTV footage taken from the reception area of the massage parlour. We are starting at time point 13.34.'

The video started. After about sixty seconds, Malina appeared, scurrying towards the reception computer, her mobile phone in her hand. Wilson watched the footage wide-eyed. Warren watched Wilson.

'What is Malina doing to the computer, Silvija?'

'No comment.'

'Are you giving her instructions? We know that she's on the phone to you. Her handset is on the table, next to her. What are you telling her to do?'

'No comment.'

'When was the rear security camera broken, Silvija?'

She cleared her throat. 'A few weeks ago.' She swallowed. 'I've been meaning to get it fixed for ages you know, for the insurance … I just never got around to it.'

'Not according to our Forensics department. You know, they really are good. Apparently, the camera was broken at 13.34 the day of the murder. We know this because they recovered the footage that Malina deleted at 13.37, under your direction.'

'No. That didn't happen.'

Warren's voice turned stern. 'Yes, it did. DC Ruskin?'

Obediently, Ruskin turned on the video again.

'I'm showing Mrs Wilson exhibit 2015/12/NH6382-65, recovered video footage from the rear-facing camera from the massage parlour. The time point is 13.36.'

Warren had already watched the video, so again he turned his attention to Wilson, whose hand was now over her mouth.

The camera showed a wide-angled view of the yard behind the parlour. The door opened and Malina emerged, carrying a chair, which she placed directly below the camera. The last clear image was that of Malina's face, as she swung what appeared to be a small fire extinguisher at the camera's lens. The glass cracked and the viewpoint tilted wildly. A second blow shattered the glass entirely, leaving the camera facing towards the sky. The footage stopped and the screen went blank, a red error message flashing 'No Signal', as the cable was pulled from the back.

'What were they trying to hide, Silvija?' asked Warren.

She said nothing, her hand still over her mouth.

'There was no man in black was there?'

She put her head in her hands.

'Stevie Cullen was murdered, we believe, at about ten past one. Malina and Biljana panicked and called you, although Malina had the presence of mind to phone you on your business phone, rather than your personal number. I guess all those *CSI* episodes were time well spent.'

Wilson remained silent, refusing to look up; Warren continued regardless.

'You received the call and rushed over to the massage parlour. What happened during that phone call, Silvija? What did Malina tell you? Did you speak to Biljana as well?'

Wilson's shoulders started to shake.

'Whose idea was it to delete the security video? Was it yours or one of the girls'?'

Warren waited for a moment, but nothing was forthcoming.

'Just so you know, Silvija, a little over an hour ago, the Crown Prosecution Service authorized me to charge both Malina and Biljana with murder and attempting to pervert the course of justice.' Wilson gave a strangled cry. 'From what I've seen, I will be asking for permission to charge you with attempting to pervert the course of justice as well.'

'No. They didn't murder him. They couldn't ...'

'Mrs Wilson, I can't stress how much trouble your nieces are in. We shared everything that we've shown you this morning with them before charging. Both of them are declining to comment.'

Now the tears were in full flow.

Warren gave her a few moments to compose herself.

'Silvija, I know that you love your nieces very much. They are refusing to say anything. You need to help them to help themselves.'

He passed over a tissue. 'Both you and your nieces claim that there was nobody else in the massage parlour that day. We both

234

know that was a lie. We have a witness who tells us that was a lie. Tell us who else was there. I need to speak to them. They might have witnessed something that could explain Mr Cullen's death.' He paused. 'They might be able to help your nieces. And you.'

She sniffed loudly but said nothing.

'DC Ruskin, can you show the suspect the recovered security video, starting at time point 13.00? Show it at eight times normal speed.'

The video started again, the camera showing the backyard again.

'You can see that nobody enters through the rear gate in the run-up to Mr Cullen's murder. Nobody climbs through the window. The back door to the property remains closed.'

The video sped towards 13.10, and Warren ordered the video slowed to normal speed. The backyard remained empty.

Suddenly, the rear door burst open. Two dark-haired women, dressed in blue coveralls, raced out of the building. Reaching the back gate, one of them fumbled frantically, trying to open it. Finally, she succeeded, turning briefly towards the camera as she opened it. Even from a distance, the girl's dark skin and tiny build was apparent, fear contorting her petite, Asian features.

'It looks as though your nail technicians did report for work that day, after all,' said Warren.

Silvija Wilson's face was a study in conflicting emotions. Emotionally, she was at a decision point. Either she would come clean and tell them what they needed to know, or she would clam up and start no commenting again.

Warren decided to help her.

'These two women could be vital witnesses. They must have heard what happened.' Warren paused. 'They might be able to help your nieces.'

Wilson shook her head but remained silent.

'We also know that there was another potential witness. DC Ruskin, start the tape again.'

'I'm showing Mrs Wilson security footage from the rear of the massage parlour on the morning of the attack, starting at eight-twenty-five,' said Ruskin.

'According to the CCTV footage in the reception area, and the tracking data from your mobile phone, you and your two nieces arrived at the massage parlour at that time, entering through the front door,' supplied Warren.

The footage showed the empty backyard again, a black-wheeled bin against the rear wall.

At eight-twenty-seven, the gate opened, and a slim female figure wearing a dark coat came through, a key in her hand. Her head was down, her face partly obscured as she pocketed the key. Turning to her right, she grabbed the handle of the bin and dragged it back through the gate, disappearing from view for almost a minute. Re-entering, she closed the gate behind her again, this time taking the key from her pocket and inserting it into the lock. She didn't turn it, leaving it protruding. Crossing the yard, she headed to the rear door, which was opened from within. Maddeningly, she didn't look up towards the camera as she entered, wiping her hands down her coat. Only her short dark hair was visible.

Ruskin paused the video.

'Who is that?' asked Warren.

Wilson paused. 'It must be Billy.'

'Biljana came through the front door with you and Malina. She didn't leave again.'

Ruskin increased the playback speed to maximum. He slowed it to normal speed again at eight-fifty.

The gate reopened. This time, the two Asian nail technicians entered. They closed the gate behind them, one of them locking it and removing the key.

This time they knocked on the rear door; it was opened from the inside again.

'That's three potential witnesses that neither you nor your nieces admit to being there at the time of the murder,' said Warren. 'If we watch the remainder of the video, we can see that none of them leave the property until the murder takes place.'

Wilson looked sick. It was clear from her face that she knew what was coming next.

'DC Ruskin, can you restart the video again at 13.24, please?'

Ruskin manipulated the controls again.

'I'll remind you that the two nail technicians have already left at this point,' said Warren. On the screen, the back gate was fully open.

'According to the mobile phone data, you have just ended your call to Malina, and arrived back at the massage parlour.'

On the screen, Silvija Wilson suddenly appeared at a half-jog. She crossed the yard and went straight through the back door. Warren left the video playing.

'Why did you enter through the rear door, Silvija?' asked Warren. 'You have a parking space at the front of the building. The alleyway at the back isn't wide enough for a vehicle; that's why your bins need to be dragged to the kerbside. Surely it makes more sense to come in through the front?'

'No comment.'

Even at maximum speed, the time passed slowly, but eventually, eight minutes after she had entered the building, Wilson re-emerged. This time, she had her arm around the unidentified dark-haired woman. The woman was sobbing uncontrollably, and Wilson all but dragged her across the yard and out of the rear. Wilson was carrying a black plastic bin bag.

Ruskin stopped the video again.

'We've looked back through the past two weeks of recorded footage on both cameras,' said Warren. 'Every day starts the same. You and your nieces arrive for work first thing in the morning. Two minutes later, this young woman walks through the rear gate. She obviously has a key because she unlocks it, but leaves

237

the key in the lock on the inside. A few minutes after that, your two nail technicians arrive, and use the key to lock the gate again.

'It seems that the young woman only works mornings, as she usually leaves before one p.m., again by the rear entrance – I assume that she is working for you?'

Wilson managed a 'No comment'.

'At the end of the day, the two nail technicians leave, again by the back entrance, before you and your nieces lock up the parlour and leave by the front door again. Does that sound about right?'

Warren sat back. Wilson was close to the edge, but she still needed a further push.

'Why do this young woman and your two nail technicians always enter by the rear entrance?'

'No comment.'

'Is it to keep them off the reception camera?' Warren produced a top-down plan of the reception area, made by the forensic team.

'You see, we've been grumbling about how badly aligned your reception security camera is. But that's deliberate isn't it?' He pointed at the diagram. 'This semi-circle shows the field of view for the camera. It covers the front door and the reception desk, and the visitor seating. The carpeted area. What it doesn't cover is the area with the wooden floor. That includes the two nail stations and the exit to the massage rooms.

'Why is that, Silvija?'

Warren wanted her to admit it.

She didn't.

'This whole set-up is designed to hide any evidence of these workers, isn't it? Your nail technicians are under strict instructions not to cross that line, aren't they?'

'No comment.'

'Of course, it would be safer not to have any cameras at all, but I imagine your insurance provider insists upon them. It's easy enough to position the camera in the reception so that it still covers the front door to keep your insurers happy, but doesn't show the nail techs, but you're kind of stuck with the camera at the rear. How often did you practise deleting any incriminating footage?'

'No comment.'

Warren pushed a sheet of paper across the desk.

'Your accounts make for interesting reading. The spreadsheet that you use to record your expenses doesn't match your hand-written ledger. At first, I assumed that you were just under-reporting your figures to dodge a bit of tax. But you aren't, are you? You're deliberately keeping some cash back to pay the wages of your illegal workers.'

'No comment.'

'Which also explains why you had the presence of mind to tell Malina to smash the rear camera and delete any footage from that camera. That's why she phoned your business phone isn't it? This was a well-rehearsed plan in case you were raided by the Home Office or Revenue and Customs, wasn't it?'

Wilson repeated, 'No comment.' But Warren could see in her eyes that he'd worked out her plan.

'Where did you take that young woman, Silvija?'

'No comment.'

'What was in the bin bag?'

'No comment.'

Now his tone softened. 'It would help you, and your nieces, if you could tell us, in your own words what really happened that day,' said Warren.

By now, Wilson was crying, her fist pressed into her mouth.

'I think we should have a break,' said Wilson's solicitor.

Chapter 31

The air in the office was quietly triumphant when Warren and Ruskin came back in. Even DSI Grayson was in a good mood.

'Good work, Warren,' he said. 'My gut tells me that we're going to finally figure out what happened that day. I suspect we're also going to make some people in Immigration very happy.'

Warren thanked him. By contrast, he wasn't quite so sure; Wilson had been beaten and thrown against the ropes, but he'd seen the determined set of her chin, and witnessed the stubborn streak that ran deep through her family. Whatever Wilson was going to tell them after the break, he suspected that it would be a carefully controlled version of the truth.

Silvija Wilson's break with her solicitor lasted until shortly after midday. When they finally signalled their return, it was clear that they had been busy.

'I would like to read a statement on behalf of Mrs Wilson,' stated the solicitor formally for the record. He had a small laptop in front of him, which he read from.

'Mrs Wilson would like to state categorically that she did not play any part in the death of Mr Stevie Cullen, on Monday the 2nd of November. Nor, to the best of her knowledge, were her two nieces, Malina and Biljana Dragi , responsible. The person she believes responsible was a casual employee of the parlour, a Serbian national known only to Mrs Wilson as "Annie".

'On the day in question, Mrs Wilson drove her two nieces to the parlour as normal. Annie arrived shortly after, entering through the rear entrance. Mrs Wilson also rents space in her parlour to two self-employed nail and beauty technicians. She knows them only as "Lilly" and "Yên". They arrived just before nine a.m., as witnessed on the security footage.

'After Mrs Wilson departed for the bank that day, Malina and Biljana were left in charge of the parlour, as is normal practice on a weekday. Mrs Wilson then went to the River View care home to visit her father-in-law. Her understanding – as she was not there – was that Mr Cullen visited the parlour for a massage, as scheduled, just before one p.m. Ordinarily, Annie would have finished at midday, but she did a second run of the washing machine to clean some new towels before use. For reasons that Mrs Wilson is not aware of, Mr Cullen attacked Annie, and she defended herself, killing him in the process.'

Warren watched Wilson carefully. The woman closed her eyes, her shoulders slumping.

'Malina and Biljana heard Annie's screams and ran in to see what was happening. It was immediately apparent that despite the best efforts of all three women, Mr Cullen could not be saved. Malina and Biljana panicked, and instead of calling the ambulance as they should have done, they called Mrs Wilson for advice.'

Wilson shifted in her seat, her eyes still closed.

'Mrs Wilson admits that she, and her two nieces, made a serious error of judgement. The two girls were very traumatized by what they had witnessed, and frightened for Annie, to whom they had become very close. They persuaded Mrs Wilson to help Annie flee the scene and concocted a story about an unknown intruder.

'At this point, Mrs Wilson would like to make it clear that the actions of all of them that day, whilst misguided, were a sincere

241

attempt to protect their friend who had been the victim of an unprovoked attack and merely defended herself, with tragic consequences. They were concerned that Annie's uncertain immigration status may result in her being treated unfairly by the police, a belief that Mrs Wilson acknowledges has no basis in fact.'

The solicitor took a sip of water, before continuing. Wilson sat unmoving.

'After arriving back at the massage parlour, Mrs Wilson helped her nieces rearrange the crime scene, in an attempt to support the false narrative of an unknown intruder. She then took Annie back to her nieces' flat to pick up some clothes and a bag. She then drove Annie to the train station, giving her some cash. That was the last time she saw Annie.

'Mrs Wilson is prepared to acknowledge that she should have investigated Annie's immigration status more carefully and should not have paid her cash in hand. As she did not employ Lilly and Yên directly, she did not believe that it was her responsibility to check their right-to-work. The positioning of the security camera in the reception area was not deliberate, and Lilly, Yên and Annie only entered through the rear of the parlour for convenience.

'Mrs Wilson admits to calling Mr Cullen on several occasions before the day of the murder, as he was supplying her with cheap beauty products for the salon. She realizes on reflection that she should have inquired more carefully as to the origin of these products. This was why she denied previously knowing Mr Cullen.'

The solicitor sat back, and Warren thanked him for the statement. Wilson looked both relieved and nervous at the same time. It was the most cooperative that she'd been since her arrest, and Warren was unwilling to let her mood change during yet another break, and so looking over his notes, he decided to start questioning immediately. Beside him, Ruskin was busy writing down questions that he'd also thought of. The constable's handwriting was clear enough that Warren could see that he was thinking along much the same lines.

'You say that Annie was responsible for the killing of Mr Cullen. Obviously, locating Annie has now become our priority. Where did she catch the train to?'

Wilson shifted in her seat, glancing over at her solicitor. 'She didn't say. I dropped her off at the station and she left without telling me where she was going.'

Warren wasn't entirely surprised at the answer. Wilson's statement had been carefully crafted to give the appearance of openness and cooperation, but it was clear that much had been left out. Why was she protecting Annie? The two sisters were non-EU nationals, meaning that the Foreign Office had taken an interest in the case. According to a liaison officer, an emergency visa had been granted to the parents of the two women, and they were expected to arrive later that day. Warren made a note to see if they could shed any light on the identity of the mysterious woman. Did the two sisters have another sibling?

'Perhaps you could help us then, Mrs Wilson. How did you meet Annie?'

'She came to the massage parlour a few months ago, asking for casual work.' Wilson shifted uncomfortably. 'We needed a bit of help about the place. Cleaning, washing uniforms and towels, that sort of thing. I agreed to give her a few hours each morning. She was clearly a bit down on her luck and I wanted to help her.'

'How did she know about the massage parlour?'

'The Serbian community is quite close-knit; I suppose somebody recommended me.'

That might explain why none of the young people they'd traced from Malina and Biljana's social media posts had admitted to knowing the identity of the young woman. They would have been unwilling to incriminate somebody working illegally.

'Where did she live?'

'I don't know; she never said.'

'So, I assume that you were paying her cash in hand?'

They already knew from Wilson's bank and financial details

that Malina and Biljana were the only workers drawing a salary from the massage parlour. If Annie had been paid formally, she would have needed a National Insurance number, and Wilson would have needed her address.

Wilson nodded, looking even more uncomfortable.

'Mrs Wilson has already admitted that she should have been more careful about ascertaining Annie's immigration status, before employing her,' said her solicitor.

'Do you know how she arrived at work each day?'

Wilson shrugged. 'I have no idea.'

It was clear that Wilson wasn't going to help them any more than necessary.

'Why did you take her back to your nieces' flat, rather than taking her home to pick up her own clothes?'

'She said her flat was on the other side of town.'

That implied that she probably needed to use public transport to get to work each day. Warren made a note to get Mags Richardson to check the CCTV on the buses. Between the video footage of her arriving for work each day, and images of her on social media, they had several clear headshots that they could use to locate her.

'You say that Mr Cullen attacked Annie. What can you tell me about that?'

'I don't know anything about it.'

'Surely Annie said something to you?'

'She was too upset to speak.'

'But you said that Malina and Biljana saw the attack. They must know what happened?'

'They haven't said anything.'

'Nothing at all?' Warren allowed a note of scepticism to creep into his tone.

'You are asking Mrs Wilson to speculate on events that she did not personally witness,' interjected the solicitor.

Again, Warren wasn't surprised. Malina and Biljana hadn't said anything since being charged. Wilson had clearly been advised not to say any more than necessary, to avoid contradicting their statements.

Warren slid more pages of Wilson's call logs across the table to her.

'You made multiple phone calls, to several different numbers, between one-forty-five and three o'clock, before driving to the train station. Who were you calling?'

Wilson looked over at her solicitor. 'No comment.'

It was the first 'no comment' since she had made her statement. Warren made a note. Identifying the owners of those phones would be a priority.

'When you left the massage parlour with Annie, you were seen carrying a black bin bag. What was in it?'

Wilson paused. 'Her uniform top. It was covered in blood.'

'And where is that top now?'

He could see that Wilson was immediately regretting answering the question.

'She took it with her.'

Beside her, her solicitor maintained a professionally neutral face. It wasn't his position to tell her to stop talking.

'What happened to the murder weapon, Silvija?'

'I don't know.'

'Was it in the bag with her uniform?'

'I don't know.'

Warren made a show of noting down her answer. Wilson watched, chewing her bottom lip.

'According to the mobile phone tracking data, once you dropped Annie off at the train station, you went for a bit of a drive, before receiving the call on your personal phone from Malina at three-thirty-five – the time that she supposedly informed you of the incident. Where were you going?'

Warren could see the conflict on her face. It was obvious that her instinct was to 'no comment', but she clearly saw that would look suspicious.

'I was stressed. I wanted some time to think and clear my head.'

Warren made another note. Ruskin slid his pad across so that Warren could read the question he had written in big letters. He nodded.

'You said that neither Biljana or Malina witnessed the initial altercation between Annie and Mr Cullen,' said Ruskin.

'That is what they told me,' said Wilson.

'The attack happened at about ten past one, I believe?'

'That is what I was told.'

'Mr Cullen's massage started at one p.m. You said in an earlier statement that depending on the treatment, it might only last half an hour, then he would be left to relax for a bit?'

Wilson bit her lip. 'I can't remember.'

'You did,' said Ruskin, firmly. 'It's on the record.'

'I guess so.'

'I've not had many massages over the years,' Ruskin continued, 'but it would seem that ten minutes is a short treatment. Where was Biljana when the alleged altercation between Annie and Mr Cullen took place?' He emphasized the word 'alleged'.

'I don't know. I wasn't there.'

Warren took over again. 'Perhaps the two nail technicians can tell us? They obviously heard or saw something; that's why they ran out.'

'They had left by the time I arrived. I haven't seen them since.'

'Then perhaps you could help us track them down.'

'I only knew them by their first names: Lilly and Yên.'

'Perhaps your two nieces can help us,' suggested Warren. 'After all, they did work with them all day.'

'I don't think so. They didn't speak English.'

'Where were they from?' asked Ruskin.

'Vietnam, I believe.'

'Perhaps you could give me their home addresses, or a contact phone number. They could really help us here. And your nieces.'

Wilson shrugged. 'They are self-employed. I don't know where they live.'

'How did they come to work at the parlour?' asked Ruskin.

'They turned up a year or so ago and offered to rent our chairs. My previous nail technicians had left, and the space was empty, so I said yes.'

There was something about the confident, fluent way that she said it that didn't sit right with Warren.

'How did they hear about the spaces?'

'I suppose word gets around.'

'If they didn't speak English, how did you communicate?'

'They spoke a few words,' said Wilson.

'What about payment?' asked Warren.

'They charged the customers directly. I charged them a flat fee for use of our facilities. It's the same arrangement as self-employed hairdressers renting a chair in a salon.'

'How often did they pay?' asked Ruskin.

'Weekly.'

'How much?'

Wilson looked uncomfortable. 'One hundred pounds.'

'And do you supply the products, or did they?'

'They do.'

'Do you get any commission?' asked Ruskin.

Wilson again looked uncomfortable. 'About fifty per cent of their takings.'

'We've looked at your business accounts, Mrs Wilson, and there are no weekly payments into your account, other than those in your customer ledger. There are no nail treatments listed in that ledger.'

'They paid cash,' said Wilson quietly.

'The turnover of your parlour only just covers your overheads,' said Warren. 'Your salary is barely more than what you pay your nieces, and their salary is below minimum wage.'

'I rent the flat to them for free, so they are paid above minimum wage,' said Wilson indignantly.

'About that,' said Warren, 'we've also had a look at your personal bank account. You have been paying the mortgage on the flat that you rent out to your nieces for years. You also pay the mortgage on the house that you live in, and you drive a very nice, brand-new Mini Clubman. When I look at those outgoings, and compare it to the salary you pay yourself, the two figures are almost identical. Aside from a small occupational pension from your late husband, I can't for the life of me work out how you afford to eat or even put petrol in your car. Perhaps you could explain to me how that works?'

'That's none of your business,' snapped Wilson.

'I would suggest that the way Mrs Wilson chooses to run her business is beyond the scope of this investigation,' said her solicitor.

Warren ignored him. 'So, two strangers that you have never met before, who don't speak English, turn up at your parlour and ask to rent space. You don't have an address or contact details for them, and have no idea whether they are entitled to work in this country. They pay their rent in cash. Is that about the size of it?' asked Warren.

'No comment,' said Wilson, finally.

'Mrs Wilson, you and your nieces are in a lot of trouble. Far more trouble than you seem to appreciate. The way things currently stand, you are all potentially looking at very lengthy prison sentences.' Warren let that sink in for a moment.

'Look at it from our perspective. The victim was a regular visitor to your parlour and sold you cut-price, probably stolen, beauty products. You lied about knowing him. You and your nieces are claiming that his murder was carried out by a mysterious woman called Annie, who you claim to know nothing about but who you helped escape the scene. The only two witnesses are two nail technicians, possibly Vietnamese, who again you claim to know nothing about, and are unable to help us locate. For the past week, you and your nieces have covered up what really happened and lied repeatedly to my team.

'This goes far beyond your dodgy business practices. Frankly, I'm not interested in whether you paid your workers cash in hand, didn't pay tax on the income from the space that you rented out, or if your beauty supplies fell off the back of a lorry. What I care about is what went on in that back room on Monday the 2nd of November and bringing those responsible to justice. And at the moment, all the available evidence is pointing towards the culprit or culprits being your nieces.

'I suggest you have a think about that. Interview suspended.'

'She's still protecting herself and her nieces,' said Grayson. He'd been watching the interview, alongside the rest of the team. The large briefing room was standing room only, with a mixture of Middlesbury-based detectives and visitors from Welwyn. Karen Hardwick had slipped in at the back, keen to hear her colleagues' take on the interviews that she'd watched on the screen. She was a big fan of the new video systems that had been installed in her absence.

'And she's also protecting this young woman, "Annie", assuming that's even her real name,' added Hutchinson.

'I agree,' said Warren, 'but I think she's torn. I think her first loyalty is to her nieces, so she'll pin the blame on this Annie, but at the same time, she isn't going to help us find her. We need to know who this woman is. Why is Silvija willing to risk her and her nieces' freedom to protect her? Could she be family also?' Warren looked over at Grayson. 'Can you get onto the Foreign Office, Sir, and see if somebody can speak to the sisters' family about whether they know somebody called Annie?'

'I wouldn't hold your breath,' said Grayson.

'That's why I asked you,' said Warren. 'You command more respect than me.' There were a few chuckles around the room.

'Of course, we don't know that she is protecting her,' said Richardson. 'If her nieces were responsible for Stevie Cullen's murder, then this Annie is a convenient scapegoat. If any of what Silvija Wilson told us is true, then it's not hard to imagine her convincing an illegal worker that the last place she needs to be is at the heart of a police investigation. The two nail technicians have already scarpered, now she just needs to get rid of the only remaining witness.'

'Then we need to track down all three women,' said Warren. 'Wilson implied that Annie lived some distance away. Hutch, get a team together to check with the bus companies, and see if we can work out where she got on. Question regular passengers waiting at the bus stop and see if any of them recognize her. If we can figure out where she was living, we might be able to work out where she's run to.

'The same goes for those two nail technicians. Mags, go back through all the security footage we have and get the clearest face shots available. Hutch, arrange for the drivers to be questioned. Even if we can't pick them up on the CCTV, two young Vietnamese women catching the bus each day might jog a few memories.'

'What if they didn't catch the bus?' asked someone from the rear of the briefing room. Warren couldn't remember their name.

'Then spread out into the local area around the massage parlour. See if any of the residents or business owners recognize them, Sergeant …?'

'Jameson, Sir.'

'Should we release their pictures to the press?' asked another detective. 'DC Henderson, by the way.'

'Not just yet. I don't want to spook them any more than we need to. The last thing we want is for them to go into hiding.'

'We should prioritize identifying those mobile phone numbers that Wilson called before she went to the train station,' suggested someone from the back. 'I'll bet she was calling friends and trying to find somewhere for Annie to go. I can't believe she just took her to the train station and waved goodbye.'

'Good suggestion. Rachel, get on it; work with the phone

companies. Whilst you're at it, contact the train station. She may have bought her ticket before she travelled. Failing that, they may be able to work out which train she caught.

'Next up, murder weapon. We've not found it at the massage parlour, or in any of the bins nearby. Nothing yet in the sisters' flat. We don't even know what it looks like, since they aren't speaking. The smart money is on it being in that black bin bag that Silvija Wilson was carrying.

'Those who know me, know that I try not to underestimate human stupidity, but I can't believe that this Annie clambered on a train with a bloody knife and her soiled uniform stuffed in her backpack. She – or Silvija Wilson – ditched them somewhere. If they didn't do it at work, or the sisters' flat, then it either happened en route to the train station, or when Silvija Wilson went for her calming little drive.'

'Could she have disposed of them on the train? You know, chucked them out the vestibule window or something?' asked another voice.

'Let's hope not. Depending where she went, that's a lot of track to search,' said Warren. 'We'll cross that bridge when we've identified the train that she caught. If the CCTV cameras in the carriages are working, we should be able to catch her in the act.'

'If they are working, it'll be the only bloody thing that does work on those trains,' said a different voice, to scattered laughter.

Warren smiled; he knew that a number of officers from Welwyn were regretting their decision to travel up by train that morning.

'Could Wilson have disposed of them at home?' asked another voice.

'Like I said, I try not to underestimate human stupidity, so there are teams searching her house and garden, and that rather nice car of hers,' replied Warren. 'We have enough to extend Wilson's custody. I don't want her going anywhere near a phone until we've tracked down this "Annie". I don't believe she has no idea where she went.'

Chapter 32

Pymm had spread a series of photographs across the table. 'These are the photographs containing the mysterious young woman that Shaun identified in the background of the pictures he retrieved from social media.'

'OK,' said Warren.

'These are scene photos taken from the search of the house that Biljana and Malina Dragi lived in. What do you notice?'

Grimshaw spotted it first. 'All of the social media pictures are taken in the house.'

'Isn't that what we'd expect?' asked Martinez. 'We know that these photos were all taken at house parties. Presumably, Aunty Silvija's place was the place to hang out.'

'Not all of them were taken at parties,' said Pymm, pulling over one.

The photo was a selfie, Biljana's arm stretching out towards the lens. She and her sister were clearly playing with Instagram filters, their images overlaid with cartoon bunny ears and noses. In the background, the unknown woman had her hand up, trying to avoid being in shot.

'So?' Grimshaw looked confused. Martinez shrugged.

'They're wearing pyjamas,' said Pymm, impatiently.

'Oh.' Grimshaw paused. 'Slumber party?' He smirked. 'I've read about those.'

Pymm sighed, but Ruskin beat her to it. 'Look which room it's taken in. It's in a bedroom; you can see they're sitting on a bed. But look at the walls; no posters or pictures, so it's not Biljana's or Malina's room.'

Grimshaw squinted at the picture. 'That's the sofa bed in the living room.'

Meera Gupta's report from the search of the flat confirmed the team's suspicions.

'The sofa bed in the living room was definitely used recently,' said Gupta. 'There were dents on the carpet that correspond to the fold-out legs.'

'Could it have been from someone staying over occasionally?' asked Martinez. 'We know that the house was a bit of a party destination.'

'Perhaps, but there were a lot of overlapping fingerprints, mostly from the same person, on the mechanism inside the sofa. I'd say that the bed was opened and closed regularly. The same fingerprints also appear all over the bathroom, the kitchen and the crockery and cutlery, alongside the girls' prints and a few from their aunt.'

'It could have been a regular visitor,' countered Martinez. 'Presumably their guests used the bathroom, and if they ate there would be using plates and bowls.'

'The fingerprints were on clean crockery and cutlery in the drawer. Unless the guest also regularly washed up and put things away in the cupboards, I can't see how they would have left their prints behind.' She smiled tightly. 'And who invites a guest over and gets them to wash the rolling pin and chopping board?'

Grimshaw smirked at his friend's discomfort. Martinez was rightly playing devil's advocate, but Gupta wasn't having any of it.

'We also looked in the bathroom. The medicine cabinet has three shelves, one of which is empty and has marks suggesting bottles have been removed. The wire basket hanging over the back of the shower stall also has room for more bottles. It's not exactly a spacious bathroom, and there was a bag with different, half-used shower gels and shampoos tucked next to the loo, with Malina and Biljana's fingerprints on them. Why wouldn't they keep all those bottles to hand in the shower or the cabinet?'

Martinez looked as if he was about to object again but thought better of it.

'And the kicker, we found evidence of a third person's hair in the shower trap.'

She pushed a high-resolution image across the desk. 'At first we though that the hairs belonged to one of the girls, but when we looked under the microscope, you can see that there are three distinct hair types.'

The picture was clear: a blonde hair labelled 'Malina', a dark brown hair labelled, 'Biljana' and another, darker hair, with a thicker shaft, labelled 'unknown'.

'DNA?' asked Warren.

Gupta shook her head, 'No, none of the hairs we've found so far have a follicle, so we've nothing to extract.'

'Then any idea who the prints belong to?' asked Hutchinson.

'Nothing in the database, so they've not previously come to our attention.' She smiled. 'But they do match some prints found in the kitchen area of the massage parlour, and on the handle of the wheelie bin that belongs to the business.'

'Annie,' said Warren and Richardson immediately. The mysterious young woman who only appeared in the background of the sisters' selfies was living with the two sisters.

Chapter 33

'Sir, we've got a witness who saw people coming in and out of the rear of the massage parlour on the day of Stevie Cullen's killing.' David Hutchinson looked excited.

'Where did they turn up?' asked Warren, in surprise. Over a week had passed since the killing. In the days following the murder, Hutchinson and his team had scoured the local area looking for witnesses from that day, as well as looking for evidence and the murder weapon. They had been unsuccessful, and when the CCTV from the rear-facing cameras had been restored, and it had become apparent that the masked intruder was a myth, the search had been wound down.

'He walked in off the street,' said Hutchinson. 'Apparently he's a rough sleeper by the name of Joey McGhee, and he kips down in the rear alley behind the massage parlour.'

'Why has he only just come forward?' asked Warren. 'The murder was a week ago.'

'Well the first thing he mentioned was the reward put up by Crimestoppers.'

'OK, to be fair, that's what the reward is there for,' allowed Warren, trying not to sound disappointed. The rewards were a double-edged sword. On the one hand, they were sometimes the catalyst that could convince a person to come forward with vital evidence, but on the other hand, they increased the number of fantasists and chancers wasting police time. Hutchinson knew all this, but he still sounded excited and he wouldn't have brought it to Warren, unless he thought it had merit.

'We found an empty sleeping bag, and some clothes lying in the alleyway the day of the murder. The CSIs examined it at the scene, to check the killer hadn't tossed the knife in there, and took away the clothes to check if they had been worn by the attacker.'

Warren remembered the detail from the report; nothing of value had been found.

'So, where does our witness come in?' asked Warren.

'He said that he's been sleeping down there for ages; he's found himself a little hidey-hole behind some bins and some bushes. It's out of the way and he reckons that as long as he keeps his head down, he's out of sight of most of the people living and working in the area, and nobody bothers him.

'On the day of the murder, he was in his sleeping bag eating his lunch. He said he knows most of the people who come and go each day by sight, but on that day, there was a lot of fuss around lunchtime, with people coming and going. He reckons he would recognize at least some of them if he saw some pictures.'

'That could be useful,' said Warren, 'but where has he been?'

'Well he says that he was watching all the activity but had no idea anything serious had happened. But when he heard the sound of police sirens, he decided he didn't want to stick around, and went for a walk. When he came back later that evening, he found that the alleyway was all taped off.'

'So, where did he go?'

'Unfortunately, this is the bit the defence team will like,' said Hutchinson. 'He's rather hazy on the exact sequence of events, as he had rather a bit too much cider. He'd lost his sleeping bag and the alleyway was still taped up, so he went for a wander and ended up in a fight. He's spent the last few days in hospital. Now he's out, and he says all of his belongings have gone and his shelter has been dismantled.'

Warren winced. The last thing that the CSIs would have considered was that they'd just dismantled a person's home. Even if McGhee's sleeping bag and belongings had been retained and not thrown away, they would be stored as evidence. The poor man had lost everything.

'Where is he now?' asked Warren.

'Downstairs scoffing biscuits.'

'Well let's hope that he has something useful to say,' said Warren. 'That Crimestoppers reward money should buy him a new sleeping bag at least.'

Joey McGhee was a scrawny-looking man of indeterminate age. His hair was a dark grey colour, and the lower part of his face was covered by a thick, similarly coloured beard. A large sticking plaster covered his right eyebrow, with a smaller one attached to the bridge of his nose. The purple colour of his matching black eyes was fading to green. His bottom lip had scabbed over, where it had been split.

'Looks painful,' observed Warren.

When the man spoke, his Scottish accent had a whistling note from his missing teeth. 'Bastard head-butted me. Never even saw it coming.'

'Thank you for coming in,' said Warren.

'What do I have to do to get my reward? That sleeping bag was right comfortable. Some bloke gave it me, said he'd bought a new one to go climbing. It was much better than the ones they hand out in the shelter. And what about my clothes?' He gestured to the cagoule he was wearing. 'I spent ages finding that coat, now I only have this thing to get me through the winter.'

'I'm really very sorry about what happened to your property.

considerate.'

McGhee acknowledged the apology with a grunt.

Warren felt sorry for the man. He'd spent time with members of the homeless community on a previous case, and he knew how hard their lives were. On paper, there were enough spaces in shelters or emergency accommodation for all of Middlesbury's homeless community, but in reality, the available places were unsuitable for many of those who found themselves on the street. Some didn't feel safe living in such close proximity to complete strangers; others had complex mental health or social problems, such as addictions, that meant they struggled to cope in such a space. For many, sleeping rough was the best option available to them.

Warren wondered what McGhee's story was. It was clear from his appearance that he'd been living on the streets for some time. He seemed reasonably alert and focused, suggesting that he wasn't under the influence of drugs at that moment, and although Warren could smell stale alcohol, it seemed to be from the man's clothing, rather than his breath. However, it was impossible to be sure.

'Why don't you tell me what you saw,' said Warren.

'At first, it was just a normal morning. There's a pretty, dark-haired girl that turns up first; she opens the back gate. Mondays she drags the bins out. Then two little oriental girls turn up. I reckon they get dropped off.'

'Why do you think that?'

'They come up the alleyway from the direction of the road. A white van goes past the mouth of the alley a few seconds later. Happens every morning, so it ain't a coincidence.'

Warren made a note. They hadn't yet found how the nail technicians arrived at work. Was somebody dropping them off?

'Can you describe the van?'

McGhee shrugged. 'Just a van. I only see the side of it. It's white.'

'Do you see where the dark-haired girl comes from?'

'She comes the same way, walking. I can't see if she's being dropped off.'

That would fit with what the team already knew. It was obvious that Silvija Wilson didn't want her illegal workers caught on the reception area's camera. When she drove to work in the morning with her two nieces, she must have dropped Annie around the corner, so that she could go in via the rear entrance.

'What happens then?'

'Well usually, not a lot happens until about lunchtime. I normally do the crosswords in the papers from the day before. Then the dark-haired girl comes back out and walks to the road.'

That agreed with what Wilson had told them in the interview. Annie usually finished her duties by noon. The day of the killing, she'd been working later than usual.

'What about the two oriental women?'

'If I'm around, I see them leave about five o'clock.'

'Do you see how they leave?'

'They walk down the alley again.'

'Do you know if they're picked up?'

McGhee thought for a moment. 'Probably. I've seen that white van go past afterwards a couple of times.'

'So, what was different about last Monday?'

'Well the dark-haired girl and the two little oriental girls arrived about the same time as usual, but I didn't see the dark-haired girl leave at her usual time. Then about lunchtime, the two oriental girls suddenly ran out the gate. They were shitting themselves. They legged it down the alley and down the road.'

'Did you see the van again?' asked Warren.

McGhee shook his head.

'What happened next?'

'Well it all went quiet for a while, and I thought "show's over", so I carried on doing the cryptic crossword in *The Times*.' He scowled. 'I'd nearly finished it when you lot turned up. I should have took it with me.'

'What then?' Warren prompted.

'This middle-aged woman comes running around the corner, all huffing and puffing and legs it in through the back gate. She's in there maybe ten minutes? A bit less? Then she comes out with the dark-haired girl, who's all sobbing and that.'

'Where did they go?'

'Down the alley again, towards the road.' He thought for a second. 'They turned right at the end. The same direction the older woman came in.'

That would have taken them away from the main road, which explained why nobody had seen Silvija Wilson's car parked outside the massage parlour. She was certainly a cool customer, thought Warren.

'Again, I thought, "show's over" and went back to my crossword. Then about ten minutes later, I heard loads of sirens. I figured something was happening and so I decided to take a wander out to the road and take a look-see.' He glared at Warren. 'If I'd have known that you lot were going to tape the alley off, I'd have taken everything with me.'

So far, McGhee had confirmed what they already knew. Nevertheless, he figured he could probably fudge it so that McGhee could claim a reward from Crimestoppers; it was the least they could do, after they took away his clothing and bedding.

'Did you see anything else suspicious that day? Did anyone else come by?'

McGhee frowned in concentration, before snapping his fingers. 'There's a northern bloke that comes by every so often. He arrived that day a couple of minutes after the older woman turned up. He didn't go in the gate, but he spoke to her when she came out with the dark-haired girl, and she handed him something.'

'Did you see what he gave her?'

McGhee thought for a moment. 'It was small and black. Could have been a mobile phone or something.'

Warren felt his pulse rise; Cullen's business phone was still missing.

'What did he say to her?'

McGhee frowned. 'I didn't hear most of it. I was trying not to be seen, you know. I figured something was going down, so I buried myself in my sleeping bag.'

'What did you hear?'

'Something like "just do everything I said, and I'll sort it".'

'What did the woman say?'

McGhee shrugged. 'Dunno, the girl was making a right bloody racket.'

'What happened then?'

'The woman and the girl walked down the alley. The bloke hung around for a moment, then walked off the same way.' He paused. 'It looked like he didn't want to be seen with them.'

Warren felt a stirring of excitement. Silvija Wilson hadn't mentioned meeting anybody else, and it looked as though the man had done his best to avoid being seen on the security camera. If McGhee was correct, the man had been a regular visitor to the massage parlour. Why?

'You said you'd seen the man before. Can you be more specific?'

McGhee looked into space. 'He turns up every few weeks. He never goes in, but the middle-aged woman comes out to speak to him. She usually gives him something.'

'Like what?'

McGhee shrugged. 'An envelope or something. I don't really pay any attention.'

Warren was starting to have his suspicions. Silvija Wilson claimed that both 'Annie' and her illegal nail technicians had simply walked in off the street, and she'd offered them a job, or let them rent a nail station. But what if they weren't self-employed? Could Wilson be paying a middleman?

'Would you be able to describe the man to a police sketch artist?'

'Maybe. I don't really pay that much attention. He usually wears a hoodie, so I can't see his face. I'm not great with English accents, but I know he's a northerner.'

It was certainly worth a go, decided Warren. If the man was some sort of fixer, then if they tracked him down, they might be able to locate the nail technicians. Warren had a feeling that they might be vital witnesses. He wondered if Organized Crime might be able to identify him?

Suddenly, McGhee sat bolt upright, looking over Warren's shoulder at the clock.

'Shit, is that the time? They'll be out of food.'

'Who?'

'The Sikhs. They serve food at this time of night.' He got to his feet. 'I've got to go. If I hurry, there might still be some food left …' He swore again. 'It's curry tonight as well.'

Warren cursed the bad timing. He knew that the Sikh community centre served *langar* to the homeless community every evening. The centre was on the other side of town; McGhee would need to get his skates on, if he was going to make it in time.

'Perhaps I could get you something to eat?' suggested Warren.

McGhee looked away. 'Nah, you're all right. Got to see a mate first.'

It was obvious why he needed to see his 'mate', and it wasn't exactly something Warren could help him with.

'Will you be able to come back tomorrow?' he asked. He desperately needed McGhee to help him identify the mysterious man. 'I'd really like to help you earn that money from Crimestoppers.' Warren hoped that the sweetener would ensure the man returned.

McGhee shrugged. 'Maybe.'

The man's focus was clearly elsewhere now. Warren could hardly blame him. He'd lost pretty much everything; getting a bellyful of food was probably next on his agenda, after scoring his fix.

Warren walked him out of the interview suite and back to reception to sign out.

'What'll you do if there isn't any food left?'

'Dunno. I might be able to beg and get enough money for some chips.'

Warren looked out of the window; he could see the rain pounding the window. A sudden gust of wind picked up a carrier bag and blew it across the car park.

'Where are you staying tonight?'

'I might be able to scrape enough to get into a shelter.' He shrugged. 'If not, I can probably find somewhere to kip down by the arches.' He grunted. 'I could really do with that sleeping bag, right now.'

Warren looked at the man in front of him. He was potentially a vital witness in the case; they really needed to look after him. But more than that, the man was living on the very edge, even more so now that the police had thoughtlessly taken away his shelter. Again, Warren wondered what McGhee's story was. How had he fallen so far? He claimed to regularly do the cryptic crossword in *The Times*, so he was no intellectual slouch. What had gone so wrong in his life?

For a moment, he considered fabricating a charge that would get McGhee a place in a cell for the night. It would be warm, he'd be fed, and the police doctor would come by and at least change his dressings. He dismissed the idea as soon as it occurred. There was too much paperwork that could come back and bite him, and he couldn't ask the duty sergeant to bend the rules that much. Besides, it was increasingly obvious that McGhee needed more than a hot meal.

'Hold on a minute,' he said, as McGhee headed out the door. The man turned in exasperation, clearly desperate to go.

Warren took out his wallet. Tucked amongst the receipts and

shopping lists, he found two ten-pound notes, a twenty and a fiver. He held out the wad of notes.

'Get yourself some food and a bed for the night,' he said.

McGhee looked at the money in surprise, before taking it and shoving it in his pocket.

'I'll see you tomorrow, yeah?' asked Warren.

McGhee nodded. When he spoke, his voice was thick. 'You're all right for a copper.'

Warren wasn't sure how to respond to that, as the man gave a half-wave, and walked through the door.

'You know he'll just spend it on drugs, don't you, Boss?'

Shaun Grimshaw was standing at the edge of the reception area.

Warren shrugged; he didn't have the energy to argue with the man. 'Well, that's just a chance I'll have to take.'

Chapter 34

There was a frisson of excitement in the main briefing room after the interview with Joey McGhee, although Grimshaw seemed to be doing his best to dampen the mood.

'That's the last you'll see of him,' predicted Grimshaw.

Warren disagreed. 'He still needs to claim his reward from Crimestoppers. From his perspective, it's easy money.'

'He could just call it in to the tip line,' countered Grimshaw, 'then it's anonymous. They give him a code and he takes it to the bank.'

'He's already turned up to the station,' said Pymm. 'Why would he suddenly decide he wants to be anonymous?'

Grimshaw shrugged. 'He already walked out of here with a wad of cash.'

'And you don't think he'll want a second bite of the cherry?' said Pymm, barely trying to hide her irritation at her colleague's obtuseness.

'Well we'll just have to see,' said Warren, calling an end to the debate before Pymm and Grimshaw started arguing again; he knew that Grimshaw took a perverse pleasure in winding up his workmate.

'Our priority at the moment is to follow the leads he gave us.

If the two nail technicians were being dropped off each morning, it would explain why we can't find them on public transport. Mags, get your contacts in Traffic to see if we can identify the white van.'

'I'll get on it, but it won't be quick,' she warned. 'There are no ANPR cameras near the massage parlour, so the area we'll be looking at will be huge, especially if we don't know which direction they came from, or the make and model of the van. There are also several builders' merchants and other businesses in that area, so there will be plenty of white vans pottering about the area at that time.'

'McGhee thinks they were dropped off the same time each morning, so you should be able to trim the list to those vehicles that appear at the same time each morning,' suggested Warren. 'Do what you can. See if you can get it prioritized.'

'I'll do my best.'

'And what about this man with a northern accent?' said Warren. 'When McGhee returns tomorrow, I'll try and get a better description from him. If he is a fixer, then Organized Crime might have some intel. They might even have some headshots we can shove under his nose.'

'I'll take that,' said Martinez. 'I know the team in Welwyn.'

'What about the phone that McGhee says he thinks Silvija Wilson handed him?' asked Hutchinson.

'Could it have been Cullen's business phone?' asked Warren.

'We have the location data for the burner phone that we think Cullen was using,' said Pymm, 'and its last location before being turned off was in the massage parlour, shortly after we believe he was killed.'

'I suppose it's too much to hope that the phone has been turned back on,' said Hutchinson.

Pymm shook her head. 'No. Nothing since then.'

'It's probably at the bottom of a river somewhere,' said Grimshaw.

'What about trying to trace Northern Man's phone?' asked

Richardson. 'For him to have arrived so quickly, presumably somebody called him?'

'There are a number of unaccounted-for phone numbers on Silvija Wilson's call logs,' said Pymm.

'Start there then,' said Warren. 'If he was her fixer, then presumably she called him periodically, so focus on numbers that she called on more than one occasion and the window of time between the killing and her leaving.'

'Well that's easy,' said Pymm. 'Almost all the traffic on her phones was between her and her nieces. Off the top of my head, there's only one number unaccounted for in the half-hour after the killing, an unregistered pay-as-you-go. She actually placed Malina on hold briefly to call it.'

'That has to be the one. Raise a warrant for its phone logs, and its records.' Warren pinched his lip. 'And I think we have a good enough case for a real-time intercept. I'll go and see DSI Grayson and see what we can do.'

The excitement level in the room had suddenly changed. In the course of the last few hours, they had not only had the sequence of events on that day confirmed by an independent witness, they also had a new suspect, and potential leads for the two outstanding witnesses.

Warren just hoped that Joey McGhee didn't let them down.

'Silvija Wilson used her credit card twice on the day of the murder,' said Pymm. 'She drew out five hundred quid in cash from a cash machine in the newsagent's at Middlesbury station. She must have been desperate; it's one of those dodgy private ones that charge you two quid to get your own cash out. Plus, the interest payments on cash withdrawals for that card are eye-watering. I'm requesting CCTV from the card machine provider, to check it was her.'

'Wilson admitted to giving Annie some cash. What was the second transaction?' asked Warren.

'It looks as though she bought a train ticket, for £154.45. I'm raising a warrant to get the train operator to release the details of the ticket, but it'll take time, there are so many bloody train companies, nobody's even sure who processed the payment.'

'Great. Any ideas on how else we can work out where she was going?' asked Warren.

Pymm raised an eyebrow, and he apologized. It wasn't her fault. He took a deep breath to calm himself. The mysterious Annie had fled the scene a week ago. If she was an illegal worker, she probably went straight to the airport and flew back to Serbia. A few more hours' delay would hardly matter.

'I looked at the trains that were leaving within an hour of her arriving at the station,' said Pymm. 'In rush hour the train companies might take the piss and charge a hundred and fifty quid for a forty-five-minute train journey to central London but there are so many different permutations, there's no way I can figure out where that fare would have taken her, especially if the ticket was a generic "London Terminals". All the other destinations were to smaller, local stations, so a ticket costing that much would mean she then took a connecting train.' Pymm sighed in frustration. 'Then she could be anywhere.'

'Do we have CCTV yet from the platforms?' asked Warren.

'Mags has a team on it, but we're struggling with resources at the moment.'

Warren was all too aware of the pressures on the video evidence team down in Welwyn; he'd received an email from the head of the unit that morning, with the exact same email forwarded to him again from John Grayson ten minutes later. As usual, there were multiple operations across the region, all with video footage that needed analysing, and Warren was being asked to consider the immediacy of his ongoing requests. Warren was starting to worry that if the case began to lose momentum, his team would find its jobs sliding down the priority list.

Tuesday 10 November

Chapter 35

Dawn was breaking as Karen Hardwick sat in her tiny kitchen, Oliver lying against her chest. The smell of his warm skin mingled with the scent of his freshly laundered Baby-gro. She took a sip of her tea. The letter from the university sat on the table. She cursed herself again for leaving it out in plain sight when her parents had come around the previous day. She hadn't even folded it up, so she couldn't accuse her mother of snooping when she'd read it and then passed it to her father.

They had been hurt that she'd not told them about the interview, and even more distressed when they realized that she must have told Gary's parents where she was going. Karen had had no choice. Gary's parents were her only links to Nottingham and so they had wanted to know why she was leaving Oliver in their care for the day and going into Nottingham dressed in her best suit. She'd downplayed the importance of the visit, but they hadn't been fooled.

Her mother had been upset when she realized that if Karen did accept the studentship, not only would she definitely not be coming back to stay in her grandmother's old flat, she would also be moving even further away from them than she was now.

And then there was the complex range of emotions that the previous day had awakened in her.

Revisiting Middlesbury CID had been hard. The team had moved on; she understood that, but she feared that her return had reopened old wounds. Colleagues that she hadn't seen since the funeral had approached her, although none seemed quite sure what to say. The table in the corner of the canteen where she and Gary had eaten lunch had been taken over by a group of uniformed constables, none of whom she recognized, although of course they all knew who she was; she could tell by the way their conversation became stilted as she walked past. Would that ever change? Would she always be 'poor Karen Hardwick' the woman whose fiancé was killed on duty; who heard every detail of his sudden death as she spoke to him on his mobile phone?

And what about the people she would be working with every day? Even aside from the influx of seconded officers working on their current case, the core team had changed. Pymm and Ruskin appeared really nice, but it seemed strange without Tony Sutton. Warren Jones had become less awkward as the day had worn on, but still the station was filled with memories of her and Gary; his ghost seemed to haunt the office the same way that it haunted the flat.

Yet despite everything, she'd felt the pull of the job again. She'd known little about the case beyond what she'd seen in the papers or on the TV, but she soon found herself being sucked into the drama of the investigation. Live video feeds from the interview suites meant that she had experienced the thrill of watching DCI Jones picking apart Silvija Wilson's story, and her eventual, partial capitulation.

She'd forgotten the surge of adrenalin you experienced when the pieces fell into place; she'd been with Pymm and Richardson when they realized from the photos that 'Annie' had been living with the two sisters.

That was what she loved about policing. Could she give that up?

She needed advice, and she could only think of one person she trusted enough to give it to her. She looked at the clock. It was too early to call now, but as soon as it was a decent hour, she'd pick up the phone.

Across town, Warren was glad to be in the office, where he didn't feel quite so useless. He'd got up early and made both his and Susan's breakfasts and packed lunches for the day, loaded the dishwasher and the washing machine, and tidied the dining room. But he still couldn't do anything to help his poor wife, whose retching in the downstairs toilet could clearly be heard over the sound of the kitchen radio. He didn't envy Susan her morning sickness, but like expectant fathers everywhere he felt guilty that it was a burden borne solely by her.

'The good news is that we received authorization for a real-time interception of what we assume is the unknown northern man's mobile, along with the past twelve months' worth of call logs,' he started the briefing. 'Cell-tower location data is being processed as we speak. The bad news is that the phone has been turned off since shortly after it received a call from Silvija Wilson's business phone on the day of the murder, so we can't use it to track the phone in real-time.'

Although disappointing, few in the room had expected locating Northern Man to be that easy.

'In better news, the phone called Wilson's business phone every couple of weeks, which would fit with the pattern of visits that Joey McGhee claims to have observed. She rarely called him. Furthermore, the phone also called Stevie Cullen's phone.'

The mood in the room shifted immediately.

'This now links Wilson, Cullen and Northern Man together. We will need to figure out just what that relationship is. And in even better news, we know where Annie was going on the train.'

273

'She, or rather Silvija Wilson, bought a one-way ticket to Manchester Piccadilly,' said Rachel Pymm.

'Do you know what route she took?' asked Martinez.

'There are two choices from there. Down to London Kings Cross, take the underground to London Euston, then direct to Manchester Piccadilly.'

'That's assuming that she even went all the way,' said Martinez. 'She could have got cold feet and disappeared into London and ditched her connection.'

'Don't forget all the other stops on the way,' said Grimshaw. 'She could have jumped the barriers at any of those stations and done a runner.'

Pymm clicked her mouse, shifting the display on the main screen. 'That's eleven stations on the way to Kings Cross, and five more from Euston to Manchester Piccadilly.'

'What about the other route?' asked Warren.

'That one's not much better,' said Pymm. 'Five stops to Stevenage, another stop between there and Doncaster, then three more stops to Manchester Piccadilly.'

'Well until we know what route she took, we'll hold off informing British Transport Police. They're not going to be impressed if we ask them to trawl the CCTV footage of all the stations and it turns out she didn't even go through them. Anything back from Mags' team on the CCTV at Middlesbury station?' asked Warren.

'I just sent them the departure times for those trains; that should narrow down the possibilities.'

'Keep us posted.'

Back to waiting.

274

Chapter 36

News that search teams had made a discovery came at lunchtime and was enough to make Warren drop everything and head out to the scene.

Sergeant Hallam Pierson greeted Warren as he pulled up at the side of the road, in a lay-by already crammed with Scenes of Crime vehicles and two vans used to transport the search teams. 'According to cell-tower data from Silvija Wilson's phone, she went for a bit of a drive in the time between dropping off this mysterious Annie character at the train station, and her niece Malina calling her on her personal mobile phone to officially tell her about what had happened at the massage parlour.'

Warren nodded to show he was listening, as he struggled into a protective paper suit.

'The data shows that she stopped moving for about ten minutes at a spot within 200 metres of where we are standing now. Given that she was in a car, and this is a fast road, it was likely that she used this lay-by.'

'Makes sense,' agreed Warren. The road was long and straight. On one side there was farmland, separated from the road by hedgerows. On the other side of the road, the land was undeveloped, natural woodland. The lay-by was the only safe place to pull off the road.

'Ten minutes isn't really long enough for her to dig a hole and bury something, so we've been searching the verges and the wooded area. We found it about a hundred metres from the road.' He looked down at Warren's feet. 'You might want to swap those shoes for some boots, Sir; it's a bit of a mess down there.'

That explained the mud in the footwell of Wilson's Mini, and the filthy pair of shoes they'd found in her house. A comparison with the mud in the woods might be enough to place her at the scene forensically, if needed.

After borrowing a pair of boots, Warren followed Pierson into the trees.

'Ten minutes allows for a maximum travel time of five minutes each way, assuming that she didn't dick about in the lay-by before she set off. If she is at all familiar with the area, and wearing decent shoes, that could be a fair bit of ground to search.'

Warren grunted in acknowledgement, as he pushed away a low-hanging tree branch that was threatening to poke him in the eye.

'Fortunately, she didn't go too far back; she just found a bit of a depression and a bush and hid them here.'

Ahead of them, an area had been demarcated with blue and white police tape. Two white-suited CSIs were squatting down, examining a black bin bag.

'She had the presence of mind to shove some heavy stones inside to stop it being blown around, but it was never going to stay hidden forever. I guess she just hoped that nobody would stumble across it anytime soon. If she'd had any sense, she'd have dumped the bag in with the massive pile of waste some bugger's fly-tipped a quarter of a mile up the road; the chances are it would have been off to the council landfill within a couple of days of it being reported, and nobody would have ever found it.'

Which, given what they knew about Stevie Cullen's illegal business dealings, would have been ironic in the extreme.

'What have you found?' Warren asked one of the technicians.

'We'll have to look at it properly when we get back to the station, but it looks like a black coverall covered in blood and some women's shoes.'

Had they found Annie's work uniform? Presumably the blood would match that of Stevie Cullen, although Warren wasn't going to take that for granted until the tests were done. Hopefully there would also be some trace evidence that could conclusively link it back to either Annie, or perhaps even one of the two sisters. Warren still hadn't ruled out the murder being committed by Biljana, or even Malina, with the mysterious 'Annie' set up to take the fall.

'Is there anything else in the bag?' asked Warren.

'Not as far as I can tell,' responded the technician.

If that was the case, then where had she dumped the murder weapon?

'We know that our mysterious young woman from the massage parlour, Annie, made it all the way to Manchester Piccadilly,' said Warren. He'd just finished relaying the search team's findings to the rest of the group. 'Mags Richardson's team down in the video processing unit in Welwyn, working with Rachel Pymm, determined that she took the 16.48 train, via Stevenage and Doncaster, arriving fifteen minutes late at five to nine. CCTV from Middlesbury, Stevenage, Doncaster and Manchester stations showed that she was wearing the same clothes and carrying the same bag throughout her journey and didn't dump anything in any of the bins at the station. She remained in her seat throughout, only making a single toilet stop on the Stevenage to Doncaster leg of her journey.'

Warren wrinkled his nose. 'You'd never know it from the state of them and the smell, but the train company assures me that the toilets are inspected regularly and there is nowhere she could have ditched the knife. CCTV in the vestibule shows that she didn't throw the knife out of the window.'

'What happened when she got to Manchester?' asked Grimshaw. 'Piccadilly train station is covered in CCTV.'

'That we don't know. We have footage of her walking from the main concourse, past the shops, and down to the taxi rank. Then she keeps on walking left, out onto Fairfield Street, where we eventually lose her.'

'Picked up?' asked Hutchinson.

'Our colleagues in the Greater Manchester Police are kindly processing the ANPR data from the area, to see who was driving around there.'

'What about the bus?'

'The GMP are checking that for us too.'

'What about a cab?' asked Grimshaw. 'She had a wad of cash in her pocket from Silvija Wilson.'

'Possibly, although she walked past the main taxi rank,' said Warren.

'That doesn't mean anything,' opined Martinez. 'There's no shortage of dodgy cab companies around there.'

'I know, my uncle used to run one.' Grimshaw chuckled.

'Why doesn't that surprise me?' said Hutchinson.

Grimshaw stretched his back and gave a big yawn. 'Well if you need someone to pop up there and take a look around, you know who to ask. No rush though, City aren't playing at home again for another week.'

Chapter 37

'I think we can make an educated guess who picked up Annie from Manchester Piccadilly train station,' said Pymm.

She pointed at the list of Silvija Wilson's mobile phone calls.

'She did a lot of phoning around in the hour or so before she took Annie to the train station. This number here is the final one she called. She phoned it at 14.50 for four and a half minutes. She then called it again, ten minutes later. That number then called her back, twelve minutes after Annie arrived in Manchester.'

'So, she was ringing around trying to find someone that Annie could go and stay with,' said Warren. 'This person agreed – probably after some persuasion – to collect her. Silvija then calls again, presumably after checking the time of the next train to Manchester, and then this person calls her back to confirm that Annie has arrived.'

'That's how I would interpret it, Sir.'

'Excellent work, Rachel. Now who does the phone belong to? Please don't tell me it's another unregistered pay-as-you-go.'

'Sorry, Sir. Shall I request the call logs and cell-tower data? Maybe we can work out who it belongs to and where they are staying,' said Pymm.

'Do it,' ordered Warren. 'You could also forward the number

to the GMP and see if they have any ideas. The owner of the phone might already be on their radar.'

'What are we going to do with Wilson?' asked Pymm. 'We're approaching her custody limit again. Do we have enough to charge her, or should we release her?'

Warren had spoken to Wilson earlier. She'd refused to say anything else.

'Let's keep her in, until we've found who she called. I'll ask DSI Grayson to arrange for another extension. We've got enough to charge her with perverting the course of justice, but I want to see if we can get more.'

Picking up his notepad, he headed for his office.

'DCI Jones, there you are.' Janice was uncharacteristically flustered as she scurried towards him. 'I have your wife's school on the phone. They say it's urgent.'

Warren made his way to the hospital in record time. On the way, he tried calling Susan's mobile phone repeatedly, but it kept on ringing out and diverting to voicemail.

Snatching a ticket from the machine, Warren risked scraping the roof of his car on the still-rising barrier, as he drove into the multi-storey car park. Knowing from experience that he could waste ages hunting for a space on the lower levels, he headed straight for the nearly empty roof. Eschewing the elevator, he then took the concrete stairs two at a time, shoulder-barging his way through the heavy wooden fire door on the ground floor. A light drizzle had started, but Warren barely noticed it as he raced across the hospital campus.

Following the signs, he headed towards the nurses' station. He must have introduced himself, as the nurse on duty used his name several times as she explained to him what had happened, but he could no longer process the information that she was imparting.

Despite his lack of comprehension, he continued to nod,

knowing that the sooner she was satisfied, the sooner she'd let him see Susan. Finally, she relented and led him to a small, private room off the main ward.

It didn't matter how little he'd understood of what the nurse had told him, the tears coursing down Susan's face told him everything he needed to know.

Wednesday 11 November

Chapter 38

The hospital had allowed Warren to sleep in a chair beside Susan's bed, although he'd spent most of the night holding her hand whilst staring at the wall.

The extremely patient nurse who'd greeted him when he'd entered the ward repeated everything that she'd told him when he'd first arrived. With what he'd got from the school, and Susan's testimony, Warren eventually pieced together what had happened.

Apparently, Susan had been feeling a little off-colour all day, with a slight temperature and stomach cramps. Nevertheless she'd taught a full day's worth of lessons, and attended a meeting of department heads after school; all of the school's cover supervisors were deployed teaching lessons for colleagues already absent and she didn't want to pull anyone off a free period at such short notice to take her lessons.

It was shortly after that meeting that she'd suddenly been violently sick. After cleaning herself up in the staff bathroom, she'd used the toilet. It was then that she'd noted several spots of blood.

Trying not to panic, she'd gone to the reception desk to ask if somebody could call her a taxi; she still felt sick and didn't trust herself to drive the several miles to the hospital. Despite Susan's protestations, the school receptionist insisted on alerting the school nurse, who was listening to Susan still downplaying the event even as she fainted. Given Susan's condition, the nurse decided to call for an ambulance and phone Warren.

By the time somebody tracked down Warren and he arrived. at the hospital, the consultant had confirmed their worst fears. They were unable to detect a pulse for either baby. This early in the pregnancy, an emergency delivery was out of the question, and so with the aid of drugs, nature was helped on its way.

By late morning, Warren and Susan were no longer expectant parents.

Despite the traumatic events of the previous twelve hours and the slight bump on the head she'd received when she'd fainted, Susan was pronounced fit to go home by midday. The loss of a pregnancy this early on was sadly not an unusual event, the consultant had gently explained to them. Given the couple's years of IVF attempts, they would run tests to see if a cause for the unexpected termination could be found, but as far as she could tell, Susan was fit and healthy. She recommended a few days' rest to get over the shock and handed over some leaflets for charities that helped bereaved parents deal with their loss.

The journey home was tense. Warren knew his wife well enough to know that against all logic and medical opinion, she would be blaming herself. She'd done exactly the same when their early attempts at IVF had failed. He knew that they would need to discuss it, to bring their emotions to the fore, but he didn't know how to start the conversation.

After pulling up outside their house, Warren walked around the car to open the passenger door, but Susan was already out. He knew precisely how things would unfold over the next few days: Susan would act as though nothing major had happened. She'd quote statistics about how common early miscarriages are and would point out that the shock to her body was not nearly as devastating as it seemed. A couple of days off to get over the turmoil, and then it was time to go back to work. In short, she was fine, and she would rather everyone stopped making a fuss.

Nevertheless, she allowed herself to be led into the living room. Warren knew that she wouldn't contemplate going to bed at such an early hour. She turned on the TV, whilst Warren headed into the kitchen. There was nothing else he could do but boil the kettle and wait for Susan to come to him when she was ready.

Out of habit, he opened his email on his phone, but closed it again almost immediately. He couldn't face the case with everything going through his head at the moment. He'd spoken to John Grayson late the previous night, telling him that Susan was unwell, and the DSI had stepped in to keep things running smoothly for the next few days. The man had many faults, but he would drop everything to support one of his officers having personal problems.

The rattle of the letter box and the flat thwack of letters on the doormat signalled the arrival of the post.

Warren padded to the door and picked up the pile of papers, leafing through them as he returned to the kitchen. A letter from Lloyds Bank exhorting him to apply for a loan he didn't need, an envelope addressed 'to the occupier' inviting him to sign up to a new broadband provider, and the offer of a free evaluation from an estate agent made their way straight into the recycle bin.

The final envelope was pale blue, its size and shape suggesting a greeting card. Too early for Christmas or either of their birthdays – he turned it over. Addressed to both of them, the familiar spidery handwriting made his heart clench.

How were they going to tell Granddad Jack what had happened?

Thursday 12 November

Chapter 39

Warren couldn't remember a day when he had less wanted to go to work. All he desired was to curl up in bed beside his wife and tell her everything was going to be all right. And one day it would be, of that he was certain. But it certainly didn't feel like it today.

In the end it was Susan who had insisted that he go to work. She was taking the rest of the week off, but physically, she was mostly OK. Today she just wanted some time to herself. Warren resolved to keep his mobile handy; he would leave at a moment's notice if she called. He hoped he was doing the right thing.

John Grayson had taken the hint and not enquired too much about the reasons for Warren's sudden escape two days earlier, or his absence the previous day, but had made it clear that Warren could come and find him at any time.

Whilst Warren was gone, the case had continued to progress, with support from Bergen and the SOC unit, but there had been no significant breakthroughs. The Foreign Office had spoken to Malina and Biljana Dragi 's parents and confirmed that they didn't have any other sisters, or indeed any close relatives that matched Annie's description. That at least seemed to rule out one motive for their willingness to face trial to protect her.

For her part, Silvija Wilson had declined to say anything else.

She refused to admit that Annie had been living with her nieces, and they too denied that she had stayed with them. Warren suspected Wilson's solicitor had told her to keep quiet and wait out the custody clock. With no new evidence that Wilson had played a more active role in the death of Stevie Cullen, she had been charged with perverting the course of justice and released on bail, on condition that she didn't contact her nieces. Grayson had arranged for a real-time intercept on both her mobile phones, and her landline, so if she did try and contact anyone, they'd know about it. His request for a surveillance team had been denied outright, but a block had been placed on her passport. Warren doubted she was a flight-risk; it was clear to him that she wouldn't leave her two nieces to face the music alone.

'They've had the metal detectors out, scouring the area where the bloody work clothes were found, but it's looking less and less likely that she disposed of the knife in the same place.' David Hutchinson sounded frustrated down the phone line.

Warren shared his disappointment. A good defence might be able to cast doubt on who was wearing the blood-covered overall at the time of Cullen's murder, particularly if the three young women shared each other's uniforms. To Warren's eye, the three women were close enough in build that they might do so.

However, fingerprints or other trace evidence on the knife, linking it to one of them, would be harder to argue in court.

Hanging up, Warren chewed the end of his pen, as he worked through the sequence of events in the days following the killing. At some point, that knife had to have been disposed of.

Had Annie taken it all the way up to Manchester with her? Surely not. They had to assume that she might be stopped by the police, in which case the last thing she'd want is the murder weapon on her.

Forensics had finished searching the massage parlour and the sisters' flat, and there was no sign of it. Similarly, Silvija Wilson's house had been searched, with the same result. The problem was that there had been a significant delay between day of the murder, and the arrest of the masseuses and their aunt. That potentially left the three women ample time to dispose of the knife.

Warren pulled over his notepad, trying to order his thoughts. Whilst there had been plenty of time to dispose of the weapon, his gut was telling him that it had been got rid of quickly. Wilson had dumped the bloody clothes as soon as she could. Surely, hiding the murder weapon was an even more pressing concern?

The two sisters had been escorted from the massage parlour immediately after the police had arrived, and whilst the exact details of what happened during the unaccounted-for minutes between the killing and the police attending were still unresolved, it was obvious that neither woman had left the premises.

Then there were the two nail technicians. It seemed unlikely that they were involved, given the speed with which they left the scene of the murder. They were obviously terrified, and Warren couldn't imagine them being persuaded to take the murder weapon with them.

Which left Silvija Wilson, and the mysterious northern-accented man that Joey McGhee had seen arriving minutes after the killing.

McGhee claimed to have seen Wilson hand him something after he arrived, and heard him promise to sort things out. Could that object have been the knife? McGhee thought it was probably a mobile phone, and that would certainly account for Cullen's missing work phone. Could she have passed him the knife also?

It seemed unlikely. They knew that Silvija Wilson had left with a bin bag containing the bloodstained work clothes to dispose of. She was already incriminated in that respect. Would this mysterious northern fixer have been willing to take the murder weapon? If he had any common sense at all, he'd have steered well clear of it. Unless he and Wilson had a relationship that went beyond the professional, then it was hard to imagine Northern Man taking the knife off her.

Which meant it all led back to Wilson.

The mobile phone tracking data for both of her phones showed that she went directly from the massage parlour to her nieces' flat. The search teams were confident that the weapon wasn't at the sisters' home. The route went straight through the busiest part of town. Could she have discarded it in a waste bin along the way? The data showed that the car only stopped for the briefest of moments at traffic lights. Even if Annie had jumped out, the contents of all the litterbins along that route had been seized by the search teams. Somebody could have returned at a later date and moved the knife, he supposed, but it seemed a bit elaborate, especially given the amateur way in which the bloody clothes had been disposed of.

Wilson then stayed at her nieces' flat, presumably helping Annie pack and arranging for her to leave Middlesbury. It seemed that whatever personal items Annie had been unable to take with her to Manchester had been dumped alongside her bloody uniform. The phones then travelled to the train station. The same argument about a lack of opportunity to discard the knife en route applied here also.

Which meant that Wilson, if she still had the knife, most likely got rid of it on her drive to the area where she had dumped the clothes.

Warren traced the route that the phones took with his finger. A crude calculation of the car's average speed showed that it was travelling a little below the speed limit. Did that figure show that she was travelling slowly, perhaps not to attract attention, or whilst she scoped out likely spots to dump her incriminating packages? Or did the low average speed mask a brief stop as she threw the knife out of the window?

Teams were scouring the verges, looking for a bladed implement that could have killed Cullen.

Warren continued to trace the route with his finger, before pausing, an idea starting to form. He couldn't believe he hadn't thought of it before.

He switched to Google Earth; the map replaced with an overhead satellite shot. Changing the display to Street View, he traced the path the Google imaging vehicle had travelled.

Hutchinson answered his phone on the second ring.

'I know where she dumped the knife,' said Warren. 'According to the phone location data, she stopped for several minutes at a turning circle, before heading back along the road she had just travelled, taking a detour past her father-in-law's care home to firm up her alibi. We assumed that she was just waiting for the call from Malina to her personal phone, pretending to tell her about the killing, before she headed back to the care home to firm up her alibi. But she received the call from Malina *after* she left the turning circle. She was at that circle for ages.'

'We have a team up there searching, but no sign of it yet. Besides, there's nowhere to dump the phone within the radius of the phone location data.'

'She didn't have her phone with her,' said Warren. 'We know it was paired to her car's Bluetooth hands-free kit. She must have left it in her vehicle. I've just looked at Google Earth and it looks as though there's an overgrown footpath that cuts through the treeline, about three hundred yards from where she stopped. That's outside the radius of the phone's location data. Looking at Street View, it doesn't look as though it's easily visible from the road, but if she was familiar with the area, which she probably is, since her father-in-law's care home is along that road, she might know about it.'

'Shit.'

'Send a team down the footpath, and start searching,' Warren ordered. 'I'll get onto DSI Grayson and get him to authorize an underwater search team. That footpath leads right down to the river Herrot.'

Chapter 40

It had been three days since Joey McGhee, the rough sleeper who had been living in the alleyway behind the massage parlour, had given his interview. He hadn't been seen since.

'I've spoken to the rough sleeper unit, and they know Joey, but he hasn't been spotted in any of his usual haunts for the past few days,' said Ruskin. 'I also took a wander down to the Sikh Community Centre to see if he attended *langar* the night he left here. They can't remember seeing him that evening and reckon that if he left as late as you said he did, he probably didn't make it in time.'

'Damn, that's frustrating,' said Bergen. 'I'll bet that this Northern Man joker is buried somewhere in our files. I was going to get McGhee to do an e-fit and run it through our system.'

Warren frowned in concern. Joey McGhee was their only confirmed sighting of the man that they were calling Northern Man. If he was right about what he saw, the man could be a key player in Stevie Cullen's murder. He might also lead them to the missing nail technicians, potential witnesses to the stabbing.

Warren knew that members of the homeless community often led disordered, chaotic lives, but McGhee had been organized enough to turn up at the station to offer information. It seemed strange that he wouldn't follow up on his deal, especially when there was potentially a substantial reward.

Another thought struck Warren. What if McGhee had been lying? Giving the police some fabricated evidence, in the hope that they paid him? He could then have got cold feet.

Yet he had given them details that matched what they had already seen on the CCTV footage. Had he then embellished his story to make it more attractive?

If Joey McGhee had disappeared, or had been lying, then a promising lead had just gone up in smoke.

'The cell-tower data is in for the phone that we think Silvija Wilson called to arrange the pick-up of Annie,' said Pymm, squinting at the screen. 'The phone spends most of its time in a suburb of Manchester called "Chorlton". Wasn't there a kids' TV program called that?'

'Chorlton and the Wheelies,' supplied Warren.

'The phone travelled to within a few hundred metres of Piccadilly train station, arriving just before Annie's train was due to arrive. It then sat there, for about twenty-five minutes because her train was late, before moving off a little over five minutes after Annie was spotted walking along the concourse. The phone then returned to its starting place.'

'Lucky he or she didn't get a ticket,' said Grimshaw, who'd wandered over, eating a packet of cheesy Doritos; Pymm wrinkled her nose at the smell. 'The buggers are really cracking down on parking around there,' he continued.

Martinez joined him, biting into an apple.

'What do you two know about Chorlton?' asked Warren.

'It's a nice area, with some quite posh houses,' said Grimshaw.

'There are some really good restaurants and pubs,' added Martinez.

'So not a den of criminality, then?' asked Warren.

'Not really, you'd have to go to where Shaun was brought up for that.'

Grimshaw shrugged. 'Don't knock it, there might have been drug dealers and pimps hanging around near the school, but at least we didn't have any Man United players as next-door neighbours.'

Martinez rolled his eyes. 'One player, and he moved out of his mum and dad's house when he got signed.'

'I'll bet the house prices shot up when he left,' said Grimshaw.

'When you two have finished ...' said Warren.

Pymm had opened Google Maps on one of her screens, switching to satellite view. 'Most of the houses in that area are large and detached, with big gardens. I think we can narrow the phone's usual location down to a single property, or at least their neighbours either side. Number 42 is the most likely candidate.'

Grimshaw let out a low whistle. 'Somebody is doing all right for themselves.'

The red location icon was hovering over a large house, surrounded by generous gardens. At the time the photograph had been taken, the driveway had three cars parked on it, with enough room for at least another two. Even from above, it was clear from the image that the house probably had at least four generous-sized bedrooms.

'See if you can find out who owns the house, and if the occupants are in our system. Look at the neighbours either side as well in case the resolution of the cell-tower data is poor,' said Warren.

Pymm opened another browser window, navigating to a website listing the electoral records. She entered the address and postcode for number 42.

'No need to look at the neighbours,' she said when the results popped up.

'I'll contact Greater Manchester Police,' said Warren, 'and get them to raid the house. There's no way that's a coincidence. Let's just hope she hasn't already left the country.'

The call from Greater Manchester Police came through to Warren's desk later that afternoon.

'Smooth as a baby's bottom,' Warren's opposite number, DCI Omara, said. 'We have Mr Aleksej and Mrs Zorana Dragi sitting in custody as we speak, along with a young woman, who currently only answers to "Annie".'

'Fantastic work,' said Warren.

'Nothing to it – they were sitting in front of the TV when we rang the doorbell.'

'Have they said anything, yet?'

'Not a lot. Mr and Mrs Dragi speak perfect English and are clearly very pissed off at being dragged into this affair by Mr Dragi 's cousin, Silvija. Annie speaks good enough English to say "no comment", but refuses to say another word.' Omara cleared his throat. 'You'll have to decide what to do with them sooner rather than later, DCI Jones; we can't hold them indefinitely.'

Warren smiled at the none-too-subtle hint. GMP had done them a big favour, picking up the suspects, but the three individuals would each require a solicitor, not to mention space in a cell. The sooner Hertfordshire Constabulary took them off the hands of their northern colleagues the better.

'I'll send a team up to fetch them back here,' he promised.

DSI Grayson agreed with Warren's suggestion that a little local knowledge wouldn't hurt, and happily authorized the cost of sending Shaun Grimshaw and Jorge Martinez up to Manchester that evening, with the aim of questioning the three suspects, and then returning Annie to Middlesbury the following day.

Warren suspected that he also fancied getting rid of the

Brownnose Brothers for a bit. With the date of their Inspector exams fast approaching, the two men had been competing harder than ever to look good in front of their Superintendent.

Warren had spoken to Silvija Wilson already, telling her that they had Annie in custody. The news had placed the woman in a very difficult position. After speaking to her solicitor, she had given a carefully worded statement admitting that she had lied about not knowing where Annie had travelled to, and that she had arranged her travel plans. Nevertheless, she had insisted that her cousin, Aleksej, and his wife Zorana, knew nothing about the identity of Annie, or her role in the murder in the massage parlour.

For their part, the Dragi s had maintained since their arrest that the call from Wilson had been entirely unexpected. They claimed that Wilson had made no mention of why she wanted somebody to offer a bed to help out a young Serbian woman who had suddenly decided to move to Manchester for a fresh start. They had both refused to comment when asked about why they thought Annie needed Silvija's assistance, or what their thoughts were when the news broke about the stabbing at Wilson's massage parlour.

Warren had instructed Grimshaw and Martinez to question them when they arrived to pick up Annie, but with little evidence of their active collusion, he expected them to be bailed pending further inquiries.

Grimshaw had been delighted at the prospect of a brief, over-night trip to Manchester, and had urged Martinez to hurry up, so they'd have time for a few pints after interviewing the Dragi s that night.

As the two of them made their way to the car park, Grimshaw could be heard excitedly telling Martinez how much he was looking forward to supper from the best fish and chip shop in the country.

'What's a "barm cake"?' asked Pymm when the two men had left.

'What you call a bread roll in these parts,' said Bergen.

'And "Manchester caviar"?' asked Ruskin.

'Mushy peas, I think,' answered Hutchinson.

'And you'd have that with gravy as well?' said Ruskin.

'I wouldn't, but it sounds like Shaun would,' said Bergen.

'The Canadians put cheese curds and gravy on their chips,' piped up Pymm, 'and yes, it's as bad as it sounds.'

'Give me a chip batch and a scallop any day,' said Warren.

'I didn't think you liked seafood,' said Richardson.

'And what's a "batch"?' asked Ruskin.

'It's the proper name for a bread roll, and in Coventry, a scallop is a slice of potato, covered in batter and then deep-fried,' replied Warren.

The Scotsman thought about it for a moment. 'To be fair, that's not the strangest thing I've heard of being deep-fried.'

Friday 13 November

Chapter 41

Grimshaw and Martinez arrived back at Middlesbury at lunchtime, with 'Annie' in tow. The two officers had made an effort to interview Silvija Wilson's cousin and his wife up in Manchester, but they had stuck to the same story; that they had known nothing about Annie before receiving a phone call from Wilson begging for a favour. They were bailed pending further inquiries.

Annie still refused to comment. A local translator had ensured that she was fully aware of what was happening to her, and so the following morning she was bundled into the back of a police car, handcuffed to a female police officer. Jorge Martinez had then driven the car back to Middlesbury. It would have made more sense for Grimshaw and Martinez to split the driving between them, but Grimshaw's reddened eyes suggested that he'd been as good as his word and found at least one pub serving a decent pint, and might not be fit to drive. A green stain on his left leg implied he'd also found a decent chip shop that served mushy peas. For his part, Martinez was dressed in a clean, freshly pressed shirt and trousers, his suit jacket looking as smart as the day before.

As Annie was booked in, the two officers reported to Warren, who was fighting sleep after spending the night awake. Susan had still been in her pyjamas when he'd arrived home the previous evening; something that she only ever did when feeling really ill. The deep shadows under her eyes that morning as he'd got ready for work testified to her own lack of rest.

He forced his attention back to Grimshaw and Martinez, ignoring the acid burn in his gut from too much coffee.

'I had hoped that the drive home would loosen her tongue a bit,' said Grimshaw, 'but nothing's doing. She's really tearful, but we can't get anything out of her. She's clearly terrified. Hell, she even seemed nervous of Jorge – must be the aftershave.'

Martinez ignored his friend. Unlike Grimshaw, who seemed to have enjoyed a taxpayer-subsidized road trip back to the North West, Martinez was frustrated to have been away from the action.

'Have the two girls said anything, now that they know we've arrested Annie?' he asked.

Warren shook his head.

'I haven't told them yet. I figured I'd wait to see what Annie said first. Now that they've been charged, they've been moved to remand at the Mount Prison.'

'We should try and play them off against each other. I reckon the younger one is most likely to crack first,' said Grimshaw.

'Let's not forget the aunt,' said Hutchinson. 'She's been changing her story left, right and centre, every time we pick a new hole in it. I'd say that Annie is a pretty big hole.'

Warren pinched his bottom lip thoughtfully. The three young women were being held separately, to minimize contact between them. Nevertheless, there was a limit to how long that could last in the overcrowded prison system. So far, Wilson had kept her head down, and had wisely decided not to phone her cousin.

'Right, we'll speak to Biljana and Malina first, see what they have to say for themselves. If Silvija Wilson is correct, her nieces are protecting this Annie, for whatever reason. Now that we have her in custody, we might be able to persuade them that there's no point doing so. If they are guilty and Annie was a witness, we

306

may be able to persuade them to cooperate. We can imply that Annie is singing like the proverbial bird, and that they don't want to be caught in a lie.'

'What about Silvija Wilson?' asked Richardson.

'We'll bring her in and speak to her afterwards. As Hutch has said, she's been changing her story repeatedly. It's clear that her loyalties lie first and foremost with her nieces. I don't know who this Annie is, but I suspect that if push comes to shove, Wilson will throw her under the bus to protect her family.'

The woman known only as Annie looked small and frightened, as she sat opposite Mags Richardson in interview suite two. Warren watched the interview on the live feed.

According to Martinez and Grimshaw, she'd been scared and unwilling to talk on her journey back from Manchester. Warren wondered if a sympathetic female officer might have more luck. Beside her, an older woman acted as translator. Warren hoped that she too, alongside the female duty solicitor, might have a calming influence.

It wasn't to be.

The woman answered 'No comment' to every question put to her, including her name. The custody sergeant had been forced in the end to list her as 'Annie', with no other biographical details.

Warren had faced more than his fair share of obstinate, unco-operative suspects, but this was different. The woman was clearly petrified.

And whatever she was frightened of, it was clearly worse than the prospect of life in prison for murder.

They would have to hope that their other interviewees were more fruitful.

'Well that was a waste of bloody time,' opined Moray Ruskin, as he and Warren drove away from the Mount Prison.

The two men had just spent a fruitless two hours trying to

persuade Silvija Wilson's two nieces to open up and admit to what had really happened the day of Stevie Cullen's murder. So far Friday the 13th had brought nothing but bad luck.

Warren had been hopeful at first. Both women had looked shocked, and then resigned when he told them that they had Annie in custody. Unfortunately, both of them requested the opportunity to speak to their solicitor, and both had returned and made no further comment.

'Bloody lawyers,' said Ruskin. 'I'll bet they were told to keep their gobs shut until they knew for certain that Annie or their aunt had spilled the beans.'

'What the hell happened in that room? And why are they keeping quiet? They must realize how much trouble they are in,' hissed Warren. The question was rhetorical, but Ruskin tried to answer it, regardless.

'As far as we can tell, there were five people present at the time of the murder, aside from Cullen. I reckon we can rule out the two nail technicians; I can't see Wilson or the sisters protecting them to the point that they could go to prison.'

Warren agreed; it seemed unlikely.

'Which leaves the two sisters and Annie,' said Ruskin. 'From what we can tell from the security footage, Malina was responding to a disturbance happening in the back room. Does that mean that Cullen was being killed by Biljana or Annie and she went in after the fact, or was she involved in the killing herself? Is she covering for the other two girls, or did she take part?'

'Maybe we need to be asking who would protect whom? And why did they send Annie away?' said Warren.

'The way I see it, there are two reasons to send Annie away,' said Ruskin. 'Either she was a witness, and they wanted her gone before she could be interviewed, or she was responsible and they were helping her to escape.'

'So, who is she then?' asked Warren again. 'If their plan worked, she would have got away scot free, leaving the sisters to carry the can. Why would they – and their aunt for that matter – do that?'

'If their plan worked, we'd still be looking for some mysterious man in a hoodie,' said Ruskin.

'That's true,' admitted Warren, 'but as soon as we started picking that story apart, you'd expect them to ditch it and either come up with a new one or tell us what really happened.'

'Unless, one or both of the sisters were involved in the killing. Then their best bet would be to say nothing, for fear of implicating themselves or their sister. I'll bet they made a pact to keep their mouth shut.'

'Unfortunately for them, they didn't plan what to do if we found Annie,' said Warren. 'That's thrown a real spanner in the works.'

'They also didn't count on their aunt blinking first and starting to change her story,' said Ruskin.

'I think the weak link is Wilson,' said Warren. He hoped that she would break today's run of bad luck.

Silvija Wilson looked exhausted. Warren doubted that she'd slept very much over the past few days. He hoped that the stress of the situation would be enough to make her talk.

'We have arrested Annie. She's in our custody. We've also recovered a black bag containing a bloodstained uniform. We'll be performing forensic tests to see who was wearing that uniform.'

Wilson deflated. She clearly hadn't wanted to risk calling her cousin now that she knew that her calls were being monitored. The news was obviously an unwelcome surprise.

'It's time to tell us what really happened, Silvija,' said Warren, his tone gentle. 'You aren't helping your nieces now. And they aren't helping themselves.'

Wilson's eyes were filled with tears.

'At the moment, all we know is that at some point, Stevie Cullen was murdered in the back room of your massage parlour. You claim that this Annie was responsible for his death, but you won't tell us who she is or what she means to you. If you and your nieces are lying to protect her, you need to tell us why.'

The tears were now trickling down Wilson's cheeks.

'Your two nieces won't tell us what really happened. Either they still think they can hide what happened that day, or they are hiding their own involvement. Regardless, as it stands, they have both been charged with murder. If they really had nothing to do with it, then you need to tell us everything you know. If I can go in there and tell them what I think really happened, then they can start cooperating and dig themselves out of the mess they've got themselves into.'

Wilson closed her eyes. The tissue that she had been using to dab away her tears was screwed up into a tight ball.

Warren said nothing; it was up to Wilson now.

Moments passed before finally, Wilson let out a shuddering breath. 'No comment.'

'We've got it!' David Hutchinson sounded elated. 'A six-inch hunting knife, wrapped in a black bag, with flecks of what appears to be blood on the blade. It wasn't even in the water. There's a stone wall between the end of the footpath and the river. She must have completely duffed throwing it into the river and either not realized, or not been able to climb over the wall and have another go. Even better, the area is covered in footprints, including ones that look suspiciously like they might match the shoes that Silvija Wilson was wearing that day.'

'Brilliant news,' said Warren. Modern forensic techniques were sensitive enough to retrieve trace evidence from even the most compromised crime scenes or suspect objects, but days immersed in water would test even the most skilled technicians. Warren looked forward to reading the report from the lab. Could this be the breakthrough they needed to finally determine what had happened that day? Perhaps Friday the 13th hadn't been a complete disaster after all.

Saturday 14 November

Chapter 42

'We think we've found the white van that dropped off the two nail technicians at the massage parlour,' said Mags Richardson. The former traffic officer had been pushing the video analysis unit in Welwyn hard for days, and it was a relief to finally have something to show for it. Warren and Grayson had been fielding an increasing number of requests to justify the amount of resources they were expending, and a positive finding vindicated them to some extent.

She called up a still image from a video on her tablet's screen.

'This was taken on a traffic camera a little over a mile from the massage parlour. There isn't a lot of detail, but we have the licence plate number.'

'Are we sure that it's definitely the van?' asked Martinez. 'You said yourself that the camera coverage in that area is patchy and covers a large area. A mile is a long distance.'

'Reasonably confident,' hedged Richardson. 'It's true that there is a lot of traffic in that area, but when we narrowed it down to white vans that appeared regularly each day at about the time that the parlour opens for business, and returned at the close of business, the number was surprisingly few. Joey McGhee said that it was a van, not a minibus, so we were able to discount a fair number of hits – besides, it seems unlikely that our nail technicians were hitching a lift with the Middlesbury Over-Fifties Ring and Ride service.'

'Who is the vehicle registered to?' asked Warren.

'That's where it gets tricky,' admitted Richardson. 'The registered keeper has been dead for years. It looks as though the van was sold on privately after his death, and the details never updated on the DVLA database. The new owners are still using the original owner's details for insurance and tax purposes and using dodgy backstreet garages for its MOT. DVLA process so many registrations every day, as long as the paperwork looks about right, they just rubber-stamp it. If the van doesn't get pulled over or done for speeding, or unpaid parking, nobody will ever realize it's dodgy.'

'There's a builders' merchants near there,' pointed out Martinez. 'I'll bet there are plenty of dodgy vans driving around the area.'

'You're probably right, Jorge, but it's a hell of a coincidence,' said Warren. 'Good work, Mags. Any idea how you can track down the new owner?'

'I've got some ideas,' said Richardson. 'Now we know the van's plate number, we're working backwards to see if we can figure out the van's regular route. If it stops at the same places each day, we might be able to get a team down there asking questions. If we're really lucky, we might even be able to intercept the van as it does its rounds.'

'That's a good idea,' said Warren, 'although we don't want to spook them.'

'I'll speak directly to Ian Bergen in SOC,' offered Martinez. 'I'm sure he'll help us out. The van might already be on their system. For operational reasons, they don't always make intelligence on ongoing operations freely available on the PNC or HOLMES.'

'That should speed things up.'

'Unfortunately, there is no useful pattern yet in the location

314

data for the phone that Silvija Wilson called that day, and which we believe belongs to Northern Man,' said Pymm.

The room groaned.

'The phone is typically turned off more than it is turned on and is only active during the daytime. When it is turned on, it is moving around constantly. At no point is the phone ever stationary for more than an hour or two in the same location.'

'Sounds as though they know exactly what they're doing,' said Hutchinson.

The man was right. Tracking where a phone spent lengthy periods of time could be used to identify a suspect's regular haunts, such as their place of work. Long periods overnight in the same place might indicate where the suspect lived.

That the suspect apparently knew this suggested a worrying degree of sophistication.

'We're sharing what we have with Organized Crime, to see if any of the locations that the phone lingered in flags anything, but as you know, that channel of communication isn't always two-way.' A ripple of frustrated agreement went around the room.

As the team trudged out of the room to start their day, Warren overheard Grimshaw muttering to Martinez. 'Better hope that down-and-out that the boss has been chatting up comes through, or this one's dead in the water.'

Warren suspected that he might be right.

The report back from the forensics lab on the knife found discarded by the river Herrot came in early evening.

'The knife was definitely the murder weapon,' said Harrison. The CSI had already emailed his report to Warren, along with photographs, but he always liked to speak in person, and had called immediately after sending the report.

'The blade had been cleaned, but there were enough traces of blood at the join where the blade meets the handle for us to do a fast-track DNA match to Stevie Cullen. The dimensions of the blade are also consistent with the wounds inflicted on the victim, including the nick to his rib.'

Warren could hear a 'but' hanging in the air. He could guess what the man was going to say next.

'However, the handle had also been cleaned. There were no prints or other trace evidence that could tell us who used the knife.'

Warren sighed. 'I suppose that would have been too easy.'

'However, we lifted some prints from the black bag it was wrapped in, and they match Silvija Wilson.'

Along with the footprints found near the dumping site, it confirmed that Silvija Wilson had been the person to dispose of the weapon, but it still didn't tell them who had wielded it and killed Cullen.

'Is there anything useful you can tell us about the knife itself?'

'Yes and no. It has a six-inch, non-serrated blade with a distinctive, olive wood handle, about two inches shorter than the blade. It's a high-quality product and well used. Olive wood is very durable, but there are some old scratches. The blade is sharp and well cared for; it's been sharpened regularly. I'd say the owner was proud of it. The bad news is that it's mass-produced and sold throughout continental Europe, but not in the UK.'

Warren pondered what Harrison had told him. If the knife was unavailable in the UK, that might indicate that it had belonged to one of the two sisters or to Annie, but it was hardly conclusive.

After thanking Harrison, he hung up.

If the murder weapon had been brought to the scene, rather than simply being the nearest weapon to hand, that raised all sorts of questions surrounding motive or premeditation. They really needed to find out who the knife belonged to, and some independent witnesses to corroborate the series of events that day.

316

Sunday 15 November

Chapter 43

Sunday mornings in the middle of a murder investigation are like any other morning of the week. Nevertheless, Warren had decided that he could afford to head to the office a bit later. Susan had taken the rest of the week off work, but he knew that she hadn't slept any better than him, tossing and turning until well-past midnight. She was now slumbering quietly beside him.

He looked at his phone. No voicemails or emails had come in overnight. The display showed half-past seven. Despite Susan's lack of rest, he knew she would be awake soon.

Moving quietly, he slipped on his slippers and dressing gown and padded softly downstairs.

A look in the fridge revealed eggs that needed using and some fresh apple juice. There was some nice sourdough bread in the bread bin.

The smell of scrambled eggs on toast and the aroma of fresh coffee was enough to bring Susan downstairs. As she slipped her arms around his waist and kissed the back of his neck, it was almost as if the past few weeks hadn't happened, and Warren allowed himself to relax.

'I assume you are going to ruin those lovely eggs with Worcestershire sauce?' she teased.

'Of course. Would you like some on yours?'

She turned up her nose. 'I married a barbarian.'

Warren smiled. He said the same thing about her when she smothered toast in Marmite.

Plating up, he sat down opposite Susan. He knew it couldn't last, but for the next couple of hours he just wanted to pretend it was a normal Sunday morning. To pretend that neither he nor Susan had any work to do that day and had no plans beyond where to go for lunch and how to spend the afternoon. To pretend that they hadn't just lost the babies. The contented look on Susan's face as she spread butter on her toast and poured them both a glass of juice gave Warren hope for the future.

Or at least the next few hours.

He'd eaten only two mouthfuls of eggs and taken only a sip of coffee when his phone rang.

They both froze.

It rang a second time.

Warren shovelled another forkful of eggs into his mouth.

The phone diverted to voicemail. Neither of them said anything.

Warren took a slurp of coffee and cut into his toast, sawing hard against the sourdough's springy texture.

The phone rang again.

Susan reached across the table and touched his hand. 'Answer it.'

'They left a voicemail,' he mumbled as he chewed.

Susan squeezed his hand. 'It's Sunday morning. You know they wouldn't be calling unless it's urgent.'

He sighed and picked up the handset. 'Jones.'

The caller chose to ignore his curt tone. 'A body has been found. Farley Woods.'

Farley Woods was a densely forested area stretching for a couple of miles along the edge of the A506, forming a natural barrier between the busy trunk road and the farmland beyond. By the time Warren arrived at the lay-by near to where the body had been found, one of the two carriageways had been cordoned off to make space for the police vehicles. An articulated lorry with Polish licence plates was parked up, its rear doors open to show that there was no cargo worth stealing as the driver slept in his cab overnight. A small, red Citroen sat in front of it.

'The body's been there a while,' said the officer who'd been first on the scene.

'Who found it?'

'Two walkers. They said they were geocaching, whatever that is.' She pointed towards a couple in their forties holding the lead of a medium-sized, orangey-brown dog with white markings on its face. Warren had no idea of its breed.

'What about the lorry driver?'

She shook her head. 'He was asleep in his cab when he heard the walkers come running out of the woods.'

'Is the scene secured?'

She looked at her clipboard. 'A Detective Sergeant Grimshaw took charge. He's taping it off now. Scenes of Crime are about ten minutes out.'

Thanking her, Warren walked towards the couple, introducing himself.

'We were looking for a cache,' said the husband, who introduced himself as Steven Spencer, an IT worker from Cardiff on a weekend away with his wife, Tina. The couple were dressed in thick, outdoor clothes, making the bright blue nylon forensic booties they wore appear even more incongruous. Their hiking boots had already been taken for forensic analysis.

'I'm not sure what you mean,' admitted Warren.

'We were geocaching,' said his wife. 'It's a bit like orienteering. People leave boxes in hidden places and post the GPS co-ordinates online for others to find. It's very popular,' she said in response to Warren's slightly bemused expression.

'You travelled from Cardiff to Hertfordshire to find a box. What's in it?'

'Well nothing, really. Just a logbook. You write your name on it, and the time you found it, then put it back for others to find. Then you record that you found it online.'

'Oh.' Warren still wasn't entirely sure what it meant, or if it was relevant to the investigation.

'We like walking to keep fit,' explained the husband. 'We were visiting some old university friends in Middlesbury and whilst they were sleeping off their hangovers, we decided to get some fresh air. We saw that there was a cache nearby, and figured it was as good a reason as any to get out of the house. We offered to take their dog, Keji, for a walk.'

'OK. Well did you find the box?'

'No. According to the GPS, it's a kilometre further into the woods.'

'Take me through what happened.'

The husband pointed toward the red Citroen. 'We used the GPS to find the nearest lay-by. We parked up in front of the lorry, then got out and headed into the woods through that gap in the tree-line.'

'What time was this?'

'About seven a.m.'

Warren was impressed. His occasional get-togethers with his university friends rarely saw anyone surface before mid-morning, and that was usually to hunt down a full-English in a local café.

'We hadn't gone very far,' continued his wife, 'when Keji started barking and then raced off deeper into the trees. We tried calling him back, but he wasn't paying any attention, so we went after him.'

'We couldn't face the awkward conversation if we lost him,' said her husband; despite the attempt at humour his eyes were bleak. He placed his arm around his wife's shoulders, as he took over the story.

'He disappeared so we just followed the sound of his barking, until suddenly he stopped and started whining. I was worried that he'd hurt himself, so I started to run …' He took a deep breath. 'Keji was circling this old tree with a big patch of bushes and brambles at the base. He's a Toller, a sort of gundog, so I figured he'd found a dead bird or something.'

After a short pause, he continued. 'Anyway, I stuck my head into there … the smell … I saw some clothes … blood …' He stopped talking and put his hand over his mouth at the memory.

His wife took over. 'It was obvious what it was, so we grabbed Keji, went back to the roadside and called the police.'

'Did you touch anything?'

The husband shook his head. 'No, and I told Tina to stay back.' He paused. 'I may have caught my sleeve on some brambles.'

'We'll need to take some samples from your coat to eliminate it,' said Warren.

The man nodded numbly, already unzipping it.

'Did Keji go into the bushes? Do you know if he disturbed the scene at all?'

'I don't think so, although I admit I lost sight of him for a bit.'

'Would you be able to contact your friends and get permission for one of my team to take a clipping of his fur, just in case?'

'I'm sure they'll be happy.' His wife spoke up. 'It's not like he hasn't got plenty to spare.' As if he knew that he was being spoken about, Keji's ears pricked up.

Warren thanked them both and arranged for them to be taken away by the officer in charge of the scene.

Repressing a sigh, he trudged back to his car to retrieve his paper suit and murder bag. This far from Welwyn, Warren and his team at Middlesbury would be expected to at least start any investigation into the circumstances surrounding the death. But they had enough on their plate already with the Cullen murder. He looked forward to passing it over to a different team to bring to completion.

Until that happened though, DSI Grayson – and thus by extension Warren – was *de facto* Senior Investigating Officer and he needed to make sure everything was done properly.

'I reckon it's been there for weeks or months,' said Grimshaw. 'It's pretty decomposed, and there's lots of growth around it.'

Like Warren, he was dressed in a paper suit. Upon arriving at the scene he'd done everything correctly. Access to the body was limited; nevertheless he'd arranged for the scene to be taped off in a rough circle a couple of hundred metres in diameter, lest other early morning walkers found themselves trampling through the area in search of Tupperware boxes.

However, that seemed unlikely. The muddy trail that the Spencers had followed was overgrown and almost non-existent in places; it didn't look as though many people had been there recently.

Ordinarily, Warren would be worried about the scene being compromised by too many officers. Despite their best efforts, anyone entering or leaving a crime scene runs the risk of removing valuable trace evidence or inadvertently introducing contamination from outside. Ideally, metal walkways would be installed and a clear path to and from the site would be established to minimize the risk of footprints and other impressions being obliterated.

Not only was that impractical in such an area, if what Grimshaw said about the age of the body was true, then any such evidence was long gone. The paper suits they wore were designed not to introduce foreign fibres, and the facemasks and hairnets stopped them shedding hair.

Grimshaw was right about the age of the body. Much of it had rotted away, or been eaten by scavengers, with bones poking through what little flesh remained. It was impossible to tell if the body was male or female. The scene would need to be subjected to rigorous investigation, but Warren's practised eye noted the brambles that had grown through holes in the body's clothing.

A forensic botanist might be able to use that to help narrow down how long the body had been lying there.

Grimshaw pointed towards the corpse's left leg. The dark blue jeans were stained a dark colour.

'I reckon that's blood. Lots of it.'

'It looks that way,' Warren agreed. He stood back slightly. In addition to the jeans, the body was wearing a dirty white T-shirt. Warren couldn't make out the logo. The corpse's left foot wore a dark, battered training shoe. As did the corpse's right foot, although that foot was no longer attached to the bottom of the right leg and was sitting a short distance away.

The corpse was slumped against the base of the tree, its arms partly around it, as if hugging it. Had it been a slow death? Had the victim held on to the tree for comfort as they bled out?

If that was so, how had they ended up in the middle of a dense patch of shrubs? And what had caused such a significant injury?

There were a dozen tragic, but innocent scenarios that could explain how this person had found themselves in such a predicament, but Warren's gut had that familiar tightening. He looked over at Grimshaw, and saw the same thoughts mirrored in the man's eyes above his facemask.

'I'm declaring it a suspicious death,' said Warren.

Monday 16 November

Chapter 44

The previous night had been the coldest of the year so far. The air had been heavy with the smell of de-icer, as Warren and his next-door neighbour scraped the frost off their cars.

Warren hadn't seen his gloves since the previous winter and could barely feel his fingers as he drove into work. The journey was almost over by the time the hot air blowers finally stopped blasting ice-cold air into the car and started to do their job properly. His thoughts turned to the whereabouts of Joey McGhee. It had always been a long shot, hoping that the man would return, and Warren was resigned to the fact that a potential lead had vanished. He knew from previous experience that some members of Middlesbury's homeless community were often happier living under the radar, and that despite the best efforts of outreach workers could be almost impossible to track down if they really didn't want to be found.

He was surprised though. McGhee had actually approached the police directly, and although he was clearly prepared to sleep rough when necessary, he was engaging with the support workers. On top of that, he had yet to claim his reward money from Crimestoppers. The forty-five pounds that Warren had given him wouldn't last long, and it seemed strange that he hadn't returned to earn more money. No tips had been received via the anonymous helpline, suggesting that he hadn't decided to earn the money that way.

Parking up, he saw Ruskin's bicycle in the bike rack, and knew he would be showering downstairs. After he and Mags Richardson had both managed personal bests in the local half-marathon the previous spring, the man was now training for a triathlon. Where he found the time to train, work so much overtime, and organize a wedding was a mystery to Warren. Did he ever sleep?

The briefing room was standing room only, with Warren's Middlesbury-based team outnumbered more than two-to-one by seconded officers from Welwyn. Warren recognized many of the faces from previous investigations, but a substantial number of the junior officers were new to him. He'd decided to place Shaun Grimshaw and Jorge Martinez in charge of dividing the visiting detectives into smaller work groups headed by his own, Middlesbury-based team. It was the sort of job that they would be expected to do as inspectors.

The meeting started with some positive news from Rachel Pymm. 'The knife that was used to kill Stevie Cullen belonged to the victim.'

She projected an image of the weapon recovered from the riverbank. Beneath it, a second image was recognisably the same knife.

'Stevie Cullen was arrested for driving without a licence or insurance two years ago. The arresting officers searched his vehicle and found this knife in the boot. They photographed it as a matter of routine, but since it was in the boot and hadn't been identified as used in any crime, it was returned to him.'

'Why would he have had it on the day of his murder?' asked Hutchinson.

'Forensics have examined the blade and the handle, and they think it was a working knife. His best friend, Benny Masterson, claims that Stevie brought it back from France years ago after a family holiday and rarely went anywhere without it. He used it all the time when he was on the farm. He shouldn't have been carrying it in a public place but as we know, the Cullens weren't really ones for following the rules.'

'If Stevie Cullen was killed with his own knife, then maybe Silvija Wilson is right, and it was self-defence?' said Pymm.

Warren pinched his bottom lip.

Unfortunately, it wasn't enough on its own to exonerate Annie. An initial extension to custody had been granted already, and the time was soon approaching that she would have to be charged with murder or released. He would check with the Crown Prosecution Service, but it was obvious that as things stood, she met the threshold for charging.

'Moving on, many of you may have heard that the decision has been made for us NOT to hand over the investigation of yesterday's find in Farley Woods to a different team,' said Warren.

He raised his voice above the chorus of groans, and muttering. 'The reasons for that will hopefully become clear in a moment, and it isn't because the powers-that-be think we have too much free time on our hands.'

There had been numerous finds overnight by the forensic teams out the in woods, and arrangements had been made for the body to be transported to the Lister Hospital in Stevenage for a post-mortem later that day. A new discovery had made the examination of the body the pathologist's number-one priority.

'Cause of death won't be fully determined until the PM has been completed, but an *in-situ* examination of the body reveals that the injury to the victim's left leg appears to have been caused by a shotgun,' revealed Warren. The announcement was news to many of the team who had only just started their shift.

'Any progress on identification?' asked a DS from Welwyn.

'Not yet, though the victim has been provisionally identified as an adult male. Fingerprints are unlikely, due to the decomposition of the body, but DNA should be possible, and the jaw is intact, so dental records are an option. The body hasn't been moved yet, so we haven't been able to check all of his pockets, although the uppermost pocket doesn't appear to contain a wallet.'

Warren switched the image on the wall projector to one of the corpse. It was clear that the elements had not been kind. Lying with its right-hand side against the tree, much of the exposed soft flesh had either decomposed or been eaten. A cap of what appeared to be dark brown hair partly covered the exposed skull.

'Is that a logo on the T-shirt?' asked Moray Ruskin. 'I don't recognize it.'

'We'll get clearer photos when the pathologist removes the clothing during the PM, but from this angle it appears to be foreign,' said Warren.

'The badge on those trainers doesn't look British, either,' somebody from the back commented, 'although it's hard to tell these days, with all the budget brands now available on the high street. I did some work a few months ago on a case that required shoe identification. I'd be happy to take a look.'

'Thank you. I'll leave that to you, DC?'

'Marshall, Sir.'

Warren highlighted the body's left leg. 'It looks as though the victim was not shot where he was found. As soon as it's light, a team will be looking to see if they can find any blood residue to track back to where he was originally injured, but even in the past few weeks there has been plenty of rain. If we're lucky we might find more pellets, or even a cartridge casing.'

Warren flicked to another image, this time of a pair of what appeared to be garden secateurs lying next to the body.

'These secateurs were found next to the body. We won't know for sure until Forensics have finished analysing them, but we are currently operating under the assumption that the victim accessed the woods from the direction of the nearby farmland, rather than the road.'

He flicked to the next slide, showing a plastic-coated mesh fence, with a hole snipped into it large enough for a person to squeeze through.

'This fence acts as a barrier between the woodland, and a field owned by Ray Dorridge, a local farmer who was seen arguing with Stevie Cullen shortly before his death. We had all but eliminated him from that inquiry, but this is too big a coincidence to ignore. A possible link between this unexplained death and Mr Cullen is why we are currently investigating the two deaths in parallel.'

Warren switched to a close-up of the jagged hole.

'The cutting blade on the secateurs showed evidence of regular sharpening, so probably could have cut the fence if enough force was applied. Forensics have found a number of different fibres on the fence edges, which we will be seeking to match to the clothing on the body. They have also found what appear to be traces of blood; they'll be testing the samples to see if it is human, and if so, whether it matches our victim.'

The next photograph was taken from a slightly different angle.

'There is also what appears to be some animal fur caught on some of the bottom strands. It's probably from local wildlife traipsing through the gap in the fence, but again, we've sent it off for testing.'

'Any ideas yet how long the body has been lying there?' asked Hutchinson.

'Too early to say, but as you can see it's significantly decomposed. We're getting entomologists in to collect insect samples, and we're waiting for a botanist to assess if the local flora can give us some indication how long the body has lain there.

'The main priority in the meantime is to revisit our old friend Mr Dorridge. Two hours ago, an extended search warrant was executed to search his entire property again, including his fields, outbuildings and any vehicles. He has a licence for two shotguns, both of which have been seized, and we'll be looking for anything else that might link him to the killing of Stevie Cullen. I'm still not entirely convinced that he wasn't involved in some way. He's currently downstairs awaiting his lawyer. I can't wait to hear what he has to say for himself.'

Chapter 45

Ray Dorridge sat across the table from Warren yet again. The harsh fluorescent lighting highlighted the man's lack of sleep, although to be fair, the face that had stared back at Warren that morning as he shaved hadn't looked much better. At least his hair had less grey.

Dorridge looked nervous. He said nothing as his solicitor read a short statement.

'My client wishes to make it categorically clear, yet again, that he had nothing to do with the death of Mr Stevie Cullen. So far, the evidence that the police have against Mr Dorridge is entirely circumstantial. Unfortunately, the late Mr Cullen was a very unpopular man, and there are many who might harbour a motive to kill him. My client has agreed, voluntarily, to questioning to clear this matter up, once and for all.'

'Thank you, Mr Dorridge, your cooperation is appreciated,' said Warren, 'however, we are not here to discuss the death of Mr Cullen. Rather, we would like you to help us with another matter.'

Dorridge nodded, warily.

'I believe that your land backs onto Farley Woods?'

Dorridge squirmed in his seat. 'Yes, although it's public land. I don't ever go into it; there's a perimeter fence.'

'I'm sure you are aware that there is significant police activity going on there at the moment.'

'I fail to see the relevance,' interrupted the solicitor again. 'Mr Dorridge's property is separated from that land, which if memory serves, is fully accessible to the general public. I fail to see the link between Mr Dorridge and whatever you are currently investigating.'

Warren opened the folder again and took out a photograph. 'Are you aware that a large hole has been cut in the fence between the woods and your field?'

'No. I haven't been down there since the summer. I'm not due to start planting down there for weeks.'

'Have you been in Farley Woods recently?'

'No. Like I said, it's not my land.'

'So, you don't know anything about the dead body found there yesterday? A dead body that may have accessed the land via the hole cut in your fence?'

Dorridge went white. 'I need a bathroom break.'

They'd deliberately held back on announcing the discovery of the body to the public until they could interview Dorridge again. He'd been shocked at the revelation of the discovery, but it was unclear if that reaction was because he knew nothing about the body, or because the crime had been uncovered.

'Do we have anything more from Scenes of Crime?' asked Warren.

'Nothing much yet. The soil samples will take a while to process for blood, so we won't know where he was shot for a while,' said Pymm. 'A search team with metal detectors is looking for more pellets, or discarded cartridges, but it's slow going. They have his guns, so we can check for a match if we find anything.'

At the moment, Dorridge was the single point of contact between both murders, a coincidence too big to ignore. His fate would likely be determined by the outcomes of the search warrant and the forensic analysis of the body and the area surrounding its discovery, but that would take time.

'Well let's just hit him with what we know so far, and see if he gives us anything else,' said Warren.

'OK, Mr Dorridge, let's turn to the body found at the edge of your property.'

Some of the colour had returned to the farmer's cheeks, although his eyes still appeared hollow.

'The body found in the *publicly accessible woodland* at the edge of his property,' reminded the solicitor.

'We believe that the victim accessed the wooded area from a hole in your fence. What can you tell us about that?'

Warren was gambling now. Forensics hadn't yet confirmed that the victim and the hole cut in the fence were related, but the presence near the body of a pair of sharpened secateurs, capable of cutting such a hole, certainly pointed that way.

'I don't know anything about a body in the woods,' said Dorridge.

'The body has been there for some time, as has the hole cut in the fence. Can you remember anything unusual happening down there?'

'No, nothing.'

Dorridge was sitting with his left leg crossed over his right. Warren glanced down at his foot. It was twitching, but not dancing as violently as it had in previous interviews when he'd been lying.

'When was the last time you went down that field?'

'Back in the summer, when the fruit was ready to pick. I haven't been back since.'

'What fruit were you picking?'

'Gooseberries.'

'And when did you pick them?'

'End of June, beginning of July – I can't remember exactly. I pick them before they fully ripen, so that they have more pectin for the jam manufacturers.'

'And you didn't see a hole in your fence then?'

Dorridge frowned in concentration. 'I didn't notice a hole in the middle of June, when I went down to check if the gooseberries were ripe enough to pick.'

If what Dorridge was saying was true, then that meant the victim had been killed after that time. But when?

Then there was the question about whether Dorridge was actually complicit in the killing. The victim had been shot with a shotgun, of which he owned two. Would ballistic analysis be able to provide a match?

And if they did, what was his motive? Could he have found the victim trespassing on his fields? It seemed a rather extreme reaction, particularly if the victim was already running away, into the woods. Forensics were looking for any blood traces on Dorridge's side of the fence, although Warren wasn't expecting anything. Months had obviously passed since the shooting; the likelihood of any blood being found was slim on such exposed ground. They might find something in the forest, but again, his hopes weren't high.

And then there was Stevie Cullen. Dorridge was the sole link so far between both murders. Warren couldn't dismiss that.

For the time being, Dorridge had to remain on the suspect board.

'Interview suspended.'

Warren only had enough time to drink a quick coffee and force down a sandwich, before his next interview. He went through the strategy Grayson had outlined. He'd considered passing the interview over to someone else, but he was desperate to meet the suspect himself, and the clock was ticking. Within reason, Grayson was happy to let Warren do things his way, even if it was unusual for such a senior officer to get so involved.

The young woman known only as Annie looked even more exhausted than Silvija Wilson. At first glance, she bore more than

338

a passing resemblance to Biljana, with short, dark hair and a slim build. It was now obvious that she'd been visible at least once on the reception CCTV footage, but the team had mistaken her for Biljana from behind. Mags Richardson's team were going back over the CCTV footage from the massage parlour's reception area to see if they had made any more misidentifications and whether this affected their timeline of events. Annie was unquestionably the young woman appearing in the background of the two sisters' social media posts.

Up close, however, she was several years older than they'd thought. Her nose had also been broken on at least one occasion, and one of her front teeth was chipped. Her left eyebrow was demarked by a small scar.

If what Silvija Wilson had told Warren was true, and the woman sat before him had been acting in self-defence, then she was worthy of his sympathy. However, they only had Wilson's word about events that she hadn't personally witnessed. On top of that, the woman's story had changed so many times, anything she said had to be taken with a generous pinch of salt.

But Warren's gut was telling him that they were getting closer to the truth. He just needed Annie to tell him her version of events.

'Annie, can you look at me?' said Warren, his voice gentle. He hoped that even if Annie was relying on the translator for the meaning of his words, she would pick up on his tone.

She looked up slowly. Her eyes were swollen from crying, the tip of her nose reddened.

'Silvija has told us what she thinks happened that day, but we need you to explain your side of it.'

Annie shook her head. 'No comment,' she mumbled.

Warren tried again. 'Biljana and Malina are in a lot of trouble. They need you to help them.'

Annie frowned, and looked over at the translator, obviously confused.

'It's true, Annie,' said Warren. 'Biljana and Malina have refused to tell us what happened. They then lied about a man dressed in black climbing through the window and committing the murder.'

Annie said nothing.

'The problem is that we have no evidence that they weren't involved. All we know is that the three of you were in that massage parlour when Stevie Cullen was killed.'

Warren leant forward, catching Annie's eyes. 'What Silvija has told us isn't enough. She wasn't there. We've had to charge them with his murder.'

Annie gasped, speaking for the first time. Even without the immediate translation, it was obvious what she had said. 'No. They had nothing to do with it.'

'Well they are prepared to go to court and perhaps even prison,' said Warren. 'They refuse to admit that you were even there.'

Annie was shaking her head. 'No. That's not fair; they didn't kill him.'

'Then who did kill him, Annie?' Warren repeated, his tone firm. 'Unless you can give me another suspect, then they are going to go to prison for you.' Warren's voice softened again. 'They are prepared to sacrifice everything for you. Can you let them do that?'

Tears coursed down Annie's cheeks. 'No. They didn't do it. Neither of them did it.'

'Then who was it, Annie? There was nobody else there. The nail technicians had already left. There were no other customers, and we know that the man in black doesn't exist. That only leaves one person.'

When she spoke, her voice was a sob, but it was clear enough for the translator. 'I did it. I killed him.'

Chapter 46

Unfortunately, Annie's unexpected revelation had not opened the floodgates. Quite the opposite. After dissolving in tears again, she eventually composed herself enough to continue answering 'no comment'.

After an increasingly frustrating thirty minutes, Warren had eventually admitted defeat, and sent her back to her cell whilst they awaited the CPS to authorize charging. With his afternoon suddenly free again, he decided to take a trip to the Lister hospital to meet with Professor Jordan.

The post-mortem on the adult body found in Farley Woods had been performed as a priority case. Even a liberal application of Vicks VapoRub on his top lip failed to fully disguise the smell of decomposition, although Warren admitted that the odour might be psychological. He'd only managed a light lunch, and had resisted the urge to have a snack, but his stomach still made an ominous gurgling noise.

'The deceased is definitely male,' said Jordan. 'I'd say in his late twenties. Approximately 185 centimetres tall, but significantly underweight. Unfortunately, exposure to the elements and scavengers has made gross examination of his internal organs of limited use.'

The body had been laid out on a steel table. With the clothing removed, Warren could see the full extent of the body's decomposition.

'I'll need to run more tests to rule out other causes, but at the moment I'd say he bled to death from a shotgun wound to his left thigh.'

Jordan pointed to the remains of the leg. The remaining flesh was peppered with several black pellets.

'One of the pellets looks to have nicked the femoral artery. The kneecap is also dislocated, although I would suggest that is more likely to be due to the body falling awkwardly.'

'Before or after he was shot?' asked Warren.

'Impossible to say, although the joint is swollen, suggesting that there was a significant delay between the injury and the cessation of the heart pumping. The damage to the artery is relatively minor – if the bullet had entered a few millimetres to the left, it would have missed it entirely, so the exsanguination took some time.'

'Long enough for him to crawl away from the location he was shot?'

'Possibly.'

Warren eyed the man's hands. He didn't even need to ask if fingerprints were possible. The skin on the remaining digits had all but disappeared. His stomach gurgled again at the sight of obvious bite marks.

'Any clues about ethnicity?'

'I'd say white, Caucasian, although the skin discoloration makes that tentative. His hair is a dark brown, and there is some of his beard left, although a lot is missing.' Jordan's tone was grim. 'Doubtless a search of any local nests or burrows will find more of it. I've taken samples for DNA analysis, and dental X-rays, so if he's in the system we may get a hit.'

'Have you had a look at what he was wearing?'

Jordan nodded, leading Warren over to a paper-covered table where the man's clothing had been neatly laid out.

Under the bright, fluorescent lighting, the man's trousers appeared to be dark blue jeans.

'The label shows the inside leg to be 31 inches, which is consistent with the man's height. But the waist is 34 inches. Even with the state of the body, I can see that's several inches too wide. Either he lost a lot of weight since buying them, or the trousers didn't originally belong to him. I'd suggest weight loss.'

Jordan lifted a battered, black leather belt. 'It looks as though at least two more holes have been made in the belt to make it tighter.'

He returned to the jeans. 'Aside from the significant staining from the blood, and the mud, I'd say that the jeans were already very dirty when the victim was shot.' He pointed to a black mark on the right knee. 'That looks like engine oil to me.' He pointed at another, white stain. 'And that looks like paint.'

'I'll get them analysed,' said Warren.

'The T-shirt also hasn't seen the inside of a washing machine in a very long while.'

Up close the once-white material was stained and grimy. The neck and the cuffs were both heavily frayed.

'I'd say the staining on the inside is probably sweat. It's not just grubby, it's filthy. It's what I'd expect to see from someone who has been living rough for some time with no access to washing facilities.'

Could the mysterious man have been homeless? Living in the woods? In that case, how had he been shot? And why was he only wearing a thin T-shirt? In Warren's experience, homeless people tended to wear most of their clothes regardless of the weather; they couldn't exactly hang them up in a wardrobe.

Warren recalled the observation from the briefing. 'I don't recognize that logo,' he said, peering closer at the T-shirt's chest.

'It looks as though it might be foreign. Is there a label inside?'

'Yes, although it's a fairly standard multi-language European wash label. It's a UK extra-large. Again, a couple of sizes bigger than I'd expect someone of his build to wear.'

Forensics would be taking the clothes away for further analysis, but Warren snapped a picture of the logo and the label on his phone so he could start someone looking on the clothing databases to identify where it came from. Jordan obligingly turned the jeans over, so Warren could photograph the size label and leather tag on the rear waistband. Again, it looked unfamiliar, although the raised lettering had been worn down to almost nothing from rubbing against the belt.

'There are some seeds and what looks like small fibres stuck to the turn-ups. I'll recommend that Forensics use sticky tape on the surfaces and see what they find. If they are different to the plant species near to where he was found, they might provide a clue to where he was before he died.'

'What about the pockets?'

'Empty as far as I can tell. I'll leave the trace evidence team to poke around inside for anything small, but there was no wallet, phone or keys, coins, notes or even scraps of paper that I could see.'

That was also unusual. Even homeless people tended to accumulate pocket litter over time: receipts, bus tickets and tissues were a ubiquitous part of daily life. Had the man's pockets been emptied?

'What about underwear?'

'Filthy again.' Jordan held up a pair of stained, black briefs. 'Be glad of your facemask; they're pretty ripe. Urine stains at the front, faecal stains at the rear. He could have urinated as he died, but I see no evidence that he defecated. Judging from the state of the rest of the clothing, and the obvious age of the underwear, I'd say the victim had worn these for weeks or even longer.'

344

There was no obvious logo on the underwear, and again, Jordan held them aloft as Warren photographed the care label.

'Let's have a look at the footwear,' he suggested.

'Socks are unbranded and very well worn.' Jordan pointed to two holes in a white sports sock. He flipped one over and showed Warren a badly repaired hole on the heel.

'Who darns their socks these days?' asked Warren.

'Not homeless people,' said Jordan, 'far easier to pick up a new pair from a clothing bank. For that matter, why would the victim keep the same clothes for so long? You can get clean, second-hand clothes from homeless shelters or churches, no questions asked.'

Remembering the offer from DC Marshall at briefing, Warren took photographs of the black trainers from several angles, including inside the shoe. Up close, it was clear that the footwear was also very well worn; with the tattered rubber soles peeling away from the uppers. The laces were frayed at the end, the aglets missing. There appeared to be the remains of a pattern on the insole, but Warren couldn't get a clear picture. He'd ask Forensics to dismantle the shoe and photograph it under different light sources to see if it could provide any clues.

Finishing up, Warren thanked Jordan, before removing his protective clothing. He'd deliberately worn old clothes, but as he left the morgue and headed back to his car, he felt as though he carried the stink of death with him. He'd have to shower when he got back to the station and change into his spare suit.

Warren finally made it back to Middlesbury late afternoon. As he entered the office, Moray Ruskin got up to greet him, his face grave.

'A call just came in a couple of minutes ago. They've found Joey McGhee. It's not good.'

The main train line between London and Cambridge ran through Middlesbury. The express service could deliver commuters to the centre of London in as little as forty-five minutes at peak time.

To the south of the town, the line was raised up on a viaduct to pass over the river Herrot. It was underneath the arches that held the tracks aloft that the body of Joey McGhee was found by a cyclist. Looking at the way the cyclist was dressed, and the way that Ruskin was admiring the man's bicycle, Warren wondered if the two of them were training for the same event.

'Looks like an overdose,' said CSM Gupta, as she clambered up the embankment to greet Warren and Ruskin. 'He was pronounced dead at the scene. I haven't had a chance to look at him properly, but he's surrounded by drug paraphernalia.'

Over her shoulder, Warren could see a bright red sleeping bag. He hoped that the man had at least been warm.

'How was he found?'

'Apparently, he was pretty much blocking the towpath. The cyclist had to dismount to go around him. He said it isn't unusual for there to be rough sleepers down here, but they are usually tucked against the wall out of the way. The man's a medical student, and he said that something didn't feel quite right, so he had a look-see. That's when he called it in.'

Warren felt deflated. McGhee had been a potential witness. He cursed himself for not trying harder to keep him at the station the evening he'd shown up. But what could he have done? McGhee had been determined to leave. Even if Warren had managed to find him a warm place in a cell and plate of hot food, he knew that McGhee would probably have turned it down. He'd clearly been wanting more than just a hot meal, and he wouldn't have been able to do what he wanted in a police station.

He also felt a sense of guilt. It looked as though Grimshaw had been right. How much of the forty-five pounds he had given the man had he injected?

Tuesday 17 November

Chapter 47

Warren's day hadn't started well. His first duty had been to drive down to Welwyn to deliver a press conference about the body found in Farley Woods. It had been a depressing affair. It seemed that the press had jumped to the same conclusions as Warren's team, and assumed it was a homeless person: sad, but never mind, these things happened. Warren knew that news of the death of Joey McGhee would be similarly received when it was announced.

The decision to hold back that the cause of death was likely to be a shotgun wound had been deliberate. They didn't want to give too much away at this stage. Ironically, the inclusion of that titbit would likely have pulled in more journalists – gun crime in the UK, particularly outside major cities, still being rare enough to cause excitement.

With no images of the deceased available, or even a ballpark figure for when he died, the only concrete information that they had been able to include in the press pack had been photographs of the foreign-branded T-shirt and trainers. Depending on what other news happened that day, Warren suspected that the best they could hope for was a few seconds on the local TV news and radio, and perhaps an inside page in the *Middlesbury Reporter*. Hopefully, the website would at least show the pictures.

Warren's day didn't get much better after he returned to the office.

'I'll need to get the blood tox results back, obviously, but I'm prepared to go out on a limb and say that it was almost certainly an overdose. Heroin by the looks of it.' Ryan Jordan was on the phone to Warren.

The post-mortem had been performed first thing that morning, at Warren's request. Aside from some cracked ribs and facial bruising consistent with the injuries sustained in the fight that had landed Joey McGhee in hospital the day of Cullen's killing, there were no signs of a violent struggle, or other obvious cause of death. His stomach contained the barely digested remains of chips and a battered sausage. At least he'd had a hot meal.

'Any indication of when he died?'

'Difficult to say as always, but decomposition had started. Given the cold weather, I'd have to put it at more than twenty-four hours before he was found.'

Warren thought about that. The cyclist who'd found the body hadn't cycled that route for a few days before his discovery, so the body could have lain undisturbed for some time. Could he have been there since the night that he'd attended the station? Since the night that Warren had given him the money that he'd probably used to buy the drugs?

He asked Jordan.

'It's possible.'

Warren felt sick. Could he have been responsible – indirectly at least – for the man's death? Warren was all too aware of the ongoing debate about the pros and cons of giving homeless people money, rather than other support. Some said that giving money to a person who might well be suffering addictions was potentially dangerous and irresponsible, no matter how well intentioned. Others said that such an attitude infantilised such people, taking away their right to self-determination. Warren was on the fence. There were times when he'd given money to beggars, whilst other times he'd scurried past, head down. He and Susan gave money to the local homeless shelter at Christmas, and he'd helped organize the office's collection for the local food bank. He'd made a donation to the Phoenix Centre after his dealings with them the previous spring, but was that enough?

Money in the hand would give a homeless person independence, allowing them to make some small choices about how they lived their lives – something that homeless people were often unable to do. But once he'd handed over that money, did the responsibility for what that money was used for transfer solely to the recipient, or did he remain morally culpable for any outcomes? He just didn't know.

Jordan continued, unaware of Warren's turmoil. 'There is something that doesn't quite sit right with me, though.'

The man's voice pulled Warren's attention back to the matter in hand. 'Go on.'

'I've emailed you a picture of the inside of the man's arm.'

Warren opened it up.

The crook of the man's elbow was covered in scars and old track marks. The median cubital vein in the centre had been used this time, a spot of dark red blood showing where the needle had been inserted.

'Zoom in on it,' instructed Jordan.

Warren followed his instruction. 'There are two marks. Was that his regular injection site?'

'Yes, but it looks as though he injected himself twice in quick succession.'

'Twice? Could that be why he overdosed?'

'Quite probably. There also appear to be two strap marks on his bicep, as if the tourniquet was loosened, then reapplied.'

'Is that normal? Maybe the first dose didn't quite hit the spot, and he decided he needed some more?' said Warren.

'That's what I'm not sure about. The thing is, even if the first dose wasn't enough to satisfy him, it would probably still have knocked him senseless. He'd have had to come around, then prepare a fresh batch of heroin and reload a fresh needle. The needle he was found with was single-use. It then looks as though he reinjected himself at almost exactly the same site.'

'There was only one needle found at the scene,' said Warren, 'although he could have chucked it in the river, I suppose.'

Warren thought about what Jordan had told him. The sequence of events, although unusual, weren't impossible. Maybe the heroin was poor quality, and McGhee had decided to give himself a second dose, inadvertently overdosing.

But if that was the case, where was the second needle?

The other possibility was that McGhee hadn't administered the second dose himself. Maybe he had been with someone else when he died. In which case, who was that person and where were they now? If they realized that they'd accidentally killed him, that might explain why they had fled the scene and hadn't called an ambulance.

But what if it hadn't been an accidental overdose? What if the second person had tried to kill him deliberately? What if it was murder?

Warren shook himself. What he was suggesting was madness. Drug users overdosed all the time. Especially drug users who'd got forty-five pounds burning a hole in their pocket. And who knew what other drugs were sloshing around McGhee's system after his recent spell in hospital? McGhee had clearly been in pain, when he'd appeared at the station. He could have been on painkillers; could they have combined with the heroin to deliver a fatal dose? Was Warren's own sense of guilt encouraging him to look for another explanation for the man's death?

Nevertheless, he decided that he needed to know one way or the other.

'Do me a favour, will you, Ryan? Fast-track the toxicology reports. And check the potency of the traces of drug left in the needle.'

Chapter 48

The telephone call that Warren received just after lunch ensured that a day that had started badly, continued to get worse.

Sergeant Jan Adams, a specialist dog handler searching the surrounding area for more evidence, had made her gruesome discovery in Farley Woods in a natural dip about 250 metres to the east of where the first body had been found. It lay just outside of the initial cordon established by Grimshaw the morning that the unknown body had been found.

The search dog was a German shepherd, by the name of Barney, its handler a middle-aged woman with a no-nonsense air, and the remains of a Scouse accent. The dog was quiet, sitting patiently as it had been trained to do, but his handler was fussing over it unnecessarily, distracting herself from the find. Warren couldn't blame her. No amount of training or experience prepared you adequately for that sort of discovery.

'In the dip, underneath that pile of leaves.' The woman's voice was thick. 'He didn't go in and disturb the scene.'

Warren nodded his thanks. Despite the chill air, he felt hot and light-headed. His facemask felt sweaty, and he struggled to breathe.

The trek through the trees had involved a slight incline. Warren would be the first to admit that he wasn't as fit as he should be; that middle age had added a few pounds more than he would have liked around his midriff, but his heart shouldn't be pounding in his chest, the blood roaring through his ears.

Was this how Tony Sutton had felt after his stroke? An image of his friend as he lay gasping, eyes rolling as his heart struggled to maintain a regular rhythm, flashed before Warren's eyes.

He pushed himself forward, forcing his gaze towards the tiny pile of leaves. He tasted metal in his mouth.

He took another step. Warren had been a police officer for twenty years. In that time, he'd attended dozens of unexplained deaths. As a uniformed officer, he'd been the first on scene many times; as a senior detective he was usually called in after the first responders had assessed the scene. He'd witnessed everything from natural causes, to accidents, to suicides and brutal murders. All of them were seared in his memory. All of them had left their mark.

The death of a child or a baby was something different. Those were the ones that stayed with him the longest. Those were the ones that haunted his dreams and hung over him like a dark cloud for hours after he awoke.

A change in wind direction rustled the few leaves that remained on the trees and delivered the familiar smell to his nose, and he felt the bile rise in his throat.

He tried to take another step, but suddenly his legs wouldn't work.

Behind him the handler was saying something to him, an urgent questioning note in her voice.

Another gust of wind whipped the pile of leaves, finally revealing the tiny form lying hidden beneath.

That was the last thing Warren remembered.

Shame, horror and embarrassment all competed for primacy as Warren perched on the rear tailgate of the dog handler's van, his paper suit rolled down to his waist. The hot, sweet tea warmed his hands, the sugar hit chasing away his light-headedness.

'Happens to the best of us, Sir.'

The dog handler's tone had been kind but had done nothing to minimize Warren's feeling of humiliation.

In two decades of front-line policing, he had never before compromised a crime scene. The facemask had caught most of the vomit, and the handler had caught his arm, stopping him from fainting directly into the dip. Nevertheless, he worried that he'd made the CSI's job harder. Had his weakness destroyed valuable evidence?

The scrunch of gravel signalled the arrival of another vehicle. Warren looked up and groaned. Could the day get any worse?

John Grayson was dressed for an evening at the golf club.

Warren closed his eyes briefly. It was bad enough that he'd thrown up and passed out in front of the dog handler and CSI team, but now he was going to have to brief his superior on what had transpired.

'I heard what happened,' said Grayson, his tone awkward. 'Happens to the best of us.'

If Warren heard that one more time ... He nodded his thanks silently.

Grayson looked around. The lay-by and carriageway were now filled with more than a dozen vehicles, and a similar number of personnel, all studiously pretending to ignore the two men. He motioned toward his car. 'Let's talk.'

Warren drained the last of the tea and stood up.

'Would you mind ...' Grayson nodded toward Warren's paper suit, splattered as it was with mud and traces of sick. Warren removed the paper suit, and placed it in a biohazard waste bag, before joining Grayson.

The interior of the Mercedes was warm, comfortable and – most importantly – soundproof.

'Warren, what's going on?' Grayson's tone was kind, but firm.

'Sorry. I had scrambled eggs for breakfast. Today was their use-by date ...'

Grayson easily saw through the lie. 'That's not it, Warren.' He took a deep breath. 'I'm not daft. For the past year or more, you've been taking half-days here and half-days there, booking personal time. A week ago, you received a phone call about Susan and raced out of the office as white as a sheet, then took personal leave the next day ...'

'I've made up the time,' protested Warren.

'That's not what this is about. You're one of the hardest working officers I know. But like I said, I'm not daft. All this personal time, then today you are unexpectedly faced with ... that scene, and you suddenly take ill.'

Grayson paused, before awkwardly reaching out a hand to Warren's shoulder. 'You don't have to tell me anything. Your private life is your private life, but if you want to talk ... I think I know what you're going through, and I am willing to listen.'

Warren stared out of the window. Ever since he'd joined Middlesbury four years previously, his relationship with John Grayson had been complicated. On the surface, Grayson could be seen as venal and even lazy, more concerned with securing one last promotion before he retired, to ensure a bigger pension. Tony Sutton had never warmed to the man; he still suspected that Grayson's commitment to maintaining Middlesbury CID's unique position as a first-response unit was only as strong as his perception of its usefulness in advancing his career.

It was certainly true that Grayson spent an inordinate amount of time with top brass, either down at headquarters in Welwyn, or out on the golf course, rather than in his office in Middlesbury. He invariably delegated the role of Senior Investigating Officer to Warren, happy to leave most of the legwork to his DCI, whilst taking credit for the team's considerable successes over the years. It was also true that he loved appearing on television and giving interviews to the press, his immaculate grooming closer to the media-loving prosecutors in the US than the typically more reti-cent officers running British policing.

But outside of work, Grayson had a kindness that few witnessed. The two men were far from drinking buddies; Warren didn't know one end of a golf club from the other and his knowl-edge of fine whisky was non-existent, yet Warren would always be grateful for the care and understanding that Grayson had shown to him when his beloved grandmother had passed away. And he could never forget how the man had thrown open his home to Warren, Susan and her parents during the horrific Delgado affair years before.

And who else could Warren talk to? Tony Sutton had too many problems of his own for Warren to confide in him at the moment. They had yet to break their sad news to Granddad Jack and Susan's parents. With his own parents long dead and no remaining relatives that he was close to, who could he speak with? It had been so long since Warren had heard from his brother, that he now thought of himself as an only child. Even the best man at his wedding now lived overseas, their once close relationship eroded by the passage of time.

'We've been trying for a baby.' His voice was thick, and he cleared his throat.

Grayson said nothing.

'It hasn't been easy, but a couple of months ago Susan finally fell pregnant.'

Warren continued to look out the window. Beside him, Grayson maintained his silence.

'Twins.'

The car was silent.

'Last week, Susan ...' His voice petered out.

'I'm so sorry,' said Grayson quietly.

'It's OK. It's just one of those things. That early in the preg-nancy it's a lottery still.' He rubbed his eyes, still staring out at the trees beyond.

'That doesn't make it easier,' said Grayson. There was a slight catch in his voice. 'Refilwe and I … we had a couple of false starts before the boys came along,' He paused. 'You assume that when it finally works the pain will go away. You have your family now. Those first losses were just a bump on the road. You think that it'll be like winning the World Cup; nobody ever remembers that you lost your first couple of games in the group matches.' He sighed. 'But it's not. You'll always wonder "what if?" What would they have been like? Would you have continued trying if you'd been successful the first time? Would you have had the kids you have now? How would life have been different?'

Warren turned in his seat. The sun had long since disappeared behind the trees, but he could see that Grayson's eyes were shining in the shadows.

'Have you been to see a counsellor about it yet?' Grayson asked.

Warren shook his head. The doctors had given them leaflets about charities and support groups, but he'd been too busy.

'You should.' Grayson raised his hand to forestall any argument. 'I didn't want to go. I didn't think I needed to, but Refilwe insisted.' He smiled. 'As always, she was right, and I was too stubborn to admit I was wrong. I'll authorize any time that you need.'

'Thank you,' said Warren, meaning it.

After a short pause, Grayson cleared his throat.

'We need to decide what to do with your caseload. I can arrange for someone else to take over the team, to give you and Susan some time.'

Warren shook his head again. 'That won't be necessary. At the moment, I want to keep on working.' Even to Warren's ears, his voice sounded weak and uncertain. It was true that his workload was mounting exponentially, with four unexplained deaths to deal with, at least two of them murders, but then that was what he had his team for.

The fact was, Warren's instincts were telling him that all of the deaths were connected in some way. It looked as though Stevie

Cullen's murder was all but solved, given Annie's confession, but he still wasn't convinced that he had the full story. Yet again, Ray Dorridge had reared his ugly head. Today's find again lay on ground adjacent to his land. It was too much of a coincidence, and Warren couldn't let that drop until he was satisfied. He couldn't just hand it over to someone else. He had to see this through to the end.

Grayson was silent for a few moments, before finally conceding. 'Have a sleep on it. Tell me your decision tomorrow.'

Warren already knew what his decision would be.

Despite Warren's protests, Grayson eventually pulled rank and sent him home for the day. Warren's team needed to expand, and quickly. It would take some hours for the new personnel, based both in Middlesbury and down at Welwyn to be brought up to speed. Grayson would oversee that. Warren had until the following morning to decide if he wanted to remain as the SIO on the various investigations.

'Go home and sleep on it,' the Superintendent had advised.

Sleep on it. Not a chance.

Susan was still out, attending a school concert, when he arrived home. After cleaning his teeth to get rid of the taste of vomit, he'd taken a long, hot shower. Towelling himself off, he'd been dismayed to find that smell of death still lingered. Cleaning his teeth a second time, he got back in the shower, turning the temperature up still further and covering himself with liberal amounts of strongly scented lemon body wash.

The smell was still there when he emerged.

The clothes would have to go, he decided.

Placing his shirt and trousers in a black bin bag, he debated about whether to throw away his tie as well. It was a cheap one that had come pre-packed with the shirt, so he decided to ditch that also. After a moment, his socks and underwear joined it.

Slipping on a T-shirt, shorts and dressing gown, he walked

outside to the bins, wincing at the sharp gravel under his bare feet.

On his way back inside, he spied his shoes by the front door.

He'd worn plastic booties over them at the scene, but the thin nylon had snagged and torn as he'd walked through the thick vegetation. Mud covered the soles and vomit splatted the leather uppers.

The shoes were only three months old; even after a hefty sales discount, they'd cost almost a hundred pounds. A scrub with a brush and some polish would have them looking as good as new.

They joined his clothes in the bin.

His third shower drained the hot water tank.

Susan had arrived home from the concert and tried to talk to him about his day, but Warren had avoided the conversation. How could he tell her what he'd seen? After all they'd been through, he couldn't do that to her. He'd forced himself to eat the curry that she'd picked up from the garage on the way home, but he'd hardly tasted it.

Eventually, frustrated, she'd gone to bed. Warren had stayed downstairs flicking sightlessly through the TV channels, until he knew she'd be asleep. Or at least pretending.

The bedroom was pitch black; the blackout blind that they'd recently bought perfectly blocking the streetlight outside. Even the annoying red LED on his phone charger had been blotted out by a strategically placed T-shirt.

He'd cleaned his teeth again before climbing into bed, the strong mint mingling with the residual flavour of the curry, and the Belgian beer he'd finished in front of the TV.

Lying there, he tried to force his mind away from that brief glimpse of what lay beneath the leaves, trying to conjure up positive memories to replace the image seared into his brain. Nothing worked.

After what seemed like hours, he heard the tempo of Susan's

breathing change, as she finally fell asleep. Turning, he touched his phone. The screen lit up, painfully bright even on the night setting. A quarter past one.

Susan murmured something in her sleep, but otherwise didn't stir.

Carefully opening the bedside drawer, he rummaged for his headphones. Loading up the BBC iPlayer radio app, he navigated to the list of archived 'In Our Time' episodes. Susan jokingly referred to the program as the insomnia killer. It was true; whilst the weekly show examined some fascinating topics, it also discussed some desperately dull and esoteric subjects that were all but guaranteed to grant Warren and Susan sleep when it eluded them.

Two hours later, Warren knew far more about a poet he'd never heard of, and an obscure battle that few remembered, but was no closer to sleep than when he'd started.

By three-thirty he gave up.

Moving as quietly as possible, he went to the bathroom, before heading downstairs, treading carefully in the dark.

Making himself a cup of coffee, he headed into the living room and sat on the sofa with his laptop, resolving to at least do something useful. It was becoming clear to him that he couldn't work the case. He'd tell Grayson first thing.

Opening his email, he saw that he'd received another nagging missive from finance about last month's expenditure. He sighed and opened up the attached spreadsheet.

'Warren. Warren. WARREN!'

Susan's voice jerked him awake. His laptop lay on the floor, the spreadsheet having finally done what Melvyn Bragg and guests had been unable to accomplish.

Susan looked down at him with concern. Her hair was tousled, and she was clad only in the T-shirt that she'd worn to bed. The living room clock read five-thirty.

361

'You were having a nightmare. I could hear you shouting from upstairs.'

'Sorry,' he mumbled. His mouth tasted of copper and stomach acid again.

She sat next to him, forcing him to look at her.

'What happened yesterday? You have to tell me,' she pleaded. 'You haven't said a word since you came back. The bathroom looks like a steam room, and that brand-new tube of toothpaste is half used. Why is there a bag of your clothes and that pair of nearly new shoes in the wheelie bin?'

'I'm sorry,' he repeated, resisting the urge to hold his sleeve against his nose, the smell of his dream lingering in the air.

She took his hand.

'Tell me,' she said softly. 'Tell me about yesterday.'

But he couldn't.

'It was nothing. Just a bad day.'

'Then what about the dream? Was it the usual one?'

Warren shook his head. The dream about his father – the dream he'd had since he was thirteen years old – rarely plagued him these days. Those demons had been largely exorcized after he'd learnt the truth about his father's death; how he hadn't killed himself through shame, leaving his family behind to deal with the fall-out.

'Then what?'

'I can't remember,' he lied. Even as he said it, fragments came back to him. He closed his eyes, but that just made them clearer.

The pile of leaves. The smell in the air, and the taste in his mouth were just as he'd remembered before he'd passed out the day before. It was as if he was watching a movie. But this time, the cast was different. The dog handler was gone; in her place stood Susan, staring down at the pile of leaves.

Despite his best efforts, he found himself joining her, looking down into the depression. A sudden gust of wind and the leaves were blown away, this time revealing not one tiny form, but two.

362

He clapped his hand over his mouth, trying not to vomit.

'Warren, what is it?' Susan's voice dragged him back to reality.

He took a few deep breaths. 'Serves me right for eating curry and watching late-night TV before bed.' The lie sounded weak even to his ears.

'Maybe you shouldn't go in today,' she suggested, squeezing his hand.

Warren shook his head. 'No, I'll be fine.'

At some point over the past couple of hours, he'd changed his mind again.

He couldn't hand the investigation over to someone else.

Something tragic had taken place in those woods, and there was no way he could rest until he knew what had happened.

Wednesday 18 November

Chapter 49

DCI Ian Bergen had a somewhat distracting habit of twisting the ends of his moustache as he spoke. A rather impressive affair that clearly required a lot of care and attention, it made Warren want to go downstairs and buy him a cup of the foamiest latte they served, just to see what it would look like coated in milk. That was probably why Bergen stuck to plain, black coffee.

It had taken Warren several minutes to convince Grayson that he was fit to continue the case. In the end, the DSI had relented, probably from practical necessity as much as anything. Nevertheless, Warren had felt the man's eyes boring into his back as he left his office.

'This white van that you have been tracking is a potential goldmine for us, Warren,' the man gushed. 'It doesn't appear anywhere on our database.'

He passed over his laptop, a paper-thin machine that doubled as an extra-large tablet. Judging from the quality of their hardware, it was plain to see that Organized Crime enjoyed a more generous equipment budget than Warren's own department; his laptop was so old the latest version of Windows had slowed it to the point that he could now make a cup of coffee whilst he waited for it to boot up in the morning.

Bergen's enthusiasm was in stark contrast to Warren, who had been deeply disappointed when Jorge Martinez had returned from Welwyn with the news that Organized Crime were unable to shed any light on the ownership of the vehicle they now believed delivered the missing nail technicians to the massage parlour every morning.

Bergen continued. 'These confirmed sightings of the van each day are consistent with our belief that there is a gangmaster supplying illegal workers to businesses in and around Middlesbury.'

He pointed to a location on the map displayed on the computer's screen. 'This camera here is within two hundred metres of a hand car wash we've had our eye on for some time.'

Warren was familiar with the car wash, although he'd never used it himself. He said as much.

'They're dodgy as anything. Next time you drive past, look at the prices they're charging, then look at the length of the queues, the number of workers that work on each car, and the time it takes them to do the job. Then do the maths and tell me how they can afford to pay minimum wage? And that's not taking into account the business's overheads. The only way the owners can make any profit is by paying illegal workers two-thirds of fuck-all.'

For the first time since meeting the man, Warren saw a flash of something other than cheerful enthusiasm.

'So why don't you shut them down?' asked Warren.

Bergen sighed. 'If only it was that simple. The buggers always seem to be one step ahead of us. Whenever we swoop in and do a raid, there are only a couple of workers there – all legal and swearing blind that they're paid minimum wage. We just don't have the resources to mount the surveillance necessary to gather the evidence we need to prosecute.' His mouth twisted. 'Unfortunately, this sort of thing doesn't even make the top ten of my priority list.' He swept his arm in a vague, encompassing arc. 'The sad fact is that out there, in this pretty little market town, there are young women – girls – being forced to turn tricks for the bastards who trafficked them into the country. There are vulnerable people that have had their homes taken over by teenage drug dealers from London so they can set up a local supply point. Car washes and nail bars are the least of our worries.

'And even, just suppose, we did try to take them to court, they'd simply pack up and disappear. Two months down the line, another business will set up in their place, supposedly run by somebody different, and we'll be back to square one.

'The only way we'll ever be able to justify mounting an operation to gather enough evidence to satisfy the CPS, is if one of the workers comes forward as a whistle-blower.'

'How likely is that?'

It was a rhetorical question; nevertheless, Bergen answered.

'Why would they? They'd be biting the hand that feeds them – and probably houses them. The gangmasters aren't stupid; they pick their workers very carefully. There's a reason they employ illegal workers who don't speak English. They take their passports if they have one, fool them into signing a "contract" that means they think they owe the bosses outrageous sums for housing them five to a room in some flea-infested hovel, and tell them if they come to the attention of the authorities, they'll spend six months in Yarl's Wood awaiting deportation back to whatever country they escaped from. Mrs May's "hostile environment" is hardly helping matters.'

'So, you think these nail technicians are part of the same group as these car wash workers?'

'I wouldn't be surprised. Car washers, nail technicians, private cleaners, farmhands, you name it. Wherever there are low-skilled workers working cash in hand, there are exploited people.'

He pointed to the laptop screen.

'There's little point raiding these places; it's just a mopping-up exercise. What I really want, are the people in charge.'

'Such as Northern Man,' supplied Warren.

'Exactly. From what your witness has told you, at the very least he's some form of fixer. If we can track him down, we might be able to bring some sort of prosecution.'

'And I might get access to these two nail technicians, who are potential witnesses to Stevie Cullen's murderer,' responded Warren. 'We'll pass over everything we've got, but I warn you now that the van hasn't been seen since McGhee gave his statement, and he's now dead. I suspect that it's been disposed of. I doubt we'll see it again.'

'Do you have any idea where it is coming in from each day?'

'Not really,' admitted Warren, 'we pick it up on a fixed ANPR camera coming in from the north of the town via the A506, and it leaves the same way, but once it's left the town's limits there's not much we can do to track it. There are a couple of safety cameras on the way out to Cambridge, but it hasn't been caught speeding. It's semi-rural out there, with lots of small roads and tiny villages. They could be going anywhere.'

'Perhaps Mrs Wilson and her two nieces can shed some light on the situation. Perhaps the threat of a fine and some jail time for employing illegal workers might loosen Mrs Wilson's tongue some more?'

Warren doubted it. Wilson was looking at a lengthy spell for perverting the course of justice, and her two nieces had been charged with murder. He couldn't imagine Bergen could threaten them with anything more than they were already facing.

Still, it couldn't hurt.

Chapter 50

'They've located the dealer who sold Joey McGhee his heroin,' said Rachel Pymm, as soon as Warren left Bergen.

'How did they manage that?' asked Warren.

'Forensics found some partial fingerprints on the drug paraphernalia found with McGhee. They ran it through the system and got a match. I wouldn't rely on it in court, but it's a hell of a coincidence.'

'Good work – where is he?'

'It's a she, and uniform have her downstairs. They picked her up first thing.'

Warren remembered a conversation he'd had with Pymm some months ago about her role within the team.

'Fancy a bit of good cop, bad cop?'

She pushed back her chair. 'I thought you'd never ask.'

Leaving her stick behind, she took Warren's arm as they walked towards the lift.

'Just one thing,' she said. 'I want to be the bad cop.'

'There was never any question.'

According to her police record, Kourtney Flitton was twenty-eight years old, but despite the acne covering her cheeks, could easily have passed for twenty years older. She'd been known to the authorities for over a decade, first for soliciting, and then for minor drugs offences. A short spell in prison had only served to deepen her dependency, and by the time she returned to the street, she'd developed a full-blown heroin habit.

After a brief period sleeping rough, she'd taken up with another user and now rented a squalid bedsit on the other side of town. It was hardly a fairy-tale ending; her boyfriend was, to all intents and purposes, also her pimp, and according to the file, responsible for her missing front teeth.

'I ain't done nothing,' she insisted, her arms crossed defiantly. Beside her, the duty solicitor made notes on her pad.

Warren passed a headshot of Joey McGhee across the desk. It had been taken by a mortuary technician after Jordan had finished with his body.

'Do you know this man?'

'Never met him,' she said, not even looking at the photo.

'Look at it properly, please,' said Warren, his voice quiet, but firm.

Flitton gave a dramatic sigh and looked at the photo. Her eyes narrowed. 'I might have seen him around.'

She was too smart to make an outright denial; if Warren then produced evidence showing the two of them together, her lies would look bad.

'Did you sell him heroin on, or after, Monday the 9th of November?'

'No comment.'

Again, she wasn't going to commit herself.

Warren pushed another photograph across the table. 'Your fingerprints were found on this plastic bag, which chemical tests have shown contained traces of diamorphine, better known as heroin.'

Flitton paused, before clearly deciding it wasn't worth denying the accusation. 'He's a mate. I just gave him a spare baggie I found lying around.'

It wasn't a bad shot at a defence; a search of her bedsit, after it had been raided immediately following her arrest, had revealed only enough heroin for personal use, and no money to speak of. Her boyfriend had been nowhere to be seen. Warren's opposite number in the drug squad, DCI Carl Mallucci, had suggested that the couple were such small dealers, their supplier probably only gave them a couple of days' worth of supply at a time, and the boyfriend was off buying their next batch. If Warren had waited a few hours, he might have caught them with more. He ignored the implied rebuke; he and Mallucci had butted heads in the past over Warren's insistence that a murder inquiry was more important than a drugs investigation.

'When did you last see Joey?'

She shrugged. 'A few days ago.'

'And that was when you sold him the heroin?'

'I didn't sell it, I *gave* it to him.' She glared at him. The distinction was a fine one, and few people would believe that she gave her product away freely, but she was clearly going to stick with that line.

'That's very generous of you,' said Pymm, mildly.

Flitton shrugged.

'How much is a bag of heroin worth these days, Kourtney?' Pymm continued.

'I wouldn't know. I don't sell it.'

'But you must pay for it when you buy it,' said Pymm.

Flitton licked her lips. 'My boyfriend gets it for me.'

It was clear that Flitton thought that she had been pulled in on a charge of possession with intent to supply, and that by refusing to admit that she was selling or buying drugs, she might just get them to drop it. Warren decided to increase the pressure.

'Joey was found dead, from a heroin overdose, two days ago. This plastic bag – with your fingerprints on it, was found next to his body.'

373

Flitton paled, her acne standing out even more. Possession with intent to supply was one thing, but the death of a client from product that could be directly linked to the dealer was something entirely different. The judge would probably consider a tariff at the higher end of the sentencing guidelines.

'No way – that ain't possible.'

'Why isn't it possible, Kourtney?' asked Warren.

'There ain't enough there to kill someone,' she said.

'How do you know?' asked Pymm.

For the first time since being arrested, Flitton looked scared. 'Because I've taken it myself. It's the same batch.' She shook her head. 'Send it to the lab – the stuff's shite. We cut it with paracetamol to make it go further.'

'Which is probably why he used two lots,' said Pymm. 'He injected himself twice. The heroin you sold him was so poor, he decided to do a second bag – that's why he overdosed.'

Flitton relaxed slightly. 'Then you're barking up the wrong tree. I only sold him one bag.'

'Really?' Pymm didn't try to hide the scepticism in her voice. 'So he went and found another dealer, and bought a second bag? Is your reputation that bad, he didn't even buy the second bag from you?'

'I don't know where he got the second bag, but it weren't from me,' snapped Flitton. 'He only asked for one bag and he only had a tenner on him.'

McGhee had been found with a twenty-pound note and a ten-pound note in his sock, and a few pence in his pocket. Flashing your cash in front of a drug dealer was rarely a good idea. However, it meant that unless he'd found some money from somewhere else, he'd only bought one bag of heroin with the money Warren had given him, spending a few pounds on a chip supper, and saving the rest. Warren felt a little better, knowing that his money hadn't been used to buy all of the heroin that McGhee had overdosed on.

'Tell me, Kourtney,' said Pymm, 'do you charge extra for the needles, or do you give them away for free?'

'What do you mean?'

'Joey was found with a needle that matches the ones that you keep in your flat.'

'Well there you go,' said Flitton. 'I never gave him a needle. He never asked for one. Either he got it from the same place I do, the needle exchange at the chemist on Troot Street, or he got it from whoever he bought that second bag of heroin from. The dodgy batch, the one that killed him,' she emphasized.

'Are you sure you didn't give him the needle?' asked Warren.

'Yes. I got a couple of spares on me, if people ask, but I ain't a fucking charity.'

'Then why,' asked Pymm, 'were your fingerprints on packaging for the needle that Joey used to inject himself with?'

'She didn't see that coming,' said Pymm in satisfaction.

Flitton had requested a break to speak to her solicitor, and they'd taken the opportunity to make a hot drink.

Pymm watched Warren spooning coffee into his cup approvingly. 'See, I told you that you'd get used to decaf. It's much better for you.'

Warren kept his mouth shut, pushing away the feeling of guilt at his deception. There was no way that Pymm could know he'd simply poured normal coffee into a decaf jar to stop her nagging. Pymm took a slurp of her own drink, a pale-yellow concoction that smelt like a packet of extra-strong mints.

'You're right, she didn't see that coming, and that's what worries me,' said Warren, 'in fact, I'd go as far as to say that she looks as though she thought what we said wasn't possible.'

'What do you mean?' she asked.

'The look on her face suggested that she knew absolutely nothing about that needle.'

'Well that's just silly – I know the fingerprints were only a partial match, but the odds that we'd get two unrelated partial matches on the same case, when we know that she and McGhee have a relationship, are incalculable.'

'Exactly. And that's what worries me.'

'What else is worrying you?' Pymm asked. 'You're looking at the honesty jar like you've never seen it before.'

'I could have sworn there was more in here yesterday.'

'I wouldn't know. I bring my own tea bags.'

'I'd hardly call it tea.'

'Funny man.'

'Seriously though, I could have sworn there was at least thirty quid in here. I was going to do a run down to Tesco to buy some more coffee and biscuits.'

'Are you sure? Maybe people haven't had as many cups of coffee as you thought, so not as much money has been put in the jar.'

'Now who's being funny? You know I'm the only person who puts any bloody money in here.'

Pymm peered into the jar. 'There's a five-pound note in there. Maybe someone swapped it for a load of coins for the vending machine?'

It wouldn't be the first time it had happened; Warren had been fighting a losing battle for years to get his colleagues to contribute to the coffee fund. Most completely ignored the jar, whilst some of the cheekier ones used it as a ready source of change.

'The fiver's mine. I didn't have any coins. There was definitely a load of fifty-pence pieces in there.'

Flitton still looked worried when she finally returned with her solicitor, after an hour-long break. She also looked twitchy and uncomfortable; she was evidently starting to need her next fix.

'I never gave Joey a needle, and I only sold him one bag of heroin.'

'Then how do you explain the fingerprints, Kourtney?' asked Warren.

'I dunno,' Her eyes narrowed. 'I reckon you're trying to stitch me up. Somebody killed Joey and now you lot are trying to pin the blame on me. I ain't stupid, I've read about this sort of thing on the internet. You lot do this all the time.'

Warren repressed a sigh. Desperate junkies needing a fix, and conspiracy theories were not a good mix. From the look on her solicitor's face, her own legal counsel wasn't a fan of her client's premise either.

'I can assure you, Kourtney, neither I, nor my officers, have any reason to try and falsely implicate you.'

'Then how did my fingerprints get on the needle packaging?' she demanded. 'I never gave him a fucking needle. Unless he nicked the needle off the bloke that turned up after him, I can't see where he got it from.' Suddenly she brightened. 'Maybe that's what happened! Maybe he mugged my next customer, stole his drugs and needle and then overdosed.' She sat back, crossing her arms in triumph.

'What bloke?' asked Pymm.

'Oh, I dunno. Just some bloke. He turned up a couple of minutes after Joey. He bought a bag, and then asked if I had any spare needles.' She shrugged. 'Cheeky bastard, but what you going to do?'

'Did you know him?' asked Pymm.

'No, never seen him before.' Her tone was firm. Warren wasn't sure if he believed her or not.

'Can you describe the man?' asked Warren.

She thought for a moment, before shrugging. 'Not really. It was dark, and he had his hood up. I didn't see his face.'

'What about his build? Was he tall or short? Fat or thin?'

'I don't know,' she whined. 'It was late, and I'd been smoking weed – you know, just to take the edge off.'

Pymm sighed and took her glasses off. Rubbing them on her

377

jumper, she looked over at Warren. 'I think she's wasting our time, Boss. She's just trying to save her own skin, so she doesn't go down for ten years.'

'No I'm not,' squeaked Flitton. 'I'm telling you, I only sold Joey one baggie and I never gave him that needle. There's no way he overdosed on one bag of heroin.'

Warren sighed. He steepled his fingers in front of him. When he started speaking, his tone was sympathetic. 'Look, Kourtney, you've got to help us out here. It's really not looking good for you. Joey died after injecting two bags of heroin, both of which came from you. He used a needle, which again was supplied by you.'

'But he stole them off some other guy. That's not my fault, is it?' She turned to her solicitor who shrugged.

'You claim that this man exists, but you can't give us a description. Did you keep the money he paid with?'

'No, of course not.'

'So no fingerprints then. The only prints on the packaging were yours and Joey's.' Warren turned. 'I think you may be right, DS Pymm, I'm not sure this person even exists.'

'He was wearing gloves.'

'What colour?' asked Warren quickly.

'Umm, black. Leather, I think.'

'What was he wearing?'

She paused. 'A hoodie, I think.'

'What colour?'

'Black? Maybe?' She put her face in her hands. 'I don't know, I can't remember.'

'Is that all?'

She nodded, for the first time tears starting to form in her eyes.

'I think we've heard enough for the time being,' said Warren. 'Interview suspended.'

'No wait,' she suddenly shouted.

'I remember now, he was northern.'

'What does "northern" even mean?' asked Grimshaw.

Kourtney Flitton's interview had sparked significant debate amongst the team.

'This far south, anywhere north of Cambridge,' said Martinez. The man had a point: Warren had been fighting a losing battle for years to convince his colleagues in Hertfordshire that coming from the West Midlands didn't make him a northerner. To make it worse, Karen Hardwick thought he sounded like Lenny Henry, who was from Dudley, part of the Black Country!

'It's still a hell of a coincidence though,' said Hutchinson, who was himself from Newcastle, but after years of living down south only sounded like a Geordie after a few beers. 'She blurted it out unprompted.'

'Coincidences do happen,' said Martinez, 'but leaving that aside, do we even believe her? She's desperate to save her own skin. If she sold Joey McGhee enough heroin for him to kill himself, she is looking at the top end of the sentencing guidelines for intent to supply.'

Martinez did have a point. Warren turned to Bergen. 'Any thoughts, Ian?'

Bergen shrugged. 'I don't know what to say, Warren. Northern accent, black hoodie? There's no point even running that through our files. I'll put the word out to Carl Mallucci's team, but if this guy isn't even a regular user and just bought it as a one-off to kill Joey McGhee, I doubt he's even known to them.'

Warren thanked the team.

It was frustrating, but he knew that there was little he could do about it. He couldn't even justify keeping Flitton in detention beyond twenty-four hours. They had enough to charge her with intent to supply, but deciding if she was in any way responsible for McGhee's overdose would be the coroner's job. In the meantime, she would have to be released on bail.

He just hoped that she decided to stick around and face the music. If they ever did track down Northern Man, he'd like to run some mugshots past her; hopefully she might not have been as stoned as she claimed.

Chapter 51

Warren was talking to Ian Bergen in the car park when Janice came and found him, to tell him that Ryan Jordan had just phoned. Warren made it back to his office in record time to return his call.

The pathologist's voice was weary, his American accent more pronounced than usual.

'I just finished the PM on the baby.'

Warren steeled himself, the image of the tiny bundle under the leaves flashing back to him. He felt the heat rise in his cheeks.

'What did you find?' Warren managed.

'The remains were almost skeletal, but it's clear the baby was nonviable. From the size and development of the long bones, I'd estimate between five and six months' gestation.'

'How …?'

'There were traces of what appears to be placental tissue, and the remains of the umbilical cord. I'd say the mother gave birth very prematurely.' Jordan's tone was professional, but Warren could hear the tenderness in his voice. 'We'll probably never know for sure, but the baby was likely stillborn. Even if it wasn't, I doubt it survived very long.'

The pathologist's voice faded into the background, drowned

out by the sudden roaring of blood in Warren's ears. He felt light-headed. Grasping the edge of his desk, he forced himself to focus on Jordan's voice.

'… too decomposed to work out the baby's sex, but a chromosome count will tell us that when they do the DNA. I've also taken a sample from the placental material; with any luck we'll also get a maternal profile.'

Somehow, Warren forced his mouth to thank the man before he hung up.

Six months old. Warren and Susan's unborn children had been much younger than that, but he still couldn't get the image of what had lain beneath the leaves out of his head. Would the babies have been recognisable at that stage? How big would they have been? Susan had not yet begun to feel the babies kick and move. Did that mean they were too small or were they already struggling to survive?

Suddenly Warren was on his hands and knees, scrabbling under the desk for the wastepaper bin. He'd eaten hardly anything all day, and the vomit left the taste of acid and coffee in his mouth. Was it too late to hand over the case to someone else?

'Warren, I need a word.' John Grayson looked grim, as he ushered Warren into his office. Warren hoped that the mints he had eaten disguised the smell of vomit on his breath. At least he'd managed not to be sick on his tie.

Grayson sat down behind his desk and steepled his fingers. The atmosphere in the room was heavy. Warren braced himself.

'Joey McGhee. Care to tell me what happened?'

'He was found dead, from a suspected overdose on Monday.'

'I see. And this was after your interview with him, the previous Monday.' It wasn't a question.

'Yes.'

'What happened after the interview?'

Warren sighed. Grayson hadn't invited him to take a seat or

382

offered him coffee. It was clear that a bollocking was on the cards.

'I walked him to reception. He had probably missed evening meal down at the Sikh Community Centre and had nowhere to stay that night. I gave him some money so he could buy some food and get into a shelter.'

Grayson looked pained. 'Christ, Warren, have you taken leave of your senses? The man was a heroin addict, and you gave him money? Money that he then spent on drugs that killed him.'

'That's a bit unfair,' said Warren. 'I couldn't have known that he was going to spend it on drugs.'

'It was a bloody good bet,' snapped Grayson.

'When he was found, most of the money was unspent. He didn't buy enough heroin to kill himself,' countered Warren, feeling the heat rise in his cheeks.

'According to his dealer,' said Grayson, 'who has something of a vested interest in claiming that she wasn't responsible.'

'We believe that he was injected a second time …'

'By some mysterious northern bloke, that we still don't have evidence even exists,' interrupted Grayson.

'There was only one, single-use needle found with the body, and only one plastic bag …'

'He'd been lying next to the river for God only knows how long. The bag could have blown away or he could have thrown the needle into the river.'

'Look, I'm sorry, Sir. It was pissing down with rain that night. He'd missed the last chance to get some food and had nowhere to sleep. He didn't even have a sleeping bag, after we dismantled his shelter. It was the least I could do. You can't tell me you haven't given money to homeless people in need.'

'Not in the sodding reception area of the police station,' said Grayson.

Warren sighed. He wasn't going to win the argument. It wasn't the first time he'd butted heads with Grayson, and he doubted it would be the last. He decided to take the reprimand on the chin and get on with his day.

'Yeah, OK. I probably shouldn't have done. And I feel bad that he used some of that money to feed his habit. I'll try and be more careful in future.'

Grayson picked a golf ball off the decorative stand at the edge of his desk. He contemplated it carefully, before placing it back where it belonged. Warren steeled himself.

'It's not about the drugs,' Grayson said quietly, 'as tragic as that was. It's about you giving money to a key witness in your investigation.'

'Oh, come on …'

'Warren!' snapped Grayson. 'Let's suppose this mysterious northern gent does exist. His defence team will have a bloody field day with this. You'll be accused of bribing a witness.'

'That's ridiculous; you know I'd never do that.'

'It doesn't matter. It's about appearances. You've potentially scuppered that whole lead.'

'It won't come to that,' said Warren. 'We have McGhee describing what he saw on video before I gave him any money.' Warren swallowed. 'And now he's dead, he's not going to be cross-examined by the defence anyway.'

Warren felt dirty even saying it. He'd made an error of judgement, he knew that, and he'd been beating himself up about it ever since. But whilst he would have to live with the tragic outcome of his decision, he could see no way that the defence would ever be able to use the decision against him.

'Unfortunately, Professional Standards don't see it that way.'

'What have they got to do with it?' asked Warren, incredulously.

'There's a video.'

'What?'

'The security camera in the reception area picked up the whole exchange. Unfortunately, there's no sound, and we can't see your lips, but the two of you are clearly having a conversation, and the footage of you taking money out of your wallet is as clear as day.'

'I don't understand ...'

'They received an anonymous tip-off yesterday, and they seized the footage this morning.'

Grayson paused. 'It doesn't look good, Warren.'

Warren felt as though he'd been punched in the gut. His knees felt weak.

'Warren, you've been under a lot of strain lately ...'

'That's not fair ...'

'You were right next to Gary Hastings when he died. Then there's the health worries about your grandfather, and Tony Sutton. And now the baby ...'

'That's got nothing to do with how I do my job.'

'I think it does. I also saw you taking your wastepaper bin down to the gents toilets minutes after receiving a call from Professor Jordan.'

'What, are you bugging my calls now?'

'Don't be bloody silly. Janice stopped me in the corridor and asked if I'd seen you. When did you last see your counsellor?'

'That's none of your business,' snapped Warren.

'Yes, it is,' countered Grayson. 'According to Occupational Health, you haven't been to see them for weeks.'

'I haven't needed to,' said Warren. 'I saw them weekly after Gary died, and then after the murders at the abbey. They told me to come back if I felt I needed their support again. I've been fine.'

It was a lie, and both men knew it.

'Warren,' started Grayson, his voice quiet, almost kind, 'I'm telling you this as your boss and as your friend. You are not fine. You're on the edge. You haven't had a proper day off for weeks, and you're living off coffee. You look like death warmed over and I think your judgement is impaired. After the incident with the baby in the woods, I should never have let you continue on the case.'

'That was my decision,' said Warren.

'And it was the wrong one.'

'What are you saying?' Warren could hear the note of desperation in his voice, but he didn't care. Grayson was right. Perhaps he had been working too hard, and with all the stress over Granddad Jack, and the babies, he had been feeling a bit overwhelmed. And he knew that he – and the team – were still grieving the loss of Gary Hastings. But he wasn't letting it impact upon his work. He was too experienced for that, wasn't he?

'I'm sending you home.'

'You're suspending me?' Warren felt light-headed.

'No, I'm sending you home until your head's straight.'

'You can't do that.'

'I can and I am. You are not to set foot inside here until Monday, after you have been to Occupational Health, and they are satisfied that you are fit to return to work. I will take their views into account when deciding if you should continue on this investigation or move to another case.'

Warren reached out to steady himself on the doorframe. 'You can't demand that, you don't have the right. I'll speak to Human Resources about it.'

'Damn it, Warren, don't make this any more difficult than it already is. I'm doing this for your own good and the good of the investigation. Get yourself home and get some sleep. Arrange some counselling and for Christ's sake, spend some time with your wife and your family.'

Thursday 19 November

Chapter 52

Grayson's order to get some sleep was easier said than done. Warren had hardly slept a wink. He'd arrived home angry and upset. The case was coming to a close, he could feel it, and to be taken away from it at such short notice …

Susan had already been home, settling in for another night alone in front of the TV.

Despite his fury at being treated like a child, it was the sight of his wife in her dressing gown, her face puffy from crying, that finally calmed him.

Maybe Grayson was right. After all they'd been through, what was he thinking? He should have been here for her. Susan had decided to go back to work, and Warren supported her decision, but still, she shouldn't be on her own at night, watching crappy television, wondering what time her husband would finally show up.

'Maybe it's for the best,' she'd said after hearing Warren's account.

He hadn't intended to share with her the story of the baby in the woods, but she'd seen the evening news and immediately pieced together what must have happened.

'Maybe John is right: you are too close to this. After everything you've ... we've been through, you need time to get your head straight.'

Warren winced as she parroted Grayson's words.

'Take the time off. Go and see Tony tomorrow – you haven't seen him for weeks. Then we can go to Coventry at the weekend and tell Mum and Dad, and Granddad Jack about the babies.'

Warren had nodded, unable to disagree. The loss of the babies was like an open wound. Intellectually, Warren knew that they couldn't start to heal properly until they told their family what had happened. For the past week he'd flinched every time the phone went, or he came home to find post on the kitchen table – who knew how many people had been told the couple's good news? The card from Granddad Jack had been like a knife twist, and he'd buried it at the bottom of the waste bin before Susan even saw it.

Bernice, Dennis and Jack would be heartbroken, and he didn't have the emotional energy to tell them that they were no longer going to be grandparents again. But he couldn't put it off forever. They had to tell them, and it wouldn't be right to share that news over the phone.

'And why not go to Occupational Health? You know what they said last time you went. If you start having bad dreams again, you should go back for more counselling. It really helped after Gary's death, and the murders at the abbey last spring.'

Susan, as ever, was right.

'Grayson said he would arrange for an emergency appointment. I haven't checked my emails.'

'Then clearly he wants you back as soon as you're fit. You're his best officer, Warren. And he cares for you.'

Again, he couldn't fault his wife's logic. Nevertheless, neither of them had slept properly, and it had taken all of Warren's willpower to avoid checking his email until Susan had left for work that morning.

It was clear from the size of his inbox that Grayson hadn't

told the team why he was absent that day, and he spent an hour forwarding messages to others to action whilst he was out of the office, his sense of frustration growing. Occupational Health responded at nine a.m. with the offer of an appointment first thing Monday. Grayson had obviously pulled some strings – over the past few years, the counselling service had borne the brunt of the government's sweeping cuts to the policing budget. He and his colleagues been asked to do more and more, with fewer and fewer resources, and a significant decrease in personnel. Front-line services were stretched beyond breaking point, taking an inevitable toll on officers' health and mental wellbeing. Waiting lists for counselling appointments were at an all-time high.

Warren still felt annoyed that Grayson had forced his hand, but the sooner OH gave him a clean bill of health, the sooner he could be back at his desk. In the meantime, he vowed to try and enjoy his enforced rest. Walking into the living room, with a cup of tea and a handful of custard creams, he perused the couple's 'to be read' bookcase, groaning with books that he hadn't had time to even look at. Deciding on the latest Lee Child, he settled into the comfy leather armchair. Some days he envied Jack Reacher. No attachments, and few worries beyond what motel to check into that night – the lifestyle of Child's nomadic character seemed almost idyllic, and he looked forward to escaping into that world for a few hours.

By lunchtime, Warren was going stir-crazy. For the first time he could remember, he'd been unable to focus on Lee Child's sparse, yet descriptive prose, finally giving up barely thirty pages in. Reacher hadn't even punched anyone yet.

A flick through the TV channels had revealed nothing more diverting than some middle-aged people getting overly excited about bidding at an auction for some junk found in an attic, and some deeply unpleasant individuals being goaded into fighting over the results of a paternity test by an even more unpleasant studio audience. After another cup of tea, and a cheese sandwich, Warren gave up. Grabbing his coat, he headed out into the chilly autumnal air.

'Warren! What a lovely surprise.' Marie Sutton greeted Warren with a warm hug. 'Tony, Warren's here,' she called back over her shoulder.

'I'm not interrupting anything am I?' Warren's hadn't thought to call ahead and he'd no idea if Sutton was busy.

'Of course not.' She lowered her voice. 'He's going mad stuck in doors all day. He'll be delighted to see you.' She glanced over her shoulder. 'And you'll be doing me a favour. He's as grumpy as sin.'

'I heard that,' came Sutton's voice, as the living room door opened.

It had been a month since Warren had last checked in with Tony Sutton. Technically, Warren shouldn't be performing line manager visits with his sick colleague, since he himself was signed off also, but he'd been friends with Sutton too long to worry about such formalities. If anyone asked, he was visiting a mate.

The mini-stroke that had felled his friend six months previously had left no permanent damage, thankfully, but the heart condition that it had uncovered had left its mark.

'You look well,' said Warren.

'Bollocks, I look like shit.'

Since his collapse, Sutton had been in and out of hospital. In the past months, he'd lost a significant amount of weight, and his pallor had improved. But Warren noticed that he was still out of breath, as he led the two of them into the living room.

'I'll put the kettle on,' said Marie, as she disappeared into the kitchen.

'Decaf only,' Sutton apologized. 'You get used to the taste, but I miss the kick.'

'Probably for the best,' said Warren. 'At least Rachel Pymm will be pleased.'

Sutton grunted. 'She won't be happy until we're all pouring hot water over the contents of the garden waste bin. What's she drinking these days?'

'I assume it's mint tea, either that or she's boiling mouthwash.'

'Hah.'

The two men sat down.

'So how is everyone?'

'Fine. Busy and overworked as usual, but they're ploughing on. Moray's training for a triathlon and stressing about his wedding; he and Alex are trying to agree on whether they should both wear the same style suit or do their own thing. The problem is, there's almost a foot difference in height, and five stones weight between them. I'm glad I didn't have to worry about that when Susan and I got married.

'Rachel is doing well. She's recovered from her last relapse. I just have to make sure she doesn't overdo it again.'

'Good luck with that. What about Hutch?'

'He's bought himself a new motorbike.'

'Mid-life crisis?'

'That's what everyone reckons.'

'And Mags? Is she still running?'

'Yeah, she's doing parkruns with Moray most Sundays. She's hoping to get a place in the London Marathon, raising money for the NSPCC.'

'That's a good cause,' said Sutton. Warren agreed. Since the appalling events of the Middlesbury Abbey case, earlier that year, the team had been raising money for children's charities. That investigation had really got under everyone's skin.

'How's Susan?' asked Sutton.

'She's fine,' said Warren quickly, 'but what about you?'

Sutton made a so-so gesture with his hand. 'Good days and bad days.'

'What do the doctors say?'

Sutton let out a puff of air. 'I'm permanently in arrhythmia; my pulse rate is all over the place.'

'Have they still got you on those beta-blockers?'

'No, thank God. They really disagreed with me. I was huffing like an old man. They've put me on some new ones, and they're going to try another cardioversion, to see if they can shock me back into a normal rhythm.'

'And if they can't?'

Sutton sighed. 'Different tablets and the possibility of an ablation, to kill off the piece of heart tissue that is causing the abnormal rhythm.'

'Christ.'

'It's not as bad as it sounds,' said Sutton. 'They go in through a blood vessel; it's not like open-heart surgery.'

The door opened, and Marie appeared, carrying a tray with two steaming mugs. 'Sorry, Warren, decaf only.'

'At least Marie lets me have the decent biscuits when we have guests,' said Sutton.

'Ignore him,' ordered Marie. 'You'd think I had him living on gruel and warm water.'

'So, any idea when you'll be back?' asked Warren, after she'd left.

'I take it the Brownnose Brothers aren't living up to expectations?'

'That's not what I meant,' said Warren.

Sutton grunted, his eyes narrowing.

'They're … different,' Warren allowed.

'So I've heard.' Sutton paused. 'Their reputation precedes them. Word on the grapevine is they're ambitious.'

'They're certainly that,' said Warren diplomatically. Despite his years of friendship with Sutton, he was uncomfortable bad-mouthing other members of the team. Grimshaw and Martinez certainly had their faults – Grimshaw in particular – but slagging them off was unprofessional. Warren had spoken to Grimshaw on more than one occasion about his choice of language when discussing victims or suspects in their cases. He also had a habit of making crude jokes that were more suited to the pub with like-minded friends, than an office environment. Everyone on the CID team was a grown-up, and dark and often adult humour was a common way of dealing with what they saw each day. Nevertheless, there was a line between what was appropriate and what was too much, and Grimshaw didn't seem to know – or care – about that line. If the man ever wanted to make it as an Inspector, he would have to work on that.

By contrast, Martinez was the polar opposite. Rachel Pymm had once described him as 'smooth, like an estate agent'. Given the difficulties she and her husband had been having trying to sell their house, that wasn't a compliment. Warren didn't really know much about him, other than his love of football, and the fact that he apparently came from a wealthy background.

'Anyway,' continued Warren, 'you didn't answer the question. When do you think you'll be back?'

'Is this an official question?' asked Sutton.

Warren was shocked. 'Of course not. You know that's not how it works.'

Sutton waved a hand in apology. 'Sorry, ignore me. I'm just sick and tired of sitting around doing nothing.' He looked towards the closed living room door.

He lowered his voice. 'To be honest, I don't know if I'll be back.'

Warren sat back in surprise. It hadn't really occurred to him that Sutton might not return to duty. Tony Sutton loved his job, and he loved Middlesbury CID even more. Warren's predecessor, Gavin Sheehy, had fought tooth and nail to keep Middlesbury independent throughout the mergers and cutbacks of the past decade or so, and Tony Sutton had been a vocal proponent of that approach.

Warren realized that he couldn't imagine Middlesbury without Sutton. The two men had certainly had their ups and downs, particularly during their first few months, but Warren had come to regard Sutton as one of the finest officers he'd ever worked with.

'Welwyn have been really good to me these past few months,' said Sutton. 'Since I was taken ill on duty, they have extended my sick pay at full rate past the six months. But I'm going to have to make my mind up sooner, rather than later.'

'What does Marie think?' asked Warren.

'She wants me to put in for ill health retirement.'

'And what do you think?'

Sutton sighed. 'I don't even know if I'd be eligible; just because I can't go legging it after suspects, doesn't mean there aren't plenty of other roles I could still do. Look at Rachel Pymm. When she was diagnosed with multiple sclerosis, they supported her retraining as an officer in the case.'

'But?'

'But that isn't me. I know my way around a computer, but sitting behind a desk all day ...?'

'So, what would you do, instead?' asked Warren.

'That's just it, I don't know.' He clenched his fist in frustration. 'All I ever wanted to be was a copper. You know that. My old man was in the police, and his old man before him. I've never been able to see myself in any other job. I'm not even fifty yet. What will I do? I've spent six months trying to keep myself occupied and failing miserably.'

He took a mouthful of his coffee. 'And of course there's the money. Ill-heath retirement is half-pay at best. I'd have to get another job, or Marie would have to work extra hours. And not to mention Josh; me and his mum are still helping him out.'

'Teaching's a good career,' pointed out Warren.

'Well that might be on the back-burner for a bit.'

'Really? Susan says he was very enthusiastic when she arranged for him to do some work shadowing in the history department.'

'He was, and he'll probably go into it one day, but he's just been offered a place on a master's course, with the possibility of extending it to a PhD.'

'Ouch.'

'Exactly. He's applying for funding, but there's so little available for the humanities. And even if his course gets funded, he probably won't get more than a pittance to live on. We've said he's welcome to stay here, since his mum's new husband has three small kids of his own, and their place is a bit of a zoo, but that's going to be hard if I'm on reduced pay.'

Warren looked at his friend with concern. Sutton saw his expression.

'Don't worry, I'll figure it out. The first thing I need to do is get this heart thing sorted though, there's nowhere quiet in the office for my afternoon nap.'

A few hours later, and it was clear that Susan had been right. Warren felt more relaxed than he had done in days. Susan had a parents' evening to attend, and it hadn't taken much to persuade Warren to stay for dinner.

After helping Marie clear the table, Warren had settled back down in the living room with his old friend.

Sutton took a swig of his alcohol-free beer and made a face.

'I won't be getting that one again,' he said. 'I've worked my way through most of the ones they sell in Tesco. Some are better than others.'

Warren agreed. He quite enjoyed some of the alternative brews, but this one was trying too hard to be a real ale and failing miserably. He stifled a burp. It was far too gassy.

Sutton put his glass down. 'Have you spoken to Karen?'

Warren felt his gut clench. 'Yes, she came in for her keep-in-touch day. It was good to see her.'

Sutton looked at him carefully. 'And has she spoken to you about returning?'

'No, I imagine that she needs to speak to HR about that.'

Sutton gave a sigh. 'She's not told you, has she?'

'Told me what?'

'She might not be coming back. She's been offered a PhD studentship. She doesn't know if she wants to accept it or not.'

Warren slumped back in his chair. 'I guess I can't blame her. I saw her face when she came into the office ...' his voice quietened '... when she saw me.'

Sutton shook his head, vehemently. 'No. We've been through this before. She doesn't blame you for what happened to Gary. Nobody does.'

'But how can she not? It was my fault. If I had just waited for backup ...'

'Stop it,' ordered Sutton. 'You did everything by the book. You couldn't have known what was waiting for you. Nobody could have.'

Warren said nothing. Eventually Sutton continued. 'She came to see me a few days ago. She's worried what you'll think if she accepts the offer.'

Warren was confused. 'Why is she worried what I might think?'

'Because she knows that you still blame yourself for Gary's death. And she doesn't want you thinking that she's left the police because she can't stand to be around you.'

'I don't know what to say,' said Warren finally.

'She has another couple of weeks to decide whether or not to accept. She wanted my advice.'

'What did you say?'

'What could I say? She's a hell of a copper, but she's got Oliver to think about now. Doing a PhD isn't easy, but she's been offered a part-time contract, so the hours are more regular. And she won't be putting herself in harm's way. I said that I thought it would be a big loss to Middlesbury if she left, and an even bigger loss to policing. But she has to follow her heart.'

'Shit.'

'Yeah.'

Sutton cleared his throat. 'And now we're onto the difficult topics, I see you have some time on your hands.'

'How do you work that out?' asked Warren.

'Well first of all, it's a Thursday in the middle of a major investigation, and you've been sitting in my living room all day.'

Warren glared at him.

'And someone might have said something.'

There was no point asking Sutton who had told him; he'd never say. Warren could probably make an educated guess anyway.

'What have you heard?'

'That you left Grayson's office late yesterday, with a face like thunder, and that you've been reassigning duties by email all morning.' Sutton's voice softened. 'What the hell happened, Warren? The rumour mill is going crazy. Mysterious absences, being sick at a crime scene ... Need I go on?'

Warren felt his cheeks flush. He hated that he was the subject of gossip. He was about to tell Sutton to mind his own business, when he suddenly felt the energy drain out of him. This was why Susan had pushed him to visit his old friend. She knew that she was too close to help him; that he needed somebody else he trusted to act as a sounding board. It also explained why Sutton had been at home that day, and Marie had enough ingredients to cook a lasagne big enough for three, before disappearing to her sister's for the evening.

'Warren, I can't begin to tell you how sorry I am,' said Sutton, after Warren had finished. 'I should have realized that something was up.'

'How could you have?' asked Warren.

Sutton looked helpless. 'I don't know. I just … sorry, mate, I wish I could have done something.'

Warren thanked him, already feeling better. The cliché was true: a problem shared was a problem halved.

Sutton left to go to the bathroom, before returning with a bottle of wine and two glasses.

'Alcohol-free Chardonnay. According to the label, it's as good as the real thing.'

He served the two men a glassful each. They each took a mouthful each.

'Christ, that's even worse than the beer,' said Sutton. 'I figured that even if it didn't taste like wine, it would at least taste like grape juice.'

'Well don't chuck it,' said Warren. 'Winter's coming, you can use it to de-ice the car.'

'It'll damage the paintwork.'

The two men laughed, before each taking another sip.

'It's not going to grow on us is it?' asked Warren.

Sutton shook his head. 'No, and based on the evidence so far, I'm not even going near the alcohol-free gin I was reading about.'

He settled back in his chair. 'I've been thinking about what you told me about the case, and I'm worried.'

'How so?'

'Don't you think it's a bit suspicious that you've been removed from the investigation at this point?'

'What do you mean?'

'Well, that footage didn't find its way to Professional Standards by itself. If you ask me, somebody wants you out of the way.'

Warren thought about it. If he was honest, the thought had crossed his mind. He'd even said as much to Susan, who had convinced him he was being paranoid.

'Who?'

Sutton thought about it for a moment. 'How well do you know Ian Bergen?'

'Bergen? I can't say I do. I've only started working with him recently.'

'I knew Ian back in the day. We worked together back when we were starting out in CID. I moved back to Middlesbury, and he went to work in Organized Crime. Worked his way up to DCI, I heard.'

Warren said nothing. Sutton had a look in his eye. One that Warren had grown to trust over the years, and one that he had missed in recent months.

'Let's look at the Cullen family. I've been hearing their names bandied about as long as I can remember, but nothing ever seems to stick. Why is that?'

Warren thought back to his conversations with Bergen. 'Lack of evidence. As far as we are aware, they steer clear of drugs and aside from their old man doing time for looking after the proceeds of a Post Office job years ago, they aren't involved in armed robbery or car theft. With the cutbacks they just aren't a priority.'

'And what happens when SOC do try to get evidence?'

'All the farm workers they meet are legal and claim to be on minimum wage.'

'As if they've been tipped off?' said Sutton.

'That's a hell of an accusation,' said Warren.

'Hear me out,' said Sutton. 'Where was Bergen when you met that homeless bloke?'

Warren thought for a moment. 'He was around. He had watched us interview Silvija Wilson earlier in the day, but I didn't see him in reception.'

'But his old mate Shaun Grimshaw was there, wasn't he?'

'Shaun did say that he thought it was a mistake giving Joey McGhee that money.'

'And from what I hear about the less polished member of the Brownnose Brothers, he isn't exactly discreet.'

Warren conceded the point. He could well imagine Grimshaw griping about him within earshot of Bergen.

'A bit circumstantial, don't you think?'

'Maybe. But I've been thinking about this "Northern Man" who seems to keep on cropping up.'

'That's how Joey McGhee described him, although he was Scottish and he admitted that he isn't always sure about English accents.'

'Have you seen Bergen's car?'

Warren blinked at the strange question. 'Sure. A red Volvo, I think.'

'What has he got plastered all over the back?'

Warren thought for a moment. 'Some stickers. Rugby maybe?'

'Thought so. Well assuming he hasn't changed his affiliation in the past twenty years, he's probably still as fanatical about rugby league as he used to be.'

Warren shrugged. It meant nothing to him.

'Down here it's all about rugby union. I used to play with Pete Kent until we both got too old.'

'Sorry, you'll have to spell it out to me.'

Sutton sighed at his boss's sporting ignorance. 'Rugby league is played in Northern England. If I remember correctly, Ian Bergen moved down south when he was a kid, but he's still mad about his home team, Wigan Warriors. He used to travel up at the weekend to watch them play whenever he was free. I'll bet he can turn his Lancashire accent back on enough for even a Scotsman to realize he's from up north.'

'Bergen has the most spectacular moustache you've ever seen, and he's almost bald. Surely somebody would have mentioned that?'

'Did either of your witnesses see his face?'

Warren thought back to the interviews with McGhee and Flitton. Both had claimed that 'Northern Man' had been wearing a hoodie, his face concealed.

He said as much.

Warren leant back in his chair. Sutton's theory was decidedly flimsy, but he couldn't dismiss it entirely.

A buzzing came from his coat pocket.

'Probably your missus wondering where you are,' said Sutton.

Warren looked at the screen before answering.

Sutton watched him over his glass of wine, his face twisting as he remembered why he hadn't drunk any more of it.

After a few seconds of intent listening, Warren ended the call. 'I'll be right there.'

Chapter 53

Warren parked outside the Black Bull pub, an ancient, sixteenth-century affair, full of tiny rooms and uneven floors. Tony Sutton climbed out of the passenger seat, wrapping his coat tightly against the cold night air. The DI had been adamant that there was no way he was staying at home after what Warren had told him about the phone call. Nevertheless, Warren watched him carefully out of the corner of his eye. The last thing he wanted was a late-night trip to A&E.

On the drive over, Warren had been thinking hard about the situation he found himself in. Grayson was clear that he hadn't been suspended; instead he was on sick leave. Professional Standards were looking into the allegations against him, but they too had declined to suspend him. Therefore, as long as he obeyed Grayson's instruction not to step inside the station until Occupational Health had declared him fit to return to work, he wasn't *technically* disobeying orders. He suspected Grayson's opinion on the matter would depend on whether it served his purposes or not.

Ducking to avoid an exposed, blackened beam, Warren entered the tiny room at the back of the bar. Moray Ruskin was waiting there nursing a pint of lager, alongside David Hutchinson sipping from a bottle of Newcastle Brown Ale. They greeted Sutton enthusiastically.

'Just keeping you in the loop, Sir,' said Hutchinson in response to Warren's inquiry. 'I'm sure that you'll be back soon, and it'll save us all a lot of time if you're kept up to date.' He was polite enough not to ask the reason for Warren's absence.

'What happened?'

'Robbery gone wrong, by all accounts,' said Ruskin. 'The front door was kicked in, and the place was ransacked. Drawers overturned, seats slashed, all the usual. If she had any drugs or cash stashed there, then it would seem to have been successful; there's nothing left.'

'You look unsure,' said Warren.

Ruskin took a swig of his pint. 'I attended the scene, alongside Martinez.' He paused. 'Kourtney Flitton had been tied to a chair and gagged. It looks as though she had been hit on the head to knock her out, and then stabbed in the heart.'

Warren winced.

'Exactly my thoughts,' said Hutchinson. 'Moray said he thought it was too brutal for this type of crime, that it looks like an execution. I agree. As far as we know, Flitton was a low-level junkie who sold just enough gear to feed her and her boyfriend's habit and turned a few tricks on the side. I can't believe she pissed off somebody enough for that. I get that she might be robbed, or even beaten. But tying her to a chair, then killing her? Seems excessive.'

'What did Jorge say?' asked Warren.

'He reckons that given the circles she moved in, it wasn't unexpected,' said Ruskin. 'He says that when he and Shaun worked Organized Crime, they saw a rise in the violence that the drug gangs are prepared to use. Her death will have minimal impact on their profits in this area, so it would be worth sacrificing her to send a message. DCI Bergen agreed.'

Warren mulled over what he had said. Jorge and Grimshaw

had worked for years down in Welwyn. They probably knew more about the drugs scene than anyone on his team, and recent intelligence briefings had flagged an increase in the degree of violence witnessed in such events. Nevertheless, he felt uncomfortable that Ian Bergen was already involved in the investigation.

'What about witnesses?'

Hutchinson snorted. 'No chance. Nobody saw or heard a thing. Even the person who reported it.'

'What about suspects? Where was her boyfriend?'

'Unknown – we're trying his usual haunts.'

'There's more,' said Ruskin. 'We have what we believe to be the knife used to kill her. Jorge spotted it sticking out from under the bed.'

'You're kidding?' Warren was incredulous. 'They killed her and then dumped the murder weapon at the scene?'

That didn't seem to make any sense. In fact, the whole crime seemed to be implausible.

On the one hand, the killing seemed to be organized and professional. The assailant or assailants waited until she was alone, then burst in, bludgeoned her to subdue her, then tied her to a chair, before executing her.

But on the other hand, Flitton was a low-level dealer, unlikely to have much in the way of drugs or money on her, making her an unexpected target. They had then discarded the murder weapon at the scene – the hallmark of someone panicking.

In Warren's mind, that left four possibilities: the first being that Flitton wasn't the right target. Perhaps they thought she was somebody else or believed that she was further up the food chain than she really was.

Alternatively, perhaps they were right and SOC were wrong – maybe Kourtney Flitton or her boyfriend were more important than they realized. Warren thought back to the case over the summer; it wouldn't be the first time Mallucci and his team's intelligence was out of date.

The third possibility was that the robbery was just what it seemed, and that those carrying it out had panicked or lost their cool. These things all seemed so straightforward on the TV or in films; perhaps the team that had done it were inexperienced and weren't able to cope when they realized that they'd chosen the wrong target.

The final possibility was the one that worried Warren the most. Kourtney Flitton had been attacked – seemingly out of the blue – only days after being arrested. That seemed an awfully big coincidence, especially after what he and Sutton had been discussing earlier that evening.

Yet another coincidence, in a case that seemed full of them.

DSI John Grayson lived in a large, five-bedroom house on the outskirts of Middlesbury. Powerful security lights illuminated the driveway as Warren drove through the powered gates. Grayson's wife, Refilwe, was a prominent human rights barrister, currently pursuing high-profile politically motivated arrests in her native South Africa. In the past, she had also represented clients against Robert Mugabe's government in Zimbabwe – the high security was more for her protection than her husband's.

John Grayson answered the door dressed in corduroy trousers and an open-necked shirt, wearing a pair of novelty slippers that resembled bear's feet. He was not pleased to see Warren. He was even less pleased to see Tony Sutton.

'Which part of "don't come in until Monday" did you not understand?' he greeted Warren. 'And you are supposed to be on sick leave, Tony.'

'Sorry about the late hour,' said Warren, 'but this couldn't wait.'

Grunting, Grayson led the two men into the kitchen. Much to Warren's surprise, his coffee-obsessed boss offered them a choice of decaffeinated blends, before heading to his study.

On the drive over, Warren had thought long and hard about how to share his concerns with his superior officer. In the end, he just poured out all of his suspicions. Grayson remained passive throughout.

'You're basing a lot of assumptions on the fact that Ian Bergen knows what a barm cake is,' he said finally.

'I know,' admitted Warren, 'but it makes a lot of sense. The Cullen family have dodged prison for years. Bergen himself claims that they always seem to know when they are going to be raided. You know how close to their chest SOC play their cards. If the Cullens were being tipped off, it had to have come from inside SOC.'

'And don't you think it a bit odd that Bergen has been hanging around Middlesbury so much, recently?' pressed Sutton. 'I can't remember a time that SOC gave two hoots about what we were up to. They spend most of their time holed up in Welwyn.'

'Unusual, yes, but Bergen has a legitimate interest in this case,' countered Grayson. 'Stevie Cullen's murder is finally shining a light on the family in a way that SOC and Bergen have been unable to justify in the past. You've seen how excited he is at a legitimate opportunity to poke around their farm.' He turned back to Warren. 'Weren't you complaining just the other day that you were worried we were going to do all the work, and then SOC were going to swoop in and take the credit?'

It was true; nevertheless Warren was undeterred. 'I know it's flimsy, but there are too many coincidences here. If Bergen is Northern Man, then everything makes sense.'

Grayson placed his mug down on a coaster and folded his arms. He stared hard at his two officers. Warren and Sutton met his gaze.

Eventually he gave a big sigh. 'I agree, it is flimsy. But, when you lay it all out, I can't dismiss it.' He paused. 'And I admit that something hasn't felt right about this case from the start; there are a lot of coincidences here.'

He stood up and started to pace. 'Even assuming that he is Northern Man, I can't take Bergen off the case. I don't have that

408

authority, and even if I did that would potentially tip him off that we are onto him. The last thing we want is him alerting the rest of the Cullen family and having them destroy evidence.'

'So report him to Professional Standards,' said Sutton. 'They can start a preliminary investigation. If he's clean, he'll never even know they opened a file.'

Grayson's lip twisted. Warren couldn't blame him. Professional Standards' Anti-Corruption Unit were a law unto themselves. They served an invaluable role, but by bringing Bergen to their attention, they were potentially ending his career. Warren had had his own run-ins with Professional Standards over the years, and they had been bruising encounters. The Anti-Corruption Unit was even worse. If they felt that there was a case to answer, they would turn Bergen's professional and private lives upside down. It felt disloyal.

But then Warren remembered what Ruskin and Hutchinson had told him that evening. Kourtney Flitton's murder had been brutal and unnecessary. She didn't deserve that. Nobody deserved that.

And what about Joey McGhee? The man had been a homeless drug addict. Yet he had the decency to seek out Warren and tell him what he knew. His motivation may have been financial, but he didn't have to come and give evidence in person. He could just as easily have phoned Crimestoppers and claimed his reward anonymously. A team of officers in Welwyn had yet to find any of his relatives. When he was eventually buried, who would come to his funeral? Who would mourn his death?

If Ian Bergen was corrupt, then he was responsible for their deaths. Not only that, he had facilitated the Cullens as they also brought misery to countless innocent people. And for what? Brown envelopes stuffed with money? Warren fought to control his anger. He would have to work alongside Bergen in the coming days, and he couldn't risk tipping him off.

'If you can't take Bergen off the case, then you can't let him out of your sight,' said Sutton, flatly. 'You have to let Warren back in.'

Grayson took a deep breath. 'You're right, both of you. Warren, I want you back in the office first thing tomorrow. I will call Professional Standards and let them know of our concerns.' He smiled grimly. 'Technically, you weren't suspended after giving that money to McGhee. Signing you off sick was a line-manager decision, although Standards dropped some pretty big hints.'

He turned to Sutton. 'But you *are* on sick leave. Don't even think about setting foot in that station.'

'Oh don't you worry about that, Sir. I've got plenty to keep me occupied. *Bargain Hunt* and *The Jeremy Kyle Show* grow on you after a while.'

Friday 20 November

Chapter 54

Warren had no intention of letting Grayson change his mind about letting him back on the case, and so he was at his desk by six a.m., long before the superintendent usually made an appearance. Susan had not been happy when Warren explained why he was going back in.

'Warren, just let it go. Let's spend a long weekend together, just the two of us.'

After Warren had explained why he had to go back and finish the job, Susan had been even less happy.

'Warren, if you're right, and someone wants you off the case, then is it wise to challenge them? Next time they might try something more extreme. You've told John Grayson everything. You should stay away and let them think they've won. Your team can keep on working in your absence. You could even direct the investigation from here; keep a line open with John.'

Warren could see her point, but he couldn't skulk at home. He was a police officer, involved in a lawful investigation. Attempts to take him off the case just showed how close he was to the truth. He had a duty to stay on the case.

No matter who wanted him off it.

*   *   *

Despite his bravado, Warren was no fool. He'd driven in by a different route that morning, and he'd arranged for a couple of uniformed officers to keep an eye on the house, and escort Susan to work. She'd refused to consider taking the day off.

Warren's first phone call of the day was from Ballistics, who had been comparing the shotgun pellets recovered from the unknown man in the woods, with Ray Dorridge's shotguns.

No sooner had he hung up, than Rachel Pymm rang, calling him over to her desk.

'I've been cross-referencing Ray Dorridge's financials with his mobile phone records, and I've spotted an interesting pattern.'

Warren stood silently whilst she talked him through her discovery.

By the time she had finished, Warren could feel the excitement coursing through his veins. Both findings confirmed what he had begun to suspect.

'That's fantastic work, Rachel. It looks as though we'll be having another chat with our old friend Ray Dorridge.'

Warren had sent a team of uniformed officers to Ray Dorridge's farm. As before, they would be inviting him to attend voluntarily – Warren was always loath to start the custody clock ticking until he had to. Not only did it impose a deadline on proceedings, it also meant that some of those precious hours would be wasted in the company of the custody sergeant. Furthermore, Warren wanted to surprise Dorridge during the interview. It was harder to do that, if you had already read out the grounds for the arrest.

But if he didn't cooperate, they were under orders to cuff him and bring him in, whether he wanted to come or not.

As he was preparing his interview strategy with Moray Ruskin and John Grayson, Janice poked her head in.

'Sorry to interrupt, but DS Hutchinson is on the phone. He says it's urgent.'

414

Warren took the call in his office.

'Sir, DSI Grayson asked for a team to canvass the local hospitals.'

Warren thought back to the request; Grayson had ordered it in his absence, and Warren had almost forgotten about it.

'Go on.'

'A young woman turned up in A&E at the Lister back in the summer. She was very distressed, dressed in filthy clothes and didn't speak much English. She'd been picked up by a couple wandering around on the side of the A506, a couple of miles from Dorridge's farm.'

'What happened to her?'

'Admissions couldn't get a lot out of her. Apparently, they tracked down a nurse who spoke the same language, and she took her into a cubicle to check her whilst they waited for a consultant to come down and assess her. The nurse says she left to get some more bandages and when she came back, the young lady had done a bunk.

'You've seen the Lister on a busy Friday night. Security were alerted, but they couldn't find her on the CCTV, so they just logged it.'

'Go on,' said Warren. Hutchinson wouldn't be in such a good mood if that was where the story ended.

'As luck would have it, the nurse in question was just coming on shift when I was talking to the admissions desk. She was a bit reluctant to speak at first, but in the end agreed to speak to me as long as we didn't tell her employers what she did. I said "no promises", but by now I think her conscience was troubling her and she really wanted to talk.'

'I think I can guess where this is going,' said Warren. He fought down rising bile in his throat.

'Yeah, the woman had just given birth to a stillborn baby. The nurse did a thorough exam, and said that aside from a little bleeding, she was essentially fit and healthy.'

Warren felt light-headed, memories of that night with Susan flooding back. Dealing with such a tragedy as a couple had been devastating. To deal with it on your own, in a foreign country …

'I assume that she didn't stick around, because she was in the country illegally?' he managed.

'Got it in one.'

'I don't suppose you got a name?' said Warren.

'I can do a lot better than that.'

Warren hung up his phone, already planning his next move. The story was nearly finished, with just a few more details needed. As if on cue, his phone went again. Rachel Pymm.

'Sir, I just got the DNA back from the baby found in the woods.'

Warren knew what the results would be before she even said them. It was the only explanation that made any sense.

He left his office, heading straight for Richardson, Grimshaw and Martinez.

'Shaun and Jorge, arrest Silvija Wilson. Mags, I want you to take a trip out to the Mount Prison.'

Ray Dorridge was in a very bad mood. He was sitting next to his solicitor with a face like thunder.

'This is verging on harassment, DCI Jones,' started the lawyer. 'My client is a very busy man. Farming runs to a tight timetable and he can ill afford to spend the better part of a day cooped up in here. If you have more questions to ask Mr Dorridge, I would ask you to please consider calling him, or visiting him at his home at a mutually convenient time.'

'I'll bear that in mind,' said Warren, before turning to Dorridge.

'First of all, ballistic analysis has shown that the pellet that killed the man found in Farley Woods came from a shotgun cartridge incompatible with either of your guns. I will arrange for your guns to be returned to you.'

Dorridge acknowledged Warren with a grunt but didn't look any less annoyed.

'The last time we spoke, you denied any knowledge of the hole in the fence between your field and the woods.'

Dorridge sighed, a little too dramatically. 'Yes, that's correct.'

'When were you last in that field?' asked Warren.

'As I said previously, when the fruit was being picked, back in early summer.'

'And there was no hole in the fence then?'

'Again, not that I saw.'

Warren made a note on his pad. Dorridge eyed it nervously. He'd already demonstrated that he wasn't a natural liar; by ostentatiously recording the man's words, Warren hoped to keep him on edge.

'It's a pretty big field. I imagine that you employ people to help you pick the fruit before it goes off.'

Dorridge shrugged, saying nothing.

'When we interviewed you previously, you said that you were alone on the farm and that you hired workers "as and when you needed them".'

Dorridge paused for a few seconds, before answering, his tone wary. 'I guess so.'

'Perhaps one of those workers saw the hole in the fence. Could you give me some names?'

'I can't remember.'

'You must have records.'

'I chucked them out.'

'Why?'

'I probably won't use the firm again; they were too expensive.'

'What was the name of the firm?'

'I can't remember.'

Warren looked at him for a few seconds, but Dorridge said nothing.

Warren pushed a sheaf of papers across the desk towards him.

417

'Your bank statements for the past twelve months. Personal and business accounts. Interesting reading.'

Dorridge stared fixedly at a spot above Warren's shoulder.

'It looks as though you're barely breaking even.'

Dorridge shrugged. 'I'm hardly alone. Between cheap imports from abroad, and the supermarkets forcing us to accept less and less money each season, farming's a dying business.'

'We've been through these entries with a fine-tooth comb, matching them to all the different companies and people you've paid. Most of it's pretty much what I'd expect.' Warren ran his finger down the list. 'Utility companies, feed suppliers, specialist equipment providers, an agricultural vehicle repair firm – that was an expensive one.'

'The gearbox broke on the tractor. It was still cheaper than buying a new one.'

'The thing is, I can't find any companies that supply farm labourers.'

Dorridge shifted uncomfortably in his seat.

Warren continued, 'However, I have found some very large cash withdrawals. Almost daily back in the summer. Would I be correct in assuming that you paid cash in hand?'

'That's not an offence, DCI Jones,' interrupted Dorridge's solicitor. 'Farming is a casual business, and it's the employee's responsibility to ensure that all relevant taxes are paid.'

'It might not be an offence, but it's not exactly best accounting practice, is it?'

'I hardly see the relevance ...'

Warren pulled another sheet of paper out of his folder. 'What's really weird, is that if you had put these payroll payments through your accounts properly, you could have offset them against your profits and reduced your tax liability. I'm not self-employed, so I don't fully understand these things, but as far as I can tell, that's pretty much free money. Why wouldn't you do that?'

Dorridge cleared his throat. 'I'm not a very good businessman, I didn't realize I could.'

'Surely your accountant would have told you this? I see you pay an annual fee to a reputable accountancy firm that specialize in farming and agriculture.'

Dorridge said nothing.

'How many workers do you employ to pick fruit on a field that size?'

Dorridge glanced over at his solicitor, who looked more interested in Warren's line of questioning than his client's discomfort.

'It depends.'

'Well I had a chat with the National Farmers' Union. They reckon that for a field that size, you'd be looking at about ten workers, probably working for about twelve hours a day in the peak season.

'Now my maths isn't great, but that's one hundred and twenty paid hours each day.'

Reading upside down, he used his pen to circle the daily cash withdrawals on the statement. Each amounted to four hundred pounds.

'Tell me Mr Dorridge, what's the current minimum wage for a person over eighteen?'

'Again, I hardly see the relevance ...' interjected the solicitor.

'Please answer the question, Mr Dorridge.'

'I'm not sure.'

'Before October's change, the rate was six pounds fifty per hour for adults. Even assuming your workers were under twenty-one, the rate was still five pounds thirteen pence. Now I'm willing to accept that I may have overestimated how many workers you employ, and how many hours they work per day, but you don't have to be Einstein to see that four hundred quid doesn't come close to a full day's labour costs.'

'What's really interesting is what we find when we compare

your mobile phone records with these cash withdrawals.' Warren produced another sheet of paper.

'Every one of these big cash withdrawals is preceded by a phone call to Stevie Cullen a day or two before. Why is that, Mr Dorridge?'

At Dorridge's request, they had agreed to take a break. This was fine by Warren, who was keen to hear back from the rest of his team.

'Detective Sergeants Martinez and Grimshaw are booking in Silvija Wilson as we speak,' said Janice. 'DS Richardson is out at the Mount, still interviewing.'

Warren felt as though he was spinning multiple plates at the same time. For the first time since the miscarriage he felt truly alive.

Ray Dorridge was a beaten man, but at the same time, there was a lightness to his posture. Dorridge knew that he was in a lot of trouble, yet he was clearly relieved to be unburdening himself.

'Stevie Cullen supplied a van load of workers at knock-down rates during the fruit-picking season, and casual labour as and when I needed it.'

Warren and the team had guessed as much, but Dorridge's apparent willingness to cooperate made things a lot easier.

'How much?'

'Four hundred quid a day, for eight of them.'

Not even close to the minimum wage.

'And where did he source the workers?'

Dorridge shrugged. 'I honestly don't know.' He paused. 'I didn't ask.'

'How did it work?'

'Stevie had been hanging around like a bad smell, ever since we came to our … arrangement over the fly-tipping. Anyway, I used to use a bloke over towards Baldock. But he was getting too expensive.'

'How expensive?' asked Warren.

Dorridge squirmed. 'He wanted eight hundred a day.'

Warren did the sums in his head; depending on overheads, that was probably a lot closer to minimum wage.

Dorridge's tone turned pleading. 'I'm a small business. I'm barely breaking even. I can't afford that sort of money.'

'So, Stevie Cullen offered to undercut them?'

'Yeah.'

'What's the name of this firm?'

'North Herts Labour Recruitment.'

Warren made a note to check that Dorridge was telling the truth. 'How did it work?'

Dorridge shrugged. 'The usual arrangement. They all turned up in a van first thing. I showed them the field where they would be working. I supplied the tools and the equipment, showed them where the portaloos were and then left them to it.'

'Who drove them in?'

'Stevie dropped them off, and left his brother Frankie behind to supervise.' Dorridge snorted. 'Not that he was any use. He used to just crack open a bottle of cider and play on some hand-held video game. As long as the workers didn't leave the field without his say-so, they could do jack shit, and he wouldn't say a word.'

'I assume that's what you and Stevie were arguing about in the White Stag?'

'Yeah. Some days, he even pissed off and left them to it. Lazy bastards would just down tools. They wouldn't do anything unless I stood and watched them work, but I'm too busy to waste my time standing over some bone-idle farm worker.'

Warren resisted the urge to suggest that you got what you paid for.

'What did Stevie say when you confronted him in the White Stag?'

'The bastard just told me to suck it up.'

'So, what happened at the end of the day?'

'Stevie would turn up with the van again, and they'd all pile in and disappear.'

'Where were they going?'

'No idea. None of them spoke English; they were all Eastern Europeans and I never asked.'

'Can you describe the van that he delivered them in?'

Dorridge thought for a moment. 'White, no windows.'

'So, it wasn't a minibus?'

He squirmed slightly. 'No, but I guess it must have had seats inside. I'm sure it was legal.'

Warren was equally sure it wasn't, but they'd deal with that at a later date.

Warren had an envelope of photographs in front of him. Unfortunately, a mug shot was out of the question, but the clothing that the victim had been wearing had been photographed. Hard work by DC Marshall had narrowed the man's trainers down to a make sold across Eastern Europe. The logo on the T-shirt had been similarly identified, again to a cheap brand sold in several Eastern European countries. Marshall had found some images online of models wearing the same garments. Hopefully, they might jog Dorridge's memory.

'The man found in Farley Woods was dressed in these clothes,' said Warren. 'Do they look familiar?'

Dorridge looked at the pictures for a several seconds each. 'I'm sorry. I might have seen them, but I can't be certain.'

Warren wasn't too disappointed; it had been a long shot.

'Forensic analysis indicates that the body has probably been lying where we found it since the summer. Did you have workers employed in that field around that time?'

Dorridge sighed. 'Yeah.'

'Remind me what they were harvesting?'

'Gooseberries.'

That matched the hairs found in the turn-ups of the victim's trousers. They were awaiting analysis of the victim's stomach contents.

Warren pushed across the picture of the hole in the fence. 'There were fibres from the victim's clothing, and traces of blood that match him on the jagged edges of the hole. We are confident that the victim pushed himself through that hole.'

Dorridge looked frustrated. 'I'm sorry, DCI Jones, I really can't help you.'

In the grand scheme of things, it didn't really matter. All the evidence seemed to point towards the victim coming from the direction of Dorridge's field, having cut a hole in the perimeter fence, before climbing through, catching himself on the jagged edge. Dorridge had admitted to having employed illegal workers in that field, at approximately the time that the victim was believed to have died. The clothes suggested that he was from Eastern Europe and the gooseberry hairs matched those from his field.

It was clear to Warren that the victim had been one of Stevie Cullen's illegal workers, who had presumably decided to make a bid for escape.

The question was, how complicit had Dorridge been in the death of the worker? They knew that neither of the guns recovered from Dorridge's property had fired the fatal shot, but that didn't entirely exonerate him.

'According to our previous interview, you said that you own a dog. What breed is it?'

'Collie,' Dorridge looked at Warren curiously. 'Why do you ask?'

'There were dog hairs, from a short-haired breed like a Rottweiler, found on the edges of the hole in the fence.'

Dorridge frowned. 'I don't own a Rottweiler but ...'

Warren held his breath.

Dorridge brightened. 'Of course, I completely forgot.'

'Forgot what?'

'Because the workers were so lazy, we got behind in the fruit-picking. I ended up having to borrow some arc lamps and a generator from a mate so we could work after the sun went down. It cost a fortune in bloody diesel and extra wages, but it was better than letting the unpicked fruit ripen too much.'

'Go on.'

'Well Stevie wasn't happy about it, and so he brought his dad and his other brother, Paddy, down with a couple of dogs. Rotties I think.' Dorridge looked ashamed. 'I guess they must have been worried that the workers would do a runner in the dark.'

Dorridge damn well ought to be ashamed, thought Warren. Legitimate workers didn't run away as soon as they got the chance. He fought to keep his face neutral.

'The last night they were here, there was a hell of a big fuss. I heard the dogs barking and shouting coming from the field, then what sounded like gunshots. I was in the kitchen, and ran outside, but Seamus, Stevie's old man, told me it was fine, and to go back inside.' Dorridge looked down at the table. 'It wasn't a request.'

'What happened?'

'I don't know. After about ten minutes they reappeared and loaded the van up with everyone and then cleared off sharpish. That was the last I saw of them. They didn't come back the next day. Fortunately, the job was pretty much done. I managed to finish picking the last bits of fruit myself.'

'Why did they leave so quickly?'

'I'm not sure, but a helicopter with a searchlight was flying around. I think that might have spooked them.'

Warren was now almost certain that he knew what had happened that night, but he had a couple more loose ends to tie up.

'In addition to Stevie and Frankie, were there any other people involved in the operation?'

'Not really, old man Cullen drove the van one morning, but that was it.'

424

For the first time since he'd started talking, Dorridge looked away.

'Nobody else at all?' pressed Warren.

'Nobody.'

Warren looked down at the man's foot. Dorridge was lying.

Chapter 55

Warren sat opposite John Grayson, bringing his superior officer up to speed on the day's events, before the upcoming raid on the Cullen farm.

'The full name of the young woman that we have in custody is Anica Vukovi . She killed Stevie Cullen by accident when they wrestled over a knife, after she defended Biljana Dragi from a serious sexual assault.

'Apparently, Stevie Cullen was a nasty piece of work. According to Wilson, he always asked for a massage from Biljana, and was often sexually suggestive. She says that Biljana had kept his behaviour to herself, since she was worried that if she complained to her aunt, Cullen would wreck her business. She didn't even tell her sister.'

'It's always the same bloody story,' muttered Grayson. 'Shits like Stevie Cullen think they can do whatever they want.'

'Wilson says that when she spoke to Biljana, she said it had been happening for months. Until then, however, she had managed to fend him off. On the day in question though, he wouldn't take no for an answer, and threatened her with a knife if she didn't give him oral sex.'

'So how was Annie involved?'

'She doesn't usually work that late, but she was doing an extra load in the washing machine. When she heard strange noises coming from the back room, she decided to investigate. That was when she found Biljana on her knees with a knife to her throat, and Cullen had his pants down. She claims not to remember what happened next, just that she found herself wrestling with Cullen over the knife. At some point, Cullen lost control of the blade and he was stabbed.'

'Why didn't Malina hear anything?'

'Wilson says that she was watching a music video on her phone.'

Grayson frowned. 'Why have the sisters kept quiet? They are literally facing life imprisonment.'

'Wilson says that the girls have become really close to Annie, but more than that they felt that Annie had risked her life to save Biljana and they couldn't let her go down for murder. She claims that she tried to talk them out of continuing the lie, but they refused to back down.'

'Do we know what Annie's relationship is to the sisters and Wilson?'

'They didn't even know each other until a few months ago. Silvija Wilson initially claimed that Annie turned up at the massage parlour needing work, and that she agreed to give her some casual labour, cash in hand, and not ask too many questions. She now admits that was a lie.

'Annie came to the UK about three years ago, on a temporary visa. She won't go into details, but it sounds as though she had a pretty bad home life back in Serbia, and she's clearly trying to escape something. She came here to work illegally, ending up working in a café in Newcastle with some other Eastern Europeans, and doing cleaning in the evening. Again, all cash in hand. From what she's said, it wasn't actually too bad. The people who employed her were pretty dodgy, as you'd expect, and housed them two to a room in some run-down terraced house, but otherwise they treated her all right. It was better than what was at home and she made some good friends, or so she thought.'

'So how did she end up down here?' asked Grayson.

'She'd been putting away a bit of money and was thinking of moving on to something better. She thinks that she may have told the wrong person, who then let their gangmasters know about it. One night, as she was walking back home, a white van pulled up alongside her. The person inside asked her for directions in Serbian – although she now realizes that their accent and pronunciation were all wrong. The next thing she knew, somebody grabbed her from behind, shoved her in the back of the van and closed the door. They put a knife against her throat and pulled a bag over her head.'

'And drove her to the Cullens', completed Grayson.

'Basically, yes. That was about two years ago. When they let her out, they had all of her belongings from her room, which was how she knows that she was betrayed by someone she lived or worked with.' Warren shook his head in sympathy. 'The poor woman didn't even know which part of the UK she had been moved to. All she knew was that the people here spoke a lot differently than the customers she'd worked with up in Newcastle.'

'I'll bet,' said Grayson. 'I suppose that's part of the way they control them. Keep them completely in the dark, so they have no idea where they are or where they can seek help.'

'The Cullens house – or rather imprison – about a dozen workers, men and women, mostly Eastern European, and a few from the Far East, in converted shipping containers on their farm. Stevie seems to be the mastermind behind the whole affair, although the rest of the family are also involved. When she first arrived, they were mostly helping the Cullens on their own farm. But a few weeks later, they started working on other farms, as well as non-seasonal work, such as car washes or private cleaning. There were also a couple of Vietnamese women working as nail technicians at Silvija Wilson's. She wanted to help them escape, but they were too scared, and they don't have a common language.

Fortunately, they kept her presence at the massage parlour quiet.'

'So, where do the dead bodies in Farley Woods come into the picture?' asked Grayson.

Warren sighed. This was where the story became even more tragic.

'The male and female workers were kept in separate containers and weren't supposed to fraternize, but human nature ...'

'She got pregnant,' finished Grayson.

'Yes. Another worker, by the name of Emil ...' Warren paused. 'He's our victim in the woods, and the baby is his.'

Grayson closed his eyes briefly. 'That poor, poor woman,' he said quietly.

'Annie intimated that she wasn't the first person to fall pregnant.' He swallowed. 'The Cullens didn't let them complete the pregnancy.'

'Bastards,' said Grayson. 'I suppose that's why they tried to escape?'

'Yes. They had no choice, and by the summer she was starting to show, it wouldn't be long before someone figured it out. And then she started getting twinges. She knew that it was far too early and that she would need medical attention, so they had to work out what to do.

'The escape was Emil's idea. They were fruit-picking at Ray Dorridge's farm. They'd got behind with their work, and so they were working late at night under electric lighting. Emil had managed to cut a hole in the fence one afternoon when Frankie was too drunk to pay any attention. That night they made a run for it. But she went into early labour and couldn't run very fast. Stevie, Frankie and their father, Seamus, came after them with shotguns and dogs. Emil was shot. He crawled back towards the Cullens to distract them whilst Annie tried to escape, but she collapsed and went into labour. What we know now was a purely coincidental flyover by a police helicopter chasing joyriders on A506, frightened the Cullens off. She gave birth in the woods, but she knew that the baby was stillborn, so she hid it and managed to find her way to the main road, where she was picked up by a passing car. She had no idea what happened to Emil.'

Grayson shook his head. 'How did she end up in her current situation?'

'Sheer chance. When she arrived at the hospital, she managed to tell them that she spoke Serbian, so they tracked down a Serbian-speaking nurse. When Annie explained her situation, and that she didn't want to go home, the nurse agreed to help. She had an aunt who had looked after her when she first came to the UK. That aunt had also been a registered midwife before she decided to set up her own business.'

'Silvija Wilson.'

'Exactly. They smuggled her out and Wilson took her back to her own house at first, until she was better, then let her move in with her nieces.'

'Christ,' muttered Grayson, 'what was she running from back home that meant she would rather go through all of that, than go back to Serbia? She might have been here illegally, but she was the victim of a serious crime. She might have been deported in the end, but you'd think that would be better than staying, after all of that.'

'Neither Annie, Wilson nor her nieces are saying,' said Warren.

'So how confident are we that this is the final version of events?' asked Grayson. 'Silvija Wilson has changed her story more times than I've changed my socks.'

'I think we need to speak to the sisters again. If they contradict what she's said, then we'll know that we still don't have the full story.'

'But even if they do, they could just be telling whatever version they agreed upon that afternoon,' pointed out Grayson.

'Which is why we need to speak to those two nail technicians; they are currently our only independent witnesses. Let's hope that they are on that farm.'

Grayson leant forward in his chair and lowered his voice. He glanced at the window, as if looking for eavesdroppers. 'You've done a fantastic job, Warren; under circumstances that can't have been easy for you.'

'Thank you, Sir.'

'But there are still questions that need answering.'

'Northern Man,' stated Warren.

'Exactly. Who is this person? Are we sure he even exists?'

Warren nodded his head, vigorously. 'We have independent sightings from both Joey McGhee and his dealer Kourtney Flitton, and the mobile phone evidence is compelling. But it's everybody else's reaction that convinces me. Ray Dorridge, Silvija Wilson, Annie, Malina and Biljana. All of them deny his existence and all of them are lying. I can see it in their eyes.'

'Have you shown them photographs of Bergen?'

'Among others, but they refuse to even look at them. They're terrified, Sir. Bergen is a senior officer in the SOC. I can't begin to imagine what he's threatened them with. And to think I let Bergen have a go at interviewing them ...'

'Christ,' muttered Grayson, 'we can't justify a raid without him, and Professional Standards aren't ready to move. But if he is bent, who knows what sort of information he could be feeding back to the Cullens?'

'Which is why we need to raid that farm as soon as possible. There is an immediate threat to wellbeing, and it'll give him less time to prepare.'

Grayson nodded. 'Then get it done now.'

Saturday 21 November

Chapter 56

Four o'clock in the morning is the time that most people are in their deepest sleep. It's the time that they are at their most vulnerable. Police forces around the world know this, and that's why they strike at that time.

Sitting beside Warren, Ian Bergen was all business as the procession of vehicles bounced and jounced its way up the Cullens' untarmacked driveway. For safety reasons, Warren and Bergen followed behind two Armed Response Units, and a van with a Forced Entry Team. The Serious Organized Crime Unit were experts at this sort of raid and Warren had no choice but to let him take a lead in executing the search warrant. Besides which. Organized Crime, the Armed Response Units and the Forced Entry Team had access to night vision goggles that allowed them to navigate the Cullens' driveway at high speed, with their headlights turned off. It was an experience that Warren, who wasn't wearing a pair, was finding disconcerting to say the least.

At Grayson's insistence, the raid had been planned quickly, with little notice. Warren had kept Bergen in his sights for most of the night, even managing to stand next to him at the urinal one last time before they left. Time would tell if Bergen – or somebody else he was working with – had managed to tip off the Cullens.

The convoy's arrival was announced seconds before it pulled into the yard by the sudden barking of the dogs chained up inside the main yard, and the flare of the security lights. As planned, the vehicles split into two groups. Grinding to a halt, Warren, Bergen, Grimshaw and Martinez headed towards the main house. The Forced Entry Team arrived seconds before them, barely pausing before smashing the front door clean off its hinges, allowing a quartet of Authorized Firearms Officers to pile in.

Another FET, and their accompanying AFOs, were already snipping the heavy-duty chain that secured the farmyard's main gates. Specialist dog handlers, led by Sergeant Adams, were ready to deal with the furious Rottweilers awaiting them. Ruskin, Richardson, and a trio of officers from Welwyn hung back, waiting for the handlers to secure the animals before searching for evidence.

Four a.m. or not, the occupants of the house were awake now, and Warren could hear yells and cries of surprise, interspersed with shouts of 'Armed Police' and orders to 'stay down'.

Before the raid, Warren and the team had pored over maps of the property made by the search team the night after Stevie Cullen had been killed. The house was an old-fashioned farm-house, extended repeatedly over the years to accommodate the sprawling Cullen brood. Stevie Cullen had occupied a large, upstairs bedroom next to his parents' double room, with another, larger room shared by the two sisters. Now that they had flown the nest, the room was a guest room, filled with Stevie Cullen's exercise equipment.

On the ground floor, the rear of the house had been extended to provide another two generous-sized rooms, inhabited by Stevie's twin brothers. As previously agreed, Martinez and Grimshaw followed the firearms officers to the downstairs bedrooms. Warren and Bergen headed after the AFOs upstairs to Rosie and Seamus Cullen's master bedroom.

They didn't receive a warm welcome, and matters didn't improve when Warren served the couple with the search warrant.

Warren's radio crackled. It was Martinez. 'Sir, there's no sign of either Frankie or Paddy; their rooms are empty.'

Warren turned to Rosie Cullen, who smirked.

'Where are they, Rosie?'

'No idea.'

'Seamus?' asked Warren.

'Fuck off.'

'Search the grounds,' ordered Warren. 'Paddy and Frankie Cullen must be somewhere. Take care, they own shotguns and we know they can be violent.'

'We'll check the barns,' said Martinez, motioning towards an AFO and Grimshaw. They trotted off towards one of a number of outhouses.

'Moray, take an AFO and search the cottage and its grounds.' Warren pointed towards the small, single-storey house that Saffron, the youngest of the Cullen children, shared with her husband and children. The burly Scotsman jogged towards the small building, waving at the two members of the Forced Entry Team who were already standing outside with an incandescent Saffron, her husband and three very scared toddlers.

Warren toggled his radio. 'DCI Bergen? Any sign of Frankie or Paddy Cullen?'

'Negative. We're heading towards the shipping containers. Somebody has gone to the trouble of fitting a standpipe outside one of them, and what looks like power cables. I'll keep an eye out for them.'

Warren was frustrated. The point of the early morning raid had been to apprehend everyone on site as quickly as possible, before they had the chance to destroy evidence. But despite their precautions, Frankie and Paddy were missing, clearly tipped off about the raid. Assuming they were even still on site, who knew where they were, or what they were doing? Warren decided to go and join Bergen, uncomfortably aware that the man had been out of his sight for several minutes.

Suddenly, Warren heard shouting, and a gunshot, followed by the revving of an engine.

There came another shot, followed by an incoherent cry then a third shot.

Spinning on his heel, towards the barn, he saw the wooden door burst open, and the glare of headlights. Behind the lights, he could just make out the boxy shape of a van, as it accelerated hard towards him. The headlights bounced as it drove over something, and Warren threw himself out of the way as the van hurtled past, heading for the main gates.

'Stop that van,' he ordered over the radio, as he started to run towards the parked police cars at the front of the farmhouse.

He lifted the radio to his mouth, but it crackled into life before he could say anything. Martinez's voice burst out. 'Officer down. Oh, shit, officer down. Get an ambulance, Shaun's been shot.'

Time seemed to slow down, and Warren felt as though he was running through treacle. His chest felt tight. Officer down. Memories of the previous summer flooded back: Gary Hastings covered in blood as Warren screamed into the radio for assistance.

Please, not again, Warren prayed as he skidded towards the remains of the barn door.

The first person he saw was the firearms officer, lying in a mangled heap, partly illuminated by the light from security lamps in the yard. Crouching down by the man, Warren was relieved to see that despite his injuries he was still breathing. Toggling his radio, he called for medical assistance for the shot and run-down AFO and for Shaun Grimshaw.

Resisting the urge to run further into the pitch-black barn,

Warren forced himself to listen as his eyes adjusted to the gloom. The air was thick and musty, the dry smell of hay and animal waste overlaid with the fresh, metallic smell of blood.

'Jorge,' he whispered, 'where are you?'

No reply.

'Jorge,' he repeated more loudly.

'In here. Get an ambulance. Frankie shot Shaun.' Martinez's voice came from deep within the barn. 'Oh, Jesus. Come on, mate, don't die on me.' Martinez raised his voice, almost to a shout. 'Come on, where's that fucking ambulance?'

'It's on its way, Jorge.' Warren could hear the sound of feet behind him, and he raised his hand to pause them.

'Where's Frankie now, Jorge?'

'In the barn. I think he's dead.'

'Are you sure? I can't send anyone in if he's still a danger.' Warren wanted nothing more than to race in and tend to his fallen colleague, but it would be suicide if Frankie was still in there with a gun.

'Yeah, I shot him.' Martinez's voice rose again, a note of panic. 'Shaun's stopped breathing. Stop pissing about, we need an ambulance now.'

Ian Bergen and two AFOs skidded to a halt beside Warren. Two members of the Forced Entry Team, both carrying medic packs, joined them, the first immediately kneeling next to the injured AFO.

'Ambulance is three minutes out,' he said quietly.

From what Martinez said, Grimshaw might not have three minutes.

Warren turned to Bergen and the AFOs.

'We can't just leave him.'

The entry to the barn was fast and violent. The night vision goggles that the SOC drivers had worn to mask their arrival revealed two warm patches. The one on the left appeared to be a body lying on its back. The other, to the right, was in the shape of a person, with another crouched over him: Frankie to the left, and Martinez and Grimshaw to the right.

Bursting in, two firearms officers raced towards the body of Frankie. After what seemed like minutes, but could only have been a couple of seconds, one of the AFOs shouted 'weapon secure!' – the cue for Warren and one member of the Forced Entry Team to head directly for Martinez and Grimshaw. Bergen ran towards Frankie. Warren closed his eyes briefly, as the barn was suddenly lit up by the headlights of two police cars positioned outside.

When he reopened them the sight before him was carnage.

Grimshaw lay sprawled on his back, his head a bloody mess. Martinez had already removed Grimshaw's stab vest and was performing vigorous CPR.

'Come on, mate. Come on, ambulance is on its way.'

Another officer with a medic pack skidded to a halt, ripping the bag open.

Warren crouched on his heels, forcing back the bile in his mouth, resisting the urge to turn away as Grimshaw's bloody face was replaced in his mind by the face of Gary Hastings.

He'd been too late to do anything for Gary; the trauma had been too great.

He felt a touch on his arm and looked over. The officer with the medic pack shook his head. It was plain to see that there was nothing more to be done.

'Jorge,' said Warren quietly, 'it's over.'

'No,' said Martinez, as he leant over and pressed his lips to Grimshaw's mouth, exhaling forcefully twice, before resuming the chest compressions.

'Somebody get that fucking defib out, come on, don't just stand around!' he shouted.

Grimshaw's face was a bloody mess. It was clear to everyone that the projectiles had gone through the rear of Grimshaw's skull and exited through his face. There was nothing that could be done.

'Jorge, he's dead,' said Warren, more forcefully.

'Not until the paramedics call it,' insisted Martinez.

Warren looked over to the officer with the pack, who gave a small shrug. It was pointless, but it couldn't hurt. He started to unpack the automated defibrillator.

A shout rang out from the team working on Frankie. 'Shit, he's still alive.'

Everybody stopped what they were doing.

'Get the medic pack over here,' Bergen yelled. 'He's still breathing.'

The choice was clear, the answer even clearer. Keep on trying to resuscitate a dead man or try to save the life of somebody still alive?

'No!' howled Martinez, stumbling to his feet, trying to grab the pack from the officer holding it. When that failed, he started running towards Frankie and Bergen.

'Somebody stop him!' shouted Warren.

Bergen looked up in surprise as Martinez grabbed the discarded shotgun, from where the AFO had placed it.

'You killed my friend, you fucker,' screamed Martinez.

'No!' shouted Warren as Martinez brought the gun to bear and pulled the trigger.

Martinez sat in the back of a police car, wearing a white paper suit and clasping a mug of hot, sweet tea. The door locks had been activated to stop him escaping and attempting something else. However, the look in his eyes was one of defeated resignation.

To one side of the car, Grayson, Warren and Bergen spoke in hushed tones.

'No shot was fired, the gun was empty,' Bergen repeated.

Warren agreed. 'Technically we don't need to fill in a discharged firearm report, because the gun wasn't discharged.'

Grayson pinched the bridge of his nose, wearily. 'I can't just brush this under the carpet.'

Bergen folded his arms and stuck his chin out. 'Well I didn't see anything, and neither did any of my team.'

Grayson let out a sigh. 'Shit.'

'Look, there's plenty to be getting on with here,' said Warren. 'Let's wrap everything up and decide what to do in the morning.'

'It's already morning,' pointed out Grayson, although there was no conviction in his voice. 'I'll have a quiet word with ACC Naseem, see what he thinks.'

It was the best they could hope for. Bergen excused himself and went back to his team, who were busy organizing a thorough search of the farm. Warren watched him go, still feeling uneasy that Bergen was unsupervised. If he was Northern Man, this was the perfect opportunity for him to clear away any incriminating evidence. Warren was grateful at least that he had managed a quiet word with a shocked Richardson and Hutchinson, who were under orders to keep a close eye on him.

'Take me through what else you've got,' Grayson ordered.

Warren motioned towards the driveway, now filled with police vehicles, their headlamps illuminating the ditch where Paddy had crashed the white van after being shot, as he'd raced down the rutted road, firing indiscriminately out of the window.

'The van was packed with workers: nine men and five women, mostly Eastern European, but there are also two East Asian women.'

'The missing nail technicians?'

'I hope so. They're being medically assessed at the moment. It looks as though by some miracle they all survived the crash relatively unscathed, despite the lack of seatbelts.'

'Thank Christ for that; if we'd known that the van was full of workers ...' Grayson looked pale.

Warren agreed. Paddy's attempted escape in the van, firing out of the window as he went, was an immediate threat, and the AFOs

442

had made a split-second decision. There would be an inquiry into their response, and the officer who had fired had already been taken from the scene for questioning. Her decision to fire at Paddy would probably be judged proportionate, but Warren was under no illusions that had a stray bullet caught one of the workers, or they had been seriously injured in the resulting crash, she would have been hung out to dry. Not for the first time, Warren was grateful that he didn't have to make such decisions.

'I don't expect to get access to them for a while yet. The body in the woods was malnourished and neglected, and Annie has said that they received little in the way of medical care. These guys don't seem much better. I've seen bodycam footage of the inside of those shipping containers, and they are little more than prison cells. It looks as though they have electricity and there's a standpipe outside for cold water, but there's no plumbing or sewage to speak of. There are translators on the way, but it could be a while before we're ready to question them.'

'What about the Cullens?'

'All under arrest. Saffron and her family were on site, so they're in custody on suspicion of human trafficking, with the parents Rosie and Seamus. We've also executed a search warrant at the home of Lavender, the oldest sibling.'

'Good, you can't tell me she didn't know what Stevie and the rest of the family were up to,' said Grayson. 'Any word back from the hospital yet?'

'They've taken Frankie straight into surgery, severe facial wounds. Paddy has also been taken in, with a shot to the upper body. Jorge reckons Paddy shot the AFO. Frankie then shot Shaun. He then turned the gun on Jorge, who managed to wrestle it off him, and that's when Frankie was shot. Paddy then drove over the AFO as he crashed out of the barn. Fortunately, the AFO's body armour took the brunt of the shotgun discharge, but it looks as though he has multiple fractures from the van running over him.'

Grayson glanced around, before motioning Warren away from the car. He lowered his voice.

'What about Bergen?'

Warren hissed in frustration. 'I don't know. I was with him most of the evening, but they were clearly tipped off. Rachel confirms that Northern Man's phone texted Paddy Cullen just minutes before we left and was then turned off again. The location data places it close to CID.'

'Shit. What did the text say?'

'"Exit now." It wouldn't have taken long to send it, especially if it was pre-typed. But the reply didn't come for twenty minutes, which might explain why the van hadn't left by the time we raided.'

'He was probably asleep.' Grayson grimaced. 'If Bergen is dirty, we need to nail the bastard. Get Mags to secure all the CCTV footage from the station at the time the text was sent and get Hutch to do some discreet questioning. See if we can pin down his movements or find out if anyone saw him using a phone at that time. In the meantime, I've got a meeting with the Anti-Corruption Unit scheduled for later this morning.'

Warren nodded glumly. He'd done his best to keep an eye on Bergen, but he had been busy trying to organize the upcoming raid. Bergen would only have needed a few seconds to send the text.

Grayson looked back over at Martinez, who was staring straight ahead at the headrest, his drink untouched.

'Shit. I really hope the forensics supports his version of events. I might be able to persuade ACC Naseem to bury what happened after Martinez snatched up the gun, but I can't do anything to help him if it turns out that the gun didn't go off accidentally when he wrestled with Frankie, and he shot him deliberately.'

Sunday 22 November

Chapter 57

The death of another colleague. Warren felt a hollow ache inside him. It had been fifteen months since Gary Hastings had been killed, but Shaun Grimshaw's death had brought back so many of the same emotions. Grief, anger and the feeling of helplessness at the unfairness of it all were foremost. They were police officers; dedicated public servants who did their best to make society safer. Since leaving uniform, the knowledge that every new shift had the potential to bring him face-to-face with danger or even death, had receded somewhat. Despite his best efforts, Warren spent increasing amounts of his time behind a desk; his forays into the field were typically after the crime that he was investigating had finished, and the danger already safely contained.

And so it came as an even bigger shock when Warren or his team were faced with such a dangerous situation. Shaun Grimshaw had started his day like any other, never expecting that the raid on the Cullens' farm would result in anything more unpleasant than some foul language. And now he was lying in Professor Jordan's morgue being cut open, prodded and probed.

Other, even less welcome feelings vied with the grief and anger, the main one being guilt. Guilt that another colleague had been killed. Should he have waited for another armed response unit, so that each search team had more AFOs? That way, when Paddy Cullen had taken out the first AFO, there would have been another armed officer who could have protected Grimshaw and Martinez.

Then there was the feeling of guilt and hypocrisy that he should be standing here eulogizing a man that he hadn't really liked. Shaun Grimshaw had been a difficult, sometimes unpleasant, man to work with. Warren had called him into his office on several occasions to berate him for his choice of language and lack of respect towards victims and suspects alike.

Warren himself had never referred to Martinez and Grimshaw as the Brownnose Brothers – at least not in work – but hadn't he joked about them behind their back? Rachel Pymm in particular had butted heads with Grimshaw many times. Could Warren have done a better job playing peacemaker?

However, now was not the time for self-recrimination. It had been a little over twenty-four hours since Grimshaw's death and Warren had convened the team for a moment's reflection in memory of their fallen colleague.

Grimshaw had worked alongside Martinez down at Welwyn before their current posting, and so the room was full of members of Bergen's SOC team, as well as Middlesbury CID. Warren had spent the past day forcing himself to interact with the man who may well have been behind the whole affair. He hoped that any coldness on his part had been dismissed as grief and anger.

Grayson had offered to say a few words on Warren's behalf, but Warren refused to relinquish his responsibility; he had been Grimshaw's line manager, so it was his duty. Later that day, he would be meeting Grimshaw's parents to express his condolences.

Warren took a deep breath. 'Shaun Grimshaw was a hard-working, dedicated officer, who died doing what he loved.'

There were mutters of assent around the room. Warren caught Martinez's eye, who gave a brief nod. Rachel Pymm gave Martinez's shoulder a squeeze. The two officers hadn't always got on, but Pymm was too kind to let that matter at time like this.

'I only worked with Shaun for the past six months, but he proved himself to be a capable officer who I believe will … would have gone far.' Warren took a deep breath. 'As you all know, Shaun had a … unique wit.' There were sad smiles around the room. 'And despite our sorrow, I want us to remember the happier times that we shared.

'Shaun was born and bred in Manchester and was a fanatical devotee of Manchester City Football Club, as most of you are no doubt aware.' There were a few more smiles around the room. 'Now as many of you probably know, football is not my strong suit and I was born and brought up in Coventry, and so it would seem natural to me, upon seeing Shaun's branded cigarette lighter to say "Play Up Sky Blues" by way of an introduction. How was I to know that they play in practically identical kits?'

There were a few chuckles.

'At least I didn't assume that he was a supporter of Manchester United.'

More laughter.

'Working with Shaun was an education and a privilege, and I ask you to join me in a moment of silence in his memory.'

The room fell silent.

After a respectful pause, Martinez got to his feet. 'If I may?'

'Of course,' said Warren. Pymm reached over and rubbed Martinez's back encouragingly. He turned and gave her a brief smile.

'Shaun was my best mate.' His voice caught. 'We joined Herts Constabulary on the same day. Shaun was even more out of place than I was; I had at least spent three years studying criminology at Anglia Ruskin University, and was used to being so far south.' A few people laughed. 'Shaun had only been down here three months. In his own words, he'd scraped a pass after three years doing a "dossers" degree – he never said in what – at Manchester Uni. He then "followed some bird" down to Stevenage to work in Human Resources. The job ended after three months, the relationship ended even sooner, and before he knew it, he'd joined the police.'

Now the laughter was genuine. Warren found himself smiling; he could almost hear Grimshaw's voice.

'We were together from the day we started. Shaun is the only person I know who would think it entirely acceptable to turn up on his first day at training college in a Man City shirt, hungover, smelling of beer and wearing too much aftershave. I knew we were going to get on.'

Martinez's eyes were shining, and he wiped his nose with a ragged tissue. 'We worked beside each other in uniform, before both deciding to join CID. I wanted to be Inspector Morse, Shaun was "sick of dealing with dickheads on a Saturday night".'

Martinez paused, his voice softening. 'He revelled in being crude and loud, and became more northern the longer he lived down south, but he was probably the brightest bloke I knew. He loved to take the piss, but he was generous and kind when he wanted to be. He was bloody useless in the betting shop, but he'd always get a round in if he won anything. I'm going to miss him.'

A chorus of muted 'hear, hears' went around the room. A few colleagues stepped forward to shake Martinez's hand, or give him a hug.

Finally, Martinez stepped back, and raised his voice. 'Shaun was killed by Frankie Cullen, probably because his brother Paddy told him to. But they're just the hired help; neither of them could find their arse with both hands. Stevie Cullen was running a profitable modern slavery business, until he was killed because he couldn't keep his dick in his pants. But again, he couldn't do that on his own. Somewhere out there is the man behind all of this. A bloke we know only as "Northern Man". All we have his mobile phone number, but let's bring this fucker down.'

'Shaun's parents will be here after lunch,' said Warren. 'Do you want to come with me to meet them?'

Martinez and Warren were sitting in Warren's office.

Martinez sighed. 'Yeah, I think I should. I knew him the best.'

'Have you ever met them before?' asked Warren.

'No, funnily enough. He talked about them of course, Cathy and Bill, but we've never met. All I really knew about them was that they used to run a small newspaper business in the town centre, but they went bust after the 1996 bombing. He popped in to see them when we drove up to Manchester to pick up Anica Vukovi , but I didn't go with him.'

Warren puffed his lips out. 'Does he have any brothers or sisters?'

'No, he's an only child.'

Martinez looked uncomfortable. 'I don't know the code to Shaun's locker. We'll want to empty it in case there's anything we need to give to his parents.'

'I'll contact security,' said Warren. 'Whilst we're waiting though, we should empty his desk drawers as well.' He didn't relish the job. He'd emptied Gary Hastings' desk and had ended up dry-heaving in the toilets. He hoped he didn't have the same reaction this time.

'No time like the present,' he said, forcing himself to stand.

Security met them beside Grimshaw's desk. It was, Warren thought, a reflection of the man himself: somewhat messy, and apparently disorganized. Underneath the desk, to the right of where Grimshaw's knees would have been, was a three-drawer desk unit. Locked with a simple key, it was suitable for personal belongings and non-sensitive, private correspondence.

'He reckoned he could find and identify anything on there,' said Martinez, as he picked up Grimshaw's favourite Manchester City mug, emblazoned with 'Winners 2013/14'. As usual, the white porcelain was stained a dark brown colour.

'He said he didn't trust the dishwasher not to chip it,' said Martinez. 'I think he was just a lazy git and liked the taste of mould.'

The security guard used his master key to open the drawer. Beside them, Rachel Pymm appeared holding a large Tupperware box.

'It doesn't seem right to put all his belongings in a bin bag,' she said.

Clearing a space on the desk, Warren lifted the top drawer out of the unit, and placed it down.

'Anything of a clearly personal nature, place it in the Tupperware box for his parents,' instructed Warren. 'Any paperwork or force-related material, place it on this pile so that we can go through it. Anything you're unsure about, place it on this pile. I'll take the Tupperware box down to HR for vetting before we give it to his parents.'

The first drawer had little of interest: a half-empty packet of cigarettes, his Manchester City lighter, a spare tie, some betting slips, and a pile of fifty-pence pieces.

Warren placed the lighter and the tie in the Tupperware box, and placed the cigarettes and coins to one side. He'd find an envelope for the money.

He placed the second drawer on top of the first. Lying on the top was a thin, dark green, woollen jumper. Warren lifted the jumper carefully, and folded it more neatly, before putting it into the Tupperware box. Behind him, Pymm inhaled sharply.

Nestled beneath the jumper, were two mobile phones.

Forensic IT were in the office within an hour. Wearing gloves, Pete Robertson carefully removed the SIM card from the first phone.

'Neither handset is a smartphone, so there's no risk of them being deleted remotely, but I'd rather not take any chances.'

He placed the SIM into a miniature adapter, which he then plugged into his laptop.

'It'll take a minute to decrypt and read whatever's on the card,' he said, as he turned his attention to the second phone. His long, thin fingers carefully manipulated the rear off the back of the second phone, inserting the SIM card into a second adapter, which he plugged into a different USB port on his laptop.

A quiet beep signalled the completion of the first SIM card. Robertson scribbled the SIM's phone number onto a Post-it Note.

A few seconds later, a second beep and the second number appeared on the screen.

Warren's heart sank. He didn't need Rachel Pymm to confirm who the numbers belonged to.

Neither did Martinez. He sat down heavily. 'Oh, Shaun mate, what were you doing?'

One number belonged to Stevie Cullen's missing mobile phone. The other belonged to the mysterious Northern Man.

Chapter 58

Warren felt as if he'd been kicked. He sat in Grayson's office, drinking coffee. It all made sense now. Joey McGhee, the homeless man who kipped behind the massage parlour had claimed that a man with a northern accent had turned up after the killing, promising to 'sort everything out'. He'd then been given what they believed to be Stevie Cullen's work phone. Kourtney Flitton had claimed that the person who bought the drugs from her that contributed to Joey McGhee's fatal overdose had been a 'northern man'.

Both of them were now dead. Grimshaw was at the heart of the case, and his broad Mancunian accent marked him out very clearly as northern. That couldn't be a coincidence. What else had he tried to cover up?

Next to Warren sat Ian Bergen. His fellow DCI was similarly pale and shocked.

'Christ, I worked alongside Shaun Grimshaw for years. He wasn't to everyone's taste, but corrupt?' He took a long swig of his coffee.

'Now it's bloody obvious, isn't it?' Putting his coffee cup down, he enumerated the points on his fingers.

'Last year we raided the Cullen farm, alongside HMRC and

Home Office observers. There were only a half-dozen workers, all with the correct documentation. The bastards knew we were coming. I managed to persuade the bean counters to cough up enough money to sit someone at the end of their drive for a month and photograph everyone coming and going. Not a bloody dicky bird. The same goes for every other dirty little business we suspected they were involved in: car washes, nail bars, cleaning firms.'

'And Shaun Grimshaw would have been privy to that information?' asked Grayson.

Bergen flushed slightly. 'Yeah, the Cullens were so far down the food chain, they were talked about openly in the office. Anyone on the task force would have been aware of what was happening.'

Grayson diplomatically chose to say nothing; Bergen and his team would have plenty of questions to answer about their operational security.

'And we think he was on the take?' said Grayson.

'The envelopes of used twenties hidden in his desk suggest so. Forensics are fast-tracking the fingerprints as we speak, to see who else handled them,' said Warren.

'What about that pile of fifty-pence pieces you sent off?' asked Grayson.

Warren looked slightly embarrassed. 'I think he was also raiding the communal coffee honesty jar. Since I am the only person who ever puts money in there, if my prints are on the coins, we can probably assume that he stole those as well.'

'Anything a little more relevant?' asked Grayson, a slight edge to his tone.

'That neatly folded jumper in his bottom drawer had some tiny stains along the cuff that might be blood,' said Warren. 'We've sent off for fast-track DNA analysis. Smart money's on Kourtney Flitton, the drug dealer who supplied Joey McGhee, and later "Northern Man" with the drugs that killed him.'

'And was brutally killed in her flat, in what at first glance looks to have been a robbery gone wrong,' supplied Bergen.

'Wasn't the murder weapon found at the scene?' asked Grayson.

'Yes,' replied Warren, 'although I'm not too hopeful we'll find anything useful. The killer was smart enough to stage the scene; I'd be surprised if they were sloppy enough to leave any obvious evidence on the murder weapon.'

'Every contact leaves a trace,' quoted Grayson. 'Let's keep our fingers crossed.'

Bergen shook his head again. 'I just can't believe it. Shaun Grimshaw not only corrupt, but also involved in two murders.'

'He also tried to get me thrown off the case,' said Warren quietly. 'He was standing in reception when I gave that money to Joey McGhee. Who else would have known to report it anonymously to Professional Standards? Or that there was CCTV footage?'

'Christ.' Grayson's voice was tight with fury. 'He was playing us all.'

'That burner phone we found in his desk was switched on just before we raided the farm,' said Warren. 'It was located within fifty metres of the centre of this building. The text tipping off Paddy Cullen wasn't responded to immediately. If it had been, Paddy and the workers would have been gone before we even got there.' Warren paused. 'And Shaun wouldn't have been shot.'

'We also wouldn't have known who Northern Man is,' said Bergen. 'Serves him right if you ask me.'

Warren bit his tongue. Nobody in the room had slept for more than a couple of hours, and they were all stressed and tired. He doubted Bergen truly meant his harsh words.

Warren tried to think back to what Grimshaw had been doing at the time of the phone call. Had he popped outside for one last cigarette before the raid, and made the call then?

'Rachel Pymm is correlating the phone's historic location data with Shaun's personal phone. It's a match so far,' said Warren.

'So, where does Stevie Cullen's murder come into all of this?' asked Grayson.

'Very bad timing,' said Warren.

'I reckon Grimshaw had a very nice, cosy little relationship going on with Stevie Cullen and almost certainly the rest of the family,' said Bergen. 'He kept an eye out for any trouble; he let them know about upcoming raids and probably used his position as a police officer to threaten any of the workers with dire consequences if they didn't play ball.'

'Which would explain why Silvija Wilson and her two nieces are too scared to speak to us,' interjected Grayson.

'Or Annie Vukovi,' said Warren. 'Bloody hell, that poor woman. I sent Shaun up to Manchester to bring her back after her arrest. She must have been terrified when he turned up.'

'Well we weren't to know,' said Grayson, firmly.

'From the call logs, it looks as though Wilson had Grimshaw's number. She must have been beside herself when her nieces phoned and told her what had just happened to Stevie Cullen,' said Bergen.

'And so in sweeps Shaun to help tidy everything up,' said Warren.

'Although he wasn't daft enough to offer to dispose of the clothing and murder weapon,' noted Grayson. 'The last thing he'd want is any trace evidence from Cullen ending up on his clothes.'

'Mind you, holding on to Stevie Cullen's business phone was a bit of a misstep,' said Bergen.

'Cheeky sod was first on scene after the uniforms,' said Warren. 'No wonder the two sisters kept their mouths shut.'

'Any theories about his involvement in the killing of the farm worker Emil, and Annie Vukovi's escape?' asked Grayson.

Warren thought for a moment. 'Limited, I would have thought, at least at the time. I can't see why he would have been there the night that Emil tried to escape and was shot. I'll bet they never even told him. I figure they will have thought that a few quid for turning a blind eye is one thing, but that whole cock-up wasn't something they'd want a police officer involved in.'

'Which makes sense,' said Bergen. 'Grimshaw wasn't an idiot. The Cullens probably reckoned both Annie and the other farm worker escaped and so when they got scared off by the police helicopter flying over the A506, just let it go. Grimshaw would have never taken that chance. He'd have gone back in the woods and searched until he was satisfied that there were no embarrassing dead bodies lying around waiting to be stumbled over.'

'He must have been as surprised as anyone when those bodies turned up,' said Warren. 'He couldn't get inside the investigation to derail it, so the best he could probably do is go and tell Ray Dorridge to keep his mouth shut about what happened that night on his land.'

'Which is probably just as well for Annie Vukovi ,' said Grayson. 'If Grimshaw knew that Wilson had started employing some young Serbian woman who appeared out of the blue, then it wouldn't have taken too much detective work to put two and two together and realize that she was one of the escaped farm workers.'

'Do you think Stevie Cullen would have recognized her in the massage parlour?' asked Bergen.

'Who knows?' said Warren. 'But from what we've pieced together so far, Annie didn't usually work that late. She and Stevie's paths wouldn't ordinarily cross.'

'Which does raise some questions concerning what really happened that day,' said Grayson. 'The story so far is that Stevie Cullen was forcing himself onto Biljana Dragi . What if Annie just happened to stumble across Cullen having a massage and decide to rid herself of a potential problem?'

'So murder, rather than self-defence?' said Warren, the words bitter in his mouth. As a detective, it was his duty to go where the evidence led him, not to hope for a particular outcome. However, the story of what had happened to Anica Vukovi , and the workers kept in slavery by the Cullens, had moved him and his team. The rules on what constituted self-defence under law had recently been changed, but even so, stabbing a man without any immediate provocation would be a hard sell to a jury.

'At least with Shaun dead, the witnesses have nothing to fear anymore. Let's hope that they finally tell us what really happened that day,' said Warren. The other two men agreed.

'So why was Grimshaw killed then?' asked Grayson.

'I imagine that he knew too much,' said Bergen. 'If Paddy really did only receive that text message minutes before we raided, he must have panicked.' He paused. 'Well we know he panicked; he took a pot shot at an armed response unit as he tried to escape. That's not the reasoning of a man with a plan. There's nothing Shaun could have done to stop our investigation after we raided the farm, so he was just a loose end that needed tidying up.'

Grayson shook his head sadly. 'He set up his own death. If he'd not tried to warn them, and then joined in the raid, presumably to help hide any evidence, then they would all have been arrested and he'd still be alive.'

The three men contemplated that thought for a while.

Poetic justice or a tragedy?

Warren wasn't sure.

Chapter 59

'From the moment that our investigation into the death of Stevie Cullen started, we have had problems with nobody being willing to tell us what really happened that day.'

Warren was addressing the entire investigation team in the main CID office.

'One of those reasons was almost certainly the pressure placed on them by Shaun Grimshaw to keep quiet. Silvija Wilson employed illegal workers and wanted to protect herself, and them, from investigation by the Organized Crime Unit and the Home Office. Her nieces wanted to protect their friend Anica Vukovi , who was herself an illegal immigrant, albeit one forced into working against her will. When she killed Stevie Cullen, they rallied around to protect her, both from prosecution for murder and to stop her from being deported. Now that we have her, and Grimshaw is gone, I'm hopeful that all four women will no longer feel that they need to keep quiet.'

'What about the two nail technicians?' asked Richardson.

'We have identified the two young women who worked in Silvija Wilson's massage parlour, and we are hopeful that they might have seen or heard something that day which can help us.'

'Why did they head back to the Cullen farm after they escaped from the massage parlour?' asked Ruskin. 'Stevie Cullen was dead; they were free.'

'It's not uncommon in these cases,' said Pymm. 'They become so institutionalized, they don't know any other type of existence. They can't imagine any other life. Besides which, they don't speak any English, probably had no money, no passports and were working here illegally. I bet when we interview them, we'll find out that they are even more terrified about being sent to a detention centre and deported back to wherever they came from, than staying with the Cullens.'

'They had the opportunity to escape every day,' Hutchinson reminded them. 'Stevie Cullen dropped them off every morning, and picked them up that evening, with no problems at all.'

'Poor bastards,' said Ruskin. 'I can't get my head around that level of control.'

Like everyone, he had seen the photographs of the locked shipping containers that the Cullens had housed the workers in. Lit by a single bulb, with no natural light, the workers had used a small gas stove to both cook on and heat their prison. A hole cut in the side of the metal container for ventilation was the only reason that the workers hadn't suffocated or died of carbon monoxide poisoning.

Sanitary facilities were limited to little more than a bucket, with water coming from the standpipe outside. In the container used by the women, someone had managed to rig up a dirty bed sheet to provide at least the illusion of privacy. Clothes were washed using the cold water from outside. The only exception to this was the nail technicians' uniforms, a couple of which were found in a laundry basket in the farmhouse's kitchen – presumably the stained, torn garments worn by the farmhands and the car washers weren't suitable for such work.

'At least they didn't say anything about Annie to the Cullens,' said Ruskin.

'She must have been terrified when she realized who they were,' said Pymm. 'I'm amazed she stuck around.'

'I think she had completely run out of options, by that point,' said Warren. 'I don't think Ray Dorridge has been entirely open with us either,' he continued. 'We'll get him back in as well. With the whole Cullen family out of the picture, and no Grimshaw to threaten him, there are no reprisals for him to worry about.'

'What have the Cullens got to say for themselves?' asked Richardson.

'Nothing so far,' said Bergen. 'The parents, Rosie and Seamus, are not commenting, and neither Paddy nor Frankie is in any fit state to be interviewed. The surgeons reckon Frankie might never wake up. Saffron and her husband are refusing to admit to knowing anything about the illegal workers, or Grimshaw's involvement.'

'They lived on site, so that's hardly going to wash with a jury,' said Warren.

'They're a hard-faced lot,' admitted Bergen, 'but we knew that going in. Lavender, their eldest daughter, has hired a lawyer, and has released a statement claiming that she knew nothing of her family's business dealings, since she left home years go. I don't believe her for one second, so we'll start building a case against her, for conspiracy if nothing else.'

'What about the other workers?' asked Hutchinson.

'Nothing yet – they're scared and confused,' said Bergen. 'We've got the translators and the counsellors in, but it's plain to see how vulnerable they are. Two appear to have significant learning difficulties, and a number have serious alcohol dependency issues.' His mouth twisted in disgust. 'It's one of the ways the bastards controlled them.'

'Have we identified the man found dead in the woods yet?' asked Richardson.

Pymm shook her head. 'Nothing yet. Annie only ever knew his first name. Immigration are going through their records to see if they can work out when he arrived in this country. All Annie knew was that he had been with the Cullens longer than she had. He was kind to her when she first arrived, which is why they fell in love.'

The team went silent.

The whole affair was a tragedy, but the fate of Emil seemed especially poignant. Whatever his story, at least one person had loved him. After all that had happened, to bury him without even his full name seemed a cruel twist.

Especially if the only person who truly knew him, and the mother of his child, would never be able to visit his grave.

Warren had called a late-afternoon briefing to go over the new interviews that had been conducted with the principal witnesses and suspects after Grimshaw's death.

The first to give feedback were Mags Richardson and Moray Ruskin, who had visited the two sisters on the remand wing of the Mount Prison first thing.

'There was a mixed response at first,' said Richardson. 'When I told Malina that Annie had admitted to killing Stevie Cullen to protect Biljana from his sexual assault, she no commented again. But when I told her that the Cullens were all in custody, she asked to speak to her lawyer. She has now admitted that the sequence of events, as told by Annie and Wilson, was what she believed happened, although she didn't see the assault directly. She entered as Annie was wrestling with Stevie for the knife. Biljana was on the floor, trying to get away from them, her top undone. She insists that the stabbing was an accident.'

'Did Biljana confirm that?' asked Warren.

'Eventually. At first she didn't believe us when I said that her aunt and sister had told us what they believed had happened, but as agreed in the interview strategy meeting I revealed that we knew that Annie had stabbed Stevie and that there was no longer any point in trying to defend her. Like her sister, it was the arrest of the Cullens that convinced her it was safe to tell us what had happened.'

'What was her version of events?' asked Warren.

'Consistent with what we had already been told. After many months of sexual approaches from Cullen, he finally attacked her, threatening her with a knife that he removed from his back pocket. The description of the knife matches the one retrieved from the riverbank.'

'So, he brought the weapon with him,' said Warren, 'which weakens the case for premeditation. What happened next?'

'He already had his trousers down,' continued Richardson. 'Biljana called out once, but he pressed the knife against her throat. She thought she would have to give Cullen oral sex, but her cry for help must have been loud enough to alert Annie, who was next door doing laundry. She burst in a few seconds later.'

'And the stabbing?' asked Warren.

'Cullen was holding her by her hair in his right hand and holding the knife to her throat with the left,' said Richardson.

'We know he was left-handed,' interjected Hutchinson.

'When Annie came in, he let go of her hair and removed the knife from her throat. Biljana scrambled away, and so she didn't see how Annie tackled Cullen. When she turned back, Annie and Cullen were wrestling over the knife. Cullen's penis was exposed, and his boxer shorts were down around his ankles, so he was off balance. Cullen fell backwards, and that was when he was stabbed.'

'That largely fits with what Annie told us,' said Warren, 'but the sisters and Wilson were alone with Annie for a considerable amount of time before she caught the train to Manchester. They could have concocted that story between them. We need an independent witness.'

'That's where we might get lucky,' said Ruskin, with a smile. 'Biljana thinks that Malina might not have been the first on the scene after Annie tackled Stevie.'

'One of the nail technicians?' asked Warren.

'She thinks so. She's sure that she saw a glimpse of a face at the door as she scrambled to get away from Cullen.'

Warren felt his pulse rate rise. Could this be the final piece of independent evidence necessary to support or destroy Annie and Biljana's account of events?

According to Silvija Wilson, and customers to the shop, the two resident nail technicians were Vietnamese, and unable to speak English. Warren thought it questionable that they could speak Serbian either. Either way, it seemed doubtful that they would have been able to concoct a shared narrative in the few moments before they disappeared out the back door.

'Have we confirmed that the Vietnamese women rescued from the Cullens' farm were the nail technicians we are looking for?' asked Hutchinson.

'Hopefully we'll know soon enough. It's one of the first things that they will be asked once the counsellors are satisfied that they are fit to be interviewed,' said Warren.

The next part of the interview left a bad taste in Warren's mouth, but it had to be asked.

'How did they react to the news that Shaun Grimshaw is dead? Were they willing to identify him as Northern Man and explain his role in the operation?'

'That's where it gets a bit weird,' said Richardson.

By the end of the day, the follow-up interviews with all of those involved in the death of Stevie Cullen had been completed. Warren sat in Grayson's office, feeding back to him the day's progress.

'All of the stories are consistent with each other,' said Warren. The last couple of days had come after an already hard few weeks, and he was grateful for Grayson's 'special' blend of coffee. What it lacked in smoothness and flavour, it more than made up for in caffeine. The buzz Warren was feeling explained why the DSI kept those pods in his desk drawer, rather than next to his coffee machine.

'Self-defence?' asked Grayson.

'Defence of Biljana certainly and given that Annie and Cullen ended up wrestling for the knife, there's probably a good case to argue that she acted lawfully. I'm awaiting guidance from the CPS as to whether we drop the murder charges, although I suspect they'll reserve judgement until we can interview the nail technician who might have witnessed the altercation.'

Grayson drained his cup, grimacing at the bitter taste. 'I have another meeting with Professional Standard's Anti-Corruption Unit first thing tomorrow morning. As you can imagine, the Shaun Grimshaw debacle has opened a whole new can of worms. They have agreed that we need to complete our murder investigation before they come in and start in earnest, but they are watching our progress with interest.'

The combined buzz from a largely completed investigation and Grayson's super-charged coffee was already receding, and Warren felt a wave of exhaustion pass over him. He was too experienced to think for one moment that all the hard work on the case was completed, now that they knew what probably happened. However, the thought that an anti-corruption inquiry would be running in parallel to their preparation for trial was acutely depressing. Warren had been the subject of Professional Standards inquiries in the past, most recently into the decisions his team had made during the murders at Middlesbury Abbey, and before that into the death of Gary Hastings. The experiences had been stressful to say the least.

Grayson saw the look on his face. 'Warren, they are not investigating you or us. Shaun Grimshaw made his choices long before he joined Middlesbury.' He pulled a face. 'They're just going to use us to help shovel the shit onto SOC and Ian Bergen and his team.'

Serious Organized Crime and Warren's murder team had butted heads before when investigations had overlapped. Nevertheless, Warren had grown to like Ian Bergen and he was relieved that he had turned out not to be Northern Man. But the man would still be subject to an anti-corruption investigation. Yet again, Warren was reminded how much he hated the way that corrupt police officers ruined the lives of so many others. If Bergen and his team were judged to have been sloppy, or even negligent, in their oversight of Grimshaw and the flow of restricted information between team members, the consequences were likely career-ending.

'With that in mind,' continued Grayson, 'what have the witnesses told us about Grimshaw's involvement? How hands-on was he?'

Warren exhaled in frustration. 'That's where we're drawing a blank. Everyone we've interviewed gave a sigh of relief when we told them that the Cullens were all under arrest, and they needn't fear reprisals. But they are still refusing to name or even identify Grimshaw. Even Silvija Wilson, who is now desperate to unravel the mess her nieces have got themselves into, has refused to acknowledge the existence of Grimshaw, even though we have eyewitnesses placing him at the scene in the immediate aftermath of the murder, and dozens of calls to that mobile phone. Annie Vukovi burst into tears when she was shown a headshot of him and told he is dead; she hasn't spoken since.

'Ray Dorridge claimed not to recognize any of the photographs that we showed him, but he looked frightened. I also have concerns about a black eye he's sporting, which he claims came from a fall.'

'What a bloody mess,' observed Grayson. He looked at his watch and stood up. 'Well, that's not our concern. Let Professional Standards unravel Grimshaw's lies and figure out how he scared everyone so much they won't even implicate him now he's dead. In the meantime, I'm going home, and so are you.' He raised a hand to quell Warren's protest. 'That's an order.'

Thursday 26 November

Chapter 60

It had been four days since the unmasking of Shaun Grimshaw as 'Northern Man', and the arrest of the Cullens. Nevertheless, CID was still busy, as the team gathered the necessary evidence for the eventual court cases and inquests. This part of the job was at least as important as the initial phase of the investigation, since any errors or shortcomings would be pounced upon by the Cullens' legal teams. Warren was also acutely aware that the future of Annie Vukovi was far from certain. The CPS still hadn't decided whether to continue pursuing a conviction for murder, and Warren needed to know that he had given her every chance. A police officer's duty was first and foremost to find the truth. He knew his team felt the same way.

However, the sense of urgency in the office had somewhat receded and Grayson had insisted that everyone – Warren included – take some of their accumulated rest days.

Warren had just returned from two days away. Susan's head teacher had agreed to let her take a couple of days unpaid personal leave and they had driven to Coventry to finally speak to their loved ones and tell them the sad news about the miscarriage. The break had been far from restful, but the previous night he had slept better than he had in weeks.

Granddad Jack had taken the news of the end of Susan's pregnancy better than they'd feared. There had been tears from everyone, but the old man had insisted that he wanted to support them. He even went as far as pledging his savings to fund another cycle of IVF; that was a discussion for another day, but Warren had been moved to tears again by his generosity.

Bernice and Dennis had been similarly upset, but had been more supportive than Warren had expected. Bernice had hugged her daughter in a way that she hadn't for months. Whatever her religious views might be on the rights and wrongs of assisted reproduction, the two babies had been her future grandchildren and she grieved their loss. Later that evening, Dennis had taken Warren to one side and also quietly promised to help them financially if they needed it. Warren had managed to hold the tears back this time.

Before Warren and Susan returned to Middlesbury, the family had picked Granddad Jack up from his respite home, wheeling him to church, where they'd lit candles and said prayers for the souls of their two children. Warren had still to come to terms with the crisis of faith he'd experienced in the aftermath of the abbey murders earlier that year. He didn't yet know if he would ever fully return to the Catholic Church – something that he and Tony Sutton had spoken about at length. However, the familiar rituals were soothing, and by the end of the service, he could feel the change in Susan, her parents and Granddad Jack. For that reason alone, he was unwilling to dismiss a return to The Church out of hand.

The previous evening, as they'd driven back home, Susan and Warren had talked for hours – for once the traffic jams caused by the perpetual roadworks on the A14 were a blessing not a curse. Warren had already had one session with Occupational Health, although he felt that in many ways the counselling he most needed – that of his wife and family – would be the most important part of healing the wounds that the past couple of years had inflicted on him.

There was a tap on his office door. Looking up, he could see the bright red of Rachel Pymm's cardigan sleeve through the frosted glass window. He got up quickly to help her in.

'How was your break?' asked Warren as he took her sticks from her and pulled over the visitor's chair. Pymm had taken her accumulated rest days at the same time as Warren.

'I need to speak to you urgently, Sir,' said Pymm, 'in confidence.'

The uncharacteristic lack of manners, coupled with her grave tone, gave Warren pause.

He knew it wouldn't be good news.

Warren felt the shock wash over him. He sat down heavily.

'Are you sure?' It was a silly question. Pymm didn't make those sorts of mistakes.

'Definitely. I ran the licence plate of the van that Paddy Cullen tried to escape in against HOLMES as per procedure. Just tidying up some loose ends really. As usual, there was the list of previous searches for that index with time stamps.' She gave a shuddering breath. 'The last search was the one that I did when Mags first identified the van from the traffic cameras. There is no record of any subsequent searches by Organized Crime, even though we asked them to run one when it was first identified.'

'But there wouldn't be, would there?' said Warren. 'They were supposed to be running it through their own restricted files. We don't have access to that part of the database, for obvious reasons.'

It wasn't lost on Warren that Grimshaw would have had the correct permissions to access those cases back when he was on Bergen's task force, although they should have been rescinded when he moved to Middlesbury.

'I'm an officer in the case. I should at least see a red flag against a search, even if I can't see any other details.'

'OK.' Warren trusted her enough to let her continue; she wouldn't be making such serious allegations without evidence.

'So, I called a friend of mine in SOC. He ran the number through the system, using his permissions and it came back as a positive match to a van that they knew the Cullens owned.' She paused and swallowed. 'When they were asked to run it through their system previously, they were told we'd already run it through the DVLA, so just ran it through HOLMES, otherwise they'd have realized they hadn't been given a real licence plate number; it was out by just one digit.'

'Which could be explained away as human error,' interjected Warren.

'Exactly. We could have linked the van to the Cullens days earlier.'

Warren was stunned, as he thought back to the sequence of events.

'But how do you know …'

'There's more, Sir.'

The news that Grimshaw hadn't been Northern Man had hit Grayson like a bombshell.

'That bastard …'

Grayson had moved fast, agreeing with Warren's assessment that they needed to arrest immediately. By the time Warren had completed briefing the rest of the team, he'd authorised a phone intercept and arranged an arrest warrant, a Forced Entry Team was already on stand-by. Professional Standards had observers from their Anti-Corruption Unit en route, but they weren't waiting for them. The target had already had days to destroy evidence and cover his tracks, and they didn't intend to give him a minute more.

Besides which, he'd duped them all. This was personal.

'Do we know where he is?' asked Grayson, skimming through the steady stream of emails flying into his phone.

'Rachel just got the location data on his phone', said Warren. 'Assuming he's carrying it, he's at home.'

'Then let's go get him.'

The house was a two-bedroom, terraced affair, in a small cul-de-sac. Spotters had already completed a drive-by and confirmed that their target's car was parked off road, on a hard-standing in front of the kitchen window. The house was less than ten years old, and unless its owner had remodelled, the living room was at the rear of the house. This time of night, the curtains were drawn, but light leaking out of the large bay windows at both the front and the back indicated the occupant was in either the living room or the kitchen. The upstairs was dark.

'He has CCTV at the front of the house and the back. My officers are behind the garden fence. The gate is wooden and locked with a simple padlock. I don't see it being an obstacle,' said Roger Gibson, the sergeant coordinating the forced entry. 'We don't want to tip him off, so we'll enter the front and rear simultaneously.'

Warren looked to Grayson for approval.

'It's your show, Warren.'

'Do it.'

The entry was fast and brutally efficient.

On Warren's signal, Sergeant Gibson and his team burst out from behind the hedges concealing them. Despite their bulky body armour, and the even bulkier battering ram two of the team were carrying, they covered the length of the front drive in seconds.

The battering ram hit the door precisely on the lock, a single blow smashing it inwards so that it crashed against the wall. A moment later, Warren heard the sound of breaking glass as the

French windows at the back of the property received the same treatment.

Shouts of 'Armed Police, show me your hands!' were echoed over the open radio link, followed by 'Drop the knife. Drop the knife.'

A second later, Warren heard the distinctive rapid-fire clicks of a TASER being fired.

For the next few seconds, all he could hear over the airwaves was shouting. Eventually the noise died down as the entry team reported each room in the house clear of any other occupants.

Unable to wait any longer, Warren headed up the drive and through the gaping doorway. Grayson followed.

'In the kitchen, Sirs,' said the armed officer standing just inside the threshold.

Following her pointed finger, Warren entered the room.

The target lay face-down on the parquet flooring. Beside him, just out of reach, a large kitchen knife lay where it had fallen. A wooden knife block lay on its side on the countertop, the remaining blades scattered across the wooden surface. A smashed glass lay in a pool of liquid in front of the sink.

'Watch your feet,' warned the sergeant kneeling on the suspect's back as he fastened the handcuffs. 'He pissed himself when I discontinued the shock.'

Warren stepped carefully around the yellow puddle.

'Got the bastard,' muttered Grayson beside him.

Warren squatted down beside the man's head. After a couple of seconds, the prostrate man turned to look at him, his eyes still glassy from the after-effects of the high-voltage electric shock.

'You are under arrest on suspicion of murder …'

Chapter 61

It was well-past midnight when the interview started. Warren had a pile of folders in front of him. Next to him, DI Erica Leadsom, a representative from the Anti-Corruption Unit of Professional Standards, made notes on a legal pad. The suspect was flanked by his solicitor and a representative from the Police Federation. Upstairs in the main CID briefing room, there was standing room only as the interview was streamed onto the big screen.

After completing the preliminary paperwork, Warren signalled it was time for the interview to start.

'My client has a statement that he wishes to be read into the record, before we start,' said the solicitor. After agreement from Warren, she started to read from her laptop screen.

'My client wishes to state that he is categorically innocent of all the charges presented to him. It is clear that there has been a misunderstanding based on his previous relationship with Detective Sergeant Shaun Grimshaw. My client believes that this investigation is based on circumstantial evidence at best and he looks forward to a complete exoneration. He will also be pursuing a claim for wrongful arrest, excessive force, and reputational damage.'

Warren thanked her for the statement and turned his attention to the man sitting opposite him.

In the hours since his arrest, the accused had been cleaned up and dressed in a grey, shapeless tracksuit. A small bandage applied to his forehead covered the cut he had received when he had collapsed to the floor after being shot with the TASER.

In the harsh, white light, the man's face was pasty, the purple bruising surrounding his cut standing out in stark relief. Since the arrest, the only words he had spoken were to confirm his name and personal details to the custody sergeant, his voice little more than a mumble. Warren had noticed how his northern accent, usually softened from years of living in the south, had been stronger under stress.

There was no doubt in Warren's mind, that the man sat before him was the mysterious Northern Man, whose corruption had allowed the Cullen family to thrive unchallenged for so many years.

'Let's start with the murder of Stevie Cullen,' said Warren.

'My client was not involved in that murder, as you well know,' said the solicitor.

So that was how it was going to be. The suspect glared at him across the table. It was obvious that a confession would not be forthcoming. Warren ignored the interruption.

'Where were you on Monday November the 2nd between the hours of approximately one-twenty-five p.m. and three p.m.?'

'No comment.'

Warren was unfazed. He had expected as much.

'According to records from your personal mobile phone, your phone was turned off at that time. In fact, the phone was switched off moments after this burner phone, later found in DS Grimshaw's desk, received a call from Silvija Wilson. Do you recognize this phone?'

Warren showed him a photograph of the burner phone.

'No comment.'

'At one-forty p.m., an emergency call was received by 999 call handlers reporting a fatal stabbing at the Middlesbury Massage and Relaxation Centre, a massage parlour owned by Silvija Wilson. Uniformed officers and a paramedic first response unit were dispatched, and Middlesbury CID were informed that a murder had taken place. DS Shaun Grimshaw was one of two CID officers to attend the scene, arriving twenty minutes after the paramedics pronounced life extinguished.

'Where were you?'

'No comment.'

'According to an analysis of the tracking movements of the burner phone and DS Grimshaw's personal phone over the past twelve months, the two phones were in close proximity to one another ninety-one per cent of the time that the burner phone was switched on. Can you explain why that was the case?'

The suspect licked his lips and glanced towards his solicitor.

'I believe that you have already established that DS Grimshaw was the owner of this burner phone,' said his solicitor. 'I fail to see what relevance this has to my client.'

'Have we established that DS Grimshaw owned the phone?' said Warren contemplatively. 'Somebody certainly wanted to make sure we thought it was his.'

He produced a second sheet of paper, spinning it through 180 degrees so that it could be read by those on the opposite side of the table.

'DS Grimshaw's personal phone's tracking data places it in close proximity ninety-one per cent of the time that the burner phone is turned on. However, the burner phone is in close proximity to *your* personal phone ninety-nine per cent of the time. In fact, on the day of the murder, the burner phone was within fifty metres of your phone, right up until the moment that it received the call from Silvija Wilson, and your personal phone was turned off. Can you explain why that happened?'

'No comment.'

The pallor of the man across the table had now gone past white and was tinged with green. Warren hoped he didn't throw up; he hated when they did that.

'The burner phone remained in close proximity to DS Grimshaw's phone right up until the moment that the call came into CID requesting presence at the scene. It then stays close to his phone until five-past-two. At that time, the burner phone moves away from DS Grimshaw's phone. It stays within that area for the next couple of hours, but it is clear from the data that it is not being carried by DS Grimshaw.'

Warren paused to let that sink in. 'Why is that?'

The suspect paused. Warren could see the panicked calculations going on behind his eyes. He held his breath.

'He must have left it in the car.'

Warren mentally punched the air.

The wise thing to do in this situation, would be to 'No comment.' The man in front of him must know that intellectually, yet despite his hours of training and even more hours of actually performing interviews, he had been unable to help himself. He was in a corner, and he knew it. Now he would come out fighting. He had no choice.

'The phone moved around; it wasn't stationary.'

'There were lots of people at the scene. Perhaps he gave the phone to somebody else? Perhaps he was working with them or even trying to frame them?'

Warren said nothing, letting him realize what he had just said. Both the solicitor and the Federation Rep winced. Out of the corner of his eye, Warren saw Leadsom make a note on her pad.

'Where were you when DS Grimshaw was securing the massage parlour?'

'No comment.'

It was too late to backtrack now, and he knew it.

'Throughout this investigation, you supported the narrative

given by the two masseuses that a mysterious masked stranger clambered through the window of the massage parlour and murdered Stevie Cullen where he lay. During that time you were willing to entertain the idea that Anton Rimington, the fiancé of Vicki Barclay, might have murdered Cullen in a fit of jealousy, yet you repeatedly dismissed the idea that Ray Dorridge, with whom Stevie Cullen had a business arrangement could have been responsible.

'An objective look at the facts would suggest that Dorridge's motives were at least as strong as Rimington's, yet you wouldn't support that idea. Why?'

'No comment.'

'Was it because you were worried that Ray Dorridge might identify you as the corrupt member of SOC, known to us as "Northern Man", who had ensured that the Cullen family's illegal workers enterprise went uncovered?'

'No comment.'

'Did you threaten to expose Ray Dorridge's use of illegal labour if he didn't keep his mouth shut?'

'No comment.'

'And when he confessed to using illegal labour, removing that particular lever, did you then go and threaten to kill him if he identified you?'

'No comment.'

'Why didn't you kill Ray Dorridge? You killed Joey McGhee and Kourtney Flitton, to stop them identifying you.'

'No comment.'

Warren let him stew for a few seconds. 'Let's move on.'

He flicked over the pages of his notepad. 'The night of the raid on the Cullen farm. You participated in the raid; however, when we arrived both Paddy Cullen and Frankie Cullen were absent from the farmhouse. They were subsequently found in the barn, preparing to escape with a van full of illegal workers. During the subsequent altercation, Authorized Firearms Officer Bradley

Kemp was shot and run over, DS Shaun Grimshaw was shot dead and Frankie Cullen was shot and seriously injured.'

Warren took a sip of water, his mouth dry. 'Shortly before the team left, a text message was sent from the burner phone to Paddy Cullen, warning him that a raid was imminent. That text was not replied to, presumably because Mr Cullen was asleep at the time. Did you send that text?'

'No.'

Warren maintained a neutral expression. The suspect had stopped 'no commenting' again. A sign that he was getting flustered.

Warren opened the lid of his laptop and turned it so that the screen was visible. The Federation rep and solicitor shuffled their chairs around so they could see more clearly, whilst Warren read the exhibit reference into evidence.

'This is CCTV footage taken in the car park at Middlesbury Police station, two minutes before the text message was sent to Paddy Cullen. It shows the rear entrance to the station. The time stamp on the footage is accurate to within one second of those used by the mobile phone networks.'

The footage was clear, but in black and white, enhanced by passive infra-red to compensate for the lack of light.

At 03.48 the door opened, and Shaun Grimshaw stepped out clutching a packet of cigarettes. Pulling his collar up against the wind and fine drizzle, he picked a cigarette from the pack and slipped it between his lips. The camera flared white briefly as he ignited his lighter, the tip of the cigarette glowing as he puffed on it, before tipping his head back and exhaling into the night air. After a few inhalations, he swapped his lighter for a mobile phone. The screen lit up against the dark background.

After a few seconds typing, he dropped the phone down to his side again, and turned his attention back to his cigarette.

Behind him the door opened, another figure stepping out. Grimshaw nodded in acknowledgement, before turning his attention back to his phone. After exchanging a few words with the newcomer, he took one last drag of his cigarette, before stubbing it out on the lid of the metal waste bin and using his swipe card to head back inside.

The newcomer picked up his own phone, and quickly typed something, before returning it to his pocket and swiping himself back in.

'The text was sent at 03.50 and 22 seconds,' said Warren. 'Shaun stops using his phone at 03.50 and 7 seconds.'

'Maybe the text was delayed?' said the Federation Rep.

Warren wound the footage back a few seconds.

'You can see from this angle, that the phone used by Shaun is a smartphone with a touch screen – the whole handset lights up. His personal phone is a Samsung. We've looked at his phone, and his usage log shows that he was using it to check his email, specifically to respond to an offer for some cheap tickets to next week's Manchester City match. The burner phone is a cheap, standard handset, with a 2-inch square screen and keypad.'

Warren let the footage continue. Now that they were looking for it, it was clear that the newcomer's phone was bulkier, and the screen took up only a third of it. Every eye in the room was focused on the timestamp on the bottom of the screen.

At exactly 03.50 and 22 seconds, the newcomer pressed a button with his thumb, and returned the phone to his pocket.

Warren turned to the suspect.

'It was raining, and cold and nearly four o'clock in the morning. You don't smoke, so why did you go outside to use your phone, Jorge?'

Wednesday 02 December

Epilogue

'Ah, Warren. Do come in.'

Assistant Chief Constable Mohammed Naseem was all smiles as he welcomed Warren into his office at the force's headquarters in Welwyn.

Six days had passed since the charging of Jorge Martinez with the murders of Joey McGhee, Kourtney Flitton, and his friend of many years, Shaun Grimshaw, and the attempted murder of Frankie Cullen. That morning, the Crown Prosecution Service had also authorized multiple charges of misconduct in a public office, with several more in the pipeline.

Without asking, he handed Warren a porcelain cup of coffee. White, no sugar. Naseem was a man who remembered the small details, even down to the small plate of custard creams he gestured towards.

'Hell of a case, Warren,' he started as he settled back in his chair, 'conducted under difficult personal circumstances, I understand.'

'Thank you, Sir,' said Warren helping himself to a biscuit. He refrained the urge to dunk it. He didn't want to seem too familiar.

The past few days had been long, but all the loose ends had finally been tied up. There were months more work to be done before Martinez's trial in the summer, but Warren could finally relax and take some personal time. Two intensive sessions with the counsellors in Occupational Health had left him feeling, if not healed, then at least more grounded. Susan would be joining him for another session in a week or so, and Warren was feeling unexpectedly optimistic. A last-minute deal for a week in the sun immediately after Christmas would give the couple some valuable time together.

Naseem flicked open the leather-bound notebook on the desk in front of him. Over the years, Warren had become familiar with that book. It was no secret that Naseem was planning on writing his memoirs when he finally retired, and Warren's exploits were sure to feature heavily. He still wasn't entirely sure how he felt about that; he'd be the first to admit that there were aspects of this, and other cases, that he would rather not dwell on too heavily. And he certainly didn't look forward to reading about them, or having his decisions picked over by the presenters of True Crime TV documentaries.

'I hear that Martinez has finally admitted everything,' said Naseem.

'Not much choice really. The weight of evidence against him is overwhelming. His only hope now is to plead guilty and hope that his minimum tariff will see him released before he's too old to enjoy his freedom.'

'Well I, for one, hope the bastard dies in there,' said Naseem. 'He deserves everything coming to him.'

Warren had to agree. The final nail in Martinez's coffin had been from the shooting at the barn. AFO Kemp had survived being shot by Paddy Cullen, and before being run over by the van Cullen was driving, had witnessed Martinez take the shotgun off a bewildered and frightened Frankie Cullen and shoot Grimshaw in the back of the head, before turning it on Frankie.

The testimony had explained the lack of gunshot residue on Frankie Cullen's hands, and why Grimshaw had turned his back on his friend, Martinez, as he raced towards the downed AFO. That had been an incredibly heroic move, given that Paddy Cullen was still armed, and Warren had vowed to make sure that was noted on Grimshaw's posthumous citation at the Police Memorial on the edge of St James's Park.

'So, tell me how you realized that he, and not Shaun Grimshaw, was Northern Man.' Naseem carefully removed the lid of an expensive-looking fountain pen.

'It was largely down to DS Rachel Pymm,' said Warren. 'She spotted that the white van that we had identified as the one used to ferry Cullen's workers around hadn't been run through SOC's private database like we requested. Jorge Martinez had offered to phone up his old colleagues at SOC and get it fast-tracked. Instead, he gave them a false licence number, just one digit different, and told them that we had already run it through the DVLA, so there was no need for them to bother. If they had done that first, they would have realized that the number doesn't even exist.'

Naseem scowled. The sloppy procedures of DCI Ian Bergen's unit were the subject of an ongoing investigation by Professional Standards. Bergen had resigned with immediate effect the day after Martinez's arrest, but it wouldn't be enough to quell the embarrassment. Or save the careers of others in the unit. Already the press were sniffing around, and it would only be so long before the whole sorry affair hit the front pages.

'Loose lips sink ships,' observed Naseem. The moment Jorge Martinez left that unit and transferred to Middlesbury, all operational contact with that team should have stopped. It's a disgrace that he was kept in the loop as regards the Cullens.'

'In their defence, they saw Grimshaw and Martinez's transfer to the CID unit covering the Cullens' patch as a two-way exchange. A lot of the Cullens' more minor infractions came across our desk first, and Martinez and Grimshaw kept them in the loop.'

Naseem's glare stopped Warren from going any further down that path.

'So, Martinez was stringing Grimshaw along, all this time?'

Warren sighed. In some ways, this was one of the aspects that saddened him the most.

'Yes. He's quite unapologetic about that. He and Grimshaw teamed up from the first time they met at training college. Shaun was … a difficult person to get along with at times, and it seems that Jorge exploited that somewhat. He befriended him and used him as a shield to deflect suspicion away from himself.'

Naseem's lip twisted. 'Yes, the infamous Brownnose Brothers. I met them hanging around the lifts in Welwyn on a number of occasions. As I recall, DS Martinez was rather more smooth-talking than his colleague.'

Warren felt a stab of guilt; he'd fallen into that trap. Shaun Grimshaw's abrasive attitude had made it all too easy to assume the worst when the finger of suspicion had been pointed towards him.

'Yes, and we all fell for his charm. Which it now seems was a complete lie.'

'I've heard that Martinez also embellished his past somewhat,' said Naseem.

'Yes, it appears that he reinvented himself when he went to university. He portrayed himself as having a wealthy upbringing in Cheshire, when in reality he came from a poor, unprivileged, single-parent family on a housing estate in Stockport. He kept up the pretence when he joined the police, even going so far as to convince Shaun and others he met that he had grown up on the same street as a Manchester United player. That may have been his downfall. That type of background comes with the sort of trappings difficult to finance on a police officer's salary.'

'Hence the corruption.'

'Not immediately. We looked at his financial record, and it seemed that he played fast and loose with credit cards at first, and when that stopped working, turned to gambling, a habit he never really kicked. CCTV from local betting shops shows that the betting slips that we found in Shaun's drawer were actually his. Shaun liked a flutter, but nothing more. Jorge even stole money from the communal coffee jar and planted it in Shaun's drawer for us to find.'

Naseem shook his head. 'It sounds as though he stitched him up good and proper.'

'Yes, forensics on the jumper found in Shaun's drawer had traces of Kourtney Flitton's blood on it. But DNA retrieved from the neck matched Jorge. It seems that he wore it when he killed her. He then left the murder weapon where it could be found with more fibres on it for good measure. He was so anxious that the evidence was found, that when he attended the scene of the murder with the SOCOs he pissed off CSM Andy Harrison by pointing out the knife, in case they missed it.'

'That's great work, Warren. Have you managed to persuade the witnesses to name him as Northern Man?'

Warren smiled. 'Every single one of them. As soon as we told them that he was in custody, everyone rolled over and admitted he was Stevie Cullen's fixer. Silvija Wilson and Ray Dorridge have testified that Jorge put the frighteners on them to ensure that they kept their end of their bargains with Stevie Cullen. When Cullen was killed, he managed to persuade Malina and Biljana Dragi that if they stuck to the story he had concocted about the hooded killer and waited out the custody clock if they were arrested, they'd be released without charge. When that didn't happen, and they were charged, he threatened to kill their Aunt Silvija and Annie if they exposed him.

'He then convinced Silvija Wilson that he was the only hope she had of keeping her nieces out of jail. He also promised to kill Annie, if she said anything. He used the same threats with Annie when he travelled to Manchester with Shaun to arrest her. Since the four women were unable to communicate, he was able to play them off against each other.'

'Clever bastard,' muttered Naseem, 'so why didn't he kill Wilson and Dorridge, or even that friend of Stevie Cullen when he had the chance? He killed Joey McGhee and Kourtney Flitton to stop them saying anything.'

'I've been giving that a lot of thought. I think that he might have considered it but missed his opportunity. At first, he tried to shift the focus of the investigation away from Dorridge, and towards Rimington to buy himself some breathing room. When Shaun was killed, and then implicated as Northern Man, Martinez no longer had anyone to pin their deaths on. It would have been too suspicious if they ended up dead as well.'

Naseem nodded. 'It sounds like they were bloody lucky. What are they saying now?'

'Both Malina and Biljana Dragi , and Anica Vukovi , have confirmed that Silvija Wilson phoned Martinez after Annie stabbed Cullen, and that he arrived to clear up the mess. We have CCTV footage of him leaving the station suddenly, immediately after Wilson called the burner phone. He then had the balls to go back with Shaun to attend the crime scene, and also helped coach the two girls and Wilson after their initial interview to get their stories straight.'

'Cheeky bastard. What about the Cullens?'

'No loyalty from them either. They're all trying to save their skin, or at least receive a reduced sentence. They're claiming that the whole set-up was masterminded by Stevie Cullen, with Jorge involved from the outset. But that's not going to stand up in court. We've already established that the oldest sister, Lavender, did the accounts for his business. We also found his laptop in her office. IT are restoring the hard drive as we speak. The workers we rescued have said that Rosie, the mother, and the youngest daughter, Saffron, were responsible for looking after them, if it could be called that.

'Ray Dorridge has implicated the father Seamus and the twins, Frankie and Paddy, in Emil's death, saying that they turned up to keep an eye on the workers the night that he was killed trying

492

to escape with Annie. They're all claiming that Stevie was the one who fired the shotgun into the forest, and we've matched fibres caught on the hole in the fence to a jacket in his wardrobe, but I don't think we'll ever truly know who pulled the trigger and killed him. I suspect the CPS will charge them all under Joint Enterprise.'

Naseem grunted. 'No honour among thieves, eh? Still some justice at least. And fancy leaving your disabled brother to face the music. There'll be a special place in hell for Paddy Cullen.'

Warren agreed. However, he worried that the full horrors of the Cullen farm had yet to be fully unearthed. Annie had said that the reason she and Emil had decided to escape, was because other women in her position had been forced to end their pregnancy. Teams with dogs had been searching the farm, to see what else they might find. He dreaded reading the report when it finally crossed his desk.

Warren paused, choosing his words carefully. 'Speaking of which, I don't suppose you know which way the wind is blowing, as concerns Anica Vukovi and the other captives do you?'

Naseem got up and refilled the two men's coffee cups. 'That's a decision that the Crown Prosecution Service will have to make.'

Warren waited.

'But unofficially, I hear that with the testimony of the two nail technicians, including one who claims to have witnessed the whole altercation, they are minded to consider self-defence, or possibly manslaughter with a recommendation of time served for Annie. I believe that a Serbian charity has stepped in to cover her legal costs, which will help. She will be deported of course, but hopefully she will eventually be able to put it all behind her. As to the rest of the captives, their status in this country will be viewed "sympathetically".'

Warren was relieved to hear that Annie was unlikely to go to prison for murder or manslaughter. The last time that he had seen Annie had been at the small funeral for Emil and their child.

So far, neither the Home Office nor the Foreign Office had managed to identify Emil, and so he had been buried, alongside his baby boy, who Annie had named Nikola, in a council funeral. Warren and the team had donated money for a simple headstone and flowers, with enough set aside for completion of the headstone if Emil was ever properly identified. He hoped that Annie would be able to pay her respects one last time before she was deported.

Warren had also given money towards the funerals of Joey McGhee and Kourtney Flitton. Perhaps if he hadn't given cash to Joey McGhee that night, their paths might not have crossed and both of them would still be alive. Tony Sutton had dismissed that notion as nonsense, but still Warren's conscience troubled him. Professional Standards had mostly agreed with Sutton's assessment, although formal advice had been placed in his file.

Warren could live with that.

Back in Middlesbury, a chill wind whistled down the road by the shops. Karen Hardwick stood in front of the post box. In her hand was the letter from Nottingham University. It had sat on the table for weeks, taunting her with its importance, but today was the day she needed to reply. If she didn't post it now, she ran the risk of missing the deadline on Friday.

Yes or No? That was the question that she'd wrestled with all this time. Finally, after another night of no sleep, she'd made her decision, scrawling her signature and sealing the letter in the prepaid envelope before she could change her mind. Again.

Oliver snuffled quietly in the pram beside her. Wrapped up tightly against the cold in a mustard-coloured jacket, with a knitted hat covering his ears, he was oblivious to his mother's emotional turmoil.

Taking a deep breath, Hardwick pushed the letter through the slot. She heard the quiet thump as it landed on the pile of letters already inside the bright red pillar box.

Reaching down, she gently touched her sleeping son's face.

The decision she had just made would affect them both. But she knew that above all else, when it came to the future, hers was lying in front of her.

Reaching down, she gently touched her sleeping son's face. The decision she had just made would affect them both. But she knew that above all else, when it came to the limits, hers was a way of part of her.

Acknowledgements

Wow, who would have thought it? The tenth book in the DCI Warren Jones series already!

As ever, there is a huge list of people to thank, but some deserve a special mention.

First of all, my beautiful fiancée and beta reader, Cheryl, whose advice and input has helped shape this series. As I write this, we are currently in Covid-19 lockdown together – I can't think of anyone I would rather be isolated with.

Special mention also goes to my father, whose excellent proof-reading skills have minimized the number of repeated phrases and logical inconsistencies throughout the series. Two of the characters in this book were directly inspired by a conversation with him a few years ago, so thanks for that! As always, he is ably supported by Mum, whose encouragement has helped me keep on going. Love you loads, guys.

I always mention my favourite lawyers, Dan and Caroline. Again, their expertise has proven invaluable.

Steve and Tina – I hope you like your belated wedding present!

Thanks also go to Jan Adams, who generously donated to the CLIC Sargent 'Get in Character' appeal. You never know who is going to win the contest to name a character, but when Jan won,

I just knew I had to have a police dog handler – complete with German shepherd – in the book. I hope you like what I've done.

If you wish to support the valuable work that CLIC Sargent do to help children affected by cancer, please consider visiting their page.

www.clicsargent.org.uk

The gang at HarperCollins and HQ Digital have pulled out all the stops as usual, from the fantastic cover design, to the editorial team and the marketing staff. As always huge thanks for the work on this book and your help over the past six years. And if you have been enjoying these novels as audiobooks, join me in a round of applause for Malk Williams, whose narration has really brought my characters to life.

This book would not have been possible without the fantastic input of my editor, Abi Fenton. You have a real understanding of what makes Warren and his team tick, and your suggestions have been invaluable. I look forward to working with you again in the future.

And finally, thanks to my readers. So many of you have got in touch, either directly or through your reviews. It really is appreciated and makes it all worth it.

Thanks again for taking the time to read *A Price to Pay*, and I hope to see you in the future.

Paul Gitsham

Essex March 2020.

If you want keep up to date with the latest news about DCI Warren Jones and his team, visit my website www.paulgitsham. com or follow me on social media at www.facebook.com/dcijones or on Twitter @dcijoneswriter or Instagram @paulgitsham.

A Letter from Paul

Hello, and thank you for taking the time to read the latest DCI Warren Jones novel. A particularly warm welcome back to previous readers of the series – I hope this new instalment lives up to your expectations.

There are a number of difficult themes explored in this book, and at times it was hard to write. I sincerely hope that I have addressed them in a sensitive and compassionate manner. The subject of illegal workers and modern slavery is increasingly topical, and whilst the events depicted here are fictional, if anything the reality is even worse. The exploitation of vulnerable people is a source of shame to our society, and one that we can all play a role in combatting. The charity Crimestoppers can pass information to police, anonymously if desired.

On a more upbeat note, the next book in the series is well underway, with more in the pipeline.

Until then, best wishes,

Paul.

Dear Reader,

We hope you enjoyed reading this book. If you did, we'd be so appreciative if you left a review. It really helps us and the author to bring more books like this to you.

Here at HQ Digital we are dedicated to publishing fiction that will keep you turning the pages into the early hours. Don't want to miss a thing? To find out more about our books, promotions, discover exclusive content and enter competitions you can keep in touch in the following ways:

JOIN OUR COMMUNITY:
Sign up to our new email newsletter: hyperurl.co/hqnewsletter
Read our new blog www.hqstories.co.uk
🐦: https://twitter.com/HQStories
📘: www.facebook.com/HQStories

BUDDING WRITER?
We're also looking for authors to join the HQ Digital family!
Find out more here:
https://www.hqstories.co.uk/want-to-write-for-us/
Thanks for reading, from the HQ Digital team

ONE PLACE. MANY STORIES

If you enjoyed *A Price to Pay*, then why not try another gripping thriller from HQ Digital?

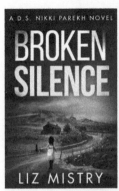

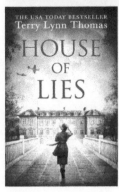